COURTING DEATH

COURTING DEATH

A NOVEL

PAUL J. HEALD

YUCCA

This is a work of fiction. Names, characters, businesses, places, events, and incidents are either the products of the author's imagination or used in a fictitious manner. Any resemblance to actual persons, living or dead, or actual events is purely coincidental.

Yucca Publishing books may be purchased in bulk at special discounts for sales promotion, corporate gifts, fund-raising, or educational purposes. Special editions can also be created to specifications. For details, contact the Special Sales Department, Yucca Publishing, 307 West 36th Street, 11th Floor, New York, NY 10018 or yucca@skyhorsepublishing.com.

Yucca Publishing® is an imprint of Skyhorse Publishing, Inc.®, a Delaware corporation.
Visit our website at www.yuccapub.com.

10 9 8 7 6 5 4 3 2 1

Library of Congress Cataloging-in-Publication Data is available on file.

Jacket design by Laura Klynstra
Jacket photo: iStockphoto

Print ISBN: 978-1-63158-101-4
Ebook ISBN: 978-1-63158-107-6

Printed in the United States of America

COURTING DEATH

To Andrea, Lewis, & Margaret

SIDE ONE

(May–November, 1988)

I.

THE CITY BY THE RIVER

Arthur Hughes pulled his battered hatchback into a Majik Market just over the Georgia state line to grab a soft drink and fill up with gas one last time before he slogged on to Clarkeston. Humid July air filled his car the moment he cracked the door, and he pumped the cheapest unleaded in a swelter absent from his last stop in the highlands of eastern Tennessee. As he paid, he noticed a pile of road maps next to the cash register and considered exiting the sticky interstate to find a less tedious route to his new home.

"I'll take this too." He gestured with a Georgia state map and pulled out his wallet again.

"That'll be five dollars." Damned expensive for a folded sheet of paper. He raised his eyebrows and frowned at the stout woman across the counter.

"Hey, it ain't called the Magic Mark-Up for nothin'." The clerk handed over the change with a wink and a broad smile of surprisingly straight teeth. "Drive safe now, hon."

He leaned against his car and studied the local roads that might carry him most directly to Clarkeston. Squinting hard in the bright sunlight, he identified the most likely candidate, Ga. Hwy 4, a thin black line that ran into the dark green leviathan of the Georgia countryside. He ran his finger along the ninety miles left to travel and decided to avoid sharing more interstate time with Midwestern families just passing through the South on the way to Disney World. Freshly divorced and still encumbered with bad mental habits picked up in law school, he wondered whether plunging off the beaten track might help scour away some of life's barnacles. With a grim smile, he tossed the map on the passenger seat and set off to explore close-up the mysterious land of witty convenience store clerks.

Traffic was light and he sailed down a series of two-lane roads through hardwood-covered hills and flatlands of exhausted cotton fields converted to pine, hay, and kudzu. Every ten miles or so a small town would appear, dotted with Greek Revival mansions on streets that could have been film sets for nineteenth-century costume dramas. But none of the tidy clapboard houses bore the haunted look demanded by gothic film makers. No inbred knife-wielding psychopaths lurked in the bushes—just children riding Big Wheels in their front yards and playing hide-and-seek behind the lattice work under their front porches. Smiling parents arrived home from work in Japanese sedans and lingered outside to gossip with their neighbors. His ex-wife would have been horrified at the thought of living there, but he wondered whether it might not be liberating. Three years in Chicago had made small towns look pretty attractive.

Arthur had interviewed with the Judge in Atlanta for his one-year clerkship and had little idea what to expect from Clarkeston. His move, therefore, hit an unpleasant bump on its outskirts when his home for the next twelve months announced itself with a K-mart and a shabby Winn Dixie Supermarket. The entire main road into town was dominated by fast food outlets and cinder block student apartments bragging about their weight rooms and cheap cable television. A brief look at the complexes—*Dogwood Terrace* (no dogwoods to be seen), *The Oaks* (zero oaks), and *Willow Gardens* (four stumps and a large pot of pansies)—convinced him to look for lodgings in a more gracious neighborhood, more like the ones he had seen earlier in his drive.

He approached the courthouse with mixed emotions. The prestigious clerkship he won had made him the envy of his law school classmates, but the interview questions posed by

the Judge about his willingness to work on habeas corpus capital cases still echoed in his head like a cracked church bell. He
stood on the sidewalk for a long while, contemplating the Latin
scrawled above the concrete pillars on either side of the front
door: *Lux et Veritas*. He took a deep breath. Time to climb the
steps and join the light and truth machine.

★ ★ ★

Ms. Stillwater, the Judge's secretary, quickly came to the rescue
on the housing front. She was a well-groomed woman with
neatly permed gray hair. He would later learn that she was in her
late sixties, but her slim figure belied her age. Lacking the girth
of Arthur's matronly Scandinavian relatives, she still managed to
send out grandmotherly vibrations as she opened the walnut
double door that led into the Judge's chambers. Why did he feel
like the gate to the Emerald City had just swung wide?

"Mr. Hughes!" She clapped her hands together and welcomed him in a voice that was as elegant as her dress. "Please
come in! I hope you had a nice drive."

"It was interesting." He nodded enthusiastically as he scanned
the hallway, an intimidating corridor of bookcases and more walnut paneling. "I took the local roads instead of the interstate."

"Well, I hope you drove carefully." For a moment he mis-
took the leisurely pace of her speech for a real chiding. "Some of
those small-town sheriffs really love to ticket cars with foreign
tags."

"Tags?" Arthur stole a glance into the huge side offices as
he walked with her down the hall. "Do I need to get some sort
of tag?"

"I assume you've already got one on the back of your car,
darlin'."

"Oh, you mean license plates."

"Of course I do!" Then, she cocked her head and snapped
her voice through the door to the left of her desk, "Judge, Arthur
Hughes is here!"

A frowning white-haired man with half-rimmed glasses pushed down his nose opened the door and extended his hand. "Good to see you again, Mr. Hughes."

Arthur reached out and was surprised by the power in the seventy-year-old grip. Here was the man who almost single-handedly integrated the State of Georgia. A living legend if there ever was one, and Arthur couldn't think of anything to say.

"Nice to be done with law school, I suppose? Ready for a year at the government rate before you head off to some big law firm?"

"Yes, sir," was the best Arthur could answer to the flurry of questions. "It's nice to be here."

"Nice to have you here too." He tipped his head back toward his office. "Now, if you'll excuse me, I'm on the phone with Judge Meriweather in Huntsville. Ms. Stillwater will get you set up. Get to bed early tonight—we'll see you in the office tomorrow at seven a.m. sharp."

He shut the door, and Ms. Stillwater settled behind her desk and shuffled through her drawers.

"Speaking of beds," she queried as she looked up and handed him the keys to his office and to the front door of the chambers, "did you have any luck finding a place to live?"

"No, ma'am." First official use of *ma'am*! "I was supposed to sign a lease today, but I got a call right before I left saying that they had let the apartment to someone else. I'll probably just stay at a hotel tonight and make some calls this afternoon and tomorrow."

Ms. Stillwater's eyes lit up. "You know, I know a young widow who's just lost a boarder. She lives on a lovely street about a fifteen-minute walk from here. Would you like me to call her?" She started writing even before he could blurt out his assent. "Here's the address . . . I'll give her a quick ring and tell her you're coming."

On his way to the house, he paused at the top of the courthouse steps and looked across the street. Straight ahead stood the historic lunch counter, integrated thirty years earlier when the Judge overturned the trespassing convictions of four black students who had dared to sit down to order hamburgers and Cokes. Although it looked unchanged since the day of the sit-in, the rest of the town had evolved over time. Two doors down from the diner stood a new Thai restaurant and a coffee shop, both of which probably owed their livelihood to Clarkeston College, which lay just south of downtown on the other side of the river. A dry cleaner, a storefront Missionary Apostolic Holiness church, a men's clothing store, and a florist's shop completed the block.

The courthouse was planted firmly in the middle of Court Street, a secondary avenue that ran a block north of and parallel to Main Street. Because the terrain sloped south down to the river, he could see over the rooftops of the buildings along Main Street to the edge of the college, which sat on a low bluff across the river. College Avenue ran perpendicular on right, connecting Court to Main before spanning the river into the tree-lined heart of the college. It was a bucolic view, incongruous with the scene from a recent made-for-television docudrama depicting an angry mob lynching the Judge in effigy on the top of the courthouse steps.

Ten minutes later, he was climbing up a dozen wooden steps to the wide porch of a large, two-story white house and twisting the handle of a brass bell stuck in the middle of a door heavy with leaded glass. A two-seater swing hung invitingly to the left next to a brightly colored chest brimming with toys. A slight breeze stirred the leaves of the two enormous elm trees standing on each side of the broad staircase. High above the moist red clay, the porch was surprisingly cool, even in the July heat. The bright aqua painted on the porch ceiling also helped keep the summer swelter at bay, although its refreshing blue-green hue was an aesthetic disaster.

He was critically examining the ceiling, head back and jaw slack, as the door clicked open behind him.

"No, we're not just tacky—the color keeps the wasps from building nests underneath the roof. They think it's water, and they won't land on it." The voice was soft and melodious, with a delicate lilt too cultured to be called a drawl.

He wrenched his head around to see her and felt the muscles in his neck spasm, but what he saw in the doorway pushed the pain into the distance. Outrageously thick hair cascaded a lustrous dark river down to the middle her back, flawless olive skin recalling dark Celtic or Mediterranean ancestors, or perhaps even gypsies. She held him in her dark eyes and waited for him to introduce himself.

Her gaze momentarily panicked him, and he scanned downward as he attempted to remember his name and why he was there. His eyes immediately encountered generous curves, tastefully and accurately shown off by a black knit blouse. Sensing danger, he snapped his head back up, jolting an electric current through his neck and down to his shoulders. The moment of agony cleared his mind.

"Hey! My name's Arthur Hughes. Mrs. Stillwater sent me . . ."

"I'm Suzanne." She wiped her hand on a dish towel and gave him a warm smile. "Martha said you'd be coming. If you'll wait out here for just a couple minutes, I'll show you the room." She glanced back into the house before she shut the screen door. "Don't mind Maria if she comes out exploring . . . She's four and as curious as a cat in a shopping bag factory."

He walked over to the swing and sat down to admire the gracious wood-frame houses that filled the neighborhood. The Queen Anne across the street had been painted by a frustrated artist who used four alternating colors on the spindles of the porch railing and four more colors to outline each gingerbread cut-out on the house's many gables. Before too long he heard the door creak, and as predicted, a stumpy fireplug of a little girl stuck her head out and glared at him.

"I want my giraffe," she demanded. Arthur looked around the porch but could not see what she was talking about.

"Where's your giraffe, Maria?"

"How do you know my name?" She squinted suspiciously at him and squirmed against the doorframe.

Long hours spent babysitting his sister and a slew of younger cousins had equipped him admirably for confrontations with marauding munchkins.

"Your mama told me that a little four-year-old girl named Maria lived here, and you look like a little four-year-old girl to me."

"She's my mama!" Maria blurted out indignantly.

"Ahhh . . . well, that solves the mystery. You two are related, huh?"

"What did you say?" She was bright-eyed and aggressive, not a china doll sort of preschooler.

"Where's your giraffe?"

She pointed at the box of toys behind him.

"Why don't you come and show me?"

She shook her head.

"Do you want me to get it?" She nodded, and he slid off the porch swing and started to rummage through the layers of junk in the container. Holding a blob of Duplos in one hand and pinning a squishy fabric doll under the same arm, he parted trucks and blocks with his free hand in a vain search for anything that looked like a giraffe. Maria slowly crept up behind him to check on his progress.

"There it is!"

"Where?" He looked around, confused by the certainty of her pronouncement. Setting down his load, he crouched on his knees to check the very bottom of the box. She sniffled and pointed with a trembling hand to the pile of Duplo rubble on the porch floor next to him.

"Oh, it was a Duplo giraffe!" Worry showed on her face, and she managed a nod. "No problem . . . I'm Dr. Duplo. I can fix him up in no time." He attempted to mesmerize her with the timbre and cadence of Mr. Fred Rodgers, and she began to calm down. By the time her mother came out, Maria was eagerly pointing out where various pieces went. She was delighted when he added a colorful plastic hat to the toy's head, and she ran to show her mother how stylish he now looked.

"I hope she's not bothering you," Suzanne said warily as she motioned him inside the house. "So, how do you like Georgia?"

With a wave back at Maria, Arthur stepped into a wide hall-way of buttery heart-of-pine planks extending the length of the house from the front door to the back porch. Two spacious rooms of roughly equal size on the left side of the hall mirrored two on the right. A broad staircase rose from the end of the hall, ascending halfway to the second floor and ending in a spacious landing before winding back toward the front and delivering them onto the second-floor breezeway that bisected the house. The four rooms on the second floor were situated as their twins below.

"This four-over-four design was very common for houses built in the 1890s," she explained.

"It's gorgeous." He spoke with genuine admiration, grabbing his neck and wincing slightly as he looked up at the brown bead-board ceilings.

"This one would be yours." She walked down the hall to the very front of the house and opened the door on the left. As she entered, he looked through the window that hung at the end of the hall: a tree-house view with patches of street and sidewalk showing between the arrowhead-shaped elm leaves.

"Maria and I have the two big rooms on the first floor. We share the living room and kitchen with Mr. Bernson, who lives on the other side up here, and with whoever takes this room."

Arthur smiled. The furniture was worn and tired, but the gleaming wood floor brightened the room and reflected its warm glow on Suzanne as he turned to nod his approval. After a quick look around, he stepped out into the hall, and she took a skeleton key out of her pocket and locked the door as if to say: *It's yours now if you want.*

But did he want share living space with an active four-year-old and two other adults? He expected the year to be exhausting, and the last thing he needed was noise and uncontrollable interruptions. His marriage had taught him to protect and treasure his privacy. Maybe a small apartment was the way to go.

But the key sold him. The thought of living in a house where he needed such an old-fashioned device was irresistible. Now, this was the real South! He could live in a sterile apartment with a pool and weight room anywhere in the country. A communal television and the patter of little feet would be a small price to pay for an authentic experience. He had done enough private stewing about the divorce and obsessing about law school bullshit. A house with skeleton keys might be the perfect therapy.

When the tour was done and a check for the first month's rent handed over, Suzanne brought them iced tea on the porch and asked him about his day.

He hesitated. "It's a lot to take in all at once."

"Where are you from?"

"Iowa, originally."

She took a sip of her tea and shook her head. "That's a long way to come for a one-year job."

"It's more than just a job," he tried to explain. Supreme Court Justices aside, the Judge was probably the most admired living American jurist. Among non-justices, only Henry Friendly and Learned Hand had as much name recognition in the twentieth century. His most famous cases filled law school textbooks. His treatise on Civil Rights law was still the standard text fifteen years after it first appeared. Case by case over a twenty-five-year period, he had become the most visible symbol of the evolution of the new South. "It's an amazing opportunity."

He began to offer examples of the Judge's fame, but she cut him off. "I know, I know," she said with a laugh. "He's my godfather." Maria helped him contain his surprise by thrusting Mr. Giraffe under his nose and demanding a hat adjustment. "Didn't Ms. Stillwater tell you?"

"I guess she forgot." He handed the toy back to Maria and scrutinized her mother. "You probably know more about being a law clerk than I do."

She met his gaze and offered him a beguiling frown. "I doubt it." Before she could say more, Maria scuttled across the porch and announced she was going to get a juice box in the kitchen. Her mother got up to follow her, gathering the empty tea glasses in a graceful motion and pausing briefly at the door. "The Judge did tell me something a couple of years ago, though . . . He said that clerking for him was the worst job in the state of Georgia."

She left him with a look of genuine sympathy, and he got up to unload the car. When he was done moving his clothes, book boxes, stereo, clock radio, and knickknacks up to the room, he leaned against the frame of the front window and stared out over the street. *Arthur*, he thought, untroubled by Suzanne's warning about the job, *it looks like you may have landed on your feet.* He looked around and was struck with the realization that his ex-wife would probably have hated Clarkeston, the neighborhood, the house, and maybe even Suzanne. It had been a day of thresholds crossed: across the Georgia border, through the Judge's chambers, and into a new home with a beautiful widow and a curious little girl.

II.

BUT THAT'S WHY YOU WANT TO BE THERE

Suzanne was psychic. At least, sort of. She occasionally sensed things would happen, and sometimes she could touch someone's mind with as much feeling as she might stroke a face or hand. The feeling came and went in no discernible pattern, and she had no control over it. This is how she knew that she would eventually sleep with Arthur, but when she told her best friend Judy about the premonition, the break room at Wee Ones Academy preschool rang with laughter.

"You don't have to be Nostradamus to figure out what happens when two attractive twenty-somethings move in together." Judy put her hand to her forehead and closed her eyes. "I see seduction in the stairwell and croissants for breakfast."

"Shut up! I haven't slept with anyone since Bill died, and I've put on thirty pounds since Maria. Trust me, nothing's inevitable . . . I just got this weird feeling when I saw him."

"Yeah, just like I get when I see Richard Gere. It's soooo ethereal." Judy poured Suzanne a cup of coffee from the communal pot at the day care center where they both worked. "What's he look like, anyway?"

"Friendly face, longish hair, cross-country runner's build. More like Nicholas Cage than Richard Gere." She sugared her coffee. "He looked pretty nice in his suit this morning, but I don't envy him the walk into town in gray wool."

"The Judge makes them dress up?"

"Oh, there's lots of rules, I think. He'll have an interesting day." The door to the break room suddenly opened, and a three-year-old boy holding on to a wet spot on the front of his pants looked in sheepishly.

"As interesting as this?"

"Are you kidding?" She gently led the boy by the shoulder toward the bathroom. "No man can handle this!"

Suzanne had worked at Wee Ones Academy for almost three years. Glad to have a job where Maria could be kept close by, it was not quite the teaching position she had aimed for when she was studying English Literature at the University of Georgia. Even so, her choice of major had led to her present position. Had she not taken Modern American Fiction, she probably would never have met William Boyd, a business major trying to finish off his Humanities requirement as painlessly as possible. They never would have married, never would have moved to Birmingham for his first job, and never would have conceived Maria. And Maria was the only reason she spent the day reading *Bongo Was a Happy Dog* to toddlers instead of Keats' poetry to Advanced Placement high school students.

Later that afternoon, she sat on the front porch, watching a light rain fall while Maria sat inside with Big Bird on the television. As she finished her second tea, she saw Arthur walking up the street, suit jacket held awkwardly over his head to keep off the rain. He looked up and sketched a wave.

"Well," she asked as he bounded up the steps, "how was the first day in chambers? Exciting?"

"Intimidating, mostly." He paused at the top of the stairs and shook his head. "I was only there about five minutes when your godfather calls me into his office to get this slightly paranoid confidentiality lecture. I knew we couldn't talk to anyone about cases, but we're supposed to keep a lid on anything that happens in chambers."

"Are you sure you should you be telling me this?" Her eyes opened wide in mock alarm.

"Probably not!" He took a quick glance under the porch, as if checking for spies. "Anyway, it wasn't what I expected."

No surprise there, she thought. The Judge cut a curious figure. With his bushy mass of snow-white beard and moustache, he would have drawn comparisons to Santa Claus but for his fierce gray eyes and slim build. He carried himself like an old soldier, and when he talked he made disturbingly frequent eye contact and gestured in deliberate motions with large, graceful hands. The newspapers sometimes described him as professorial, which she took to mean thoughtful, but the aura of authority he radiated reminded her of no professor she had ever known.

"I also had no idea how much traveling we have to do. I thought everything was in Atlanta, but the court sits all over Alabama, Florida, and Georgia."

"You want my advice? Volunteer for Savannah or Miami before you get sent to some hellhole like Montgomery, Alabama."

"I'll try, but I don't know how much choice we've got . . . It probably doesn't matter." She slid over on the swing, and he sat down next to her. "Most of the work is sitting in chambers and researching issues for bench briefs. I can't believe that we've got our own library and conference room. And you should see our offices . . . Actually, you probably have, haven't you?"

She nodded and they pushed back on the swing. The light rain had already stopped falling, and the sun was starting to peek out again.

"It's amazing," he continued. "I've got this massive oak desk, a huge oak conference table, three walls full of books, and a leaded glass window that opens out over the city. And that's not even the best office. Phil, my co-clerk, has got even more space than me."

"What's he like?"

"Pretty cool, I think. He's a Stanford grad, looks like a body builder, but super nice and really smart. We're gonna have a beer later."

She sat patiently while he excitedly described the details of his day. He struck her as wonderfully naïve. He knew what federal judges did, but only in theory. The newspaper had reported that the governor of Georgia was getting ready to sign another death warrant for Karl Gottlieb, one of the most famous serial killers in US history. Two years earlier, the Gottlieb case had left a bloody trail through the Judge's chambers. Did Arthur really have a clue what might be coming his way? He sounded a like a rookie cop in a television show, all excited to ride in the police cruiser and hunt for bad guys.

"I'm sorry," he finally said. "I usually don't talk about myself all the time . . . What about you? How was your day? Anything fun happen?"

"Does dealing with two four-year-olds with explosive diarrhea count as fun?" She smiled but her eyes dared him to suggest any problem confronted by the federal judiciary could be more challenging to solve.

The look of horror on his face said it all.

"How did you end up at the preschool anyway?"

She sighed as she considered spinning the long or the short version of her story. The sun beat down on the pavement in front of the house, and she watched the steam wraiths gather and dance. Soon a muggy haze would blanket the neighborhood, but for now the porches along Oak Street were cool and comfortable.

"Well," she started slowly, "I was living in Birmingham and substitute teaching in a couple of the high schools when I got pregnant with Maria. While Bill—that was my husband—and I were trying to figure out whether I'd keep working . . . well, fighting about it, actually . . . he sort of settled the whole debate by getting drunk and driving into a viaduct on I-85."

"God, that's shitty." He studied the porch floor, looking embarrassed to have dragged up so much drama.

"It's alright . . . ancient history." She was not yet good enough friends with Arthur to explain why the apparent tragedy did not deserve as intense grieving as he might think.

She got up and started tossing Maria's stray toys in the porch chest. "The logical thing to do was to come back here and live with my mom for a while, which was great when I had the baby . . . but then she got sick and I ended up taking care of both of them."

She shut the lid and leaned back against the porch rail. "After Momma passed away, her medical bills ate up most of her estate. We would have lost the house if I hadn't been able to find the job at Wee Ones and take in some boarders. The job doesn't pay that great, but I get to keep Maria close by, and the savings on child care are really huge."

He shook his head, looking like a solemn child. "I don't think I could do it."

"Oh, you could if you had to." She laughed as she ran her fingers through her hair, pushing it back behind her ears. "And there's something kind of liberating about putting your dreams on hold and just living day to day." He looked dubious. "It's not the lawyer's creed, I know. My father was one too—the Judge's partner before he was appointed to the bench—but that was a long time ago."

"Has he passed too?"

"When I was in middle school." Suzanne heard Maria stirring inside the house, and she took a last look back at Arthur as she walked toward the door. "What time are you meeting Phil?"

"About six."

She glanced at her watch. "You'd better get moving then."

"Wanna join us?"

He clearly did not comprehend the difficulties posed by bringing a four-year-old to happy hour. She shook her head with a bemused grin.

"Maybe next time, Arthur. Have fun." She pulled the screen door shut, watched the young barely-man hurry down the street, and felt her premonition fade. At age twenty-eight, playing Ms. Robinson just seemed a little weird.

III.

THE OLD MAN WITH THE TELESCOPE/WHERE THEY DRINK CHAMPAGNE

The Judge had not opened the curtains in his office in almost five years. He had scowled the first time he overheard Ms. Stillwater joke about *the bear in his cave*, but the drapes stayed down, obscuring a magnificent view of the river as it meandered through the town. Twenty years earlier, he had leaned against the sill and watched thousands of civil rights activists gather for the famous protest march from Clarkeston to Atlanta. Without his hastily penned order authorizing their "constitutionally protected attempt to petition the government of the State of Georgia," the event would never have taken place, at least not peacefully. His wife had stood at his side and commented that the mob was biggest darn petition she had ever seen.

Now, his wife was dead, and civil rights cases had virtually disappeared from his docket. He was a hero of the new South, but the reward seemed to be a never-ending succession of habeas corpus petitions piling up on his desk. Schools and other public services in Georgia had been successfully integrated, but the sense of progress and reform did not extend to those convicted of murder. And since his promotion from the trial court to the Eleventh Circuit Court of Appeals, he had become part of a small group of judges whose jurisdiction covered all of Georgia,

Alabama, and Florida, three states that combined a keen sense of retribution with low levels of judicial and prosecutorial competence. As a result, in the 1980s, the federal courts had become the overseers and caretakers of a deeply flawed system of capital punishment.

At first, the habeas cases seemed to share something in common with civil rights work. They both embodied complaints that state officials had acted improperly. And in both kinds of cases, ruling against the state was likely to raise public outcry, but the beneficiaries of due process in habeas corpus were not hard-working victims of racial oppression. They were murderers. Some more psychotic than others; some truly victims themselves. But few could convincingly argue their innocence. Nonetheless, they sometimes won. Several terms earlier, the Judge had granted a notorious serial killer a procedural victory that had delayed his execution for two years and counting. Unfortunately, the next appeal of Karl Gottlieb could jump out of the muck at any time. Eventually, of course, Gottlieb and most of the other condemned would run out of valid reasons to delay, and he would permit the state to act. One final desperate petition was always filed, and with the exception of very rare interference by the Supreme Court, the denial of a stay by the Eleventh Circuit was the last judicial act before execution.

Some were surprised by the Judge's complicity in the system, shocked at his failure to do to the death penalty what he had done to segregated schools, parks, and lunch counters. Critics failed to remember that he had always justified his role in desegregation litigation by an unwavering adherence to the Constitution and Supreme Court precedent. His opinions had deliberately avoided idealism and proclaimed exacting obedience to the law of land. No matter how unpleasant he found the world of habeas corpus, he could not bring himself to renege on his commitment to the rule of law. Capital punishment had been held constitutional by the Supreme Court; he had no stomach for rebellion. By the time the mideighties rolled around, he realized he no longer enjoyed judging. Even so, the curtains had stayed open until a woman had entered his life and then abruptly left it. After that, he sat in shadow.

★ ★ ★

Phil sat waiting for Arthur at the Wild Boar, sipping a beer and enjoying the view from the best table in his new favorite bar. The front of the tavern consisted of a huge plate glass window that tilted up and out when it was warm and locked down tight at night. A dark green awning extended over the sidewalk and kept the sun's glare off the drinkers. There was no outdoor seating, but several tables were placed snug to the windowsill so that Phil could lean out and watch the world go by. Since the bar was next to the Clarkeston College campus, the passersby, Phil noticed, included a steady stream of attractive students.

When Arthur approached, Phil raised his empty glass and made a gesture with his hands that he hoped traced the shape of a pitcher. A minute later, Arthur wound his way between the tables and filled both of their mugs. Phil studied him while he poured. Even after just one day working together, Phil was sure they would have a great year together. Arthur seemed to have a sharp sense of humor and definitely passed the crucial pitcher pantomime test. He seemed really smart too, but apart from his slightly nasal Midwestern accent, he didn't know much about Arthur.

"You go first," said Phil as he wiped a speck of foam from his moustache.

"You go first what?"

"Let's have your life story in fifteen words or less."

"Right!" Arthur took a drink. "Iowa farm, boring corn, ecology degree, Chicago law, environmental division of the Justice Department."

"Nice," responded Phil. "My turn: San Fran suburbs, single mom, divinity school, Stanford law, ACLU Cal Office." He counted on his fingers. "Got you by two words!"

"Divinity school?" Arthur gave him a curious look that Phil had seen more than once. "You wanted to be a priest?"

"Well, not exactly a priest." He laughed. "The Pope likes Catholics for that. I went to the Disciples of Christ Seminary outside of Sacramento for a year before going to law school."

"Disciples of Christ... hold on ... In Iowa they're whacky right wing or whacky left wing depending on the town." Arthur smiled and drank half his beer. "Which are you?"

"Neither." Phil laughed. "But we had some of both in seminary. That's one reason I quit."

"What? Too much diversity?"

"Nah. The problem was that no matter how good a sermon we heard or how great a class was, no one on the left or the right ever changed their minds. I mean never." He sighed and shook his head. "It taught me that preaching and teaching might not matter that much."

"Did you have a crisis of faith?"

That was a new record. It usually took a minimum of six beers for someone to go there.

"Not really ... not at all, actually. It was more crisis of effectiveness. I went to seminary because I wanted to help people, and I realized that I could do that much better with a law degree."

Arthur read his mind. "Just think of the Judge."

Phil nodded, happy that Arthur was not freaked out by his story. Too many people assumed that a former seminarian must be some sort evangelical nutcase. "That's exactly what I told my mom when she complained about me moving away. She kept saying that to her Georgia meant Martin Luther King, a minister, not some judge she'd barely heard of."

"Well, she's got a point, doesn't she?" Arthur said as his attention was momentarily distracted by a young blonde who sauntered past.

"Maybe. But imagine MLK in Russia or China in the 1950s and 60s." He paused until he had Arthur's full attention. "One protest and he's history, gone forever in some cell or maybe executed. Without federal judges blessing bus boycotts, marches, and demonstrations, we never would have heard of him."

"And speaking of the Judge," Phil continued, "he wanted us to do some business before we get too trashed."

"He knows we're here?"

"No, he's not quite omnipresent, but before he left, he told me to go over some things." He pulled a sheaf of typed pages out and put them on the table. "These are some sample bench memos and draft opinions written by prior clerks. The Judge gave the same stack to me when I got here last month."

"Why didn't he give them to me himself?"

"Probably too busy reading briefs for the next sitting," Phil replied. "Anyway, I've done some writing for him already, so I've got a decent feel for what he wants. The most important thing, and I quote, is *brevity and clarity*. He doesn't want us writing law review articles. He says each case is a problem that can be explained and solved in an economical fashion."

"That's weird," Arthur mused. "When you think about those huge opinions of his in our textbooks, 'economical' does not spring to mind."

Phil nodded and poured himself another beer while Arthur looked through the papers. He wondered how long it would take his new friend to see the same patterns that he had. He picked up the empty pitcher, walked to the long polished bar to order a refill, chatted with the bartender, and then visited the men's room. When he returned, Arthur appeared to have finished—he was an astonishingly fast reader. Law school must have been a breeze from someone who could read forty-five pages in ten minutes.

"This is what strikes me the most," Phil said as he spread two sets of papers in front of Arthur. "Look at this. Here's a bench memo written to the Judge by an ex-clerk named Rob Perry. And here's the official published opinion in the same case. As you can tell, there's only a couple of superficial differences between the two. A private memo written by someone just out of law school got turned into binding legal precedent. The Judge deferred completely."

Arthur looked at the papers and nodded cautiously. "So the Judge emphasizes brevity and clarity because he doesn't write his own opinions anymore."

"If my clerks were going to write my opinions," Phil guessed, "I wouldn't want them getting too creative either . . . In the old days, back in the civil rights era, the Judge probably wrote all his own stuff. Now with a different caseload, he's willing to delegate the job of opinion writing, but he's not about to authorize us to wax eloquently about what we think the law should be."

"One of my professors who clerked on the Supreme Court told me that he didn't think that any Justice had actually written an opinion in years," Arthur revealed, his mouth set in a grim line. "Their clerks do almost all the writing."

Phil said nothing, full of wonder at the level of responsibility they had so surreptitiously acquired.

"And you know what's really amazing?" Arthur continued, "On the first day of work, I'm already doing this huge class action."

"Yeah." Phil pointed to his book bag and added, "And if the case I'm working on is affirmed, all the law schools and medical schools in Georgia, Florida, and Alabama will have to change their admissions policies."

"Well, at least he tells us which way the case comes out."

"After we do all his research for him and write a memo saying what the result should be."

Arthur poured two more glasses. Phil's foamed over the top, and he blotted the spillage with a paper napkin. Arthur sipped and scanned the scene, seemingly unconcerned about the power they would be wielding.

"So, it doesn't worry you?" Phil asked, surprised by Arthur's nonchalance.

"What?"

"Well," Phil tried to articulate the source of his anxiety, "think about the death cases we're going to get." He pushed his beer away and leaned back in his chair. "Are you going to be comfortable doing the research in a habeas corpus case and then writing a memo saying there should be no stay of execution?"

Arthur frowned. "You sound like the Judge in my interview. He asked the same question."

"What did you say?"

"I said what my professors told me federal judges in the south wanted to hear: 'Judge, I have serious doubts about the way the system of capital punishment works in this country, but current law does allow for its application in appropriate circumstances.'" He spoke as if the answer were obvious. "Not too bleeding heart, not too bloodthirsty. So, you read the cases and write a memo that gets the law right, regardless of what the substantive result is."

Phil studied him for a moment, trying to figure out whether Arthur was a true believer in the death penalty or just a fan of the rule of law or just someone who would say anything to clerk for the Judge.

"Not me," Phil said. "I think the result matters."

"What did you do?" Arthur's eyes narrowed. "Lie in your interview?"

"Yes." Now that he had said it, Phil felt better. He had given the same answer in his interview as Arthur had, but he had not meant it. When faced with telling a lie or disqualifying himself for the job, he chose the former. "I went to law school to help people, not to kill them."

Arthur gave him a funny look. "Even if capital punishment is wrong, don't we have to obey the law? We might disagree with the Supreme Court, but who are we, especially as law clerks, to substitute our own judgment?"

"People with consciences." Phil looked at Arthur without flinching. "I can't leave my conscience outside the courthouse door."

"That sounds very noble." Arthur smiled, obviously unconvinced. "But isn't that exactly what we're supposed to do?"

Instead of pushing the debate, Phil forced a laugh, already familiar with the arguments Arthur was marshaling. "No! What we're supposed to do is go next door and order some pizza and another pitcher."

"Good idea, counselor."

Over food, the talk was less philosophical. Clerkships only lasted one year, so Arthur asked for a summary of the lessons of Phil's first month. He related his brief experience and passed on what little he had learned from a recently departed clerk who had been assigned to initiate him, a colorful character named Titus Grover III, a native Georgian who bragged about "polishing the library table" with female conquests that he had brought up to the Judge's chambers at night.

As they walked unsteadily back through campus, the cooling summer dusk gently dropped around them. The high-pitched buzz of the locusts and tree frogs reverberated in the muggy air and followed them back across the river and into town. As they passed through the night, they concluded that they had found the ideal job—one where a love of stories and argument could be put to productive use, well-aware that the generation of clerks before them had used their skills to advance civil rights and build a working model for nonviolent social change. Neither of them realized at the time that the merger of scholarship and justice, of law and love, was far from inevitable.

IV.

PEOPLE WHO DIED

S everal weeks later, on a Tuesday afternoon in early August, the Judge called Arthur into his office and informed him that Karl Gottlieb, the most famous serial killer in US history, had been scheduled to die in the Georgia electric chair the following Friday morning. Arthur blinked once and swallowed hard.

"Efficiency never goes unpunished, Mr. Hughes. According to Stillwater, you're the furthest ahead in your work, so this death watch goes to you. Gottlieb's lawyers are going to file a motion for stay of execution in the state trial court this afternoon. As a matter of courtesy, the clerk of the court there will fax us a copy of the brief as soon as it's filed so we can anticipate his arguments."

He grabbed a thick file folder on his desk and fingered it rythmically while he explained the habeas process. His eyes never left Arthur's.

"Death warrants are signed by the governor a week or so in advance of the execution date, so these cases pop up without much warning. The time to research them gets compressed even further because a petition is required to move through the state court system before it can be refiled in the federal district court."

The Judge waited for Arthur to nod before continuing. Was the old man looking for some sign of miscomprehension or panic?

"Because we're so high up on the food chain, the petition is usually faxed to chambers less than thirty-six hours before the execution, but we can work on it before it officially gets to us. In order to get up to speed, you should read the opinion I wrote two years ago when we granted Gottlieb a stay of execution on his first habeas petition."

"I remember that one," Arthur interrupted eagerly. "It was my second year in law school. Didn't a group of congressmen try to impeach you and Judge Garnett for granting Gottlieb a stay and sending the case back to state court?"

"He killed at least thirty young women," the Judge sighed as he leaned back in his chair, tilting past the edge of the light cast by the reading lamp on his desk. "He was finally caught after the murder of a twelve-year old girl in Macon, Georgia. After his arrest he started acting weird, so his attorney—the local public defender—moved for a psychiatric evaluation on the basis that his client wasn't competent to stand trial. Gottlieb stood up and shouted that he was completely sane. He dismissed the attorney on the spot and demanded that he be allowed to conduct his own defense. The trial judge suspended the proceedings at that point and rescheduled the hearing for the following day. He urged Gottlieb to reconcile with the PD or find someone else willing to represent him.

"Gottlieb showed up with some out-of-town celebrity attorney the next day." The Judge shook his head with disgust. "When asked about the need for a psychiatric evaluation, the new counsel replied that an interview was not desired by him or his client, and he withdrew the prior motion. In the meantime, the PD is standing at the back of the courtroom, jumping up and down and screaming to the judge that Gottlieb is certifiable.

"That was probably a breach of confidentiality," the Judge admitted, "but it put the trial judge on notice that Gottlieb might be nuts."

"But Gottlieb said he was competent and ready to proceed." Arthur was beginning to get into the story. He had no recollection of the procedural maneuvering in the case, just the gory details of the crime. It was nice to feel like an insider to a hidden history.

"Right." The Judge nodded and leaned forward to deliver the punch line. "And after Gottlieb was convicted and sentenced to death, his next new attorney filed a habeas petition arguing that the state's failure to conduct a psychiatric evaluation should result in a new trial."

A groan rumbled past Arthur's lips, and the Judge nodded his approval of Arthur's reaction.

"Judge Garnett and I found the trial judge was on notice that Gottlieb might be severely disturbed. Between his own behavior in the courtroom and the PD's protests, the judge should have ordered a psychiatric evaluation."

"Makes sense, I suppose," Arthur agreed, "especially when he had no reason to trust Gottlieb's new attorney."

"Every judge makes mistakes, but we had to send the case back."

Arthur watched the Judge carefully and stayed quiet. It was not his job to opine on judicial error—except that was precisely his job. He wondered with a morbid curiosity what role the Judge would give him in the next chapter of Gottlieb's story.

"We figured that the State would hold a new trial," the Judge continued, "but instead a court-appointed psychologist evaluated Gottlieb's mental capacity from just the trial transcripts. The psychologist found that Gottlieb had testified effectively and had delivered a brilliant final summation after dismissing his attorney. After reading the report, the state court concluded that Gottlieb had been competent to stand trial and upheld his conviction."

The Judge grinned at the audacity of the State in conducting a retroactive competency hearing without even interviewing the person whose competence had been in doubt.

"My guess," he suggested, "is that the new habeas petition will complain about this retroactive hearing. You might start by seeing if there's any precedent for doing what Georgia did."

He handed the densely packed accordion folder over to Arthur. What other secrets were in there, he wondered. One of his law professors had analogized criminal cases to plays. What would it mean to step out on the stage of such a famous and long-running show?

Before he could stand up, Ms. Stillwater burst into the chambers.

"Judge! Ms. Melanie has arrived. I told her to wait in the library."

"Stillwater!" The Judge fumed. "How many times have I told you to knock before coming in here? Arthur might have been smoking or something."

"You're the only who smokes in here," she snorted and turned to Arthur. "Come on out and say hello. She's even prettier than she looks on television."

The Judge rolled his eyes and nodded toward the door. Ms. Stillwater had told Arthur earlier in the day that his final co-clerk would be arriving soon. She had emphasized his new colleague's beauty pageant credentials—which Melanie had mysteriously not included on her resume—while Ms. Stillwater had barely mentioned her sterling law school record.

Ms. Stillwater called Phil out of his office as Arthur and the Judge followed her to the library. The four of them squeezed through the doorway and greeted their newest colleague.

"This is Melanie Wilkerson," the proud secretary announced, "the only runner-up Miss Georgia to finish in the top ten percent of her law school class at Harvard." The young woman winced and then stood up and smiled. She was more than just pageant pretty. Her lips were full and red. An unruly mound of lustrous auburn hair was held behind her head with several turquoise barrettes. Her conservative white blouse and black pencil skirt almost disguised her figure.

"Nice to finally meet you." Phil stepped forward and took her hand. "It's always good to put a face to someone you've only spoken to on the phone."

"Nice to meet you too. Thanks for switching spots with me and letting me come last!" she replied. "You're the only reason that I got to split the summer between the Justice Department and Williams & Connolly."

Arthur stared at her for a moment, then wiped his palm on his pants and extended it to her. "Have you found a place to live yet?"

"Oh, yes! Ms. Stillwater found me a lovely apartment in a brand new complex just off of the perimeter road. It's got a big swimming pool, tennis courts, health club—everything you could want." She smiled brightly. "You've probably driven by it. It's called *The Poplars*."

"Probably because they cut down a bunch of poplar trees," Arthur blurted out, remembering his visceral reaction to the sterile apartments he had seen on his trip into town. "Well, have fun out in yuppie land."

"Excuse me?" She dismissed him with a glance and turned to Ms. Stillwater.

"Never mind," Arthur mumbled under his breath.

The secretary cast him a curious look and bustled her new ward off to her office. The Judge signaled to Arthur to follow him back into his lair.

★ ★ ★

The Judge looked at Arthur and tried to figure out what went on inside the kid's head.

"You always so slick with women?" he finally asked.

"What do you mean?"

"Never mind. Just trying to make a joke." The Judge sighed. "Just trying to lighten the mood, son. Having someone like Karl Gottlieb on your plate can really be a grind."

"I know."

"You do?" The Judge glared at him. "You and I are gonna decide next week whether this man will be executed. Do you remotely understand what that means?"

"Not really, I guess."

"Not really . . ." He struggled to keep the mocking tone out of his voice. Intimidating the kid was not going to prepare him for a week of wading through a cesspool of habeas litigation.

"You know what, Arthur? As nasty as the Gottlieb case is, it's a relatively easy one. In fact, it may be the easiest death case you ever have." He held up his hand and scooted his chair smoothly across the hard plastic sheet between his desk and credenza. He opened the top drawer and pulled out a paperback book.

After studying the cover for a moment, he tossed it to Arthur. It was entitled: *An Interview with the Angel of Death: The Twisted Mind of Karl Gottlieb.* "You might find this interesting. It's supposedly the most objective book on Gottlieb. I got it in the mail after we sent his case back to state court. A very angry citizen thought that I should see what a monster we had, and I quote: *set loose on the heartland of America.*" He snorted.

"Since I figured the state would retry him and he'd be out of our hair, I went ahead and read it. It's not too bad."

Arthur nodded, but his expression suggested that he doubted the propriety of reading materials outside the record.

"You know those four girls he killed in Atlanta?" the Judge explained. "He broke into the house they were renting and spattered their brains all over the walls with a baseball bat. Apparently, he wanted to feel the squish between his toes, so he took his shoes off and waded around for awhile." The Judge made no effort to hide his disgust. "He was convicted of those murders on the basis of the footprints he left at that crime scene."

The Judge pulled out a drawer on the right side of his desk, grabbed a pack of cigarettes, and tapped them against the palm of his hand. Smoking was illegal in the building, but he had issued an informal ruling that excepted his office.

"Don't get me wrong. The fact of the Atlanta murders will not affect the impartiality of our deliberations in the Macon case. We will do our duty here, but remember that you already knew a whole lot about this guy before you ever stepped in this office." He softened his expression for a moment. "Shoot, the whole damn country does. So, if you're curious and want to know what I know, I don't think it's going to hurt anything."

V.

MY WAY

After just two days at work, Melanie had concluded that Arthur Hughes was an arrogant and self-important twit, and watching him sift smugly through the new pile of appellate briefs did nothing to change her opinion. At the next session of the court, the Judge, and two of his colleagues, would hear twenty-one appeals over two days. After dividing up the cases, each clerk would have six weeks to research and write the memoranda that the Judge would rely on at the hearing. Phil and Arthur acted like old pros and were quickly going through the stack, putting sticky notes on the cases they wanted to bid for.

"Does anyone want this sex discrimination case?" Phil slid a file across the battered walnut table in the chambers library. The room was a slightly bigger rectangle than their offices, but instead of a desk underneath the window, a set of movable bookcases stood overflowing with treatises, partially blocking the light from coming in. The conference table sat in the exact center, so broad that one could not shake hands with the person on the other side.

"Not me," Arthur replied. "I don't know why you want all this employment stuff. I didn't even take labor law."

"That's because you like trees more than people."

"You're right." He popped open the folder. "If Karl Gottlieb were a small shrub, for example, the world would be a much better place."

Melanie picked up the file and tried to decide whether she wanted to argue for the case. After reading the factual summary, she looked up at her co-clerks. Despite their different styles, they had become very comfortable with each other during the weeks before her arrival. They were both very smart, but Phil was a sweetie, and certainly the more cautious and deliberate of the two. Arthur was just as bright and sometimes pretty funny, but he was immature and his sense of sarcasm could cut too close to the bone. They both loved to argue, but their disagreements reflected a difference in approach rather than a difference in substance. And they shared another trait in common: self-confidence.

She was confident too but, being a southern girl, had always thought there was something vaguely unseemly about letting anyone see it. She had never liked the contestants who preened themselves and strutted about like peacocks in the pageant changing room. And law school was no different—even there she had found her classmates parading their IQs like her former rivals used to flaunt their boobs. In both venues, she had managed to emerge victorious without modifying the deferential demeanor that was her secret weapon. But sometime, she admitted, it might be interesting to show the judges the fire inside.

Even her parents were clueless about her drive and ambition. How did they think she gotten so far in life anyway? The power of sweetness? To be fair, she had been playing a role for them since she was a child and had learned that performing could stop their arguments. At times, following her around the pageant circuit was all that had kept them together. But that embarrassing demon was almost exorcised. Finishing runner-up four years earlier had given her a wonderful out from the stupid charade. Then, she had proven herself at the most famous law school in the country and now she would prove herself in the chambers of the most famous judge in the South.

Her reverie was interrupted by Phil. "Arthur and I have been tabbing the cases we're really interested in, and you should do the same. Everything is negotiable as long as we each end up with a third of 'em."

"Didn't the Judge say Arthur should take fewer because he's working on the Gottlieb case?"

"Yeah," Phil replied with a doubtful glance at his friend, "but he wants to the show the Judge that he can still handle a full load of regular cases too."

She nodded and flipped through some files, browsing through the obligatory *Issues Presented* section of each of the briefs. She didn't foresee too many arguments. Phil seemed to like the business and tax cases, while Arthur liked the environmental and civil rights stuff. She had no problem ceding that territory to them, especially since most of the unclaimed cases looked fairly interesting, but apart from some thoughtful pursing of her lips and calculated arching of her eyebrows, she withheld comment until she was halfway through the stack.

"I don't think we're going to have too many fights over these cases," she drawled sweetly, "but I'm wondering whether there's anything a little juicier that I haven't seen yet?"

"Well, there's some commercial stuff," offered Phil. "You could have *Resolution Trust Corp. v. Third Bank & Trust of Macon* if you're into the fiduciary duties of bank directors." Despite his plans to work for the ACLU, he seemed oddly interested in commercial law.

"No thanks, Phillip. I was thinking more in terms of some criminal cases. I really liked the criminal work I did at the Harvard clinic my third year."

"Prosecutorial or defense clinic?" Arthur asked. Many law schools offered students not only the possibility of representing indigent criminal defendants but also—for those students who were tougher on crime—the opportunity to help the state prosecute them instead.

"Neither," she replied, "I worked on a prisoner legal counseling project, helping prisoners write habeas corpus petitions and file complaints about civil rights violations."

Arthur gave her a smirky grin and pushed a file across the table to her. She took it cautiously and began to read. The case involved a repeat check bouncer named John Moyes who had been sentenced to eighteen months in prison. During Moyes's routine intake physical, the prison doctor, who spent two half days a week seeing to the needs of 450 inmates, decided to suspend Moyes's daily prescription of Haldol, a powerful anti-psychotic drug that he had been taking for several years to control his self-destructive impulses. The doctor had not seen Moyes before, nor did he make a complete inquiry into his medical history. Several days after his last dose of Haldol, Moyes took a cafeteria fork and removed his right eye during lunch.

To make matters worse, the doctor had not immediately ordered Moyes back on the drug after being notified at his office what his patient had done. Before the doctor got back to the prison the following day, Moyes had managed to break off a bit of spring from under his bed and crudely sawn off both of his testicles. The prisoner, through his legal guardian, was suing the prison and the State of Alabama for violating his civil rights.

"Okay," she said carefully, "he's not suing the doc because he's probably immune under state law. That's why it's a constitutional claim, so the issue is not whether the doctor made a mistake, but whether he should have known that his screwup constituted a violation of an established constitutional right, like maybe due process . . . or cruel and unusual punishment."

"Right," Arthur confirmed. "And if the right wasn't clearly established at the time of the incident," he added, assuming she had missed the most salient issue, "then everyone gets off. So, I've been looking for cases involving doctors and detainees decided before the date of the accident."

"What have you found?"

"Nothing, I just started."

She returned to the brief, a beatific study in concentration, eyes moving rapidly back and forth, left hand unconsciously curling and uncurling a lock of her hair.

"You can have it if you want," Arthur finally said. "The whole thing kind of grosses me out." In spite of the offer, she got the impression that he did not really consider the case appropriate for her. He added quickly, "Besides you obviously know more about this area of the law than I do."

"Uh-huh." Was he patronizing her? "I'll take it, Arthur."

He shrugged and pulled another file from the pile, but not before he shot a cryptic glance at Phil. What the fuck was that about? Maybe nothing. Probably nothing. And it didn't matter, because under no circumstances was she going to let him get to her.

VI.

EXCITABLE BOY

With Suzanne and Maria away at her friend Judy's for dinner, Arthur tucked himself into the corner of the living room sofa and read through the Judge's book on Karl Gottlieb. He got up only once, a bathroom break prompted by a cat's sudden scamper across the porch floor. Gottlieb was locked up miles away, but Arthur felt like he was gazing surreptitiously through the bars of his cell, and when a pair of car headlights passed the house just a little too slowly, it felt like the condemned man was looking back. The ancient décor of the living room did little to calm his nerves. The furniture dated from the same general era when Gottlieb was a kid, and whatever warped him may have happened in a room much like the one in which Arthur sat. He almost invited Phil for a nightcap at the Wild Boar to clear his head, but instead he warmed a couple of Pop-Tarts in the toaster oven, poured a glass of milk, and studied the sports page under the bright fluorescent light of the kitchen. Warm food dispelled Gottlieb's specter, but he was still relieved when the front door banged open and Maria ran down the hall.

Early the next morning, Suzanne waved something at him as he left for work. It was the Gottlieb book. "You need to be careful what you leave in the living room." Her expression was a mixture of concern and irritation. "Maria can't read, but some of the pictures in here might scare her, and I don't want to have to explain to her what this is about."

"I'm so sorry," he cried, remembering the black and white photos of broken women lying in shallow graves. "It won't happen again!" He pointed to the paperback as if to disown it. "I really never read this kind of crap."

"Then why are you reading it now?"

"For work, sort of."

"For work . . . then don't tell me." She made to pitch the book to him, but then took a closer look at it as she leaned her shoulder against the smooth plaster wall of the hallway. Even without makeup, her face was a beguiling study in concentrated thought.

"Oh, wait," she said, "don't tell me the Judge pulled Gottlieb's case again? I read in the paper this morning that the execution's scheduled for Friday."

"You didn't hear it from me."

"And is this relevant to the case?" She gestured with the book again. Her eyes shone and her tone was measured, absent was the vibe of the harried mother herding Maria around the house. He resisted a wild impulse to kiss her.

"It shouldn't be relevant, really," he explained. "According to the Judge, we work on these cases at a distance. No relatives of the victims or Gottlieb will ever appear. No last-minute witnesses. No hearing either. Everything happens in a flurry of memos hundreds of miles away from Gottlieb's prison cell." He leaned against the wall on the other side of the hall and sighed. "Not like a mystery novel. His guilt isn't in doubt, nor his ultimate fate, really. I can see why the Judge thinks this is an easy case."

"Easy?" She looked doubtful and gestured again with the book. "This was a bestseller, wasn't it?"

"Yeah." He nodded. "People are fascinated by Gottlieb. Or maybe they just want to be horrified or maybe they want to judge him." He shrugged and admitted his own prurient interest. "I read it because Gottlieb's always intrigued me. His background doesn't give any clues why he killed so many people. He didn't torture animals or set fires; he wasn't a bed-wetter; he had a college degree; he wasn't impotent . . . He could have normal romantic relationships with women."

"You're not going to invite him over for dinner, are you?" She cracked a smile and handed him the book.

"Hardly!" He stuck it in his back pocket and followed her into the kitchen where she poured both of them glasses of orange juice.

"You know the only black mark on his record was a charge of peeping into a neighbor's bedroom late one night," Arthur continued. "Nobody thought he was a great guy, but his friends and parents were really shocked to find out he was a murderer. Even after seeing tons of evidence, his mother and father still deny that he was responsible for a single killing, much less thirty."

"That's no surprise, I suppose."

He thought that she was going to say more, but she sat down and looked hard at him. It was disconcerting to be so firmly the center of her attention.

"I don't know." He shrugged. "He's always struck me as the embodiment of pure evil. You'd think someone would have noticed early on."

"And now you get to judge him."

"Well . . . the Judge does."

"But you're the arm of the Judge. You'll be doing the research and writing the memo." She sipped her juice and looked at him like he was going to work that morning at a nuclear plant and might come home covered in radiation.

★ ★ ★

When Arthur got to chambers, he went straight to Phil's office. With the addition of some personal knickknacks, a couple of oil paintings appropriated from the photocopy room, a small carpet, and some deft positioning of his furniture, he had given his work space the feel of a Victorian drawing room. Arthur found his friend leaning back in his chair, legs perched on the corner of his desk. He looked more like a muscular blond surfer dude than a highly educated law clerk, an image that was dispelled as soon as he opened his mouth and his rich baritone rolled out.

"Hey, Arthur,"—he laid down the folder that he had been reading—"you're late . . . I've been here since six." This was his habit. He claimed that years of waking up for early-morning swim practice in high school and college had never worn off.

"God," Arthur sighed, "it's a sick world where 7:15 in the morning is late." He pulled the Gottlieb book from his briefcase. "I didn't have a good night's sleep." He slid the book across the desk. "Bad dreams."

Phil glanced at the paperback but did not pick it up. "Well, no wonder. What are you reading that for?" He paused for a moment, and then his brow furrowed. "More to the point—why are you reading it at all? You're working on the Gottlieb case. Aren't you afraid that you'll prejudice the outcome?"

"Is there really any doubt about the outcome?"

"That's not the point." He slid his feet off the desk and rocked slightly in his chair. "Isn't Gottlieb entitled to have a clerk that hasn't filled his head with pulp fiction? And who says he's going to fry anyway? The Judge bought him two more years last time he came up."

"The Judge is the one who gave me the book."

Phil opened his mouth as if to respond, but then picked up a paper clip from his desk, straightened it out, and began poking the top of his wooden desk. "Why would he do that?" He looked up. "It doesn't make any sense."

"He thinks that Gottlieb is a goner . . . Maybe he's trying to make me feel better for writing memo that finds no stay of execution should issue." He shrugged. "It's kinda hard to read the book and feel sorry for the guy."

"How can you *not* feel sorry for someone who's so fucked up?"

"But that's the thing about Gottlieb. He's not just a victim passing the shit on down the line." He tapped the book. "His mom had a little postpartum depression and couldn't breast feed him, and it sounds like she was a little frustrated career-wise, but there's no history of family abuse."

"What about his father?"

"Kind of a cipher. He was a low-level bookkeeper who came home every night, poured himself a martini, and watched television. He might have been guilty of a little benign neglect. You know, lousy attendance at Little League games, stuff like that, but nothing remotely close to shocking."

"Not quite the serial killer recipe."

"Nope." Arthur saw his friend warming up to the subject despite his declared disgust with everything having to do with death cases. Everyone was fascinated by Karl Gottlieb. "Apparently he had a rough move just before he started middle school, and once he got caught as a peeping tom, but before he started killing women in graduate school, everything looked pretty normal."

"I was a little kid when it started," Phil remembered with a shake of his head. "Some farmer plowing his cornfield outside of Madison rakes up four bodies and suddenly there's a serial killer on the loose."

"Knocking women on the back of the head with a baseball bat, raping and sodomizing them after death."

"And it just kept happening."

"And the media probably helped him get away with it. The news kept describing a monster, but he looked and acted like some well-to-do prepster. Even after the panic, he could still chat up a girl in the coffee shop, offer to drive her home, and kill her instead." Arthur looked for a sign that his friend understood that this was a special case, that no one could really have a problem with this execution.

"This doesn't sound like an easy case to me, Arthur."

"What are you talking about? You mean this retroactive sanity hearing business is going to get complicated?"

"No, I mean that if anybody deserves to die, then it's Gottlieb. You see, if you had some poor likeable schmuck, it'd be easy to write a memo granting him a stay." He flicked the paper clip in the wastebasket. "It's going to be a lot harder to write that memo for Gottlieb."

"Goddamnit, Phil," he sputtered, "between you and the Judge, this memo's already written! He's ready to fry Gottlieb, and you want to save him."

"I don't want to save him." Phil got out of his chair and opened up the blinds behind his desk, revealing the green parade of trees along Oak Street that led to Suzanne's house. A car blasting its stereo shot past the courthouse. "I want to save you."

Arthur studied him closely, hoping that his friend was not about to get all evangelical. "You did not just say that."

"Look," Phil spoke, picking his words carefully, "Gottlieb's crime, his sin, his . . . his whatever, was killing people, right? I don't want to see you join that club. I know that in this case the state is going to say it's all right, it's legal, hell, it may even be legally compelled, but you don't have to participate. You don't have to join the Gottlieb club."

Arthur had heard all of the arguments against capital punishment, and he was sympathetic to many of them, but this was over the top. "First of all, I won't be killing Gottlieb; I'll be writing a memo to a federal judge. That's not quite the same as whacking someone on the head. Second, why don't we let the law dictate the memo? I don't have any agenda except to research the question I'm presented with. I'm just going to report the law to the Judge."

"I don't think it's that easy, Arthur." He sat down again as he spoke. "We just can't say that the only person who kills Gottlieb is a discretionless prison guard who pulls the switch on the Georgia electric chair. He'll get a call from the prison warden telling him to do it, and the warden will have gotten a call from the governor's office saying the same. Several courts, including ours, will have the chance to cut the governor off. And we have absolute power over what the governor can do. If your memo says no execution, then there won't be an execution." He offered Arthur a compassionate grimace. "You are much more on the line than the poor schmuck who pulls the switch. There's really nothing he can do to stop anything."

"Look," Arthur said, finding it increasingly difficult to be patient. "Save the poetic language and theological debate for the Wild Boar. If Gottlieb ends up in the electric chair, please feel free to blame the law or even blame the Judge, but leave me out of it. I've got work to do."

Phil nodded, and Arthur got up and walked to the door.

"Be careful, Art."

★ ★ ★

Arthur sat alone in the library, insulated from the din of the outside world by thick volumes containing two hundred years of federal court cases. The refuge slowly worked its magic, and eventually he was able to focus on Gottlieb's successful petition of two years earlier. It provided few new facts, but made for a compelling follow-up to his conversation with Phil. Once Gottlieb had quietly slipped away from Wisconsin, he had gone to Jacksonville, Florida, where over the next five years, he killed twelve young blond-haired women between the ages of eighteen and twenty-seven.

The most extraordinary aspect of Gottlieb's sojourn there had been his relationship with Nicole Thompson, a technician whom he met while purchasing glasses. They dated steadily during his last two years in Jacksonville and were engaged to be married just before the frenzy of killing that led to his ultimate capture. Thompson had no inkling of Gottlieb's criminal activities. He had successfully hidden the dark side of his personality from her. Yet, apart from his tendency to discuss his role in the killings in the third person, he had never shown any clinical signs of schizophrenia.

The end of Gottlieb's career as an anonymous killer began late one October night when he brought his Louisville Slugger to a Burger King at closing time and brutally murdered a seventeen-year old high school girl and her thirty-year-old manager.

Fingerprints left at the scene identified Gottlieb as the perpetrator, and when several of Gottlieb's coworkers identified him from pictures shown on television, the hunt was on.

Gottlieb's frantic flight from Jacksonville in Nicole Thompson's car bore no resemblance to his careful escape from Madison. He killed a night janitor behind a school in a South Georgia town and made off with thirty-five dollars from the unfortunate man's pocket. Stopping for gas only a block away, he inexplicably paid by credit card and put the police on a trail that eventually led them to Atlanta.

Gottlieb laid low in Atlanta three days before leaving brutal proof of his presence—four young women bludgeoned beyond recognition in a small rental house in the Buckhead neighborhood. Narrowly escaping being caught at the scene, Gottlieb led Georgia law enforcement officials on a furious six-hour chase down I-75 and various back roads to Macon where he allegedly killed his final victim, a twelve-year-old girl. Unshaven and barely coherent, the former MBA student was pulled from the car at a state police roadblock without a struggle. At the time, Gottlieb was twenty-eight years old and arguably the most infamous mass murderer in American history.

Be careful, indeed.

VII.

SUSPICIOUS MINDS

The next afternoon Melanie was in the library in the Judge's chambers, slogging through a district court opinion challenged by an appeal from a radio station that had been blocked from transferring its license to a potential buyer. She had a hard time getting excited about the intricacies of Federal Communications Commission law and kept gazing longingly at the police brutality case next on her docket. Phil worked across from her, seemingly content to plow through whatever the Judge threw at him. He and Arthur were both like furniture in the library, comfortable and at home in midst of musty legal history. She preferred to be writing motions and briefs, not just checking what the old Fifth Circuit had opined in some ancient precedent. Looking out the fourth-floor window onto downtown Clarkeston, she could see the post office where a group of Freedom Riders had sought refuge from an angry mob in 1961.

As she got back to her reading, the clanging of a telephone startled her out of the tiny print of the *Federal Reporter (2.d)*. She spotted an old fashioned circular dialer by the doorway and reached it before her co-clerk had a chance to get out of his chair. Funny, she had not known the phone was there until it started jangling the shelf where it was squeezed in between a row of books. She picked it up and a moment later gave an alarmed look to Phil.

"No, you can't speak with him; he's not here." She held the phone several inches from her ear and winced. "Would you like to talk to Ms. Stillwater—"

"She most certainly is not!" Melanie said indignantly. "And you should—" She forced herself to listen for a while longer, started to speak, and then gave the phone a hard look and put it back on the receiver. "What the fuck!"

"What is it?" Phil pushed his yellow pad to the side. "Who was that?"

"I don't know . . . I think maybe I should talk to the Judge first." She looked back at the phone as if it might jump off the shelf on its own. This was not exactly the excitement she had been daydreaming about. "This woman called Ms. Stillwater a 'conspiring bitch.'"

"A what? Who did?"

"A conspiring bitch! She said that Stillwater was part of a plot, along with the Judge and half the courthouse."

"What plot?"

Melanie considered whether she should say anything more. The level of anger and hysteria on the other end of the phone line had been unnerving. "A conspiracy to cover up the murder of her daughter. She said that her daughter clerked here five years ago and that someone killed her. She said a shitload more vile stuff, but that was the gist of it."

"Here? You mean clerked for the Judge?"

"That's what she said." She tapped her pencil impatiently on the table. "I wish he wasn't in Atlanta."

"It's probably just a crank call."

"It was totally a crank call, but we need to tell him anyway. I mean, wouldn't you want to know if someone was slandering you?"

"I suppose." Phil ran his fingers through his thick blond hair, and she wondered for the third time that day why she was not more attracted to him. Just a little too handsome, she supposed. Nobody has the right to be that nice and that cute. More likely her lukewarm response was a sensible defense mechanism against what would undoubtedly be a ruinous office romance.

"I'm sure the Judge has gotten a lot of crank calls in his day." He continued, "Didn't the governor of Georgia once call and tell him to give himself a barbed wire enema?" He gave her a thoughtful look. "Let's ask Ms. Stillwater. Maybe she's talked to your friend before." She nodded and followed him to the alcove outside the Judge's office. The secretary looked up from her typewriter and smiled when they came in.

"You two are looking very industrious today. Have you got something for me to type up?" Her efficiency was legendary. Even with three clerks dedicated to the nonstop production of paperwork, she never fell behind and was constantly asking them for their next round of revisions on memos and draft opinions.

"Uh ... I just got a really strange phone call, and we wanted to ask you about it."

"Ms. Stillwater," Melanie lowered her voice, "did one of the Judge's clerks die five years ago?"

"Oh Lord, you didn't get a call from Shirley Bastaigne, did you?" Ms. Stillwater's face turned pink with embarrassment. "It's been a couple of years since she called, so I didn't think I needed to warn you. What did that horrible woman say?"

"Well, mainly that you, the Judge, and the rest of the courthouse were engaged in a conspiracy to cover up the murder of her daughter." Melanie crossed her arms and then shrugged. "She was pretty hysterical."

"She usually is. Sit down, and let me tell you the story. I'm afraid this is my fault for not saying anything before." She sighed, embarrassed to be relating anything negative about the Judge's chambers.

Melanie remembered a similar look on her mother's face when she revealed somberly that one of her unmarried cousins had gotten pregnant.

"I don't really know where to begin. Carolyn Bastaigne clerked here about five years ago. A month before she was supposed to leave for New York and start a job at Cravath, Something & Something–"

"—Cravath, Swaine, & Moore?" Melanie completed the name of the famous New York City sweat shop.

"That's it." The secretary folded her hands penitentially on her desk. "Well, Carolyn worked late one evening and fell down the stairs after she left the office. A janitor found her lying with her neck broken at the bottom of the stairwell." She shook her head and sighed again. "Poor girl. She was probably the laziest clerk who ever worked here, but I wouldn't wish that on anyone. She had her whole life in front of her." Melanie nodded, eager to get more information about the tragedy. "That's it really. A horrible unfortunate accident."

"So where does the murder conspiracy part come in?" Melanie asked, remembering the hard marble of the stairwell she had climbed just the day before. "I've walked down those stairs. It's not too hard to imagine what would happen if someone tripped."

"And why's she so mad at you?" Phil added.

"Well, I suppose she's angry with me because I shield her from the Judge. After her first nasty talk with him, he told me never to put her through or give him her messages. I guess that makes me part of the conspiracy."

"But why does she blame the Judge?" Melanie asked.

"You'll have to ask him. I mentioned it to him once, and he growled at me to mind my own business." She paused and smoothed out the top of her skirt on her lap. "But if I were you, I'd just let sleeping dogs lie. I think he'd rather forget that it ever happened."

"I don't blame him," Phil said as he got up. "Thanks for the heads up, though . . .and the story." He grinned broadly and winked at Melanie. "If we get another call, we'll be sure to put her straight through to you."

Ms. Stillwater rolled her eyes and shoo'd the two clerks out of her office.

They walked in silence to the library and sat back down in front of their work. Melanie flipped through a case report, looked up, and frowned. The afternoon sun suffused the room with a yellow light, setting dust motes dancing in the air. For some reason the story of the ancient accident seemed more compelling to her than the appeal she was supposed to be working on. She had never been this distractable in law school.

"I wonder why Mrs. Bastaigne is still so emotional after all this time?" she wondered aloud.

"Some people never get over their grief," Phil replied. "Losing a child is a really hard."

"Of course, but why blame the Judge?" As someone who had admired him since childhood, she found any attitude other than hero worship hard to understand.

"Maybe she didn't want her daughter working for him in the first place. You saw that movie last year with the crowd lynching him in effigy. Maybe she's a racist who blames him and federal government for everything wrong in the world."

"Maybe," Melanie said doubtfully, "but you wouldn't think that a paranoid racist would raise a child who would go to an elite law school and then clerk for the Judge."

"Maybe Carolyn was a rebel? And who says she went to an elite law school? The Judge went to Mercer and hires Mercer clerks sometimes."

"Hmm . . . look, it's four thirty, and I need a little break." She gave her co-clerk a mischievous smile. "Let's go down to the main courthouse library on the second floor and find the story in the newspaper. The death must have been pretty big news in a town this small."

"Sorry," Phil replied with a gesture to the legal pad in front of him. "I've got to knock out this draft out by tomorrow. You go down and tell me what you find."

Melanie fetched the keys from her office in case she returned after Ms. Stillwater had locked the doors for the night and then walked down the dark, empty corridor to the elevator. She pushed the down arrow but curiosity drew her farther down the hall to the stairwell door. After a moment's hesitation, she pulled the handle and found herself standing where Carolyn Bastaigne must have passed just before she fell. The faint echo of footfalls drifted up toward her. Melanie grabbed the worn brass handrail firmly as she headed down, slightly tippy as her heels searched for a purchase on the smooth marble steps. She paused on the cold terrazzo of the third-floor landing. In the afternoon, little sunlight penetrated the eastward-facing windows, and she gave an involuntary shiver. Ms. Stillwater had not said exactly where Carolyn had been found; perhaps this was where the janitor discovered her.

At the second-floor exit, she slipped through a metal door into the brightly painted space where the communal resources of the courthouse were located. The office of the Clerk of the Court, the main library, a small vending machine room, and lounge occupied most of the space, and it was here, on neutral ground, that the law clerks from different chambers met and gossiped. The Judge hardly had the building to himself. He shared it with two district court judges, two magistrates, and another appellate judge who had retired but still was on active "senior" status. Each of these Judges had one or two law clerks. Although clerks sometimes visited other chambers, most of the socializing occurred in the library or the lounge. The judges shared an obsession with confidentiality and got grumpy if outside clerks spent too much time in chambers. Melanie thought they were all being a bit paranoid.

She sat down at the microfiche reader and inserted the card listed *Clarkesville Chronicle*, 1984. Ms. Stillwater had said that Carolyn Bastaigne had died just before her clerkship was over, so Melanie guessed that the accident must have occurred in June or July, the months when old clerks were most likely to rotate out of chambers. After a few minutes of scrolling, she found a page-three story, dated June 27.

FEDERAL LAW CLERK FOUND DEAD IN COURTHOUSE STAIRWELL

Carolyn Bastaigne, a law clerk working in the federal building on Court Street, was found by a janitor early Thursday morning in a stairwell landing between the third and fourth floors. The initial police report lists the cause of death as "broken neck." In a brief interview, a janitor, who asked that his name not be used, also described facial injuries caused by the fall. Bastaigne was seen by a courthouse employee leaving the office where she worked at 6:30 p.m. Police place the time of the accident shortly thereafter. Ms. Bastaigne, a native of New York City, was a graduate of Columbia College and Yale University Law School. She was finishing a one-year clerkship and had planned to return to New York to practice law.

Melanie read through the article twice and frowned at its lack of details. After looking at it one more time, she scrolled ahead looking for a follow-up story. In the June 30 issue, she found a report of the coroner's inquest.

INQUEST FINDS LAW CLERK DEATH ACCIDENTAL

A federal official today ruled that the death of Carolyn Bastaigne, a native New Yorker and an employee of the US Federal Court of Appeals for the Eleventh Circuit, was accidental. No evidence of foul play was found and a brief statement issued noted that the accident occurred in a secure building more than ninety minutes after it closed.

Both stories were filed by a local reporter named Sidney Dumont. Melanie skimmed through later issues of the newspaper but found no follow-up. She leaned back in the chair and contemplated the story. The death of Carolyn Bastaigne had barely caused a ripple in the Clarkeston news scene. Odd, given that very morning the *Chronicle* had considered the expansion of the animal shelter front page material.

She flicked off the microfiche reader and smiled. Now, here was a research project you could get your teeth into. In law school, she had enjoyed working in the clinic, meeting with real clients, asking them questions and trying to figure out legal strategies that might work. She liked the front end of the legal process, the fact-finding and the little mysteries. Working for an appellate judge and never seeing the actual parties to the case seemed too much an extension of her time editing the student law journal.

A few minutes later, she knocked on Phil's office door and summarized the slim set of facts for him as she sat down. "So many things bug me about the newspaper story that I don't know where to begin. First, why wasn't there more coverage? I read the *Chronicle*. You'd think that a mysterious death in the federal courthouse would warrant a hell of a lot more ink."

"Must be part of the conspiracy that Mrs. Bastaigne was talking about," Phil teased.

"You laugh," she said with a smile, "but it's just the sort of thing to fuel a mother's paranoia. Not to mention that the article never says which judge she worked for. Given the headlines he's made over the years, you'd think that the Judge would be mentioned. About the accident itself, I hate to be Sherlocky—"

"—more like Ms. Marple."

"Give me V. I. Warshawski at least!" She snagged Phil's wastebasket with her left leg and balanced a foot on its edge. "Anyway, why was she going home down the stairs? Have you ever been tempted to go down those stairs at night?"

Phil shook his head and Melanie continued.

"They come out on the wrong side of the building from the parking lot for one thing. And didn't Stillwater say that she was lazy? Sounds like an elevator person to me."

"Sounds like someone threw her lazy butt down the stairs to me!" Phil grinned.

"Will you be serious for a second? I also wonder about this 'courthouse employee' who saw her at six thirty. Apart from clerks working late, this place is empty as Ronald Reagan's cranium by five fifteen. Neither the Judge nor Ms. Stillwater would be here after six thirty."

"It was probably some janitor or security guard."

"Maybe."

"Anyway, we should tell Arthur something in the morning, in case the crazy lady calls back," she added with a hint of an eye roll. "He'll be sure to have an opinion on all this."

"I don't know." Phil grabbed a book and put pen to paper, a signal for her to leave. "He's got plenty on his mind already."

VIII

ETERNITY IN A SPACIOUS GRAVE

W hat people did not understand was the relation of process to substance. The Judge twirled an unlit cigarette in his hand as he pondered the complicated legal dance that would end in the execution of Karl Gottlieb. The clearer a criminal's guilt, the less understanding the public had of the importance of the procedures established by law. Those who thought about the problem assumed that habeas corpus constituted a safeguard for the accused. They were right in a way, but more importantly proper procedure was a safeguard for the legal system itself and the judiciary especially. "It makes it look like were doing law," he had said to his wife before she died. "Dotting the *i*'s and crossing the *t*'s with due deliberation differentiates us from the bloodthirsty mob shouting for justice."

As he waited for Arthur to enter his office, he wondered whether his young clerk understood that Gottlieb's fate this time was preordained. After the surprise victory in his previous appeal, no one could doubt that the Eleventh Circuit was impartial and fair. Any plausible procedural justification that led to execution on this occasion would be viewed as inevitable and unbiased. Yet, he would let Arthur dance the dance. Once the necessary adjustments to his naïveté and his overconfidence had been made, he might turn out to be a pretty good clerk.

"Now, that you've had some time to study on it," he asked as the young man settled down in the brown leather chair facing his desk. "How are you going to address Gottlieb's argument that he was incompetent to stand trial and his conviction should be reversed?"

"Okay." Arthur looked at the notes on his lap. "As you know, plenty of cases say it's an error for a court to fail to order a psychiatric exam, but no state has been creative enough to hold a retrospective hearing on the matter five years after the defective trial . . . at least until Georgia did with Gottlieb."

The Judge nodded.

"But I think there might be parallel kinds of cases where states have tried to remedy a mistake after the fact," his clerk suggested hopefully. "For example, defendants sometimes claim that ballistic tests should have been performed on weapons, and I've found some cases where states have conducted retroactive tests on handguns. And there should be some cases where a defendant claims that a blood test should have been done, and then the state runs a post-conviction test on the old blood."

"Interesting little problem, isn't it?"

"I guess it's all about the quality of the process."

"Exactly!" The Judge jerked his thumb toward the closed curtains and scowled. "The world out there doesn't know shit about how the death penalty really works. They think it's about surprise witnesses, last-minute appearances by family members, lawyers rushing papers to the prison warden. What horseshit! People read too many mystery novels. It's all about the process. It's complicated and sometimes it's even boring. But it happens *here*, three hundred miles from Gottlieb's cell on death row. We'll decide whether Gottlieb dies—and no one even knows where we are or what the hell we really do."

"Yes, sir." His downward glance suggested that he was beginning to get adjusted to the new weight on his shoulders.

The Judge considered lighting up, but decided to wait. Showing weakness was a mistake. The chambers would not be the same if he placed himself on level ground with his clerks. Judge Henderson disagreed and treated his like bosom buddies. He was a good friend and a good judge, but it was a dangerous idea to treat twenty-five-year-old clerks as friends, even when he had no one else he could really talk to. He dismissed Arthur with a wave.

"But don't be fooled by the physical distance between us and Gottlieb, Mr. Hughes, the wheels of justice are grinding here. Don't get your ass caught in the gears."

★ ★ ★

Phil sat in the library, flipping through a treatise on trademark law and wondering why he did not find the woman sitting across from him more attractive. Melanie had a great sense of humor, at least when she wasn't sniping at Arthur, and a lively wit was what he appreciated most. Not to mention that she was tall and athletic, with a mysterious full-lipped smile that should have been irresistible. She was also aggressive, ambitious, and clearly used to getting what she wanted, but that was no big deal. After all, his only successful romance in college was with a domineering vegan who viewed compromise on any issue, food-related or not, as unthinkable.

After lunch, he saw Arthur emerge from his office and start collecting waxy pages curling out of the fax machine. He pressed them flat on the library conference table and went to collect more from Ms. Stillwater's office. Phil took a peak at the stack and saw that Gottlieb's pleadings were finally arriving. The Judge would rely on Arthur's summary rather than read all the voluminous original documents himself.

After ten minutes of ferrying paper from the fax to the library, Arthur sat down and almost immediately commented on the proceedings.

"Fuck," he spit out. "What a bucket of fuck!"

"What's the matter?"

"I've been researching the retroactive sanity hearing all morning, and his fucking petition adds a new claim on top of that one." Arthur slammed his pencil down, and the tip went flying past Melanie's head.

"Hey!"

"Sorry . . ." He turned and explained himself. "Gottlieb's arguing that he deserves a new hearing because his death sentence was based on an invalid prior conviction–that earlier conviction for the Buckhead murders."

"I didn't know the Buckhead trial came first."

"Yeah, the Atlanta prosecutors were more efficient, I guess." Arthur said, "Anyway, a murderer is only eligible for the death penalty if the aggravating factors in his case outnumber the mitigating factors. In the Macon case I've got, Gottlieb was sentenced to death based on two aggravating circumstances. This earlier conviction in the Buckhead murders was one, and the second was that the Macon murder was 'especially atrocious, heinous, or cruel' as set forth in the capital murder statute. No mitigating circumstances were found."

"So how does that make his conviction invalid?" Even though he believed all death penalty convictions should be overturned, Phil knew how to play the game, although it left him feeling vaguely sullied. "In Georgia, if you lose 2-0 or 1-0, you still go to the chair. What's wrong with the Buckhead conviction, anyway?"

"Gottlieb says he was incompetent to stand trial, just like he said he was incompetent to be tried in the Macon case. The twist is that no one ever retroactively evaluated his competency to be tried for the Buckhead killings." Arthur rubbed his forehead with the palm of his hand. "And we've got the Judge's own published opinion from two years ago standing for the proposition that failure to order a competency hearing is error! The conviction in the Buckhead case can't be used as an aggravating factor to support his Macon death sentence."

"Well, there's still the heinousness aggravating factor." Melanie finally chimed in. "Like Phillip says, a 1-0 loss is as bad for Gottlieb as a 2-0 loss."

Arthur picked up the pleadings and shuffled through them while he talked. Phil felt a pang of pity for his friend as he struggled with the arguments. "I don't get it. Gottlieb's new lawyers are awesome . . . Why would they bother attacking one aggravating factor but not the other?"

"Good question." Phil had a feeling that the answer to Arthur's question might end up saving Gottlieb's life. He admired the persistence of Gottlieb's attorneys, undoubtedly working for free under a lot of pressure for the sole purpose of saving a life that most Americans thought was not worth saving.

Phil watched Arthur read to himself as Melanie studied him. Why was she not participating more in the discussion? She was usually interested in criminal law after all. Phil considered changing the subject and bringing up yesterday's strange phone call, but then Arthur let out another groan.

"I can't believe this . . . Gottlieb already won the heinousness argument in an appeal a couple of years ago. He's not a heinous killer."

"What?" Phil and Melanie burst out simultaneously.

"According to the Georgia Supreme Court," Arthur read, *"especially heinous killers invoke the terror of impending death in their victims."* He looked up and spoke in a resigned voice. *"Heinous murderers torture their victims first or enjoy forcing them to contemplate their own deaths.* In the Macon case, Gottlieb snuck up behind his victim and clubbed her. She probably never knew what hit her."

Phil's heart gave a little leap. He had no natural sympathy for Gottlieb. The man was a monster, but that was all the more reason that Arthur should not indulge the public's lust for retribution. There was now no reason for Arthur to be Gottlieb's last victim. "So, we're back to zero-zero . . . tie goes to Gottlieb." Phil tried to contain his excitement. "Arthur, this is great! You can write a memo telling the Judge that the execution has to be stayed. You're off the hook!"

Arthur frowned. Phil could tell from the clenched teeth and glaring eyes that he had already imagined himself as the clerk who denied Karl Gottlieb's last appeal.

"Off the hook? If you think that I'd feel guilty about pulling the switch on this guy, then you're crazy."

"He's a person, Arthur."

"That may be so, but he hasn't won yet." He pushed the papers in front of him and sighed. "But you're right, Phil. I need to just do the math and stop treating this like a game." He paused and shook his head. "I can't believe I need to report to the Judge tomorrow."

Phil watched Melanie frown and get up to leave. She paused at the library door and offered some advice. "The solution is pretty obvious, Arthur, if you just think about it hard enough."

IX.

SWEET DREAMS ARE MADE OF THESE

Maria was safely asleep and the front porch beckoned to Suzanne. The afternoon rain had come later than usual, granting relief without giving the sun time to burn off the moisture from roofs, roads, and walkways. The wind blew from the north, and she could almost imagine the relief of fall was not two long months away. She sat and rocked in the darkness, multiplying the breeze and dreaming of taking Maria to the beach for a late-summer vacation. But the thought of sand led to thoughts of beach toys and so to the toys scattered all around her and soon she was reaching down and pitching the closest ones into the toy chest and then following a trail of LEGOs around the corner of the porch.

As she picked up the last block and squinted at her neighbors' window to confirm that she was really seeing porn on their television screen, she heard the front door open and watched Arthur lean against the corner of the railing, half in shadow, half illuminated by the streetlamp. He was a handsome boy, tall and lean with a tousled mop of dark hair. She wondered what he would do if she sidled over and put her arms around his trim waist. She settled for studying him a bit longer. The contemplative pose suited him, lending a gravitas that was sometimes lacking when he opened his mouth.

"Hey," she spoke softly to avoid startling him. "If you came out to help with cleanup, you're too late."

"Sorry." He turned and shifted his stance, as if trying to decide whether he should go back in. "Is there anything more I can do out here?"

"Not really." She walked past him and dropped the final load of toys into the chest. "But you could go to the kitchen and bring me a beer."

"Sure."

When he returned, two brown bottles in hand, he sat down next to her on the porch swing and carefully wiped away the moisture condensing on the glass. He handed her one, clinked it with his own, and stared out over the street.

"Long day?" No psychic powers were necessary to divine his mood. He grunted and mumbled something inaudible that ended in *Gottlieb*.

"That can't be any fun," she replied.

He snorted. "The Macon murder has dimmed my love for baseball, that's for sure." He turned toward her and tried to explain what was bothering him. "I just finished reading the last chapter of the book that the Judge gave me. The author interviewed Gottlieb in prison a couple of times and asked him why he killed all those women."

"What sort of horseshit did he come up with?" There was no possible *reason* that he could have given.

"Well, the guy's not too introspective, so he mostly rambled on in the third person about how he killed them, but when the psychologist pressed him, he started talking about how he *possessed* his victims. That was what obsessed him, possession and control. He was playing God." He picked at the label on his bottle while he spoke, trying to unpeel it in one piece. "Gottlieb would look around a place and decide who would live and who would die. He was the ultimate decider of fates. That's why he didn't torture them or even particularly care to see them suffer. That's why he always whacked their skull from behind and then raped them. It was the ultimate possession he was after, the ultimate act of control."

"That's just sick." She took a sip of her beer, but it tasted metallic and flat.

"If you enjoy snuffing out candles, you don't want them fighting with you." Arthur finished his peeling job and held up his prize.

"That's well put," she said, "if somewhat creepy."

A car drove too quickly down the street, stereo blaring so loudly that she could not hear the beginning of his reply.

". . .I've read about a bunch of famous serial killers. With most of them, you get some sort of insight into what went wrong in their lives. Most of them were horribly abused as kids or something like that."

"But most child abuse victims don't go out and kill dozens of people," she said.

"Of course not," he agreed. "Anyway, I'm not excusing anyone. I'm just saying that you can sort of understand what might drive them. You could imagine going back in time, giving them to responsible parents, and saving the world a lot of pain. Another bunch of killers are clearly brain damaged or drugged up in some way. They're scary, but easy to understand." He frowned. "Gottlieb's different."

For a couple of minutes, they sat quietly and listened to the low drone of the summer insects sporadically interrupted by the buzz and sizzle of the neighbor's bug zapper. Suzanne shifted her body on the swing so she could see him better.

"Did you ever read Dante's *Inferno*?" she asked.

"Back in high school. I thought that all the different layers of Hell were pretty cool. Well, hot . . . whatever."

"I had to read it in college," she explained. "I've never forgotten this guy that Dante meets in the frozen lake at the very bottom of Hell.

"Dante is shocked to see a monk he'd spoken to in Italy just before he started his journey into Hell. The monk explains that he hasn't died yet; his body is still walking around Italy, doing all sorts of horrible things. It's just that when he killed all of his dinner guests one night, his soul became so evil that it plunged straight down to Hell in advance of his body." She looked out at the street. "That's always stuck with me. I imagine soulless bodies wandering around the earth committing crimes. You read about some convenience store clerk who's told to lie on the floor and gets shot for no reason. It seems like nobody's really in the killer's body at all when it commits the crime because no human could do such a thing."

She turned and looked at him. "Does that make any sense to you?"

He nodded after a moment. "I don't know whether it makes sense or not—theology is Phil's thing—but Gottlieb hardly seems human."

"He's the ultimate predator is what he is." She shivered and slid closer to him. "I shouldn't admit it, but part of me will feel relieved when he's executed."

She looked out over the familiar street and back to Arthur. He didn't look like he was going to get much sleep that night. Suddenly, she was glad of her job and its intimacy with life. She did not envy the dark business of death that got worked in the Judge's chambers.

"Whatever he is," Arthur replied, "he's not alone. People like him have probably always been out there. I kind of like your theory because it makes them unpersons, not really human at all, like some kind of dangerous virus."

She nodded and a dark intuition settled between them.

"But what if there's something fundamentally human about Gottlieb?" he continued. "What if the only difference between him and normal people is that his predatory instinct is just a lot closer to the surface?"

They watched the street in silence, considering the awful possibility that Gottlieb had somehow cultivated and fed something that lurked in all men.

★ ★ ★

When he got to the courthouse at seven the next morning, Arthur found his co-clerks waiting for him in the conference room. He had spent all night thinking about Gottlieb's petition and could come to no other conclusion than to advise the Judge that the execution had to be stayed. Gottlieb's attorneys had made both of the aggravating circumstances in his case disappear. The propriety of the retroactive sanity hearing was now irrelevant.

Phil spoke to him first. "What are you going to tell the Judge?" His plaintive look irritated Arthur. His co-clerk was sure how the case should come out, how every death penalty case should come out. It let him escape the hard thinking.

"You win." Arthur shrugged. "I don't even have to get into the question of whether the retroactive sanity hearing was okay. He wins this one on procedural grounds."

"No, he doesn't." Melanie spoke from the far end of the table, not even bothering to look up from her book. "He's toast."

"What?" She glanced up as Arthur spoke. She wore a teal jacket and an intricately embroidered white blouse. Behind the table she looked more like a television anchor woman than a law clerk.

"You're missing the forest for the trees."

Arthur sat down across from her and waited impatiently for the explanation. Phil's eyes were wide.

"You left the file here last night," she explained. "Look, this is Gottlieb's second petition, right?"

"Yeah."

"This is his second petition, right?"

"Yes." He emphasized the answer to show he had heard the question right the first time. She stared at him and blinked, as if waiting for a sign that he comprehended her secret code.

"Arthur, what's the foremost law of habeas corpus?"

"Oh, just spit it out, Melanie," Phil broke in impatiently.

And then it dawned on Arthur. He had gotten so drawn into the substance of Gottlieb that he had forgotten the importance of procedure. "You cannot make arguments in your second petition that you could have made in your first petition."

"Bingo." Her expression suggested that she was explaining something simple to a slow child. "Without that rule, you could bring an endless stream of petitions, all alleging the same claims, delaying your execution indefinitely."

Arthur nodded, feeling both stupid and relieved when he realized where she was going. "You're right. I read his first petition yesterday—his lawyer didn't raise any objection to the use of the Buckhead murders as an aggravating circumstance!"

"Exactly. Now, if you remember your federal jurisdiction class, there is one exception." She waited for Arthur to fill in the blank.

"Uh . . . let's see . . . if Gottlieb relies on a case that is a radical change in the law or that establishes a new fundamental right, then he is excused from not raising a claim in his first petition." He looked at his watch. He had to talk to the Judge in thirty minutes, not much time to assess the law of aggravating circumstances at the time of Gottlieb's first petition three years earlier. With his execution scheduled in less than twenty-four hours, there was no time to delay. As he jumped up to look for cases, he glanced at Melanie.

"Thanks!" He felt a bit foolish that she had shown him up so easily, but being bested by her was far better than screwing up something so simple in front of the Judge. The smile he got in return for his gratitude was a bit smug.

"Gottlieb's relying on precedent that's almost ten years old." She pushed a light brown book toward him with a case marked by a square of yellow sticky paper.

"What?" Surely she had not done his research for him.

"The Eleventh Circuit decided a long time ago that a court can't use a bad prior conviction as an aggravating circumstance." He read the brief synopsis of the case note and saw that she was right. "Which means Gottlieb could have made this exact same argument about aggravation in the first petition, but his lawyer forgot." She picked up her things, stood up, and walked toward the door. "You're welcome," she added with a quick turn before she headed down the corridor to her office.

Arthur glanced at Phil, who sat speechless at his end of the table; then he grabbed a piece of paper and started to write an addendum to his memo for the Judge. After a moment, he grumbled and looked up. "I don't know whether to kiss her or throw something at her."

"Forget about her," Phil said abruptly. "What are you going to do about Gottlieb?"

"I'm going to show the Judge this case that Melanie found."

"And now the retroactive sanity hearing issue is alive again. What about that argument?"

Arthur knew what his friend wanted to hear, that he too had principles. "I've found some relevant cases, I think." After running into Melanie's bulldozer, he was no longer as sure of himself. "I'll lay out what they say for the Judge and let him decide."

Phil frowned, saying nothing, but doing a poor job of hiding his disapproval.

"Look, I didn't write the law," Arthur said. He held up the book and gestured with it. "And I didn't decide these cases."

"There's no law here apart from you and the Judge."

Arthur shook his head slowly. "I don't believe that." He picked up the book and legal pad and left the room without looking back.

★ ★ ★

Contrary to public perception and thanks to modern technology, a prisoner's second (or third or fourth) habeas petition moves through the system quite quickly. In the twenty-four hours after Gottlieb's second petition was filed, it had already been denied by the state trial and appellate courts. A decision by the Georgia Supreme Court had arrived Wednesday at lunchtime. The federal district court acted next, finishing its review early Thursday morning. The Judge wanted to be ready to rule by later on Thursday, which would allow the US Supreme Court the rest of the day and the wee hours of Friday morning to decide whether or not to stay the execution and hear the case. Arthur knew that the Supreme Court heard arguments in only two or three death cases a year, so Gottlieb had no real chance if the Judge and the other two members of the panel did not grant him the stay he requested.

When Arthur walked into the Judge's office, his boss did not bother to look up. The preliminary memo lay on his desk, and he was studying it through a pair of reading glasses perched on the end of his nose. When he finished the last page, he turned his gaze to his clerk. "Do you have anything to add to what you've got here?"

Arthur could not tell from his expression whether the Judge approved of the memo or not. "Yes, sir, the issue of improper aggravation turns out to be easier than I thought. Gottlieb's law-yers should have raised it in the first petition three years ago. It's procedurally barred now, even though it's otherwise a winner." He felt a little guilty for not mentioning Melanie's role in his conclusion, but that regret faded when the Judge made it clear that he had already figured out the answer.

"Obviously." He nodded impatiently. "And what about the retroactive sanity hearing?"

Arthur hesitated for a moment, acutely aware that Gottlieb's life hung in the balance. Until that moment, he had not decided where the cases pushed him, but as he spoke, it seemed that the State of Georgia had the better of the argument and he gradually donned the robe of advocate.

"Even after going through the computer databases and all the West digests, I couldn't find a single example of a state court holding a retroactive competency hearing, but courts have fre-quently held retroactive hearings of other kinds. In one Fifth Circuit case, a gang member was convicted of murder, but on appeal he successfully argued that the state should have granted his request to run ballistics tests on the alleged murder weapon. The state performed the test three years after the crime and proved that his pistol was the murder weapon after all. Court says no problem, and he stays in jail.

"Another case involved a rapist seeking to overturn his conviction because no tests were done to prove fluids found on the victim's clothes were his. Instead of giving him a new trial, the Fourth Circuit ordered the test be conducted on evidence still in the state's possession. The blood matched, and the case says that the retroactive correction of the error was permissible.

"Why shouldn't Georgia be able to do the same with the issue of Gottlieb's competency?" Arthur asked earnestly. "The State has collected a bunch of evidence of his mental state at the time of trial, including the transcript and the testimony of his lawyers, the trial judge, and even one of his cell mates. I think the analogy to ballistics testing or blood testing is a pretty good one."

The Judge swiveled his chair sideways and stared at the curtains hiding the picture window. He smiled and nodded. "Nice job, Mr. Hughes. Your enthusiasm for this case is almost catching, but I'm afraid I don't really buy the analogy."

Arthur sat in stunned silence.

"Ballistics and DNA tests give *yes* or *no* answers. They can be performed years later with little or no loss of accuracy. Testing competency is a lot different—it's hardly an exact science even at the time of trial. Once years have passed, how can we really be sure that Gottlieb was competent?"

"But I've read the transcripts," Arthur insisted. "He's perfectly coherent, sometimes even brilliant."

"But you've read the book too, son."

But the book is irrelevant, Arthur thought. And giving me the book was probably a breach of judicial ethics.

"If he's crazy," the Judge continued, "then it's a very subtle crazy, likely to show itself in ways other than ranting and raving in the courtroom. Who knows what was running through that twisted mind of his?"

He paused for a moment and sighed. "And I'll tell you a secret. I don't even think he killed the Macon girl. The details of the crime don't fit his pattern at all, and the only witness who placed him anywhere near the victim couldn't remember a thing until she was hypnotized *after* seeing all the news reports about the famous killer in custody. It would be pretty ironic to execute him for a crime that he didn't commit."

He was watching Arthur with a look that might have been pity or sadness. "You've done good work though, excellent work. You took this further than I thought you possibly could."

Arthur shrugged. Shot down twice in one morning, he just wanted to get back to his office. The excitement and exhilaration of his first day on the job seemed long behind him. "All right, I'll go and draft an order granting Gottlieb's stay."

The Judge frowned and turned back toward the curtains. "I don't think that will be necessary." For a long moment, the only sound in the office was the distant tapping of Ms. Stillwater's keyboard and the hum of the air conditioner. "In theory, this court should issue a stay of execution and hold oral argument to give his attorney a chance to submit more detailed briefs on the issue, but that's not going to change the end result. While Gottlieb waits for a decision in this case, the governor would probably sign a death warrant for the Buckhead murders.

"The bottom line is, your work won't be wasted. Although your analogy to ballistics and blood testing isn't perfect, it's plenty for the other two judges on the panel who would never consider granting him a stay this time for any reason anyway! It's a fact of life that a judge cannot remedy all the errors he sees, especially in high-profile murder cases. We gave Gottlieb a second bite at the apple last time and bought him about two years more than he deserved."

Arthur watched wide-eyed, scarcely believing what he was hearing. At one moment Gottlieb had won a stay and in the next he was dead. Was this really the herioc figure who did battle with the governor of Georgia back in the sixties? If the Judge noticed his expression, he didn't acknowledge it.

"Don't be so shocked," the Judge continued. "Look what's happened to Justice Brennan. By becoming the Great Dissenter, by arguing every goddamn point in every goddamn case, he no longer has any credibility left for the cases that he might win.

"Go draft me a short order denying Gottlieb's petition."

Arthur went back to his office and wrote the order. He cited the Fifth and Fourth Circuit cases on retroactive testing of weapons and fluids. He wrote persuasively and realized the Judge was right about the other members of the panel. They would not question his reasoning. He reread the memo twice before making the long walk down the hall to Ms. Stillwater's office. She took it from him without comment.

"The Judge is gone," she said. "You can go on home if you want to."

He took her advice, but walked through the college campus instead of going home, tracing a meandering path through the outskirts of the town. He arrived on Oak Street two hours later than usual, exhausted and relieved to see a bright light shining in the hallway of Suzanne's house.

When he got to work the next day, he found a photocopy of a fax on his desk:

To: ALL ACTIVE JUDGES
Date: Friday, September 1
From: Mark Davis, Clerk of the Court

Subject: EXECUTION OF
KARL ROBERT GOTTLIEB

Attached for your information is the US Supreme Court order entered last night in the Karl Gottlieb case. The Eleventh Circuit panel entered an order denying CPC and a stay of execution yesterday, August 18, at 3:11 p.m.

Mr. Gottlieb was pronounced dead at 7:16 a.m. today.

X.

THE MORNING AFTER BLUES

P hil enjoyed almost everything about his new life in Georgia: the intimacy of the Judge's chambers, his tiny but funky downtown apartment, the grandeur of the old Carnegie Public Library just down the street from his place, and his favorite graduation present, a second-hand Volkswagen Rabbit provided by his mom that let him explore every corner of the atmospheric town. The only thing he didn't like was seeing a friend forced to decide whether habeas corpus petitioners should live or die.

After waiting all day for Arthur to emerge from his office, Phil walked down the short carpeted hall and knocked on his door. Hearing no response, he paused and listened for any sign of activity. He knew his friend was in there, so he rapped once again and then pushed the door halfway open.

Arthur sat with his back to the desk, looking out his window onto the courthouse square. His broad shoulders leaned hard into his chair, and his thick brown hair, uncut since he arrived in Clarkeston, bunched up against the top of his collar. Obviously thinking about the prior day's events, he presented a noble and compelling sight. Phil's heart went out to him.

"How about a pitcher at the Boar?" Phil asked, wondering if a change of venue might help slough the weight off his friend's shoulders.

"How about three of them?" Arthur turned grimly and tossed a pen onto his desk.

"Done!" Phil smiled and looked at his watch. "The Judge left early today so we should be good to go in another fifteen minutes or so."

Phil studied his friend, trying to determine the extent of the damage done by the Gottlieb case. Arthur looked tired, but maybe he would open up after a couple of beers. He didn't want to pressure Arthur into talking about Gottlieb, but he could just be there for his friend.

"Can Suzanne come too?" Arthur asked. "She said she might be free after work."

So much for an intimate tête-à-tête, Phil thought, but on the other hand, he was curious about Arthur's mysterious landlady.

"That's cool," he replied. "I'll ask Melanie too, but she'll be working late as usual."

"I hope so." Arthur grimaced. "I don't know what she's got up her butt, but she really rubbed my nose in it yesterday."

"Come on!" Phil grinned. "Think of it as a team-building exercise."

"Yeah, like adding Yoko Ono to improve the Beatles."

To Phil's surprise, Melanie dropped what she was doing, and the three clerks were soon walking together across campus, talking shop and scuffling brittle Magnolia leaves along the sidewalk. The fall semester was two weeks old, but the air was warm and students were still dressed for summer. Phil got the comforting impression that fall would proceed with delicious slowness in Clarkeston.

Although it was Friday afternoon, they had no problem acquiring a window table with an unobstructed view back to the campus. Phil bought a pitcher, and Melanie filled Arthur in on the details of the death of Carolyn Bastaigne. She seemed more relaxed after her Thursday morning victory over Arthur, and Phil wondered whether she was the type of person who needed a bit of confrontation and a win to feel part of the gang.

"We were going to tell you about this yesterday," Melanie said to Arthur as she scooted her chair closer to the table and took a small sip from her glass, "but you were busy with Gottlieb, so it didn't seem important."

No one would guess from her breezy vibe that she had pretty much cut off his balls the previous day.

"I'm really tempted to call the reporter who wrote the Bastaigne story," she continued, "and ask him some questions— like why the Judge was never mentioned and who saw her last."

"You should ask Suzanne what she knows," Arthur replied. "She might've heard something. It must have been a pretty big deal at the time."

"You'd never know it from reading the paper."

As Melanie spoke, Suzanne arrived and took a chair between Arthur and Phil.

"Hey," Melanie acknowledged the newcomer with a wave, "what I want to know is: if she was as lazy as Ms. Stillwater says, then why was she working late and why she taking the stairs?"

Before anyone could answer her question, Arthur introduced Suzanne.

"Who are you talking about?" Suzanne asked.

In her department store jeans and plain button-down shirt, she was quite a contrast from the formal elegance of Melanie. Nevertheless, Suzanne was just as powerful a presence as her dark eyes flashed, and she pushed her thick black hair behind her right ear. She probably weighed thirty pounds more than the folks at *Vogue* would dictate, but Phil could see why Arthur had described her as beautiful.

Phil watched the two women exchange glances. They were mutually wary, he concluded, but he had no immediate theory as to why.

"Carolyn Bastaigne, one of the Judge's clerks, died mysteriously a couple of years ago," Melanie explained. "We got a crank call from her mother the other day. Have you ever heard of her?"

"Yeah, but I was in Alabama when it happened. I remember my mom calling and telling me that one of the Judge's clerks had died."

"How did your mom know who she worked for? The Judge's name doesn't show up in the newspaper article about the accident."

Suzanne thought for a moment and took a sip of her beer. "Gossip, I suppose. But the lack of publicity isn't too surprising. The Judge was hated for years, including by the *Clarkeston Chronicle*, but now it's just the opposite. Unless there was a compelling reason to mention his name, I can see the paper deciding just to leave it out."

"Do you remember anything else about what happened?" Melanie asked.

"No, but I remember that week pretty well. It was just after my father died. It was also the last time I saw the Judge at my house. He used to be around all the time when I was little, but then he sort of disappeared."

"What do you mean the Judge disappeared?" Phil was fascinated by personal details about the Judge's life. The old man wasn't much for sharing, so all information needed to be gathered secondhand from clerk lore and Ms. Stillwater. Phil told himself that his father's death when he was a boy had absolutely nothing to do with his obsessive interest in the Judge.

"Well, he used to be my dad's law partner," Suzanne replied, "so he would visit quite a bit. I remember that he started smoking again about that time too. He'd stopped years before and used to lecture me about the perils of tobacco. And he stopped going to church. We all used to go to the old Episcopal Church on the edge of downtown, but I haven't seen him there for five years at least."

Suzanne's revelations made Phil wonder when the Judge had permanently shut the shades in his office. He had not seen any overt signs of depression in his boss, but he recognized the symptoms. He had a tough time reconciling his image of the Judge with any psychological weakness.

Phil looked at Arthur but could see that his attention had wandered, and he caught him staring toward the campus. He touched Arthur's shoulder. "Pretty shitty week, eh?"

"Huh?" Arthur blinked. "Oh, Gottlieb . . . I don't know. Glad it's over, I guess."

"Any regrets?"

"You mean other than not finding the case that Melanie gave me?" Arthur shrugged his shoulders and fingered his beer mat on the table. "I read the briefs; I applied the law." He started to say something about the Judge, but the aborted sentence faded to a mumble.

In the silence that followed, Melanie suggested another pitcher and Suzanne offered to pay. They argued their way to the bar together leaving Phil and Arthur seated at the table. Phil watched Arthur staring out the window again, eyes fixed on nothing or some indiscernible point far in the distance.

"You can't tell me that it wasn't hard to read the Gottlieb fax this morning." With the women gone, maybe Arthur's armor would crack a bit. After all, he had just played a substantial role in the death of another human being. He needed to vent.

Arthur turned wearily toward him. "What's hard is losing respect for the Judge."

He shook his head and gave a summary of the Judge's flip-flopping on the arguments made in Gottlieb's petition. "I think it was completely unethical. I don't give a flying fuck about Gottlieb. He got what he deserved. But the Judge . . ."

Arthur set his glass down on the table with a thump. "The only way you can have a valid system of capital punishment is to follow the law."

Phil was speechless. The Judge was his hero too.

"Fuck. I'm sorry, Arthur."

"Well, we agree on that."

Behind Arthur, Phil saw the women returning to the table. He gave his friend a look which said they needed to put off their discussion to another time and got a solemn nod in return.

★ ★ ★

Melanie sat in her apartment and stared at the phone. She really wanted to call the reporter who had covered the Bastaigne case, but she knew deep down that her curiosity was completely idle. Not to mention that an inquiry from her might well get back to the Judge. She stood up, walked into her windowless kitchen, poured herself a mineral water, leaned on the counter, and stared back into her living room. The handsy greaseball who ran the apartment complex thought she would like the "hip rattan décor," but after three weeks, she was already tired of sitting in beach furniture when the view out the window was nothing but parking lot asphalt.

She took a sip of water and, with a sudden burst of inspiration, crossed the room to look up the number of the reporter who had written the Bastaigne articles.

"Hello? Could I speak to Sidney Dumont please?" A moment later a languid and velvety voice came over the line.

"This is Sidney Dumont." He pronounced his name as the French would.

"My name is Margaret Hill," Melanie replied, hoping that her hastily concocted story would hold up. "I'm an insurance adjuster for Aetna, and we're conducting a five-year review of our liability policy on the courthouse in downtown Clarkeston. In the course of the review, I see that we paid on an accidental death that occurred within the mandatory review period. We've spoken to the courthouse administrator already, but we always like to get third-party reports whenever possible. Since you were the reporter who wrote about the case, we were hoping you could tell us what you know about the accident."

"Sure, but I doubt I know anything that the federal marshals don't. They handled the investigation." Of course, she thought to herself, local authorities would not have jurisdiction over something that happened in a federal building. And, she realized with a sinking feeling, a private insurance firm would probably not be asked to insure federal property! She scrambled quickly, hoping that Dumont would miss the gaping hole in her story.

"The marshal who handled the case is no longer there," she fabricated. "In any event, we might as well get your perspective since you're on the phone." She put her hand over the mouthpiece and mouthed "shit."

"Well, she fell down some marble stairs at the top of the fourth-floor stairwell." His voice sounded sympathetic. "All it would take is a little slip in high heels."

"Any idea why she was taking the stairs instead of the elevator? I've been in that building, and the stairs are quite out of the way."

"Maybe she was taking the stairs for her health?" His ironic laugh was a low rumble. "Sorry about that. I really don't know. No one saw her enter the stairwell."

"Who was the last to see her alive, anyway?"

"Her boss."

"Her boss?" Melanie sat up straighter.

"Yeah, he spoke with her around six thirty. She left after that, presumably down the hall and down the stairs."

"Uh-huh. Were there any signs of foul play?" She hoped she didn't sound too snoopy. "Obviously, security issues impact on our rate structure."

"Not really. She had a bruise on her chest and a banged-up face, but the coroner thought the injuries were consistent with a fall."

"Was he sure?"

"You know how those guys are." Dumont laughed again. "They won't testify about the color of the shirt they're wearing without some equivocation. *My shirt color is consistent with a range of shades from lime green to avocado green.* All I know is what the guy put in the report. I wasn't at the hearing; it was closed."

"Is that usual?"

"County hearings are always public, but this is the only death on federal property that I ever covered. Might be different rules. That's really all I know."

"Well, thank you so much for your help."

"Any time, Ms. Hill."

Melanie hung up the phone and tapped the receiver with her fingers. At least the source of Mrs. Bastaigne's paranoia was clearer. An investigation by courthouse personnel instead of outsiders followed by a closed hearing were bound to seem suspicious. Did Mrs. Bastaigne know that the Judge was the last to see her alive? Usually such witnesses were automatically suspects in murder cases, just like husbands when their wives are killed. But why would she suspect the Judge?

She poured herself another glass of water and sat down on the couch. Now would be a good time to let the mystery go and concentrate on work. But she couldn't. Her attraction to the case was visceral. The choice to work in the criminal law clinic in law school had not been a coincidence. Commercial law bored her silly, while the messy facts of murder cases held infinite appeal. Why not take on the Bastaigne case as a hobby? But just thinking about the mystery set her body tingling; that made it more like an obsession, but probably a harmless one.

★ ★ ★

On Monday, Melanie worked steadily until midmorning and then went into Ms. Stillwater's office for a cup of coffee as an excuse to see if the aging secretary remembered anything more about the accident.

"Do you ever think about Carolyn Bastaigne?" She stirred some creamer into the cup and turned to Ms. Stillwater. "I know it was five years ago, and I never even met her, but every time I walk past that stairwell now, I get the creeps."

"I know just what you mean," the woman replied. "We've still got a box of her stuff back in the storeroom. When I see her name on the side, I get a little spooked myself."

"What's in it?"

"Just some junk from her desk. The marshal's office told us to hang on to it, so we did. I suppose we could throw it out by now. They can't possibly have any use for it any more."

"Probably not." Melanie was seized by the sudden desire to rummage through the former clerk's belongings. Maybe she could look for it some evening after everyone had left.

Ms. Stillwater paused for a moment. "We asked the family if they wanted it, but it's just some office supplies, a couple of textbooks, and a pair of shoes. Nothing personal, no pictures or correspondence or anything."

"A pair of shoes?"

"Why yes, we found them in her office the morning after she died. She always walked around without 'em. She said that high heels really bothered her feet. It used to drive the Judge absolutely crazy."

Suzanne sat down and pressed for more details. "But why would she be going home without her shoes?"

"I doubt she was going home, dear." Stillwater shook her head slowly, and a smile creased her kind face. "She was probably going down to get a candy bar from the second-floor vending machines. Boy, she sure loved those Milky Ways."

★ ★ ★

"Is Sidney Dumont there?"

"Speaking."

"Mr. Dumont? This is Margaret Hill again, from Aetna Insurance. Could I ask you one quick follow-up question?"

"Sure."

"You said that Carolyn Bastaigne was wearing high heels when she tripped. Are you sure of that?"

There was a slight pause. "Well, not really. I interviewed most of the clerks who worked in the building, and I noticed that the women were all dressed to the nines. All of 'em in heels, just like lady lawyers. I just assumed she was too." His voice took on a tinge curiosity. "Is that not right?"

"I don't know." She paused for a moment. Carolyn's lack of heels certainly qualified as information not meant to the leave the chambers under the Judge's confidentiality policy. "No, I was just checking. Thanks, again!"

XI.

A BRAND NEW PAIR OF ROLLER SKATES

One Saturday morning in early September, Arthur was awakened by a high-pitched wail that bounced off the hard plaster walls and wood floors of the house and reverberated in his head like a bad hangover. He glanced at the clock and confronted the racket with thoughts of the Belgian waffles he had stored in the back of the freezer downstairs. Visions of butter and maple syrup propelled him down to the kitchen and straight to the toaster with no temptation to look in the television room to see what was transpiring with Maria. As the miracle of modern breakfast took shape, the screaming reduced itself to sobbing, then to sniffing. Finally, he could hear the drone of Saturday morning cartoons over the murmuring of mother and child.

As he stood up and responded to the ding of the toaster oven, he turned and saw Maria stomping into the kitchen.

"Good morning, Maria."

"Mommy said I could have a Pop-Tart."

Wondering whether toaster pastries had been at the heart of the morning's dispute, he considered how to respond. No sense triggering another ear-piercing eruption, especially when the core of the volcano simmered a mere six feet away.

"Mommy said I can't go to Skateland this afternoon."

Uh-oh. Here was a minefield where a false step could cause severe auditory damage. He considered various strategies but could only manage: "How come?"

Her lower lip started to tremble, and it was clear he had asked the wrong question. He desperately backtracked.

"The last time I skated," he improvised manically, "I fell down and hit my head on the floor, and I got knocked out and saw little blue cuckoo birds circling around my head just like in the cartoons! My head got pretty badly dented, so the doctors had to shave it and pound it back out. But that was really cool because all of my friends could sign their names on my head, just like a cast on a broken leg. Next time I skate, I'm going to wear one of those motorcycle helmets!"

Pause.

"You wanna a bite of my waffle?"

"You're just joking me," she sniffed and stood quietly. She showed some interest in Arthur's breakfast, but an experimental nibble proved she didn't like the malty flavor of the waffle compared to a fruit pastry. He fetched her what she wanted and offered to heat it up, but she shook her head and wandered back into the television room with it cold, leaving a trail of crumbs behind her. He let out a sigh of relief and tucked into his food.

Suzanne swished in a couple of minutes later, a royal blue terrycloth bathrobe cinched tightly around her waist. "Maria said that you were in a serious roller skating accident."

"Uh, not really. I was just trying to divert her attention." He gave her a sympathetic look. "She's suffered from a skating-related letdown today?"

"She's dying to go to this birthday party at Skateland, but my friend Judy just called and reminded me that I promised to help her do some wallpapering this morning. And I've already cancelled on her three times! I'd let Maria go without me, but the skating rink is crazy on Saturdays and the birthday girl's mother is a real airhead." She poured herself a cup of coffee. "So, she needs to come with me instead, whether she wants to or not."

Whether the trauma of similar childhood disappointments lingered in his subconscious or whether a spark of spontaneous generosity had somehow survived law school, Arthur heard himself say, "You know, I could chaperone Maria, and maybe even feed her lunch afterward and drop her off at Judy's."

Her reply came quickly. "I wouldn't want to take advantage of you."

"Really, it's no problem."

"Really?" Was she concerned about ruining his Saturday or fearful of putting him in charge of her daughter? "Skateland can be a scary place."

"I'll tell you what," he said suddenly. "If you'll go hear a band with me at the Wild Boar tonight, I'll take Maria to her party."

She gave him a look like the sugar from the waffles had addled his brain.

"Phil won't go, and I really don't want to go by myself." This was pure impulse, but after a week in chambers, a skate party and then some live music seemed like an inspired idea. And asking Suzanne wasn't crazy. They were pretty much friends now, and she hardly ever got out of the house.

"I don't know if I could get a sitter on such short notice."

He couldn't tell whether she was wavering or looking for excuses.

"What about Judy? Won't she be grateful for your wallpapering?"

"Well," she finally begrudged him a smile, "she owes me one . . . I'll ask her if she can sit and let you know when you drop off Maria."

She left to tell Maria the plan, and he was rewarded with a shriek of joy and a warning from Suzanne that they needed to be there in twenty minutes.

★ ★ ★

"Have you ever been skating before?" he asked Maria on the way to the rink.

"Uh-huh," she nodded vigorously. "You don't have to walk with me like a little baby."

When they got there and put her skates on, Maria led him to the lady in charge of the party, slid her present onto a card table, and scuttled off to join her friends. He traded small talk with the birthday mom, Jeannie McCullough, in the vestibule of the building, catching brief glimpses of Maria as she shuffled past the open entryway once every trip round the rink. With a start, he realized that Jeannie was flirting with him.

"So what do you do in town, Mr. Hughes?"

"I work downtown for the Judge." He bent his head close to hear her over the music.

"I'll bet he runs you ragged." She put her hand on his arm and gave him a sympathetic smile.

"Yeah, it's a lot of work, but the worst is having no time to exercise." She responded by giving his biceps a squeeze as if to reassure him that he was still fit enough for some important activities.

"Oh, I try to get to the gym for at least an hour every day." She had a horsey face and massive frosted hair, but she was justifiably proud of her trim and athletic body. "I used to know one of the Judge's clerks. Do you know Titus Grover?"

An image of her, one knee up on the conference room table flitted through his imagination. He thought she must be a single mother, but a discrete inquiry revealed that Mr. McCullough, a local dry cleaner, was still very much in the picture. Alarm bells clanged, and he politely excused himself to check on Maria.

Spotting her at the far end of the rink, he sat down on a carpeted bench and studied the crowd. The painted concrete rink was encircled by a raised platform of worn shag carpeting designed to make a bruiseless escape from the constant revolution of skaters a theoretical possibility. The carpet ran several feet up and over the benches that were built into the walls and then up the walls themselves halfway to the ceiling except for a gap where a small snack bar overlooked the whirlpool of motion.

An incongruous selection of disco, new wave, rock, ska, and country music propelled the stumpy legs of Maria and her friends slowly around and around the rink. None of her group could really glide properly on their skates; no wheel ever completed a full rotation before being picked up and walked forward, but they seemed happy to live vicariously through the more proficient skaters whizzing past them.

Middle-class moms taught their teenage daughters to glide gracefully with only a swish and twitch of their jean-clad bottoms, while sloppy habituées of the local Waffle House huffed hand-in-hand, clearing a wide swathe before them. Teenagers of both sexes, liberated from the scrutiny of their parents, flirted openly with discrete pass-by touchings or cool-eyed exhibitions of skating virtuosity. The occasional lone adult skater, usually a woman, quietly slid by in a world of her own. Children, however, dominated the scene, sometimes demonstrating balance and coordination well-beyond their years but more often cracking tailbones as they fell on the unforgiving concrete. Knowing their cries could not be heard over the din of the music, they resolutely picked themselves up, rubbed the damaged part of their anatomy, and rejoined the circling throng.

Maria waved and pointed him out to her friends as she passed by. One of them, a black girl with elaborately braided and beaded hair fell down as she turned to glance back at him. Unabashed, she picked herself up quickly and rejoined hands with her partners. Looking around the rink, he tried to determine the age at which Clarkeston children started to segregate themselves by race. Hand holding seemed to stop around six or seven, but mixed race groups of skaters persisted through the ten- and eleven-year-olds. Older adolescents and adults no longer came to the rink together, but they did acknowledge each other in a friendly fashion and chatted in line at the snack bar. Arthur concluded that people got along better in Clarkeston than his home town in Iowa. He doubted his friends' mothers would have let their children go to a rink where a third of the skaters were black.

When Maria started to tire, she came to sit next to him, and he soon found himself surrounded by a bevy of little girls swinging their skates back and forth and interrogating him.

"How come you're not skating with us?"

"Are you Maria's father?"

"Did you see me fall down on my butt?"

"What kind of car do you have?"

They peppered him with questions until Jeannie waved them all over to a carpeted door at the far side of the rink that led to tables covered with cake and presents.

When the hostess declined his offer to help, he sat down to cake and ice cream with the kids and regaled them with stories of his years on the professional skating circuit. They were fascinated, their moms were amused, and he got a second helping of cake. Why did his brother always complain about attending kiddie parties? Apart from some temporary hearing loss caused by an especially loud rendition of "YMCA" the outing was more enjoyable than his usual Saturday morning. He and Maria stayed until the end of the affair, and he washed down the sweets with a cup of coffee from the snack bar as Maria made a few final circuits before her legs gave out.

The little girl was too full of cake to be interested in lunch, so they drove straight to Judy's house. Her head bobbed drowsily against the back of her seat until she fell asleep against the sun-baked fabric, leaving Arthur in silence to reflect on the strange places his career was leading him.

XII.

GARDENING AT NIGHT

The shock absorbers of Arthur's Plymouth groaned loudly as they clipped the curb on the turn into Judy's driveway. He noticed Suzanne watching from the window as he helped Maria with her seat belt. As soon as she was released, she was wide awake and racing into the backyard.

"We're here!" she cried as she jumped into a plastic turtle sandbox occupied by Judy's daughter. Arthur left them to their Tonka back-hoes and steam shovels and met Suzanne at the back door.

"We survived," he said. "I think she had a pretty good time. Lots of cake and ice cream . . . no broken bones."

"Thanks again, Arthur." She gave him a warm smile and checked on Maria with a quick glance. "Now come in and see what we've done. There's beer in the fridge."

He grabbed a couple of cold bottles, and she led him toward the sound of rustling paper in a corner room at the back of the house. Judy was hanging a muted floral pattern over a ghastly shade of purple.

"Very nice!" he commented as she stretched to hold the edge of a sheet of paper flush to the ceiling.

"Well, thank you," she replied tartly, "but how do you like the paper?"

Suzanne laughed, a lilting song extended by Arthur's failure to muster a good comeback.

"Have you ever done this before?" Judy asked.

"No, just some painting."

"Then why don't you just sit down and watch while you drink your beer."

Seeing no chairs, he leaned against the wall and sank down to the floor. "How come the wallpaper only goes two-thirds of the way down the wall from the ceiling?"

"I'm gonna to run a chair rail around the room at about thirty-six inches," Judy explained, "and then touch up the chipped spots in this horrible purple."

"Why keep the purple if it's horrible?"

"It's the original paint color for the room and shows how weird people's tastes were back in the twenties." She laughed. "People used really outrageous colors. It'll be a good conversation piece for the room."

He spent the rest of the afternoon at Judy's house, learning how to paper and fetching the girls Kool-Aid and ice cream sandwiches when their moms' hands were messy. While Suzanne and Judy cleaned up, he retired to the patio and had another beer as the shadows crept over the backyard. The women soon emerged from the house with a small cooler, and he listened to their tales of motherhood and genteel poverty. They were refreshingly different from the people he had been to law school with. Their easy intimacy was world's away from the status-conscious pontificating that passed for conversation between law students. Judy asked him how many brothers and sisters he had, but not where he went to college.

"Why don't you let me treat you all to pizza?" he suggested gratefully. "And if I order from Pizza Villa, they'll deliver more beer and soda for the girls too."

"Where did you find this guy?" Judy teased Suzanne as she got up to show him the phone. Once dinner arrived, they ate on the floor of the newly papered dining room and sucked down more beer to replace the fluids that the unairconditioned house had drained out of them.

"So what band are you going to see?" Judy asked.

"Hillbilly Dracula. Have you seen 'em?"

"Nah, but I read about them in the *Flagpole*." She shook her head. "But any band that's supposed to be a marriage of Elvis and the Clash can't be all bad. I wish I could come with you guys." She bent down and picked up the empty pizza boxes. "I haven't been out forever."

"Why don't you? Is there someone who could sit for both the girls?"

"Maybe Louise?" Suzanne suggested. "She owes you big time for when Sheena was sick."

"I'll pay for it," Arthur offered.

"No, it's getting late, and I've got some more work to do. And besides, unlike your date, Arthur, I gotta do more than just run a brush through my hair to look gorgeous. It takes me hours just to achieve mediocre. Now, get out of here, or you're going to miss the show." With a wink at her friend, Judy pushed Suzanne and Arthur out of the house.

As they walked to the bar, Arthur wondered whether Suzanne thought they were out on a date. Trying to define the term had led to a memorable spat with his ex-wife years before.

"In my opinion," he had argued, "a person is not on a date unless he or she is open to romance with the person they are with."

"So," Julia had replied, "under your definition, one person could be on a date while the other one isn't."

"Exactly . . . and that would explain some shitty dates people have."

"Sorry, but I prefer the definition used by every woman I know: if a woman is out alone with a man for an evening, then she's on a date."

"Well, then many virtuous women would be surprised to learn that they continued to date even after they were married." And the argument had gone downhill from there.

★ ★ ★

Arthur had drunk to the pleasant point where he didn't care whether Suzanne would side with him or Julia on the definition of dating. She seemed utterly unbothered by the ambiguous status of their outing. As a widow and a mother, the danger of petty embarrassment seemed beyond her. She did not need Arthur to entertain her, nor did she seem concerned about his intentions. They walked the twelve blocks to the Wild Boar with scarcely a lull in the conversation.

Talking was impossible once they entered the building. The band rocked frenetically, and the small dance floor was crowded with bodies slamming into one another. They squeezed their way to the bar and leaned against it while the band churned out high-quality Clash covers and their own unique combination of thrash and rock-a-billy (thrash-a-billy?). He had heard them by accident a few weeks earlier when a happy hour rendezvous with Phil extended into an evening sound check.

He looked over at Suzanne and inclined his head in the direction of the mayhem to see if she wanted to join in. She nodded cautiously in response. As the music jolted every shred of self-consciousness from his body, he grabbed her hand and pulled her closer to the band. He was an awkward dancer, but nothing much like dancing was happening at the Wild Boar that night. Nobody had enough space to do more than bounce up and down, but even that limited art form was interrupted by the domino scrumming of those who had trouble staying upright. Unlike punk clubs in New York and Los Angeles, no one was intentionally throwing punches or NFL-quality blocks, but they were buffeted about the floor, roughly to the beat of the music, until the crowd spit them out like a watermelon seed into the hallway leading to the kitchen and bathrooms.

Suzanne rested her hand on his shoulder and pushed the hair off of her damp forehead. "I haven't done that for a long time," she yelled in his ear. "I'm getting too old for this!"

"Do you want to go?" He thumbed in the direction of the door, but she shook her head and slipped off to visit the ladies' room.

From the hallway, the band's manic stage show was framed by the edges of the door and the bobbing heads of the crowd.

The music ran through Arthur's veins, picking up oxygen in his lungs and pumping through every artery of his body with monster truck force. He felt like Superman . . . *No, I am Clerk Kent: Able to leap piles of briefs in a single bound, faster than a snap decision, more powerful than the Federal Judiciary Committee. Super Clerk, with his faithful sidekick Judgeling, was civilization's last hope against the devastating forces of anti-lawyer public opinion, the greatest threat to democracy the world has ever known.*

"What are you smiling at?" Suzanne sneaked her arm around his waist and yelled in his ear.

Before he could reply, the opening guitar licks of "White Riot" snatched him and propelled both of them back out onto the dance floor where they shared in the group seizure until the band finished its set. When the last encore was over and the houselights were turned on, they spilled out onto the street and gulped in fresh air. They sat on the curb between two cars and waited for their ears to stop ringing. He could see the street lights twinkling in Suzanne's eyes.

"Thanks so much for taking me out tonight! I can't even remember the last time I heard a band . . . or danced for that matter—if you want to call that dancing."

"But this town is so full of great music. You must go out all the time!"

"Well, it's hard to get a sitter for Maria, and it's no fun—and not super safe—to go out to the bars at night alone."

"But you must have a line of guys three deep begging to take you out."

"You are so sweet." She gave him a peck on the cheek. "And so utterly full of shit that your eyes are brown." She laughed. "In case you hadn't noticed, the ideal southern woman is rather slimmer than me and comes without a jabbering four-year old." She set forth the cultural facts without a trace of self-pity. She wasn't seeking consolation, so he offered none.

"Well, these brown eyes better start moving or they'll be waking up in the gutter. Can I escort you home, Madame?"

"Absolutely." She pulled herself up on his arm and leaned against him as they walked away.

★ ★ ★

Suzanne tried to remember the last date she had been on. It must have been sometime before getting married, but then she remembered Frank from the preschool. He was divorced and picked up his daughter every other Friday. A dinner and a movie had led to some awkward groping in his living room, where he had insisted on playing Barry White on his stereo to "set the mood." She found excuses for his subsequent overtures, and he had quietly faded into the background.

"I think I've danced off enough beer to be safe to drive us home from Judy's," Arthur offered.

She smiled at him and wondered what to do next. Arthur was difficult to figure out. He was intense and intelligent—all the Judge's clerks were high-fliers—but he honestly seemed to like Maria and seemed perfectly happy to spend the day talking with two moms about everything except law. He gave no indication that he expected a romantic interlude as a reward. Unlike the typical lawyer, he seemed to be comfortable with her calling the shots. Which brought her back to the original question about what to do next.

"We don't have to go back to Judy's," she said. "Maria can sleep over, and I don't see any reason to wake her up this late just to put her in her own bed."

They strolled through campus, talking quietly about music and listening to the hum of the tree frogs and locusts. The moonlight shone on the river as they walked over it and into their neighborhood. The house was dark as they approached.

"You want to sit out on the porch?" he asked.

"It's kinda buggy. Why don't we sit and watch videos instead?" MTV was still enough of a novelty to interest viewers whose complexions were clear, and it followed naturally from their prior conversation about the relative merits of INXS and R.E.M. and the drivel produced by Debbie Gibson and her clones.

After a few minutes in the kitchen, Suzanne emerged with two coffees and plopped down beside Arthur to watch Billy Idol zap zombies off a high rise and Peter Gabriel shock a troupe of monkeys. She muted the sound when the commercials started.

"Is working with the Judge what you expected, Arthur?"

"I don't know," he said after a short pause. "Some of my classmates from law school have great relationships with their judges, dinners at their homes, stuff like that . . . I just find the Judge a little difficult to cuddle up to."

"He wasn't always that way." She looked at him and tried to explain. His intense brown eyes stopped her, and she knew that if she got lost in them, she would do something foolish. She brushed her hair past her ear and glanced at him. He was stretched out on the sofa, lean and languid. What would he do if she ran her hand underneath his shirt?

"The Judge was one of my father's old law partners. He was a lot of fun when I was a kid, but I haven't seen much of him since Daddy died." She sighed. "There's been something uncomfortable about him for a long time. I can't really put it into words."

"So, I'm not just being paranoid? Phil doesn't understand what I'm talking about. He thinks the Judge is some kind of a foster father."

"Every year someone finds a father figure in the Judge. He has more clerk children named after him than he can possibly remember at Christmas time." She sighed again. "I don't get it. I love him, but I gave up trying to figure him out a long time ago."

As they drained their mugs, their butts sank lower into the spongy mush of the aging divan, finally fusing comfortably at the hip. While they watched and tried in vain to develop some objective criteria for judging the new video art form, they became progressively more wedged together. When Arthur made a lazy attempt to put his empty cup on the coffee table underneath their feet, he listed heavily toward Suzanne, landing his chest in her lap and bonking his head on the far armrest. He struggled to extricate himself and finally slid his legs off the coffee table, pushing hard with both hands on her armrest until he flopped back to his side.

Suzanne turned and laughed. "That may be the clumsiest pass anyone has ever made at me!" She found her lips mere inches from his as he rebounded with a grunt against her shoulder. She smiled and looked deeply into his eyes, signaling that he was equally free to offer a snappy come back or to kiss her. Arthur leaned over and pressed his lips against hers and lingered for a long moment.

"Wow," he whispered.

"Hmmm . . . pretty good . . . ." This time she took his face in her hands and pressed close against him, parting her lips slightly, tilting her head, his breath beery sweet and coffee bitter, her mouth soft and urgent. They came up for air at the same time and kissed lightly just to reestablish contact, but that kiss lingered and soon they were rolling on the sofa, reaching for each other like a couple of teenagers home alone for the first time.

★ ★ ★

"Maybe I should shut the door," Arthur gasped. "What if Mr. Bernson came down?"

"Lock it."

In truth, he didn't know what he really wanted to happen. Julia was the only woman he had ever slept with, so his experience was full of gaps. Logic dictated caution, but after weeks of being rational at work and after months of over-thinking every aspect of his failed marriage, the need to be irrational overwhelmed his common sense. He had not brought a condom. As he walked back to the sofa, she stood up and met him with a seductive embrace.

"Uh, I'm really embarrassed to admit this," he whispered, "but I don't have any protection." He moaned as her fingers stymied further coherent thought.

"That's good," she said contentedly as his pants slipped toward to the floor.

"Huh?"

"That means you didn't expect this to happen. You didn't spend all night being handsome and charming just to get me into bed. You're really sweet."

"Really sweet?"

"Um hmmmm." As his worries about birth control faded, she pushed him back down onto the couch and reduced him to a quivering mass of nerve endings. After a few ecstatic minutes, she broke contact, and he opened his eyes to find her slipping her jeans past her knees and ankles and onto the floor.

"But . . ."

"Shhhh . . ." She straddled him, rocking back and forth slowly. "I ovulated two weeks ago . . . it's okay."

One final scrap of rationality remained, a testament to an effective Sunday school program or a gifted sex education teacher.

"How do you know?"

As she laughed, she squeezed him deep inside her.

"Didn't you notice that blemish on my chin two weeks ago? I always feel a little twinge and get a big zit when I ovulate."

"Umm, where did you learn to talk so dirty?" he managed to say before he gasped again.

★ ★ ★

When they disengaged for the last time, dawn was streaming through the windows and the newspaper had already thumped upon the porch. Without speaking, she kissed him softly, slipped on her jeans and hurried to her room to shower before Mr. Bernson came down to breakfast. He dressed too, but then collapsed back on the sofa, basking in the afterglow like a green lizard sunning himself on a hot porch railing.

Arthur's ex-wife had insisted that women were very hard to please. To be merely adequate for her required Olympian stamina and Buddha-like patience. He had loved trying to satisfy her but had often fallen short of her exacting mark. She would have judged his performance very lazy indeed, yet Suzanne made him feel like some sort of slick international gigolo. After just one evening with her, he was suddenly rid of an extensive backlog of adolescent neuroses. Unable to stop smiling and very grateful that he did not have to work Sundays, he stumbled off to his room to take a long nap.

XIII

GIRLS TALK

Autumn, the Judge observed, was coming gently to Clarkeston. The tulip poplars had turned first, then lost their yellow leaves almost overnight when a cool wind gusted down from the Carolinas. Soon thereafter, the Bradford pears reddened and then turned gold. The dogwoods were almost as beautiful in the fall as in the spring, and the soft whispers of their russet leaves filled the morning air. When October melted into November, the brilliant colors of the sourwoods, elms, and red oaks carpeted the sidewalks and alleys, swishing and crunching underfoot, mixing with the perfectly formed banana-yellow gingkoes to lay a richly textured tapestry for the town.

Autumn was a feast for the eyes, but the changes pricked at the Judge's heart. For children, summer vacation was a faded memory and the promise of Christmas was unthinkably far away. Parents prepared for winter with prophylactic gardening and storm window washings, while birds and squirrels shared their obsession, flitting and scurrying as they repaired nests and hoarded food enough to the last the cold season. The whole community seemed unable to live in the moment, looking backwards or forward in a vain attempt to ignore its mortality. The presence of the ultimate artist rustling in the symphony of falling leaves alerted the Judge to the chasm between creator and created. The music of autumn was vast and wondrous, but its tonic chord sounded far in the distance.

The Judge sat in the dim light of his desk lamp, elbows on his desk as his calloused fingertips massaged an incipient headache.

Everything in chambers had been going pretty well. This year's group of clerks seemed to be working out just fine. All three were intelligent and quick, and they seemed to get along, apart from the occasional spark between Arthur and Melanie. There were no new death cases on docket. Then, Sidney Dumont had called to say that someone was asking questions about Carolyn Bastaigne.

"She said she was from an insurance company?"

"Yes, sir," the reporter affirmed. "From Aetna. Do they insure the building?"

"No." The Judge exhaled his exasperation. "The federal government doesn't buy insurance, Sid. We self-insure. This was a bogus call."

"Do you know anyone who would care after all these years?"

"Don't pull that reporter crap on me." He flicked a broken pencil tip from his desk and answered anyway. "Who the hell knows? It might be some attorney hired by her mother. Stillwater said that she called a while ago." He paused for a moment and tried in vain to come up with a benign alternative theory. "Anyway, thanks for calling, Sid. I appreciate it."

He hung up and stared at the large flat calendar lying on his desk. Chinese people named their years. For him, 1984, five years earlier, would have been: The Year of Betrayal. But there had been much more than just a treacherous clerk. The habeas cases had rained like a firestorm that spring, and he had lost his wife to cancer in the summer. The fall had brought new love and loss, and in the middle of it all waltzed Carolyn Bastaigne, the laziest and most contemptible clerk who ever worked in his chambers. Whoever was poking around was stirring up more than just memories of an unfortunate fall.

★ ★ ★

"Nope, not today." Arthur shook his head.

Phil stood in the doorway of his friend's office, unable to believe what he was hearing.

"Suzanne's gonna to show me how to make pizza dough this afternoon."

"Pizza dough?" Phil asked in amazement. "You realize that it's Friday, right? The bartender at the Boar is gonna call missing persons if we don't show up."

"I'm sorry." Despite his apology, Arthur appeared to be looking forward to spending the evening in his landlady's kitchen instead of at his favorite bar.

"Come on," Phil urged, "you've got time for a quick one before you go home."

"Next week, for sure." Arthur nodded and then put his head down and started back to work.

Phil shook his head in disgust and walked back toward his office. Going straight to his apartment after work on Friday was unthinkable, but the image of himself sitting alone with a beer in his hand was equally pathetic. He wished that Suzanne and Arthur had included him in their pizza-making scheme. Beer and pizza, even with a little kid running around, would be vastly better than the evening that now faced him.

He had his hand on the door knob of his office, ready to admit defeat, when he remembered that Melanie had come drinking the Friday after Gottlieb's execution. She was a poor substitute for Arthur, but a definite improvement on solitude. He turned back down the hall and knocked on her door.

"Come in." She was sitting in a leather chair in the corner of her office, pouring over a case that looked like a yellow peacock of sticky notes. She looked mildly surprised to see him. Although he and Arthur made regular trips to each other's offices, most of his contact with Melanie came around the conference table in the library.

"What's up?"

He looked around the room and saw no logical place to sit, so he walked over and leaned against her desk. The room looked like a Calcutta trash heap. Books, accordion files, and papers littered every square inch, including her two chairs.

"Wanna have a beer after work?"

"I don't know," she said. "Aren't you and Arthur off to the Wild Boar again?"

"Nope."

She raised her eyebrows at him, and he offered his theory. "I think he's in love." He stretched out the vowel in the *L* word and rolled his eyes. "I've been rejected in favor of a pizza-baking party with his landlady."

"Suzanne? Oh, now that's juicy." She scanned the various disasters surrounding her. "I'll be done around six thirty. If you want to hang around that long, I wouldn't mind trying out that Thai place on Court Street." She wrinkled her nose. "I'm not a huge fan of the Wild Boar."

Phil looked at his watch. Two hours more work. Still it was better than the alternative. "You're on."

★ ★ ★

The restaurant was cheaply furnished in formica tables and mismatched chairs, but it was permeated with the scent of savory spices and offered a two-for-one Singha beer special that suggested to Phil that they had made the right choice. They took their time ordering, and the kitchen took its time with the food, so four beers were leisurely shared before dinner even arrived.

"So, what's the poop on Arthur?" Melanie leaned forward, apparently expecting Phil to dish like the hostess of television gossip show. "Are he and Suzanne officially an item?"

"Promise not to say anything?"

Melanie nodded her head eagerly.

"A couple of weeks ago, he let slip that they'd slept together."

"No way!" She gasped. "She's at least five years older than him."

"Yeah, so I figured it was just a one-night stand or a unique part of his rental agreement." He gestured to her with the top of his beer bottle. "Now I'm thinking it's something more serious. You don't just blow off a standing Friday happy hour to make pizza unless there's something more serious going on."

"Poor baby!" Melanie lisped mischieviously. "Did Awety weave you awe awone?"

"No." Phil grinned. "He left me with a catty bitch."

"Ouch!" She took a spring roll and donked it into the duck sauce. "I guess I touched a sore spot. I get it, though . . . I'm sorry it's not working out with him."

Phil picked up his own roll and took a bite, the murky undertone of her comment gradually sinking in. "Not working out? What do you mean, not working out?"

She appeared to study him for a long moment. "Promise not to take this the wrong way? . . . I sort of assumed that you were gay."

"What?"

"Remember, I worked the pageant circuit for years—my antennae are pretty well-tuned." She took another sip of beer. Her completely nonjudgmental attitude made the accusation even harder to take.

He choked back his outrage. "I'm not . . . Why the hell would you even think that?"

She shrugged. "Well, you're really handsome, and you don't have a girlfriend, and you never talk about women or your former girlfriends. I've seen those Barbara Streisand cassettes in your office, and you definitely prefer Arthur to me . . . ."

"Now I see," Phil proclaimed with satisfaction, "I've never come on to the beauty queen, so I must be gay. Well, maybe, you're the one that needs the psychoanalyzing."

The main course arrived and elongated the pause in the conversation. Melanie picked at her noodles for a moment before speaking. "I'm really sorry if I offended you, but I sit with you guys a lot, and I guess I was just misinterpreting the vibe."

"I suppose," he conceded sulkily. There was really nothing to be upset about, he told himself. His best friend in high school was gay; it was nothing to be ashamed of. He put himself in her position and smiled, "Well, I did grow up in San Francisco without a dad."

"And you do have a crush on Arthur." She held her hands up, as if to fend him off, and then laughed. "Just kidding! I couldn't resist." She giggled again. "You'd make an awesome straight man. In a comedy routine! I mean in a comedy routine!"

Phil sighed and gave up. There was nothing he could do at this point except change the subject. Making a pass at her might shut her up, but he just didn't find her that alluring. "So, have you figured out yet who killed Carolyn Bastaigne?"

"No"—she paused and speared a shrimp—"but I did call up the reporter who wrote the article."

"Are you kidding? What if he tells the Judge?"

"I told him I was an insurance adjuster doing a background check." She dipped the shrimp and popped it in her mouth. "He had no clue who I am."

"Man, you are cold-blooded. I could never do that." He shook his head in admiration. "What'd you find out?"

"Not too much . . . other than the fact that the Judge was the last one to see her alive."

Phil pulled a bone out of his fish and took a large bite. The sauce was rich and thick, flecked with dried chili peppers. "So, the Judge probably killed her . . . hmm . . . I never saw that coming."

"Of course the Judge didn't kill her, you idiot. But I'll bet he knows a lot more than he's ever let on. I mean, why was he there at six thirty in the evening? Have you ever seen him work that late?"

Phil took another bite and considered her remark. "No, but that doesn't mean anything. Who knows what his work habits were five years ago?"

"You're right." She nodded and squeezed a slice of lime over her noodles. "But thinking about this case is so much more fun than work! Don't you ever get tired of writing bench memos in tax cases? I'm sick of working hard just to please other people. This job is too much like law school." She pursed her lips and frowned. "Fuck . . . this job is too much like a pageant: too many judges."

Phil laughed.

"I'm ready for the real world," she continued, "and I'm dying to ask the Judge about Carolyn Bastaigne."

"That is the most horrible idea I've ever heard." He could just imagine the explosion coming from the Judge's office when he learned someone had been poking around in his private affairs.

"I'm not going to do it . . . I'm just saying."

"And I'm just saying screwing around with him would not be a good idea." The statement came out strong, as if it were a criticism of the Judge himself.

"Whoa, I thought he was your hero." She smiled and waved for the waitress to bring them two more beers. "Did I get that wrong too?"

"No. He's awesome. Shit, you know that better than me or Arthur. You're the one who grew up down here." He stabbed at his fish while he pondered what to say next. Arthur's story about the Judge's reasoning in the Gottlieb case had put a dent in his heroic image. Phil decided to tell Melanie how the Judge had found the law in Gottlieb's favor, but had nonetheless sent him to die.

"So?" Melanie shrugged and began working on the sugared watermelon slices served as dessert in the small restaurant. "He saved everyone a lot of time and trouble. Gottlieb was gonna fry anyway for the Buckhead murders. It's not like he sent an innocent man to the chair."

"Yeah, but the way he did it really upset Arthur." He spit a watermelon seed into his napkin. "Me too, for that fact."

She sucked her fingertips and wiped them on her napkin. He took the last melon slice while she stared at him.

"You guys are upset about two different things," she said.

"How so?"

"He's pissed because the Judge took a shortcut, and you're pissed because the Judge won't take a stand against the death penalty."

"Fair enough," Phil conceded as he finished the last drops of his beer, "but I'm worried about the next death case. What happens when someone's hands get really dirty?"

Melanie got up and laid a twenty-dollar bill on the table and Phil did the same. "You're so melodramatic," she sighed. "We're law clerks. We write memos . . . I wish life were as exciting as you think it is."

"Well, you two have one thing in common." He frowned. "Neither of you take death seriously enough."

XIV.

MARGARITAVILLE

Until Arthur moved south, he had never thought to spend Thanksgiving at the beach, but an interesting proposal took shape when one of the Judge's clerks from the early sixties invited the whole chambers, plus spouses and significant others, to spend the long holiday weekend at his house on Saint George Island, Florida. When Ms. Stillwater passed the invitation around the chambers, she explained that Jack Ramsey was one of the Judge's first clerks, working for two years under very difficult circumstances. He had long been a partner in a Tallahassee law firm and had a huge eight-bedroom house right on the Gulf of Mexico. His wife had died years earlier, and since then he had been generous with his invitations to the Judge and the chambers family to spend time on the island.

"The poor dear. He was devastated when he lost his wife." Ms. Stillwater cast a quick glance in Arthur's direction. "Whom he met here in Clarkeston by the way." She took her time explaining the situation. "He doesn't seem to be interested in getting remarried and making something of that lovely house. It sits empty most of the time. You all really should go! You'll get to meet some more of the Judge's old clerks and see where you fit in."

Ms. Stillwater, whose children had long since grown, was clearly thrilled by the idea of gathering together past and current clerks. She raised a new family in chambers every year and clearly loved speculating how previous years' broods would interact. She had already spoken excitedly about two intermarriages that had produced grandchildren with clerk lineage on both sides.

"Do you think it would be okay if Suzanne and Maria came with me?" Arthur asked.

"Of course!" she replied enthusiastically. "I'll talk to Jack, but it won't be a problem. He likes a big crowd . . . and if I remember right, he was clerking here the year Suzanne was born and christened." Her eyes fairly twinkled as she spoke. "He won't mind at all."

"I was more concerned about the Judge."

"It's none of the Judge's business whom you take," she said tartly and then offered an inscrutable smile. "He hasn't gone for years. You let me worry about him."

★ ★ ★

Florida sounded good to Melanie too, but she had family in Atlanta who felt neglected by the grinding hours she put in for the Judge. After listening to her mother's pitiful mewling, she figured she had little choice but to spend the four-day break with her parents, her sister, and two nieces. The visit would be nothing but a duty call. She no longer enjoyed playing the golden girl, performing for her family and providing the focus they lacked when she was away. Her parents barely spoke to each other most of the time, but when they played her old pageant tapes on the VCR, an observer would think that their marriage was Ozzie and Harriet solid.

"You can't miss out on this!" Phil pleaded as she walked down the hall to her office.

"It sounds like fun, but I need to keep my parents happy." She sighed as she leaned against a bookcase. "They did pay for law school after all."

"It's gonna be awesome."

"Who's coming?"

"Me, Arthur, Suzanne and Maria, Jack Ramsey, Glenn Hatcher who clerked nine years ago, and April Duncan who clerked five years ago."

Phil looked meaningfully at her until she got the message.

"April must have been a co-clerk of Carolyn Bastaigne."

"Bingo."

Melanie bit her lip and thought for a moment while Phil watched expectantly. "Okay, I'll leave here on Wednesday and drive to my folks' house. I'll spend Thanksgiving Day with them and then drive down to the beach on Friday."

"I knew you couldn't resist." He chortled. "You're such a little detective."

"Shut up! I'm just curious."

"I still don't understand why."

Good question, she thought. Maybe she just wanted to solve a mystery and impress the Judge. No memo she wrote was going to distinguish her from the seventy or so brilliant clerks who had preceded her, but solving a five-year-old riddle might.

"I don't know . . . I do love to read mystery novels."

Phil looked unconvinced.

"And I do feel protective of the Judge. There's a crazy lady out there slandering him, and that bugs me. He's the one public figure in this state whose career hasn't been hit with a scandal—even Martin Luther King was slurred by the FBI sex tapes. I don't want to see the same thing happen with him."

"So, it's altruism."

"That"—she laughed at her own self-deception—"and the sheer entertainment value."

"And speaking of entertainment value, Titus Grover might show up too." He smiled at her. "Wink, wink, nudge, nudge."

"Really?" She pantomimed putting her finger down her throat and gagging. "I met him when I interviewed. I like them slightly less sleazy, thank you!"

★ ★ ★

On the Wednesday afternoon before Thanksgiving, Suzanne and Maria picked up Arthur and Phil at the courthouse in her aging Chrysler station wagon. Phil sat in the front, and Arthur sat with

Maria in the back. Shortly after their departure, he handed Phil an Elvis Costello cassette and abdicated his third of the driving chores by popping the top of a can of beer. He handed Maria a juice box, banged it against his can, and they rubbernecked happily together to the music as the south side of town faded into hay fields and piney woodland.

Three beers, two juice boxes, and six bladder-expanding hours later, they crunched onto the clamshell driveway of a massive gray cedar house on St. George Island. Maria leaped out of the car, and Arthur followed her westward into the rapidly setting sun, ignoring Suzanne's questions about where Ramsey hid the keys or acknowledging Phil's desperate pleas for a bathroom. He kicked off his shoes and walked directly to the beach, transfixed by the brilliant oranges, reds, and purples mushrooming their way across the evening sky. Maria pursued zigzagging sandpipers across the sand and played tag with the surf while he stared out over the first truly open horizon he had seen since arriving in woodsy and hilly Clarkeston.

Suzanne sidled behind him and nibbled his ear, her first overt show of affection in front of Phil, who stood relieving himself against a stunted oak tree about fifty yards down the beach. She slipped her arms around him and communicated without speaking that the sight of Maria scampering on the beach had already made the long trip worth it.

"Where's the key?" she finally whispered. "Phil's oak tree is not wide enough to hide my big butt while I pee."

"It's supposed to be underneath a brick next to the outdoor shower pipe." As she turned to go back to the house, Arthur heard an enthusiastic shout.

"Ahoy, maties!" A tall, tan ginger-haired man strode down the weathered walkway that led from the back deck of the house over a small sand dune to the beach.

"There's gin and tonic inside. The others went to town to get some snacks and beer." He extended his hand. "I'm Titus Grover, and you must be Phil or Art."

"Arthur, actually. This is Suzanne Garfield."

"Hello, Suzanne." He kissed her cheek and then added with a smile, "We met last year when I was clerking." Arthur sneaked a peek to catch her expression, but she betrayed no emotion as she excused herself to go up to the house.

Grover had flown to Tallahassee from Washington, DC, where he was in his first year at a well-known corporate firm. He had arrived earlier in the day with April Duncan, who had been Carolyn Bastaigne's co-clerk, and Glenn Hatcher, another former clerk who had spent each Thanksgiving on Saint George since leaving Clarkeston eight years earlier.

As Phil introduced himself, Arthur walked to the house and unloaded the car. He claimed two adjacent bedrooms on the second story for Suzanne, Maria, and himself, in the hope that Suzanne would sneak over for a visit when Maria was asleep.

"Good old Jack isn't arriving until lunchtime tomorrow," Grover announced as the other ex-clerks arrived with one ice chest full of fresh shrimp and another full of beer, "so I'm gonna be chef tonight and get the girls working on a roux for shrimp gumbo while I cut up some garlic for scampi." He nodded at Glenn and Arthur. "Why don't you boys go under the house and devein the shrimp."

Grover's hoarding of the women was not lost on anyone, but Glenn and Arthur were content to set up a portable stereo in the enormous carport created by the ten-foot concrete pillars supporting the house. They drank beer and talked as they pulled sticky black entrails from the mountain of seafood in the battered ice chest.

"Where do you work, Glenn?" Arthur asked.

"I do preclearance work on mergers in the Antitrust Division of the Justice Department," Glenn explained enthusiastically.

He was single, a slight young man who constantly fiddled with his glasses and lank dark hair. The rapid and abundant growth of his facial hair lent a bluish tint to his skin even though he had undoubtedly shaved that morning and maybe after lunch too. He shelled the shrimp and spoke rapidly at the same time.

"Have you decided what you're doing once the clerkship is over?"

"I'm pretty focused on environmental enforcement, right now." Arthur didn't mention that he was most interested in a job at the Office of Legal Counsel. OLC comprised an elite group of two dozen lawyers who advised the executive branch of the federal government, and since jobs there were harder to get than Supreme Court clerkships, he did not want to sound naively optimistic.

"I'm going to interview with the Environmental Protection Agency and the Environmental Enforcement Division at Justice the first week in December," he added. These, too, would be difficult jobs to obtain, but working for the Judge almost assured him of a position.

The group dined late in a screened portion of the top deck. The meal was jovial and childless, Maria having been sent to bed after devouring two dozen boiled shrimp. The lawyers were sensitive enough to the presence of a layperson to keep the law talk on the level of personalities and away from tedious discussions of cases. Even Grover, when he was not casting maddeningly indiscrete glances at Suzanne's chest, played a charming host. He was armed with an inexhaustible supply of jokes about the Judge and had his gentle drawl down perfectly.

"Confidentiality is critical," he mimicked with both his voice and his hands, "I expect my clerks to keep absolutely silent about whatever happens in chambers. If you eat a burrito in your office, I don't want to hear you fart in public!"

When they finished cleaning up, they drank coffee and watched the lights of the shrimp boats bob like fallen stars on top of the inky water. The breeze was brisk enough to keep away the sand flies, but not cold enough to call for sweaters. The group talked sporadically, heeding the amniotic call of the gentle surf during pauses in the conversation. When Grover, April, and Glenn got up to fetch more drinks, Arthur suggested quietly to Suzanne that they go for a walk alone on the beach.

"I'd love to," she whispered, "but I don't feel right about leaving Maria alone with strangers."

"I don't think they're going to bother her, sweetie," he slurred slightly, the beer finally taking its toll.

"No, you moron." She looked around to see if anyone could overhear the conversation. "What if she wakes up and finds that neither you nor I are here? This is a new place. I don't want her to freak out."

Arthur knew that this was a perfectly reasonable excuse to give, but the alcohol accentuated his disappointment and he headed moodily off to bed. Although he was all smiles as he made his excuses to the group, the look he gave Suzanne let her know he was pouting and was expecting her to hurry upstairs and comfort him. He lay awake waiting for a while and then quickly slipped over the edge of consciousness into a heavy, dreamless sleep.

★ ★ ★

Phil and April could not bring themselves to leave the balmy serenity of the back deck. The Californian had grown up close to the rocky coast south of San Francisco, but he could not think of anywhere close to his home where he could sit outside in a T-shirt in the wee hours of a November morning without freezing. April was good company too, and they abided easily the long breaks in conversation as dawn approached and the tide rolled in. The sense of family he felt in the chambers crossed time and space.

"How do you like working for the Judge so far?" April asked.

"It's cool . . . just about everything I expected."

"You love writing those bench memos, huh?"

Phil laughed. "I don't mind, especially when the Judge sits down and hashes through all the issues. He doesn't do it often, but when he does it's a pretty amazing."

"I know what you mean." She took out a cigarette and blew a puff of smoke toward the mist coming in off the Gulf. "It's a lot more interesting than the public defender work I'm doing now."

"And your year was pretty eventful, wasn't it?" Phil probed. Although he didn't share Melanie's obsession with the death of Carolyn Bastaigne, he got a charge out of being her co-conspirator. "Didn't one of your co-clerks die?"

"How did you know that?"

"Carolyn's Bastaigne's mother called the chambers about two weeks ago and started ranting about the Judge, and Ms. Stillwater, and a big courthouse conspiracy."

"I can't believe she's still doing that!" She turned sideways in the deck chair and faced him.

"Oh, yeah. And she was pretty nasty too. Melanie took the call, but I could hear her screaming from the other side of the library." He paused for a moment and took a sip from a glass of water. "Melanie was pretty shook up, so we asked Ms. Stillwater for the whole story."

"I doubt that she knows the whole story, but what did she say?"

"Just that Carolyn was a terrible clerk and that she had fallen down the stairs. She also told Melanie that Carolyn was famous for leaving her shoes in her office and walking around barefoot." April nodded but offered nothing further in response. "We pulled the old stories from the *Clarkeston Chronicle* too."

April stood up and walked to the edge of the deck. She leaned against the railing for a moment and looked out over the Gulf. "The newspaper stories didn't say much, if I remember right."

"Not really." He searched for a question to prompt her and decided to ask one that he already knew the answer to. "There's one thing we don't know: Who was the last person to see her alive? The paper mentions someone but doesn't say who."

"One of the Marshals who interviewed me let slip that the Judge was the last person to see her leave the chambers." She stubbed her cigarette out and flicked the butt into an empty planter on the deck.

Phil nodded. "That might explain why the paper doesn't say that he was the last to see her alive . . . out of respect and all."

"I didn't say that."

"Say what?"

"That he was the last person to see her alive." She turned and faced him, leaning against the weathered wood railing. "I'm only telling you this because you're a clerk too. You understand that certain things never leave the chambers." She paused for a moment and brushed her hair out of her eyes. "I've never been as convinced as Ms. Stillwater that she slipped on her way to fetch a candy bar."

"Why not?" He tried to keep the excitement out of his voice. Maybe Melanie's instincts were better than he gave them credit for.

"Well, first of all, she always took the elevator. Always. Even if it was just down one floor. And then there's the no-shoes business. There's only one place outside of the office where she went without them: Judge Meyers' chambers at the other end of the floor."

"The District Court Judge who passed away last year? Why would she go down there?" Phil got up and walked over to the railing next to April. A series of waves crashed onto the beach.

"She had a classmate from law school who clerked for Meyers. They were tight as ticks. She never did anything with me or Bob, the other clerk. It seemed like she spent half her time down there." She laughed suddenly and shook her head. "Boy, the Judge really hated that. You know how he likes to keep the chambers hermetically sealed."

"Yeah." Phil digested the news and then tested the depth of April's suspicions. "Do you think that someone from Meyers' chambers might have pushed her?"

"I'm not saying anyone pushed anybody! I have no idea what happened. I've just never made any sense out of it, that's all."

"You mean, why was she in the stairwell with her shoes off?"

"Exactly. And I can't come up with any good reason why she would be in too much of a hurry to take the elevator." She shrugged and, pleading tiredness, pushed open the sliding glass doors and disappeared into the house.

XV.

TEQUILA SUNRISE

Arthur woke up alone and stumbled downstairs at nine o'clock with a bottle of aspirin. The house was so still that he could hear the gentle pounding of the surf through the closed windows. He swallowed three pills with a tumbler of orange juice, made a twelve-cup pot of coffee, washed a pile of dishes, set the breakfast table, and prepared a huge bowl of pancake batter. If anyone remembered his early exit the night before, a fresh breakfast would erase any bad impression. But apart from Maria, who awoke soon after him, he had no customers until April emerged around ten thirty and sleepily requested two eggs over easy with her stack of pancakes.

"You're the first one down!" He handed her a cup of coffee and pushed the cream and sugar toward her. "How late did y'all stay up last night anyway?"

"Pretty late. Glenn went to bed a little after you did, but Phil and I lasted 'til about 6:00 a.m. I don't remember what time Grover and Suzanne went to bed." Cringing a little at April's choice of words, Arthur sent Maria upstairs to wake up her mom and tell her breakfast was ready.

Before she returned, Glenn came through the front door and reported that he had spent a lovely morning in the Apalachicola Waffle House reading the morning newspaper. As Arthur talked to him, Maria returned alone, and his heart skipped a beat, irrationally fearing a report of: "Mommy's not in her room."

Instead, Maria explained in a serious voice that Mommy had a headache and wanted to sleep a little while longer. Arthur breathed a sigh of relief and left a note on the counter for late-comers that there was pancake batter in the fridge. He invited Maria to walk down to the beach where he mulled over his ridiculous reaction to the imagined tryst between Grover and Suzanne. Suzanne was not his ex-wife, Julia, and there was no reason ever to indulge his sense of jealousy. Despite his resolve, his stomach churned as he remembered stumbling across love notes that one of Julia's admirers had written to her. He shook the dark memories of her indiscretions out of his head. He needed to see Suzanne; one kiss would suffice to reconnect them.

Arthur and Maria built sand castles and splashed in the surf for about an hour before Suzanne came down with two mugs of coffee and a box of fruit juice. He thanked her and leaned over to kiss her good morning, but her face tilted slightly so that he caught only cheek and no lips. His resolution to make no reference to her late-night tête-à-tête with Titus Grover dissolved like sugar in hot water.

"Are you afraid someone's going to see us?" He remembered Grover's cryptic comment the other day about having "met" Suzanne the year before. "April said you and Grover were up late last night." He gave her a querying look, but she saw right through him.

She stared hard and then spoke deliberately. "Jealousy is a very ugly thing, Arthur." She turned, looked at the ocean, and sipped her coffee. "Please get over it."

"Get over what? What is there for me to get over?"

"Well, your attitude for one." She raised her eyebrows and turned to help Maria work on the moat for her sand castle. When he didn't sit down and join them, she looked up. "Why don't you take a walk down the beach and chill out a bit."

His face burned and he sputtered a bit, but he managed to make no more silly statements before walking off down the beach. He hiked in the surf to the border of the state park at the south end of the island and started back having come to the obvious conclusion that he needed to apologize.

The need for contrition was fairly obvious, but sorting out the whole of his feelings for Suzanne required serious thought. The Socratic method proved inconclusive: Did he love her? Yes. Then why hadn't he told her during the dozen or so times that they had slept together? Good question. He had told Julia a dozen times a day, so he knew he could say it. But Julia was the only woman he had ever uttered the words to, so *I love you* sounded inevitably like a marriage proposal. Did he want to marry her? Well, he was definitely going to Washington while Suzanne made it crystal clear that Clarkeston was the only place she wanted to raise Maria. Neither of them were naïve enough to believe in long-distance romance.

Suzanne deserved a white knight, he concluded, not someone with nothing long-term to offer. On the other hand, she was hardly unaware of the situation, and she had the advantage of being more mature than him. Rapidly tiring of himself, he abandoned self-examination, wishing desperately that he had a friend to talk to, someone who understood the feminine perspective.

He found a piece of driftwood, and after a few minutes of sitting and contemplating the surf, he finally decided that the best approach would be to ask Suzanne herself for help in sorting out his feelings. He would tell her that he loved her, but remind her that he was leaving town in seven months. He would confess to being an irrationally jealous person who could only survive in a monogamous relationship. To avoid more stupidity, he needed her counsel. She was his best friend in Clarkeston, and her response to his soul-baring would tell him what to do.

Suzanne was digging a shoulder-deep hole in the sand with Maria when he returned from his walk.

"I'm so sorry! I'm totally chill now."

"It's okay."

"You know, my parents used to send me on long walks whenever I did something stupid."

She smiled and drew up a wet handful of sand to plop in Maria's bucket. "Don't worry about it."

"Maybe we could spend some time alone this evening and talk a bit?"

"Sure! Maybe we could go on that beach walk? Maria seems comfortable with everybody now." And so the day passed smoothly until after the Thanksgiving feasting was over.

The holiday host, Jack Ramsey, arrived early in the afternoon with a bag of Idaho potatoes, a marshmallow-topped sweet potato casserole, and a huge turkey, already stuffed and ready to put in the oven. He apologized for bringing store-bought pies for dessert, but redeemed himself by pouring everybody glasses of a superb Oregon Pinot Noir. The group spent an increasingly tipsy afternoon coaxing the legal equivalent of war stories out of him and answering his questions about the current state of affairs in Clarkston.

★ ★ ★

Suzanne had never met Jack Ramsey before, so she appreciated the fact that he included Maria in the conversation around the large glass dining room table, never talking down to her and eagerly showing her pictures of his numerous grandchildren. He was a natural with kids, much like Arthur was. As dinner wound down, she watched Arthur excuse himself to make coffee in the kitchen, and she decided to push his morning bout of jealousy to the back of her mind. He was such a nice guy. Handsome, intelligent, a considerate lover, and very sweet with Maria. He couldn't have known what a red button he had pushed.

"Hey," asked Titus Grover to the group as he stood up, "does anyone want to drive with me to the Magic Mark-Up on a wine run? We're about out."

Although leery of traveling alone with the famous lothario, Suzanne was out of tampons, and she knew that she shouldn't be driving herself anywhere on four large glasses of wine.

"Sure," she said, hoping someone else would join in, "I've got to pick up something."

Looking in vain for others willing to take Grover up on his offer, she saw April and Jack crawling on the floor with Maria, looking for a toy that she had dropped under the table. Her first impulse was to take her daughter with her, but that would mean moving the kid's clunky car seat. And, as cocksure as Grover pretended to be, he was just a ladies' man, not a rapist.

"Hey, can you guys watch Maria for fifteen minutes?"

They nodded happily and began to play, so she grabbed her purse from a hook by the front door and left the beach house alone with Grover.

★ ★ ★

After the gut-busting dinner, Arthur poured himself a cup of coffee and wandered down to the beach to catch the sunset. After taking several strides in the soft white sand, he heard the door open behind him and a small voice cry out, "Lemme come too!"

A moment later, April appeared behind Maria who wrenched her hand away from the young lawyer with a determined frown.

"It's okay!" Arthur said. "She can come with me."

April looked doubtfully at the pounding surf. "Are you sure?"

"Yeah." He nodded. "We'll just play in the sand like we did this morning."

With that, Maria ran down the steps, grabbed his hand, and held it all the way to the beach where she noticed a gnarly piece of driftwood sticking out of the sand and stopped to investigate. He sat in a lawn chair dragged down by someone earlier in the day and breathed a contented sigh as the molten glow of the sun's pigment pot poured slowly across the Gulf sky.

Before too long, his reverie was interrupted by Maria filling his lap with treasures revealed by the receding tide, and by the time darkness had fallen, he was in possession of a large pile of shells and the front of his pants was soaked. Gathering the debris up in his shirt, he and the weary little girl headed back to the house, stopping underneath it to store a dozen of the best shells in a corroded stainless steel sink. Arthur led her up the stairs to clean up.

A perfect opportunity to practice inner serenity arose when Glenn informed him that Suzanne and Grover had left to replenish the depleted stock of wine and were due back any minute. He was proud of his self-control. His expression never changed, and only the briefest twinge of jealousy knotted his stomach. If he were capable of a serious relationship, something that Julia had declared impossible on more than one occasion, he would have to anchor his well-being in something other than knowing the exact whereabouts of honorable, trustworthy people.

Two hours later, he sat alone on the upper deck, unable to listen to any more speculation from Glenn, April, and Jack about where Suzanne and Grover could possibly be. He escaped by offering to put Maria to bed, an unenviable task given her mother's absence. He helped her find her toothbrush and stood over her while she cleaned with deliberate if clumsy strokes. He washed her hands and stood her in the tub while he pushed up the legs of her pajama bottoms and sprayed the sand off her feet.

"That tickles!" She cried as she stamped her feet to avoid the cold water. After he wiped her off, she put her arms around his neck, and he lifted her out of the tub. She hugged him tightly and laid her head on his shoulder. Realizing with a start that losing Suzanne would mean losing Maria too, he hugged her back and laid her down gently in the bed. She grinned up at him.

"I get ten stories before I go to sleep!" He nodded and picked through Maria's Dr. Seuss collection and read until he was hoarse. Remembering a trick Suzanne had told him, he waited until the little girl started to nod off a little and then gave her a big picture book to study while he went to get her a cup of water. When he stuck his head in her room five minutes later, she was fast asleep. He turned on the closet light, diffusing its intensity by cracking the door, and then flipped off the overhead light. He tucked her in and carefully shut the door.

He had been out on the deck nursing depressing thoughts for about thirty minutes when a pair of headlights suddenly backlit the sand dunes. Moments later, two car doors slammed, and a giggle could be heard momentarily above the breeze. A muffled cheer then drifted up from below as the wine-bearing prodigals were welcomed by the thirsty crowd.

A couple of minutes later, Suzanne came upstairs. She found Arthur, the very picture of relaxation, with his legs propped up on the deck rail, contentedly sipping the last of the initial supply of white wine.

"Sorry I'm late! We—"

Arthur cut her off, not wanting to hear excuses or explanations for her three-hour absence. "Maria and I collected some shells and had a great time."

"How did you get her to sleep?"

"I just read to her. She wanted you, but the sandman won out in the end."

"You know," she replied, "you could have let her stay up. It's only ten thirty."

"I'm sorry." Could she hear his insincerity? "You normally put her down about eight thirty. I guess I screwed up."

"Don't be ridiculous! I really appreciate it."

Rather than turn to face her, he continued to look out into the dark.

"I'm just surprised you could do it."

He said nothing more, hoping that their relationship could just smoothly and without fuss devolve from lovers back to landlord-tenant. Nonetheless, his imagination served up vivid images of what must have transpired during her time with Grover. He took a deep breath. Suzanne had seen his bad side that morning, but she would see the stoic version this evening.

"You said this morning that you wanted to talk." Her inflection gave no indication that she would leave him alone to the consolation of starlight and murmuring surf.

"I did, but it's not important now . . . I just wanted to apologize again for being so stupid."

"Are you okay?"

"I'll be fine. I'm a big boy . . . I'll get over it."

"Get over what?" A hint of exasperation colored her voice. For the first time, he turned and met her eyes, wondering why she wanted to pursue this.

"What do you think?" A hint of annoyance crept into his voice, and he forced himself to look out at the ocean. "Just let it be, okay? You've got nothing to apologize for, and I don't want any apologies anyway."

"You're right. I've got nothing to apologize for, unless spending two and a half hours digging Grover's car out of the sand requires one." She waited for him to challenge her story. He glanced at her. She looked absolutely ravishing—or possibly just ravished—with her hair running riot over head, eyes flashing, and flawless skin glowing in the moonlight.

"Well, that would explain the sand on your back."

"Are you saying—"

"I'm not saying anything!" He swallowed his frustration at the fact she thought he was a fool. "And I'm not angry. I'm sitting here quietly, drinking a glass of wine and listening to the surf. Just what is it precisely that you want me to do?"

She paused before responding. "How about go straight to hell?"

She whipped around and made a clumsy attempt to slam the sticky sliding door as she stalked out. He watched the shrimp boats blink underneath the shimmering yellow moon. A sandpiper landed on the railing in front of him to snatch a crumb off an abandoned pie plate. It eyed him suspiciously, ready to fly off at the slightest movement. He sighed as it stared at him. "That went well, don't you think?"

Fifteen minutes later, he pasted a contented smile on his face and went down to the party. He leaned against the wet bar and sipped a glass of water and listened to Grover regale his audience with a story about a deposition gone horribly wrong. When he felt his presence fade to a sufficient level of inconspicuousness, he slipped miserably through the back door for a walk that he hoped would end long after everyone was in bed. As he strode barefoot down to the water, he heard the door open and shut.

"Wait up!"

He pretended not hear and strode up the beach at a steady clip. A minute later, Suzanne huffed up next to him.

"Are you deaf or something?"

He shrugged and let out a huge sigh before turning around.

"I'm sorry that you had to watch Maria for three hours—"

"Don't apologize for that. I love spending time with her."

"No, I don't mean it like that. Look, you invited me to the beach, and you've been wonderful with Maria. Then, I disappeared and yelled at you. I'm sorry for being so pissy."

"Don't worry about it. It's okay."

"Just what is bugging you then?" The twinge of pleading in her tone made the question sound almost reasonable. Rather than dissemble again or say nothing, he decided to just lay it all out as calmly as possible.

"Remember you asked for it." He couldn't look her in the eye. "When you ask questions about what's going on inside my head, you may hear some adverse shit."

He took a deep breath. The moon flashed intermittedly on the tips of the whitecaps. "I was a little bit of a jerk last night, but the way Grover had his eyes glued permanently to your chest was a hell of a lot ruder . . . I understand why you didn't run upstairs after me, but to reward him with a tête-à-tête until the wee hours of the morning is totally incomprehensible." That seemed fair and balanced.

"Then, on an evening when I ask to have a serious talk with you, you leave Maria with me so you can socialize with this same guy that you've already spent most of your time with during our vacation." He took a step down the beach and she followed. He was finally getting his moonlit walk, but it was not quite as romantic as he had planned.

"It was just supposed to be a fifteen-minute wine run."

"Yeah, yeah, I heard the story downstairs." He picked up a shell, then tossed it ahead and crunched it with his heel. "Grover thought you had time to take a quick drive through the park before the sunset, and he made the mistake of driving on some soft sand." He stopped and looked at her, making a helpless gesture with his hands, trying to convey that he could never really know the truth. "Whatever happened, you chose to take a romantic detour with a famous lecher while I babysat your child.

"That's what's bugging me, and if it shows how shallow and petty I am then . . . well, just remind yourself that you're the one who ran out here to ask."

Suzanne was looking at him, but it was a hard stare that did not invite reciprocation, so he looked down at the sand scrunching between his toes. A cool breeze whispered around them, a reminder that summer was over, even in Florida. She lifted his chin with her hand and forced his eyes to meet hers.

"You know," she said in a steely voice, "someone should really slap some sense into you."

He could not believe that she was sticking to her story.

"But since I'm used to teaching toddlers, let me explain something to you. My husband was insanely jealous. He used to come home in the evening and push the redial button on the phone to see if he could catch me having called any of my imaginary boyfriends." She snorted. "That gets old in a hurry. And guess what? I still can't stand it."

She started down the beach once again, and this time he followed her. "If you play that game with me, I'm going to lash right back and maybe even accept some harmless attention."

He stopped in his tracks, body rigid.

"Will you let me finish?" She turned and continued. "Whether you believe it or not, the thought of cheating on somebody makes me physically ill. After Bill died, one of my friends felt free to tell me that he had been sleeping with not just one, but two of his colleagues in Birmingham!"

Arthur walked down into the surf. He let the cold water quench the ridiculous hope that nothing had happened with Grover.

"I saw the signs that he was having an affair, but ignored them, and finding out hurt as much as the accident. When he died, I lost the future we had planned. When I found out he had been sleeping around, I lost the past too."

Arthur stared out over the waves. It might have been easier if she had slapped him. The story of her marriage made for compelling listening, and he cringed at the comparison between his jealousy and her deceased husband's. Maybe he just wasn't cut out for this relationship stuff.

"I couldn't hurt someone that way." She crept up behind him and rested her chin on his shoulder, circling her arms around his waist.

She almost convinced him, but the lawyer kept looking for loopholes.

"But we're not married or engaged or even officially committed as I can tell."

"It doesn't matter. Despite your idiocies, I can't help but love you, and I don't want to hurt you." She squeezed him tighter, as if she were trying to force some common sense into him. "I'm a good person, Arthur."

The sudden joy of his belief swept through him like a sandstorm, scouring away all doubt.

"I love you too." He hugged her fiercely. "I never said it because . . . it just seems so inconsistent with me leaving in June."

She told him to shut up and kissed him.

When lip fatigue finally set in, they opened their eyes and noticed the ghost crabs scuttling about them, picking the beach clean before the tide rolled in to make its nightly delivery of shells and jellyfish. They took each other's hands and walked far down the beach, away from the lights of the houses. For a long while, they strolled silently along the shoreline until at the edge of the park they found a large piece of driftwood and sat down to rest.

"So why did you and your ex-wife break up?"

Arthur warmed to the twinge of worry in Suzanne's voice. "It's a long story," he sighed dramatically, "but mostly because she caught me in bed with the neighbor's fifteen-year-old daughter."

"You creep!" She pushed him off the log and kicked sand at him. "How come, really?"

"Hmm . . . the real reason?" He eased himself back onto his perch. "Well, we argued all the time, so maybe we really didn't have much in common." He reached over and brushed some sand from her leg. He hadn't talked about his marriage for months, and he was surprised at the perspective he had gained.

"We were probably doomed before we even got married. If one of us had been able to swallow hard and call off the engagement, I'll bet the other would have sighed with relief." This rang true to him, although he had never said it aloud before. "But the inertia of a two-year engagement is really powerful. We went through with all of our fancy wedding plans, honeymooned in the Bahamas, and assumed we had a good relationship when all we did was live and sleep together.

"I think the only reason it lasted three years was because we were so focused on other stuff. She had a great new job, and I had law school. We hardly ever saw each other." He grimaced at the memory of her sixty-hour work weeks and increasingly indifferent shows of affection. "Things came to a head when I decided to clerk after graduation. She expected me to take a job in downtown Chicago like her, work hours like she did, and make a huge pile of money. She couldn't understand my desire to work for a federal judge and flat out refused to move to Georgia, even for a year."

"So you chose the Judge over your marriage," Suzanne teased. "You should mention that to him."

"In her mind, I did. In my mind, she became this materialistic bitch who was only interested in making vice president before thirty." It was nice to finally be able to talk. "She thought that I was a lazy, romantic do-gooder who tricked her into supporting me during law school. We were both being unfair, but we had plenty of ammunition to kill off the relationship."

It was an accurate, but not quite complete, picture he painted for Suzanne. He did not tell her that Julia was so pretty that she made Melanie look like a wallflower. Nor did he tell her he was so depressed after the breakup that he missed two weeks of classes or that he had desperately tried to reconcile with her on the eve of the divorce even though she had long been seeing someone else. Suzanne wanted to judge what sort of husband he had been, so there was no reason to detail the power of his attraction to Julia, nor why he had felt like such an utter failure when the marriage was finally over. Editing the story was merely doing unto others—he had absolutely no desire to hear about the good parts of Suzanne's relationship with her husband.

"So, no fifteen-year-old girls?"

"Just me acting like one . . ."

They both had more questions, and each story led them deeper into each other's lives. It took them hours to make their way back to the house, and when they finally approached it, they found the party going full force on the bottom deck.

They were greeted by a chorus of wolf whistles and cat calls from the tipsy lawyers. Suzanne had fended off Grover's advances on the beer run by bragging about her boyfriend, and Grover, taking a mild revenge, had passed this on to Phil, April, and Glenn, who spontaneously erupted with the sort of razzing heard from sixth graders seeing two of their classmates emerge together from the broom closet.

Even in the dark, Arthur could see Suzanne redden, but he accepted the hooting graciously and strode up the steps, waving to the crowd like a baseball player called out of the dugout after hitting a game-winning home run. As they sat down, Arthur ordered Grover to get them a couple of glasses of wine. He complied graciously and served them with a respectful bow.

The company was pleasant, and they lingered outside until four a.m., when April offered to treat everyone to an early breakfast at the Waffle House. Only Glenn accepted the invitation, and the rest slipped off to bed. Arthur followed Suzanne up the interior stairway with his hands on the small of her back, luxuriating in the swish and sway of her hips as she climbed. She sent him to his room while she went to check on Maria.

He stripped to his boxers and lay down exhausted, head propped up on two pillows, window cracked just enough to fill the room with the gentle pounding of the surf. Before long, he heard the click of the door knob and turned to see Suzanne in a new camisole, crawling panther-like across his bed. Luckily, the lingerie stayed mostly intact, because Maria woke them up three hours later confused to find her mommy sleeping back-to-back with Mr. Hughes in his bed. While he played possum, Suzanne yawned and stretched as if nothing out of the ordinary had happened.

"Goodness, what am I doing here?" she queried convincingly. "Let's go downstairs and make some pancakes, little girl."

He didn't roll over until he heard the door close behind them. He marveled at Suzanne's finessing of Maria, and as the sun streamed through the curtains, he wondered whether they could so smoothly negotiate the future. During their walk, he had promised Suzanne that he would do some interviewing in Atlanta and Clarkeston, promises he fully intended to keep, but he knew that no job could keep him in Georgia. The call of Washington and the opportunity to right big wrongs was simply too powerful. He made the promise to her in good faith, but with the sort of misgivings a diaphragm-toting Roman Catholic has when she promises her priest to be open to the possibility of children blessing her marriage.

XVI

WATCHING THE DETECTIVES

Melanie digested Phil's summary of Thanksgiving on the beach with interest. Post-turkey chest pains had put her father in the hospital over the holiday weekend and scuttled the proposed trip to Florida. As they sat in the library on Monday morning, she complimented Phil on his detective work and bemoaned her inability to ask April follow-up questions about Carolyn Bastaigne.

"Just call her," he suggested.

"Wouldn't that be kind of weird?"

"Nah, she's really nice, and she thinks the accident is as suspicious as you do." He laughed and then put his pinky to his mouth and his thumb to his ear. "Hello, could I speak to Ms. Marple? This is Nancy Drew."

"Shut up!"

"'I'm working on *The Case of the Clumsy Clerk*."

"Careful, or you'll be working on *The Case of the Neutered Smart-Ass*." She threw a Post-it pad at him. "Maybe I will call her. There might be something going on if she's suspicious too."

Melanie worked the rest of the day on a bench memo in a tedious search and seizure case. Drug cases not only make bad law, she decided, but dull reading too. She worked until late afternoon, fighting the urge to call April. When she finally gave in, it was 2:30 p.m. in Denver, a good time to find a lawyer in her office.

"I'm sorry you never made it down to the beach," April said cheerfully after her assistant connected her. "It was nice to meet Phil, though. What a sweetheart!"

"He really is, and he said it would be okay to call you about Carolyn Bastaigne. I know it sounds stupid, but I'm really curious about how she died."

"It was pretty strange."

She paused for a moment, and Melanie reached over for a pad of legal paper and a pen.

"What do you want to know?"

"I'm not really sure," Melanie replied. "One new bit that Phil mentioned was this connection to Judge Meyers' chambers. I really haven't heard much about him."

"He was a district court judge, totally unreconstructed southern conservative, but very well-connected politically, Clarkeston Country Club and all that jazz. The Judge must have reversed him in civil rights cases about a dozen times over the years."

Melanie could hear the sound of a cigarette being lit and waited until April took a deep drag.

"What was really galling to Meyers," April continued, "was when the Judge transformed from pariah to hero. Meyers was the darling of the local social scene in the fifties and sixties. By the late seventies, he was an anachronism. That was probably hard for him to take."

"You don't think he might have . . ."

April laughed so loud that Melanie had to push the receiver from her ear. "No way. He was a harmless old twit. It's amazing how nice a hard-core racist can be in person. Anyway, he was very frail. I can't see him pushing Carolyn down the stairs with his walker."

"What about this friend she had in Myers's chambers?"

"Jennifer Huffman? She's at Cravath in New York, where Carolyn was going to go." April paused for a moment. "They were buddies, but I never understood why. Carolyn was loud and obnoxious and lazier than a depressed sloth. Jennifer was real bright and energetic. They were pretty much Mutt and Jeff. Quite frankly, I preferred Jennifer."

"Did you ever suspect her of anything?"

"No, but I never really suspected anybody of anything. Carolyn probably just tripped. I don't know why anybody would want to do her any harm. You could call Jennifer, if you're really desperate." She gave an audible exhalation of disgust. "The two of them were pretty obnoxious together, like they were still in middle school or something, whispering and note passing . . . It was less than a perfect year, I have to say."

"Well, thanks anyway. I'm really sorry we didn't get to meet last week."

"Me too! Maybe I'll see you next time."

Melanie hung up and wondered what to do next. She was at a dead end. Ms. Bastaigne had not called back, so the threat to the Judge's reputation seemed remote, and her wild fantasy of uncovering a murder and becoming a chambers legend seemed more and more delusional. She decided to pass along April's greeting to Phil and get back to work.

Melanie peeked in the library and found him working quietly across the conference table from Arthur.

"April says hello. She's says you're a 'real sweetie.'"

Phil blushed. He really was a sweetie.

"Well, did you two solve the great mystery?" Phil asked.

"What mystery?" Arthur reached for his mug of coffee and looked up at the two amateur detectives.

"*The Case of the Clumsy Clerk.*" Phil smiled at Melanie.

"Are you guys still talking about that?"

"I'm just Melanie's sounding board. She's been doing all the sleuthing."

"Hey! You interrogated April in Florida."

"Fair enough," he said as he grabbed his own coffee. "But it's kinda fun. I don't think she was murdered, but what happened is still pretty odd."

"I suppose." Arthur looked down at the file he was reading. "It's got to be more fun working on fake murder than the real thing."

Melanie thought he was going to say more, but Phil interrupted. "I believe it. The Gottlieb case wasn't much of a whodunit, was it?"

"Nope. No mystery there." Arthur traced a pattern with his pencil on the scared surface of the conference table. "It's strange, though. You write on a piece of paper saying someone should die, then you read about it in the newspaper the next day. You look over your shoulder and you realize that no one's going to punish you for it. In fact, there's people on television cheering."

Introspection quite became Arthur, Melanie thought.

"Arthur?" Phil said.

"Yeah?"

"You need a beer."

Melanie nodded enthusiastically, and she saw Arthur smile.

★ ★ ★

Arthur wanted to walk alone to the Wild Boar, so he pleaded a fictional errand and left before the others had finished work. Hands in his pockets, he strolled slowly past the storefronts on Court Street, turned left down College Avenue, then crossed the river onto the grounds of Clarkeston College. At the top of the bluff marking the edge of the campus, the entrance road forked to divert traffic around its east and west perimeters. Rather than follow one of the branches, he crossed the road and entered the north quadrangle of the college through an enormous wrought iron gate. The Wild Boar lay on the far side of the college, where the split road reconnected.

The main quad exposed the architectural impoverishment of Arthur's undergraduate years at a Midwestern school consisting of mismatched concrete buildings squatting uncomfortably on former cornfields. The north part of Clarkeston College was encompassed by a harmonious ring of red brick, ivy-covered buildings sheltering a generous expanse of tree-lined sidewalks and a thick, carefully manicured lawn. Arched porticos connected the buildings, enabling students to make a complete circuit during bad weather without getting wet.

Arthur wandered along a shaded sidewalk, sneaking the occasional peek into the first-floor classrooms and offices. The quad was deserted except for some students reading on the concrete benches that lined the recessed areas of the cloister. Squirrels traveled overhead, leaping from branch to branch, from one side of the quad to the other without touching the ground. Oaks predominated, but dogwoods and redbuds had been planted alongside the buildings and a huge cedar of Lebanon guarded the pathway alongside the Music Building portico that led to the next quadrangle.

As he followed the sidewalk past the cedar, he turned to take one last look at the library and was surprised to hear the pure focused sound of women's voices coming from inside the music building. At least a dozen sopranos sang in unison, holding one clear sustained note on *Lux* . . . They were then joined by the altos, tenors, and basses divided beneath them, one measure behind, *Lux aeterna luceat eis, luceat domine* . . . Arthur knew the English text: *Light eternal shine upon them Lord*. The Fauré requiem mass was his mother's favorite choral work. He had sung it twice in her large church choir in high school but had not heard it since.

He was drawn through the open door of the building and sat down on a bench just outside the rehearsal room. The choir continued, voices in harmony singing the Latin mass for the dead, *Cum sanctis tuis in aeternum, quia pius, pius es.* They repeated the line, swelling to an ecstatic cadence. As the singers rested, the accompanist continued as tears filled Arthur's eyes.

He squeezed them hard, recovering his composure until the voices swelled again, *Requiem aeternam.* Pause. *Dona eis Domine.* Pause. E*t lux perpetua*, a piercing plea for eternal light that resonated to the corners of his soul and transported him back to his childhood and the green cornfields swaying behind his house. For a moment in the Clarkeston College Music Building, he regained his innocence and sat breathless and longing, outside himself, filled completely with the raw spirit of life.

He leaned his head back against the wall and took a couple of deep breaths, realizing just in time that rehearsal was now over and the choir had started to leave. He turned away, walked a couple of paces farther down the hall, and drank deeply at a stained ceramic water fountain.

He was surprised at his own sentimentality. Weddings and dead kittens on the side of the road left him completely dry-eyed, but something inherently spiritual in good music could creep up on him when he least expected it, filling him with awe and driving out tears he had not known he had been collecting. He had been moved to his core, but whether what he heard was a secular or divine absolution or simply the foreknowledge of grief, he could not say. By the time he walked back down the hall, the last of the singers were filing out, and he regained his composure enough to stick his head in the door.

A tall woman with a steel-gray bun pulled tightly back behind her head was shuffling papers behind the podium.

"That was wonderful," he called from the door.

She turned and squinted, dark eyebrows furrowed, an indel-icate face rendered more severe by her expression. "You're not a tenor, are you?"

"I'm a lawyer actually—not practicing, though. I'm work-ing downtown for the Judge." She doesn't need to know that, he told himself, but he rushed on, "I was just walking past when I heard the Fauré so I wandered in."

She looked disappointed and went back to shuffling her papers.

"When is the performance?"

"We'll be doing it two weeks from Friday in the main music building auditorium." She paused and squinted again as she gathered up her load. "You certainly sound like a tenor."

"Yes, ma'am. My mom's a choir director, and I help her out at Christmas and Easter, but I haven't sung with a group since high school." He turned and began to walk out of the rehearsal room.

"You know," her voice grabbed him from behind, "I sometimes let people from the community people sing with the college chorus." She picked up her scores and walked toward him. "I've got so many holes in the tenor section right now that the second altos are singing the first tenor line half the time. If you're interested in singing spring quarter, why don't you set up an audition at the beginning of January?" She stuck out her hand for him to shake. "My name is Dorothy Henderson."

"I'd love to, but I don't think that I'll have the time." He frowned slightly and strode into the late-summer afternoon. "Thank you anyway!"

★ ★ ★

By the following afternoon, Phil's hangover had worn off, and he was starting work on a continuing class action suit that had first appeared in chambers three years earlier. Ms. Stillwater pointed him to an enormous box of documents stored in a corner of the photocopy room.

"What are these?" he asked her. "Trial exhibits and stuff?"

"No," she said slowly, her voice carrying a hint of pity, "those are just the appellate pleadings that have been filed over the years. I'll bet the trial materials take up a whole file room in the Atlanta District Court."

"Oh my God."

"Don't worry. This was Mr. Grover's case last year, and he just read the old bench memos written on it. He said it was a lot easier than plowing through all the pleadings."

"Old bench memos? Do we have those?" Before the Judge heard the oral argument in any case, one of the clerks was assigned to write a memo summarizing the facts and law relevant to every issue presented by the parties. Phil's own work had varied in length from five to thirty-five pages.

"Of course! Didn't I show them to you the first day?"

Phil shook his head, and she marched him to the Judge's office. She rapped hard once with the back of her knuckles and charged into the room before getting a response.

"Goddamn it, Stillwater! What if I had been in the bathroom?" the Judge bellowed from behind his desk.

"Well, if you'd shut the door when you're in there, you won't have to worry about it, would you! I'm showing Phillip where you keep the old bench memos." She walked to the far side of the room to a small alcove lined with bookshelves. Every square inch was lined with small black binders crammed with yellowing memoranda. The date of the judicial term was printed neatly on a square of white paper taped to the spine. "They're only indexed by year, so you'll have flip through them to find the ones written about your case. Just go back three years and you should have them all."

"Thanks!" He grabbed the last three volumes off the shelf and carried them past the Judge's glower into the library. After fifteen minutes of skimming through the memos, Melanie sat down with several volumes of the *Federal Reporter*.

"What are you looking at?"

"Old bench memos." He stood one up on its end to show her the typed pages in the binder.

"They save them?"

"There's a whole collection in the Judge's office, thank God. I've got a massive class action where I can read the old memos instead of four boxes of pleadings." He flipped through the pages. "It's kind of interesting to see the different writing styles of old clerks."

"How far back do they go?"

"All way, I think. It sure looked like thirty-five years' worth of binders in there." Melanie's mouth curled up in an intrigued smile.

"So, I could read all of Carolyn Bastaigne's memoranda to the Judge?"

"If you wanted to." He gave her a quizzical look. "What would you expect to find?"

"Well," she mused, "what if she worked on an organized crime case and recommended to the Judge that some mafia boss's sentence be affirmed and then someone ordered a hit?"

"Wouldn't they hit the Judge?" He gave her a skeptical look. "I mean, who would know who wrote the memo?"

"I don't know." She thought for a moment. "What if someone tried to bribe her to get someone out of jail in a habeas case and she refused?" She waited in vain for an answer. "What do you think?"

"I think you need to move to Hollywood." He put down his head and started to work. "Look, if you want to read her stuff, go ahead. I'll tell you what though, most of these are pretty boring . . . but I guess we knew that already!"

★ ★ ★

Melanie waited until everyone had gone home for the day before she opened the top drawer of Ms. Stillwater's desk and took out the spare key to the Judge's office. She had seen the secretary use it several times to access his space while he was away at a hearing. In the uncomfortable emptiness of the chambers, she hesitated to use it, but rationalized that she was doing nothing that she couldn't do in full view of the Judge. The memos were not secret; they were meant to be accessible to the clerking descendants of those that wrote them. Nonetheless, she fumbled with the key in the door and cast a furtive glance over her shoulder when it opened with a loud squeak.

She walked straight over to the shadowy alcove in the back of his office, determined to make her stay in the Judge's inner sanctum as brief as possible. Carolyn had clerked during the 1983-84 term, but to Melanie's dismay, she found a gap in the row of binders where 1983-84 should have been. She slowly scanned the entire collection to see if it had been misplaced, but the volumes had been meticulously kept in the proper order.

"Damn."

She turned slowly, took one last look at the shelves, and walked toward the door, but as she passed the Judge's desk, she noticed a black binder sitting on top of a stack of papers. Without touching it, she bent over and checked the year: 1983-84. Why the hell does he have it out now? She fought the urge to pick it up. What if the Judge came back and she were caught? But the Judge never came back after supper. He arrived super early, worked hard, and left early. Calm down, she said to herself, memorized the position of the book, and picked it up, you're not stealing anything.

She turned on every light in the library to help dispel the sense that she was doing something unseemly and sat down to read the collected works of Carolyn Bastaigne. She anxiously skipped to the end of the binder, looking for the last case that she had worked on, but it turned out to be a boring review of a Federal Trade Commission merger decision. Disappointed, she went back to the front of the book and started working through the memoranda in chronological order.

Nothing jumped out at her. Carolyn worked on a number of criminal cases, but they all had been decided in favor of the defendant or involved defendants who seemed utterly unlikely to come seeking revenge on a lowly law clerk. Other cases involved the improper granting of a radio station license, a department store chain bankruptcy, and music copyright infringement. Her memos were inevitably short and devoid of the massive citation to prior case law that characterized Melanie's own work. By the time she got back to the final case, she was thoroughly discouraged. She stared at the first page of the FTC merger case and lamented the three hours she had wasted. It was already 11:00 p.m.

She was about to put the book away, when she noticed the heading of the final case:

Panel: FJM, PKA, GTB
Clerk: CB
Date: June 5, 1984
Appeal From: Central District (Meyers)

This was the only appeal from Judge Meyers that Carolyn had worked on. Melanie started to read the case again and noticed that the memo was almost three times longer than the others, with voluminous citation to other cases and even a learned discussion of law review articles on anti-trust law. She read slowly and carefully while the kernel of a theory formed in her head.

The case involved a proposed merger between two soft drink manufacturers. Because of the size of the firms, the approval of the Federal Trade Commission had been necessary and eventually obtained. Before the merger was consummated, however, a rival bottler had challenged it in court on anti-trust grounds, arguing that the combined firms would control a dangerously large share of the market. In an opinion by Judge Meyers, the merger had been enjoined and the two frustrated bottlers appealed to the Eleventh Circuit. Enter Carolyn Bastaigne, who had apparently been assigned to take the case. Her well-written and comprehensive memo argued convincingly that Judge Meyers had erred and recommended that the merger be approved.

Melanie leaned back in her chair. Why had Carolyn spent so much time and effort on this particular case? Why work so hard to overturn the opinion of her best friend's judge? She pulled her knees to her chest and set her heels on the edge of the chair.

What if her friend wanted the case overturned? Melanie had not been a star in her securities regulation class, but she remembered that when mergers were denied, the stock prices of both firms usually fell. A later approval of the same proposed merger would send stock prices skyrocketing. Carolyn would have known the decision in the case long before the media or even the parties involved. It would be very easy to make a tidy bundle on the inside information. Was this what Jennifer Huffman and Carolyn Bastaigne had been whispering about before she died?

It was nine thirty in Denver. Melanie got April's home number from information.

"Hi, April, it's Melanie. I'm sorry to bug you at home, but I was wondering if you remember anything about the last case Carolyn was working on, a big soft drink merger case."

"How'd you find out about that?"

"From an old bench memo." She flipped through the case one more time while April spoke.

"Well, I can remember how much she wanted to work on it. Our co-clerk had originally chosen it, but she bitched and moaned and offered to trade another case for it. Eventually he let her have it just to shut her up."

"Interesting."

"How come?"

"I read the memo, and it's actually good. All the rest of her work is crap. She must have really wanted the case for some reason." She tapped the binder with her pencil and scribbled a note on a yellow pad.

"Hmmm . . . I never read it. But you're right about her work. I could never figure out how she got a job with a firm like Cravath."

"Maybe she had a great summer internship there when she was a law student?"

"Maybe. But I doubt it. She was a slacker to the core."

"Thanks, April." Melanie heard the judgment in her voice and shuddered involuntarily. How could someone like Carolyn hand in work that was substandard? How could someone not care about her reputation? When you work for someone, Melanie thought, they will judge you. Life was filled with bosses, teachers, pageant officials, and parents, and if you couldn't satisfy them, where would you be? In the middle of an argument, one of her sorority sisters had once accused her of being a "pleaser." *You've got no will of your own,* she had been told. What was she supposed to do, get Bs instead of As or withdraw from a competition just to demonstrate she was a free spirit? There were enough slackers without her joining the group.

She sat for a long while and wondered what to do next. It would be nice to talk to Jennifer Huffman, but she doubted that a phone call out of the blue would be very productive. And if she and Carolyn were attempting to trade on inside information together, she was unlikely to admit it. If only she could figure out a way to get to Cravath, Swaine, and Moore.

XVII.

LOSING MY RELIGION

Suzanne knew as soon as the phone rang that the news was bad. Her hand lingered on the receiver through the fifth ring before she slowly picked it up. A shaky voice asked to speak to Arthur. Suzanne explained that he was interviewing in Washington, DC, and the caller, his sister Terri, told her that their father's car had been struck head-on by a drunk driver on US 88 in eastern Iowa. By the time Terri was done describing the massive head and chest injuries, they were both crying. The doctors were not sure that he would make it through the night.

"Do you have any idea where he is?" Terri finally asked.

"I think he was interviewing at the Office of Legal Counsel today, but I don't have the number. You should try his hotel and leave a message. I'm so sorry." Suzanne pulled Arthur's itinerary down from the refrigerator and read off the phone number. "He said it's by the airport, so he might be able to grab a quick flight."

Suzanne went out to the front porch and sat on the stoop. The air outside was cool and mild. The maple tree in her neighbor's yard set the whole street aglow. She said a short prayer for Arthur's father and then a longer one for him. This is too much death for one season, she thought. Gottlieb had taken much more out of Arthur than he was willing to admit, and news of his father's accident would be devastating. She could feel him starting to drift away.

Like a silent little monk, Maria found her mother on the porch and leaned heavily against her.

"What's wrong, Momma?"

"I'm just worried about Arthur."

"He's a long way away today, isn't he?"

"Yes, he is. A very long way away."

★ ★ ★

Arthur sat confined on the plane, stuck between two self-absorbed businessmen and wondering what his father would have thought about his recently concluded visit to the halls of the mighty in Washington. The old farmer might have gotten a kick out of explaining to his cronies at the grain elevator what his son was doing. His dad would never volunteer the information, but eventually his friends would be unable to resist asking whether his boy would be coming back to Iowa to practice law, maybe even join a firm in a big city like Des Moines. Then, he would be forced to reveal in his laconic manner that Arthur would be working at some alphabet agency in Washington, trying to talk some sense into the folks who ran the federal government.

He had spent one day interviewing at the Office of Legal Counsel, the home of the president's own lawyers, and the next at the Environmental Protection Agency. Although his commitment to environmentalism remained strong, he had decided that prosecuting the owners of leaky landfills would not be quite as exciting as telling senators which presidential documents they could examine and which were protected by executive privilege. Of course, his chances at OLC were about one out of fifty, while his chances at the EPA were about two out of three.

Now, his father would never find out where his life would lead. He remembered the last time they had spoken, a brief conversation while he was at the beach. He could not remember what they talked about. The beach replayed itself in his mind and spiraled him back through law school and Julia and college, back to the farm and fresh snow crunching underfoot on the long walk down the driveway to catch the morning school bus. He wondered what would happen if he retraced those steps, rode the bus, and sat quietly in the back of the kindergarten classroom knees to chest in a tiny chair.

Arthur's father had earned a degree in agricultural economics but had been an accountant working in Chicago when a childless uncle died, leaving him sole heir to his grandfather's farm. Tired of the city and his job, he saw farming as an honorable escape and a chance to make a fresh start. Hal and his wife turned out to be natural farmers, relishing the variety of challenges that six hundred acres provided. But the farm was his parents' domain, and soon after Arthur boarded his first bus, he made Evergreen County Comprehensive School his main stage. His favorite summer game was playing war in the thick grove of hickory and walnut trees behind the school. In the winter, he would beg his mother nearly every day to drive him to the sledding hill that gently sloped down from the gymnasium. He had long considered being a teacher instead of a lawyer . . .

"You'll have to flip your tray up, sir, while we descend." The stewardess took a full cup of Coke and unopened bag of peanuts from him, and he turned to watch the snow-powdered corn stubble blur past his window.

When he got off the plane and emerged from the gangway, he could see his sister waving, by force of habit offering a thin smile to accompany her hand in spite of the dreadful cause of their reunion.

Terri belonged in Iowa. Her pleasant, broad face bore no makeup, blond hair pulled back with a simple rubber band. A worn gray sweater and blue jeans proclaimed lack of pretense that made her Arthur's favorite sibling.

"He's still alive." She gave him a quick hug. "But he's in a coma. The doctors want to sit down with us this afternoon and talk about his condition, but even an idiot can look at the EEG and see nothing's happening." She grabbed the smaller of his two bags and started walking through the terminal.

"Well, how much brain activity is there supposed to be when you're in a coma?" he asked as he caught up to her.

"I don't know. We can ask the doctors . . . I'm just trying to get you ready to see him. It's pretty bad, and as you can imagine, Mom's a mess."

"How are you and Buddy doing?"

"I haven't had time to think about me. I've been doing all of the talking to the doctors and Dad's friends who want to know what's happening. Buddy may be a grown man out in the fields, but he's only nineteen and he's barely holding himself together right now. He's not ready to face the possibility that he's losing his father, business partner, and best friend all at the same time."

"And Mom's worse?"

"She's been vacillating between hysteria and catatonia. It's horrible for her, even after thirty years of marriage they were still lovestruck teenagers. It's a total nightmare."

★ ★ ★

Arthur and Terri found their mother and brother slumped ashen-faced in a waiting room outside the critical care unit. Sally looked all of her fifty-five years, and Arthur noticed for the first time how many strands of gray colored the brown hair that her husband begged her to keep long. She looked small and vulnerable with Buddy sitting protectively next to her. He was shorter than Arthur, but his muscular build and handsome face (girls were forever comparing him to Tom Cruise) more than made up for his lack of height. Anyone wishing to disturb his mother would have to go through Buddy first. They had spent the night at the hospital, waiting to hear how the surgery had gone and to catch a brief glimpse of husband and father surrounded by machines in one of the rooms past the nurses' station. Sally got up and hugged Arthur hard when she saw them come into the room.

"Thanks for coming so quickly . . . The doctor says he'll see us soon." She smiled weakly. "Maybe we can get something out of the docs with a lawyer around."

"And then you need to get back home and go to bed, Mom. You look exhausted."

"This is my home as long as your father is here." She sat back down, fumbled in her purse, and eventually pulled out a hairbrush. She ripped mercilessly through her hair while she gave him the details of the accident

"Some drunk drove right over the median," she explained in a relatively steady voice, "and plowed into him. He was in the left lane at the time passing someone. He never had a chance. I got a phone call from the highway patrol"—her voice finally started to break—"and they told me there had been an accident and that they were bringing your father here. They wouldn't tell me anything else, even when I begged them."

Arthur tried to divert the conversation away from the immediate horror of the accident. He pushed the hair gently back from her face and tucked it behind her ear. Had anyone talked to the pastor about getting Hal on the church prayer list? Was there anything at the farm that needed tending while Buddy was at the hospital? Had the insurance company been contacted? Had the family physician been here and had his wife finally divorced him? By the time the neurosurgeon arrived, he had managed to distract his mother a bit.

Buddy just stared at an ancient issue of *Outdoor Life*.

Before leading them into a small conference room, the neurosurgeon took them to Hal's room. Arthur did not recognize his father. The bandages on Hal's head and the ventilator sticking down his throat obscured all but a small swathe of mottled skin around his swollen eyelids. He waited to be overwhelmed by shock or grief, but no strong emotion came. Dad was gone, and Arthur had no sense of his presence. He cast a quick glance at his mom, but she was in no shape to help him understand.

The doctor gave the family a tour of the electronic equipment keeping him alive. By the time Dr. Perez was done, they could distinguish between the wheezing of the respirator, the beeping of the heart monitor, and the low hum of electroencephalogram.

Arthur reacted with a deepened sense of resignation, while his brother balled his fists and clenched his jaw. His mother seemed to process little of the substance or implication of Perez's explanations. She sobbed, unable to suffer a technical rhetoric better suited to a mechanic's discussion of what was ailing the family sedan. Although the doctor had not expressly called their attention to the sick yellow-gray pallor of his skin or the misshapen parody of her husband's head, his broken body was all she seemed to be taking in. She reached out and stroked the back of his IV-punctured hand before they left the room.

When they got to the conference room, Dr. Perez began detailing the damage caused by the collision, starting with the least serious injuries. "His left leg and arm are broken, the leg suffering a compound fracture which also seriously damaged muscle tissue in his thigh. Four ribs were broken—one punctured his left lung, another damaged the pericardial sac surrounding his heart, the other two were just cracked. The heart wound almost killed him, and it still poses a serious threat if a post-operative infection sets in.

"I'm sorry to say that the worst injury is to his cranium. He suffered a massive concussion with extensive damage to both frontal lobes of his brain. Between the impact itself and the internal pressure caused by cerebral swelling, he's lost higher-level cognitive function although the portions of the brain governing involuntary motor functions such as breathing and cardiac activity seem relatively undamaged."

Buddy cut off Perez before he completed his presentation. "So, how long will it take for Dad to get back to work? How much therapy is he going to have to do? I saw a story on *20/20* about a guy who got shot in the head, and he had to relearn how to talk and write and even walk." Arthur knew that his brother was not stupid. He was either deliberately ignoring the implications of Perez's diagnosis or simply could not accept that his father, although breathing, was gone forever.

"The highest likelihood is that your father will never talk or write or walk again. You've seen the condition he's in. The EEG indicates minimal brain activity."

"Could you give us a rough idea of his chances of ever regaining consciousness?" Arthur intervened before Buddy could bluster further.

Perez frowned, not at the difficulty of the question, but with impatience at having to spell out what he saw as obvious. "I have been dealing with cranial trauma victims for eighteen years now. I have never seen a patient with your father's injuries ever emerge from a coma with significant cognitive function."

The finality of this prognosis pushed Sally over the edge. She leaned against Terri and cried uncontrollably.

"But I saw his foot move! You're not God—you don't know what's going to happen." Buddy shouted at the doctor.

"What about your colleagues' patients or case histories that you've read about in journals or textbooks?" Arthur asked, thinking that his younger brother should hear the worst.

"We've all heard of miracle cases," Perez sighed as he shook his head and turned for the door, "but I think they are always explained more convincingly in terms of monitor malfunction rather than spontaneous regeneration of brain activity. But anything is possible, I suppose." He opened the door and escaped awkwardly. Terri held Sally and rubbed her back gently as she struggled to get a hold of herself. Buddy closed his eyes tightly and rocked himself back and forth in small, measured motions like an autistic child. No one found any words to cut through the despair that permeated the room.

The door opened again after a few minutes and a middle-aged woman wearing a name tag embossed "Leslie Blackwell, Critical Care Liaison" sat down at the conference room table. Her conservative gray skirt and matching blazer made her look more like an attorney than a nurse but her demeanor was not coldly businesslike. She fairly radiated empathy and concern as she took the seat that Dr. Perez had occupied.

"I know this is a very difficult time, but the doctor wanted me to speak with all of you together. My name is Leslie, and I'm not a nurse or a doctor, but a social worker whose job it is to help the families of patients deal with the difficult medical decisions they have to make." Arthur wondered how she would deal with his brother. "Now, I need to ask you some questions that will help our staff determine how aggressively your father will be treated."

Buddy opened his eyes.

"First of all, we need to know whether he ever executed any sort of living will or any other type of witnessed document in which he spelled out what sort of treatment he wanted to receive in the event of a terrible accident like this one." Terri and Arthur looked at their mother, who shook her head. Ms. Blackwell explained that without a living will, some options, such as ceasing tube feeding, were not available.

"Why the hell would we want to stop feeding him?"

Blackwell nodded at Buddy to acknowledge his question. "You can decide to give your father the benefit of every heroic measure modern medicine can offer, but many families are quite adamant about letting nature take its course when there is no hope of a recovery." She spoke unapologetically, directing her soothing voice at Buddy, but glancing casually at Terri and Arthur to see if they too were likely antagonists.

"Well, this is one family that's not going to kill their father, especially when the doctor says that anything is possible." Buddy's glare would have paralyzed a less experienced woman.

"Exactly what did Dr. Perez say about your father's chances for recovery?" She looked slightly perplexed.

"The doctor gave us no hope short of a miracle, which he himself didn't seem to believe in."

Terri nodded in agreement with Arthur's summary.

Buddy muttered something under his breathe about not giving up hope.

"It's not my job to tell you whether to hope, or not to hope, or what to hope for." She spoke quietly, resting the tips of her fingers on the table in front of her. "I do know that your father is injured badly enough that Dr. Perez is willing to consider several different treatment options. Any decisions must ultimately be made by Mrs. Hughes, but he thought that the children should be informed to help her think things through." They were all attentive now; even Sally had raised her head, her puffy eyes fixing on Blackwell's name tag for the first time. "You've all seen your father. Right now, we are doing everything we can to keep him alive. Although his brain has been severely damaged, his vital signs are fairly strong, and he may soon be able to breathe without a respirator. He might continue in this vegetative state for months or maybe even years, or he might develop complications tonight and pass tomorrow.

"In accordance with hospital procedure, I have checked your father's insurance. It's adequate for the short-term, even with his care here in the ICU running over two thousand dollars a day. Were he to live more than a couple of months, however, you would be facing severe financial hardship."

"Mrs. Hughes," she addressed Arthur's mother directly for the first time, "you may want us to sustain your husband as he is indefinitely, but at your request, we could cease treating him quite as aggressively as we have been. As I mentioned before, we cannot stop providing food and water, but over the next couple of days, your husband is likely to suffer from two conditions very common to patients with his sort of injuries. To be specific, the doctor said he would be very surprised if a post-operative pericardial infection did not set in. He also believes that pressure on the brain caused by its own swelling will increase dangerously.

"Both of these conditions are life threatening. If left untreated, his chances of survival are slim. The severity of the injury to his brain—the fact that he's in a vegetative state from which he is extremely unlikely to recover—gives you the option of refusing him further treatment for these two conditions."

Buddy started to say something, but Sally waved him off and asked how effective the treatment for the infection and swelling would be.

"It's hard to predict, but an aggressive round of antibiotics and further procedures taken to relieve cranial pressure might prolong his life." She stood up and looked around the room. "Please talk among yourselves here as long as you want. I'll come back this evening around seven or so, if that's convenient for you, Mrs. Hughes?" She got a nod in return. "Sometimes it's very helpful to talk to your pastor."

In the silence that followed her exit, Arthur knew that Blackwell's implicit suggestion offered the best course of action for the family. Their father should be allowed to die. He repressed a sudden impulse to tell them about Gottlieb. He knew something about death now, something about facilitating the end of a desperate life. While he tried to shake these thoughts out of his head, Terri spoke.

"Mom, did Dad ever talk about any of this kind of stuff? You know, like what he would want?"

"I don't remember him saying anything specific," she said quietly. "From things he said watching the news, I guess he disapproved of extreme measures when there was no hope, but I don't know if he'd want to be unplugged."

"We are not really talking about pulling a plug here, Mom," she replied gently.

"But you are talking about deliberately not treating him so that he'll die." Buddy stared at his family. "You're talking about it, and it makes me sick. That's our dad out there, and I don't care how mangled up he is, we should be thinking about doing everything we can to save him. This is the worst thing that's ever happened to him, and he needs all the help he can get."

Terri answered quietly and evenly in response to the rising inflection in Buddy's voice. "Do you really think that Dad would want to live for months or years like a vegetable?"

Buddy paused for a moment, sucking in a deep breath. "Of course he wouldn't, but he wouldn't want to be dead either." He clenched his teeth and hissed, "I'm not going to kill my own father. That's just murder plain and simple."

Sally looked stricken.

"Do you think you could spend a little more time thinking before opening your mouth?" Terri reached over to clasp her mother's hand. "Whatever Mom decides, we need to support her . . . even if we disagree with her decision. We don't need to make things harder on her than they already are."

Arthur nodded his agreement and revealed what he knew about his father's wishes. When he had been in college, Hal's aunt had been diagnosed with Alzheimer's disease. Although he wasn't close to her, he talked to Arthur at length about how much he feared losing his mind.

"When Great-Aunt Janice got sick, he told me that if he ever got to the point where his body still worked, but his brain didn't, someone should put him in the Chevy, point it at the Grand Canyon, and push down the accelerator." He smiled grimly. "The thought of losing his life didn't bother him as much as being a burden. He worried about us losing the farm. He worried about Mom being trapped. He even worried about the waste of public resources. You all remember how economical he was—"

"Could you manage not to use the past tense?" Terri interrupted before Buddy could.

"I'm not telling you what to do, Mom, I'm really not." He sighed. "But I don't think it's wrong to ask what Dad would have wanted."

"You can't have any idea what Dad would have wanted." Buddy stood up and shouted. "I've worked with him every day for the last four years. I know him way better than you. I think he would want us to hope and pray and do everything we can for him."

He cut off Arthur's attempt to agree with him. "You want to be totally cold-blooded and ruthless? Have you forgotten what Dad's like? When old Bear got sick, he couldn't even bring him to the vet's office to have him put to sleep. Mom had to do it all by herself, so you can't tell me he'd be on your side." He stormed out, and Arthur shrugged at Terri. Sally looked calmer than she had before. Smoothing out sibling arguments was a familiar responsibility.

"You need to give Buddy some time, Arthur. He's so close to your dad. All he ever wanted to do was run the farm with him." She brushed her hair out of her face and blew her nose. "I know that you love your father, Arthur, but you never relied on him like Buddy does. You became independent at a very young age, so you look at this a little more objectively than he can. Let me go out and talk to him."

"Mom, what are you going to do about Dad?"

"I don't know." She kissed him gently on the forehead and left.

When Terri and Arthur emerged from the room, the nurse told them that Mrs. Hughes and her son were in with Mr. Hughes. Only two persons were allowed to visit at a time, and the nurse was adamant about admitting visitors beyond the prescribed limit. Arthur suddenly felt claustrophobic in the waiting room and asked Terri if she wanted to grab a quick bite. Although she claimed the hospital cafeteria was adequate, he insisted they get out of the medical complex. They saw a sign for a Denny's two blocks away and trudged to it through the dirty snow.

"You're right about Dad." She waited until they were seated and had their drinks before speaking. "What you said in there, I mean. When I took the medical ethics course in dental school, he and I talked about some of the problems in the class assignments. I'm sure that he'd pull the plug on himself if he could."

"Why didn't you say anything?"

"Mom probably knows deep down what he would want, but I don't want to push her." She looked up at her brother. "Arthur, what if Mom's not sure and something I say changes her mind . . . ? I don't want to be responsible. I'm just a coward." She poked at her salad. "I know what he wants us to do. I just can't bring myself to be responsible for someone else's death."

"It's easier than you think." Arthur avoided his sister's questioning gaze and signaled the waitress for more coffee. "What do you think Mom will do?"

She paused. "I'm not sure, but it'd be pretty tough to deny treatment to your husband with your youngest son calling you a murderer, wouldn't it?" Arthur nodded and changed the subject.

"Are you still dating Tom Erickson?" Tom was a farmer with whom he had gone to school and whom Arthur considered to be one of the most boring people he had ever met.

"You mean Mr. Excitement, as Buddy calls him?" Terri smiled for the first time since she left the hospital. No one in the family could keep a sour face for too long. A persistent optimism and sense of the absurd would be Hal Hughes's two longest lasting legacies. "Things with Tom haven't changed much. We go to the movies once a week, and he asks me to marry him once a month. Are you seeing anyone?"

"Well, I'm sort of dating my landlady and her daughter." He replied in as off-hand a fashion as he could manage.

"You're what?"

He tried to explain how much fun he had with Suzanne and Maria. He tried to describe the charm of the old house they lived in, the seductive beauty of Clarkeston, the enigmatic and paradoxical personality of the Judge, and the intimate atmosphere Ms. Stillwater nurtured in the chambers. "You need to visit. Ms. Stillwater will fix you up with the hunky scion of a wealthy southern family in no time. You need a break from Tom and cornfields and all those patients with bad breath."

"I'd love to visit when things have calmed down here." She looked at him and shook her head. "You know, it's only been twenty-four hours since the accident."

"I know, Sissy." He picked up the tab while she was in the ladies' room, and they walked back to the hospital, shoulders hunched against the bitter wind and the situation ahead of them. As they entered the hospital, Arthur put his arm around his sister, something he never would have done before he met Suzanne. She leaned her head on his shoulder.

When they got to the room, Terri was more comfortable with Hal than Arthur was. She walked straight to his bed and smoothed back a wisp of hair that the air vent had blown over his forehead. Arthur looked at him and realized that in every way that mattered, he was already gone. He went to the other side of the bed and rested the tips of his fingers gently on the arm that had the fewest tubes protruding from it. The body was warm, but Arthur looked at his face and still could not see his father in it. Swollen, misshapen, discolored, distorted, obscured by bandages and the respirator tube, the face belonged to no one he knew. He closed his eyes and tried to imagine his father like he had been before, but the door burst open behind him and a nurse entered with a full bag of IV solution. She replaced the bag draining into his left arm.

"How come you're changing a bag that's still full?"

"The antibiotics in the new solution are much stronger." She hooked up the new bag and set the drip. "Your father has a fever that's rising quite rapidly. He needs a massive dose right now."

"Did Dr. Perez order the change?"

"Of course, only the supervising doctor can prescribe any kind of treatment. If you want to talk to him, I saw him with Mrs. Hughes and her son in the waiting room." He thanked her as she left. Terri said nothing, hands supporting her chin, forehead pressed against the side of the bed. Sally Hughes had apparently come to the only decision she could live with under the circumstances; Arthur did not think that his father would be mad at her. He would not have wanted to see guilt heaped on pain.

Terri got up slowly. "I'm going to see how Mom's doing."

Arthur sat next to his father and considered his mother's summary of their relationship. How had he become so independent over time while Buddy had just grown closer? He loved his father, and he could not think of a single man that he respected more. He shared his father's sense of humor, his politics, and his general view of the world. Yet, he knew that if his mother had been injured, he would be bawling like a baby, while his father's predicament left him introspective and depressed, but not devastated. It made no sense. This was a man worthy of grief. On the other hand, his father always admired a stoic.

Unable to focus his scattered thoughts, Arthur stared at the technology that monitored and maintained his father's vital functions. The heart monitor recorded his cardiac rhythm and provided notice of an emergency via a cable that ran from the device to the wall and then presumably to the ICU nurse's station. No such line ran from the respirator; a respiratory emergency would go unnoticed by the ICU nurses until it adversely affected the heartbeat.

Terri entered the room. "Mom told Dr. Perez she wanted him to go ahead and treat everything, like the fever and swelling . . . just like we thought." She paused for a moment. "She was willing, though, to sign a nonresuscitation order. If Dad has a heart attack or something, they won't try to revive him. Buddy wasn't real happy about the decision, but Mom stayed very calm. She had it all thought out." Her voice cracked, but she managed a crooked smile. "She reminded him that Dad always let nature take its course with the animals. *You never saw him giving mouth-to-mouth to a dying horse did you?*"

"Buddy didn't push it too hard after that. Maybe he sees a difference between denying drugs and reviving a technically dead body." She shuddered next to the technically not-dead body by her side.

"Well, I don't see the difference," Arthur replied, "but I'm glad he does . . . Mom doesn't need any more grief from him."

★ ★ ★

Buddy sat alone, flipping through a four-month old *People*, lingering for a moment on the pages that displayed a little celebrity cleavage or a well-turned leg. Arthur asked him about what needed to be done on the farm in early December and who was feeding the few livestock that he and his father kept. The biggest winter jobs involved working on the heavy machinery and attending to a backlog of repairs needed on the barn and house. These chores would have to wait until his father's condition had stabilized.

"Will you have any problems accessing the bank accounts and credit lines and all that stuff?"

"He put my name on everything last year, so Mom and I can handle stuff without his signature." Buddy stopped flipping for a moment and looked up. "You know, he put my name on the deed to the farm . . . that still doesn't seem right to me. You and Terri grew up there too." He pretended to study the comparative tar and nicotine statistics on the back cover of the magazine.

"Buddy, you know that was my idea. Dad paid a bunch of money to send me to law school and that'll give me a steady income without having to work half as hard as you. I wouldn't want to trade places with you. I'm too lazy. And Mom's estate plan takes care of Terri, so you don't need to worry about a thing except planting corn and soybeans." He studied his exhausted brother.

"Buddy, why don't I spend the night here while you go home and rest?"

"I'm not ready to leave yet, not with his temperature going up. I don't think Mom is either. Why don't you go back home and clean up and dump your bags. You must be pretty tired from your flight. The dog needs to be walked and fed too."

He nodded at his brother. Despite not being very close, they understood each other. Arthur would much rather spend time with Terri, but he admired Buddy's work ethic and had no desire be anything but a good big brother to him. Somehow that wasn't enough to make them good friends.

Terri drove him home and dealt with the dog while he showered. She yelled through the bathroom door that she would come by and take him out to breakfast and then on to the hospital the following morning. Too tired to watch television, he crawled beneath the crisp, clean sheets of his old twin bed and listened to the sounds of the cold winter night. Metal siding popping randomly as it contracted in the plummeting temperature, ice fragments tinkling down onto the roof and blowing across the hard crust of snow outside the window, a low whistle from the weather vane, nails of canine toes tapping across the floor of the kitchen, the hum and rumble of the gas furnace: all the familiar sounds of his childhood.

Although he was exhausted, sleep would not come, held at bay by a vision of his father, kept alive against his will, draining his mother's resources and spreading their agony over months and years. In the hospital, he had fantasized briefly about turning off his dad's respirator. With his mother's decision made, Arthur was the only one who could prevent the nightmare from becoming a reality. All it would take was an act of will and the ability to rationalize the intentional taking of life. He had done that before, he told himself. He had written the words, "Stay of Execution Denied" on the Gottlieb order. Gottlieb was now dead and, quite unlike his father, switched off very much against his will. The ultimate decision had not been Arthur's, but he had participated. He had been part of the process. And a decision about his father would not be his alone either. If he did anything, he told himself, it would only be because his father wanted it done. Any drastic action would only be the fulfillment of his will. Arthur imagined explaining everything to his dad but fell asleep before any response came.

Terri and Arthur spent the next day popping in and out of the hospital and running errands. Neither of them could grind out a whole day amid the antiseptic hopelessness of the Neurological Intensive Care Unit. Leaving the hospital was like coming up for air after a prolonged swim in foul water. They spent about half of the day there, observing no change in their father apart from a slight decrease in his fever. Buddy and Sally looked even more zombie-like than the day before. Arthur brought them fast-food burgers and watched them doze between bites. By late evening, they were barely able to stand and were willing to let him sit with his father that night. Arthur promised to call them if anything changed, and they left together for the farmhouse.

He bought an extra large coffee at the cafeteria and a paperback novel in the hospital gift shop. Ready for his vigil, he went up to the room and told Terri that he was ready to relieve her. He sat down on a cold naugahyde armchair in the corner and tried to concentrate on the first few pages of a thriller featuring neo-Nazis plotting to take over the world. Terri spent a long time holding her father's hand, eyes closed and whispering intently. She then kissed him on the forehead, hugged Arthur urgently, and slipped away with tears in her eyes.

The hours of waiting passed quickly. A single night does not allow nearly enough time to weigh adequately all of the arguments for and against killing one's father. He cataloged in lawyerly fashion all the reasons why he should interfere: He was certain that his father would not have wanted to remain trapped in a vegetative state. He knew that his family would be better off emotionally and financially, and that the community's burden would be lightened. Helping him die would also be living the Golden Rule. If their positions were reversed, he would have wanted his father to treat him exactly the same way. On the other hand, what he was planning was not only illegal but immoral in the minds of many good people. People that he loved and respected like his mother or sister would not do it. Acts that must be done in secret are by their very nature suspect. Gradually, the more rationally he looked at the situation, the firmer his resolve became. He would do it. As with Gottlieb, he never considered the effect his decision might have on himself.

Between midnight and three, a young nurse entered the room roughly every thirty minutes on the hour. During the first hourly visit, she read his blood pressure and temperature, noting the data on his chart with a clacking of her pen. The second visit each hour seemed to be nothing more than a quick peek to check his general appearance.

After her 3:32 a.m. visit, Arthur turned the alarm volume knob to "off" on the heart monitor and then stood and walked to the respirator. He hesitated for a moment and then switched it off. At first, nothing happened. His father's breathing slowed, but did not stop. His heart continued to beat, so no alarm sounded down the hallway in the nurse's station.

What if his father continued to breathe without the help of the machine? The tube in his throat was vented so that in the event of mechanical failure, a patient capable of breathing on his own would not be suffocated. He was not sure if he could cover the opening with his thumb. He touched the top of his father's hand as the breathing grew so shallow that he could barely discern the movement of the chest under the sheet. Minutes later, the graph line measuring the cardiac rhythm went flat and the slowing beeps were replaced by a quiet monotone buzz. Almost immediately a faint whine sounded from the nurse's station at the end of the hall.

He quickly flicked the respirator back on, not knowing whether the whoosh of air into his father's lungs would restart Hal's heart. He took two quick strides back to the chair in the corner of the room. When the nurse arrived moments later, his head was leaning against the wall. Slack-jawed, book in lap, he looked like he had been sleeping for some time.

He watched the nurse through slitted eyelids as she examined the cardiac monitor and then looked over the body. She watched Hal carefully for a minute and then switched off the respirator and heart monitor. Finally, she turned to Arthur and shook his shoulder gently. He looked up at her groggily, blinking his eyes a couple of times to get them into focus.

"I'm sorry, but your father's passed away."

He stood up slowly, approached the body, and touched it.

"Could you call my mother?"

The nurse made a note on the clipboard and left. He dragged the chair over to the side of the bed and sat down as close as he could. The body was still warm. A feeling of utter exhaustion suddenly swept over him. He sat down, rested his head against his father's arm, shut his eyes, and chased the elusive shadows flickering through his mind.

A doctor he did not recognize touched his back and asked him to leave while he performed a post-mortem examination of the body. Arthur walked past the nurse's station and found his mom and Buddy waiting for him. Their faces were lined with sorrow and fatigue, but the fierce edge of their anxiety was gone.

"How was it at the end?"

"I'm sorry." He confessed that he had fallen asleep. "It must have been peaceful—he looked just the same as when you left."

Don't worry about it," his mother said gently. "I'm sure it was a comfort for him to have you in the room when it happened."

★ ★ ★

Arthur did not remember much about the funeral service. Awareness slowly returned afterward amid the buzz of conversations racketing off the cinder block walls and tile floor of the church basement. Impatient lines of overweight, thick-ankled farmers and awkward kids stabbed at a buffet of fried chicken, polish sausages, cheese and ham casseroles, three-bean salad, German potato salad, port-wine nut-coated cheese balls, fresh fruit Jell-O molds, apple pies, cherry pies, and crescent rolls, continually replenished by a vigilant band of blue-haired church matrons. He talked to a number of the people, but on his silent trip back to Clarkeston, he could only recall two conversations. Commenting favorably on his hymn-singing, his mother told him that she wished she still had his voice in her choir. Without thinking, he replied that he was joining the Clarkeston College chorus. This brought such a smile to her face that he resolved to call Dorothy Henderson as soon as he got back. Then, before he left with his mom to go home and pack up his bag, Terri came over to hug him good-bye.

"I wish you could come over to the house tonight to eat with us." She squeezed his hand. "Are you going to be all right? I prayed as much for you during the service as I did for Dad." Was she letting him know she knew somehow and approved? "You call me if you need anything, okay?"

"All right." She gave him a weak smile and turned to drag boring Tom off to help her prepare for the next round of analgesic gorging.

When Sally and Arthur got back home, he went immediately upstairs to pack, leaving her in the living room flipping absentmindedly through the newspapers she had not read over the last several days. After packing, showering, and leaving a message on Phil's machine confirming his arrival time in Atlanta, he went downstairs to make coffee before his mother took him to the airport. He found her dozing on the living room sofa, facing the back cushion and murmuring uneasily in her sleep. He made the coffee quietly, but when he returned, he rattled the cups lightly on the serving tray to keep from startling her. As he set the mugs down on the table in front of the sofa, she rolled over and clutched a small throw pillow tightly against her chest. She whispered, "Arthur, it hurts so bad."

He lay down on the edge of the sofa and wrapped his arms around her, but no matter how he tried, he could not think of anything to say.

SIDE TWO

(December 1988– May 1989)

XVIII.

LEAVES ARE BROWN, NOW

December passed Arthur in a blur. His father's death had put him behind in his writing, and by the time he lifted his nose out of the books and filed his last memo, the court had adjourned for Christmas break and it was time to go back to Iowa. The holiday was cheerless. His brother and mother coped with his father's death by tackling an unending series of chores from morning until night, while Terri escaped to Mexico with some college friends. His own buddies eluded him. Sure, they were around, ready to have a beer or shoot some pool, but a gulf now separated him from the past. His old friends had never met Gottlieb; they had never pulled the plug on their fathers. Conversations went awkwardly and eventually he just stayed home, quietly helping his brother clean, adjust, and repair mechanical things.

He returned to Clarkeston with the odd sense of relief an infantryman feels when his furlough is over and he can finally rejoin his comrades-in-arms. The post-holiday atmosphere in the Judge's chambers was appropriately subdued, but Suzanne gave him a fierce hug when he arrived at the house. As they disengaged, she cocked her head and gave him a strange look, but before he could decipher it, Maria charged in to show him a toy she had gotten for Christmas and an avalanche of chatter soon overwhelmed him.

January did promise to provide some clarity to his future as he waited to hear from the Office of Legal Counsel and the

Department of Justice. Their timetables were somewhat vague, but each had promised to tell him whether he had made its list of finalists by February. The air of expectancy was palpable.

"I'm sorry, Justice Brennan," Phil spoke brightly into a phone, "but I doubt that Mr. Hughes would be interested in working for you. You see, he's waiting to hear from the Office of Legal Counsel. I'm also sure he'd appreciate you getting off the line as quickly as possible, since he's expecting a call from them any minute."

"You're a dumb ass." Arthur shot a pencil across the room at this friend. "You know that?"

Arthur received no important calls, phony or real, during January, but as soon as the college reopened after its holiday break, he rang Dorothy Henderson, the college choir director, to see whether she was still interested in auditioning a new tenor. She remembered her invitation and assured him that she needed men for the chorus's spring performance of Arthur Honegger's *King David*.

The next day, he knocked on her door frame, and she looked up from her piano, an old-fashioned pince nez cemented firmly on the bridge of her prominent nose. With her hair pulled back, she might have been any age from fifty-five to sixty-five, but her demeanor was not grandmotherly, nor even motherly. He felt a strong urge to impress her, but he had not sung except in church for years, nor had he bothered to warm up before coming.

"Well, how are you enjoying Clarkeston, Mr. Hughes? It must be interesting working for the Judge."

"It sure is." No matter how many times he heard the question, he never came up with a better answer.

"Why don't you tell me where you're from and what sort of singing experience you have." They talked for a while, and he began to feel a bit more comfortable. She seemed more interested in his legal training than the fact that his mother was a choir director too. She ran him through some vocal exercises and asked him to sing the melody of *America the Beautiful* and then the tenor line of the same song, which he had not sung before.

Finally, to expose his limited ability to sight-sing, she forced him to fake his way through a couple of bars of an unidentified piece of music.

"Well," she concluded with a bluntness he would come to admire, "you have an adequate range and a very nice tone, but you tend to go flat due to inadequate breath support. You also occasionally scoop to reach high notes, which is one of my pet peeves." Before he could thank her for her time and beat a hasty retreat, she handed him some papers.

"What are these?"

"The information sheets for the chorus."

"You mean I passed?"

"We don't have a full-fledged music degree program." She broke a smile for the first time. "So, most of my choristers are not music majors. I'm used to teaching vocal technique along with the music, and I expect your bad habits will fade throughout the course of the semester. And don't worry about your lousy sight-reading; that should improve too. Even if it doesn't, that's okay. Sometimes I think those who have to memorize the music follow me better anyway." She smiled again. "They, at least, tend to keep their heads up and watch."

She stood up and gave him a firm, dry handshake, welcoming him officially to the group. He wondered whether the Judge would approve of this new distraction as left the office and delivered the forms to Henderson's secretary.

★ ★ ★

"Hello? Angie? How's life at the highest-paying firm in New York City?" Melanie's New Year's resolution was to bring the Carolyn Bastaigne affair to a conclusion, and that meant tracking down the autopsy report on the unfortunate clerk, as well as any other information about her. So, on her first day back in Clarkeston, she called Angela Donaldson, a former classmate and study partner who worked at Cravath, Swain, and Moore in New York City. "Are you getting any sleep at all?"

"No, but I'm saving money on an apartment. I just crash in my office."

Melanie laughed, but then remembered some of the horror stories she had heard about life in large New York firms. "You're kidding, right?"

"Of course! I work a million hours, but they don't chain me to the desk. Time just flies—I'll be looking at my watch thinking it's like seven, and it turns out to be midnight."

"Angie, you're not doing a very good recruiting job."

"Well, you said you'd never work up north anyway." The young attorney clicked off her speakerphone. "How are things going down in the land of the KKK?"

"Not too bad. No cross burnings today. I do have a favor to ask you, though." Melanie debated whether to claim that the Judge was conducting a personal investigation into the death of Carolyn Bastaigne, but opted for being ambiguous. "This is going to sound really bizarre, but we're making an informal inquiry into the death of one my judge's law clerks five years ago. She was going to work for Cravath right before she died, and we were hoping to get a hold of her recruitment file."

"Five years ago? What happened?"

"She had an accident in the courthouse."

"Ugh." The young lawyer paused. "Why does it matter now?"

"Well, the mother of the dead clerk is a real crackpot. She thinks her daughter was murdered, and she's been calling and bugging the Judge, so we're trying to find out everything we can."

"How did she die?"

"She was found at the bottom of a stairwell. No signs of foul play, but the mom thinks otherwise. I was hoping that you could talk to the recruitment coordinator and see if we could get a copy of her file." She felt a brief pang of guilt at sucking a friend in to her unauthorized investigation. "Since she's dead, there shouldn't be any confidentiality concerns."

"But why do you need it? I'll need to give a reason." This was a question for which Melanie did not have a good answer, so she substituted bright confidence for substance.

"Well, most of all, we want to do something to impress the mother. She thinks there's been a big cover-up, and we want to build a file for her. Maybe she'll get off our back if she sees us doing something. And maybe there'll be some sort of clues about her in there. Her death actually was a little suspicious."

"Well, I'll ask the recruiting coordinator what hoops you have to jump through. I know her pretty well. She spent a lot of time convincing me to come here instead of Sullivan and Cromwell."

"Cool. Just let me know what she says."

★ ★ ★

When the Judge walked into chambers, he heard three animated voices coming from the library. They're not getting much work done, he thought. On the other hand, it was the first day back after Christmas, and this year's group of clerks was pretty productive. Nice kids too. He stood outside the library door and overhead them competing to see who had the most ridiculous eccentric relative holiday story. He wondered what they thought of him, and for a moment regretted the distance he deliberately kept from them. The Judge straightened himself, walked through the door, and sat down at the conference table. By long habit he first addressed the lone female in the room.

"Good morning, Ms. Melanie, how are you?"

"Just fine, Judge." He nodded to Phillip and Arthur and then turned back to her. "Good job on the eyeball case. I think you're right. What happened there went way beyond malpractice."

"I think so too." She flushed with pride, and he caught Arthur casting a glance her way. Did he divine something not quite chaste in the way Arthur looked at her? They would make a well-matched couple, but the last thing he needed was romantic drama in chambers.

"Judge," Arthur asked, "do you know Dorothy Henderson, the choir director at Clarkeston College?"

"Sure, her father used to be an attorney in town long ago. But she went off and studied music, worked with Robert Shaw in Atlanta, and then came back here." He smiled at the memory of Dorothy integrating her choir before any local schools had complied with *Brown v. Board of Education*. She had scandalized the Clarkeston establishment more than once. "She's gotten in almost as much trouble as me over the years."

"Do you think that I could sing with her this spring? Rehearsals start at four thirty on Tuesdays and Thursdays . . . That's why I ask."

He thought for a moment. "As long as you're caught up in your work, I don't see why not. And as long as your colleagues don't have any objections." He looked at Phillip and Melanie who shook their heads.

"That's awesome, Arthur!" Melanie was beaming. "Professor Henderson used to come to my high school every year to do a choral workshop. Singing with her is like a religious experience."

"Why don't you audition too?" Arthur said. "She might need another soprano. Ms. Stillwater told us you're a great singer."

The young woman blushed and shook her head. "No . . . I've got too much to do here." Then, she changed the subject. "Could I ask you a question, Judge? How do you deal with people who are ignorant about the South? I just talked to a friend in New York who always refers to Georgia as 'the land of the KKK.'"

He thought for a moment. "Tell her that you just read about serious sectarian violence in her part of the country. Did you all see the story in the paper about the Unitarian Klansman in Boston?"

"No."

"They caught him," he drawled, "burning a question mark in someone's lawn."

He managed to keep a straight face while his clerks sputtered and moaned. "Enjoying a joke at the Unitarians' expense, are we? That's not very open-minded. Did I ever tell you about the Catholic priest, the rabbi, and the Unitarian minister?"

"No," they answered in unison.

"Well, the wealthiest man in town bought himself a BMW 420i, and he wanted it blessed, so he sought out the leading clerics in the town. 'I want you to say a blessing for my 420i,' he asked the priest. 'What's a 420i?' the priest replied. 'It's a car,' said the rich man in disgust. 'I'll go ask the rabbi instead.' So, the rich man asks the rabbi, 'I want you to say a blessing for my 420i.' 'What's a 420i?' the rabbi asks. Disappointed once again, the rich man goes to the Unitarian minister. 'I want you to say a blessing for my 420i. And please tell me that you know what a 420i is!' 'Sure,' replied the Unitarian, 'it's a car . . . but what's a blessing?'"

"That's terrible," Arthur groaned. The other two could not get anything out at all. While they recovered, the Judge stood up, gave them a slight nod, and left for his office.

★ ★ ★

"What the hell was that about?" Melanie spoke first, still delighted that the Judge had singled her out on the "eyeball case" before he had launched into his comedy routine.

"What a total drive-by!" Phil turned his palms up and shook his head. "Who knew?"

"That was awesome." Arthur nodded. "I wonder why he's not always like that. At the beach, Jack Ramsey told me that the Judge used to take his clerks with him on a fishing trip every year. Can you imagine sitting out on a lake with just the Judge and a case of beer?"

"Not really," Melanie replied, "where the hell would I pee on a boat?"

The shrill ring of the phone interrupted her as she speculated whether the fishing trips had stopped when the Judge started hiring women clerks. The guys looked at her, and she waited four rings to give Ms. Stillwater a chance to pick up before she finally answered.

"Hello? Oh, hey, Angie ..." Melanie spoke quietly into the phone while her co-clerks went back to their work. A few minutes later, she hung the phone up and stared at them.

"That was interesting."

"What?" Phil asked.

"I called a friend of mine at Cravath and asked her about Carolyn Bastaigne." She pursed her lips and confessed. "Actually, I was hoping to get ahold of her personnel file."

"Are you crazy?" Phil accused her in a hoarse whisper.

"Apparently so, because they don't let those files out of the office. According to my friend, I'd have to go up there with a court order if I wanted to look at it." She cut Phil off before he could speak. "And no, I'm not going to forge one. But she did say something very interesting. Cravath apparently revoked Carolyn's offer just before she was supposed to start work."

"How did you find that out?"

"The recruitment person there looked at the file. She wouldn't give it to Angie, but she wanted to correct the misimpression that 'someone like Carolyn' was going to work at Cravath."

"Did she say what happened?" Phil frowned.

"Nope, just that the offer had been revoked."

"Maybe they finally figured out she was lazy."

"Maybe." She pushed back from the table and laced her fingers behind her head. "But if they asked for a writing sample or something, she would have given them something good. She was capable of writing well. The merger memo proves it."

Contemplative silence.

Then, Phil tapped his fingers on the table. "Maybe the Judge torpedoed her."

"Huh?"

"If they did a reference check and he said something negative, they wouldn't hire her." Phil paused, but no one jumped into the empty space. Melanie was well aware of the Judge's influence and what a good or a bad recommendation could do for her career. "Or . . ."

"Or what?" Melanie studied Phil and suddenly understood where he was going.

"What if your stock manipulation theory is right? What if the Judge found out that Carolyn had misused her position and planned to trade on news of the beverage company merger before it was made public." He let out a low whistle. "Talk about a breach of confidentiality!"

"I can definitely see him calling up Cravath," she said. "In fact, he might even have an ethical obligation to call."

"Yeah, but why would he know about your imaginary stock scheme?" Arthur asked. "Even if the insider trading theory is right, how would the Judge know what she was planning?"

"I don't know," Melanie replied slowly, but she still thought she was on to something big. She could sense it.

"And that's why," Melanie announced with certainty, "we've got to read Carolyn's personnel folder." She cast a glance in the direction of Ms. Stillwater's filing cabinets.

"*You* need to read it," Arthur said. "I don't need to read anything. I don't see what good can come of it. And if you look at her file, you'll be breaking the Judge's confidentiality rules too." Phil looked at Melanie seriously and nodded his agreement.

Their advice was sound, but not irresistible. The impulse to impress the Judge was simply too strong. Her co-clerks had not grown up in the State that he had dominated for decades. They couldn't understand what it really meant for a Georgian to leave her mark in these chambers. It was not enough to write excellent bench memos. She wanted to solve the mystery of Carolyn Bastaigne's death, and for the time being, the ends clearly justified the means.

XIX.

SPIRIT IN THE SKY

Late in the afternoon, Arthur left the courthouse and walked through the Clarkston College campus to his first rehearsal. Although it was barely four o'clock, the winter sun was already spent and provided nothing more than a cool orange shadow to illuminate his walk.

He followed a small group of students under the arched portico of the Music Building into the chorus room, and took a seat in the middle row of risers, just to the right of a piece of paper labeled "T."

Professor Henderson entered at exactly four thirty.

"Let me welcome you to the first rehearsal of the spring semester. Most of you have sung with the chorus before, but let me welcome those who have not." She scrutinized a group of about twenty sopranos, twenty-five altos, fifteen basses, and seven tenors. "As you can see, although we've borrowed a tenor from the federal courthouse, we could still use about five more."

Arthur saw a couple of curious altos sneak a peek at him.

"And if you know any other gentlemen who might like to join us, I would appreciate your sending them to me." She clapped her hands. "Now, let's get started. To the right, massage!"

He stood up and joined the line of choristers each rubbing the back and neck of the person next to them. His hands ran self-consciously over the soft sweater of a red-headed soprano. The students around him talked animatedly.

"My, haven't we been working out over vacation."

"Ooooh, angora, this is softer than my cat."

Everyone but Arthur seemed comfortable running their hands over their neighbors.

"Pound!"

He felt his back being rhythmically karate-chopped, neck muscles first, then over each side of his spine from shoulders to kidneys. He transferred to the soprano's back whatever was being done to him.

"To the left, massage!"

As he worked on the shoulders of the tenor on the other side, the girl behind him chided him on how tense his neck muscles were.

"Pound!" After a brief flurry of punches, the director commanded them to raise them over their heads, stretching and moving their arms down in the same motion used to complete a snow angel.

"Face forward and massage your own neck." Henderson rubbed her neck and groaned.

Arthur reached back and found the soprano was right about his muscle tension.

"Now, roll your head forward from your right shoulder to your left and back again."

The girl next to him laughed as Arthur's neck crackled and popped.

"Shake out your hands." She demonstrated by placing her hands in front her, palms facing her body, and shaking her fingers like a cat trying to flick water off its paws.

"Now, open your mouth, touch your tongue to your front teeth and pant silently like a dog. This is important. I want you to be aware of the lower abdominal muscles that provide your breath support." She spread her hands flat on her stomach, pinkies extending below her belt-line. "Put your hands on your belly and pant again. Feel that? That's where your body should work when you sing. Not your throat. Your throat should always be relaxed and open."

Then, she opened her mouth wide and vocalized a lazy yawn which started at the extreme high end of her voice and gradually descended to the lower end of her range. When she opened her mouth again and made eye contact with the choir, they took her cue, emitting a cacophony of orgiastic wails. When they quieted down, she waved her hand gracefully in the direction of a plump girl with a beautiful complexion sitting at the piano in the corner of the room. "Let me introduce our accompanist for this semester, Debbie Richardson." Raucous applause and hoots confirmed that she was a favorite of the group.

"Now, let's warm up our voices." She started them humming octaves, sliding as smoothly as they could down a scale starting at B flat. For the next twenty-five minutes, she ran them through a variety of increasingly demanding vocal exercises working their abdomens and intensifying the resonance of their voices.

"Good people." She waved them quiet after a couple of repetitions of the exercise and scanned the room for offenders. "I'm detecting a lot of shadow-singing. Do not wait to hear the person next to you initiate the pitch. Hear it in your head beforehand and enter on the beat. Be virtuous and step into the note! Faith comes before confidence."

Arthur wondered how long it would take him to develop the faith Professor Henderson prescribed.

It turned out that anyone could potentially be guilty of shadow-singing, but only the altos and sopranos could be guilty of "chirping like little girls." Exhorting the women to sing with a "cathedral space" in their mouths, she imitated Pee-Wee Herman and then contrasted his squeaking with an operatic version of the same scale. "Now, which sounds better?"

Although the professor projected well and was always dead on pitch, she did not have a beautiful voice, but this worked to her advantage in coaxing the proper sound out of the women in the group. No alto or soprano could ever claim that God did not give her the tools to sing as well as her director. If a chorister failed, it was because she lacked a spiritual commitment to Dorothy Henderson's world of open mouth, relaxed throat, active belly, and attentive mind.

In general, the women were more frequently the object of her attention than the men, but basses who sang in the back of their throats were treated to a growling imitation of their transgression. Tenors got off the lightest. She didn't want to scare any of them off. They seldom heard anything harsher than, "Sing out and enunciate! You've got the notes, but nobody is going to hear you mumble." She paid attention to everyone in the chorus. On one alarming occasion, she met Arthur's eye when he went flat and made a finger-turning motion that looked like she was trying to start a car, sending the message to tune up the pitch.

Forty minutes into the rehearsal, she set the basses humming on the tonic in the key of B flat major, tenors on the fifth, altos on the third, and sopranos an octave above the basses. Once they were in tune, she asked them to articulate "me, may, meh, mo, moo" at increasing levels of intensity until her face became transfigured like the Virgin Mary holding the slumping body of her crucified son. For one rapturous instant her body and soul were fused in an epiphany of sound, electrified, ecstatic, transcendent, filled with grace, fixed eternally in the moment. She lowered her arms, stilling all sound and movement in the room. When, she opened her eyes, Arthur felt that she was looking at him.

"That's what we're working for—those times when we are one, precisely in the center of the pitch. Consistently finding that sound will be worth all the effort you expend this semester."

She pulled out a battered score. "All right, let's learn some music. Take the Honegger *King David* out from underneath your chairs and let's look at the first chorus, marked number three."

Arthur looked up at the clock—they had been warming up for forty-five minutes. They spent the next hour going over the first chorus, a song written in unison, and the second chorus, a piece constructed in such tightly dissonant harmony that Arthur strained to hear another tenor singing the first half of each note so he could join in on the second half. Shadow-singing be damned; he was struggling for survival. To his relief, one tenor voice stood out, a bellwether for the accuracy of his guesses as to just where the line was going.

Finding the precise pitch was just one piece of the puzzle. In addition to demanding perfect intonation, she was insistent in her indication of the proper dynamic level, pronunciation, and places to breathe. "Always come to practice with a pencil," she sighed as she tossed extras to the miscreants among them. By the time they finished, his score was as heavily notated as his old law school textbooks. At five minutes after six, she dismissed them into the darkness of a moonless winter night.

As he walked home, still alive with the music, a middle-aged baritone, one of a handful of obvious non-students in the chorus, fell in step alongside him and introduced himself as the Herman Kennedy, Chair of the History Department. He was interested in legal history and asked Arthur who he worked for in the courthouse.

He was almost the archetype of a college professor. Brown plaid patches covered the elbows of a well-worn corduroy jacket, and ancient Hush Puppies fit his feet like moccasins. He was not smoking a pipe, but he did sport a beard and a battered pair of wire-rim glasses that reflected back the light from the lamps along the campus sidewalk.

"I did my dissertation on the role of federal judges in the civil rights movement," he explained, "and hedged my bets against not finding an academic job by starting law school." In spite of his garb, he seemed utterly without pretense, face beaming with good intention. "When the dissertation won a minor award, I left Penn law school for a job at Miami University in Ohio before taking the job here about ten years ago."

"I used to be a history person too," Arthur explained. "I even got a masters while waiting for my ex-wife to finish up her bachelor's degree." The two unhurried years in graduate school seemed like ancient history now. They talked until Kennedy stopped to turn down a quiet residential street.

"My co-clerk Phil and I sometimes hang out at the Wild Boar after work." They shook hands. "If you really miss talking about law, I could give you a call the next time we go."

"Please do!" He looked conspiratorially at Arthur. "That's a perfect place to go to avoid my colleagues."

Arthur walked home, humming as he crossed the river, bouncing snatches of the Honegger off the hard walls of the downtown buildings.

He entered the foyer of Suzanne's house, singing forcefully the line from the second chorus that he was most sure of, "*Saul has slain his thousands and ten thousands, David!*" His voice echoed off the acoustically live plaster, bounced off wood floors, and seemed to gather momentum off the far end of the hall, slamming him like a hurricane, blowing his hair back, and forcing him to lean slightly forward to avoid being knocked over.

"Would Pavarotti like a cup of decaf?" Suzanne's voice called from the kitchen.

"You sing really loud!" Maria exclaimed.

He laughed, wishing just loud were good enough. "Thanks, Maria."

He walked into the kitchen and handed Suzanne the music. "This is going to be really fun. Have you ever heard it?"

"No, but that doesn't really mean anything." She looked and handed it back. "My folks listened to big band and jazz stuff when I was growing up, not much classical." She handed him a cup of steaming coffee and left to begin Maria's bedtime routine.

★ ★ ★

An hour later, he heard Suzanne enter the television room where he was watching the Kentucky basketball team destroy some hapless conference foe. He felt her kiss the side of his head.

"Do you have a second?" she asked.

He watched the Kentucky center finish a fast break with a thunderous dunk and muted the television. "Sure. This is like watching Goliath beat the living crap out of David."

She sat sideways on the sofa next him and propped a leg in his lap. "You've been really preoccupied and distant, but I didn't want to say anything until you snapped out of it a little." She seemed to struggle to find the right words. "Maria and I have been trying to stay out of your way. I remember when my mom died. I just wanted to be left alone . . . I hated those sympathy cards that came every day, reminding me that she was gone."

He felt fine. He had gotten one or two cards, but that was weeks ago. Where was this coming from?

She leaned forward and touched his hand. "Are we doing the right thing with you? Or do you want to talk?"

He was at a loss for a response. He couldn't remember moping around the house or being anything except his usual self.

"Until you came into the house singing tonight, I've barely recognized you. You've been working so late and spending so much time in your room."

He shrugged and deflected her concern. "We've been really busy in chambers." He glanced at the score of the game and gave her a puzzled look. What was she seeing? "I'm sorry if I've put you all on suicide watch."

"I never said that! But I can tell that something's been eating at you." He felt her study him for a long moment. "You've been wandering around here like a ghost, never making eye contact, all wrapped up inside yourself."

He looked up, but the intensity of her expression drove his gaze back to the silent television. Was it possible that she knew him better than he knew himself? Where was she coming from with this? He'd been doing his share of the dishes and housework. Hell, he had even vacuumed the whole upstairs without being asked.

"You know," he murmured, a strategy of misdirection taking shape, "now that you mention it, I could use some serious therapy for my mental condition. Why don't we go upstairs and talk about it?"

She laughed as he pressed a series of swift and sensuous kisses on her lips and neck.

"All right," she conceded with a whisper.

He kissed her again, then took her hand and led her up the stairs. As soon as the door to his room clicked shut, their bodies pressed together, hips and mouths grinding, hands groping under sweater and shirt, sliding past belt-lines to waist and hip. Clothing dropped, then flew desperately to all corners of the room. Suzanne's bra landed askew on the ancient teddy bear perched on his desk, an odd merger of Toys"R"Us and Victoria's Secret. They burrowed under the warm covers, bypassing foreplay. Her need seemed as strong as his, relentless as never before, bulldozing over his plea to slow down after he had come with unexpected speed deep within her. As her own climax approached, he sublimated the sensitive agony of her movement and managed to cooperate just enough to help her over the edge.

"Wow," he gasped as he caught his breath, "where did that come from?"

"I don't know," she said, "maybe it's a full moon or something."

"Or something!"

After a prolonged snuggle, Suzanne slipped downstairs, but Arthur was unable to sleep. It was sweet that she was so concerned about him, even if it came from a hyperactive imagination. He put a CD in his portable player and listened to Robert Shaw's recording of the Fauré *Requiem*. The light in his room was off, and tiny dry snowflakes began to swirl down against the backdrop of the streetlamps. He cracked the window slightly and let the cold air connect him to the outside world. He leaned back with his bare feet on the sill, listening to Fauré's plea for repose eternal and wondering whether Suzanne was overreacting or whether he was in fact a little depressed. He had to admit that he hadn't yet fully processed his father's death.

Downstairs, Suzanne was awake, staring at Maria's sleeping form and praying hard that the slight twinge she felt just below her navel was not a sign of premature ovulation.

XX

LEAVE THE ROAD
(AND MEMORIZE)

Melanie sat in her office late on a Wednesday evening. The chambers were as still as her mind was restless. In a moment, she planned to reach inside Ms. Stillwater's desk, take the keys to the filing cabinet, and peek into Carolyn Bastaigne's personnel file. She hesitated, waiting for a rationalization that would justify her transgression. Unfortunately, the convenient purpose of protecting the Judge from her crazy mother provided little justification for prying into his own private papers. When she realized she had nothing to rely on but raw curiosity, she sighed, but nonetheless went into Ms. Stillwater's office.

She paused as she reached the desk and thought suddenly of her parents. They would be horrified. But maybe that was a reason to go ahead with the plan. She was tired of meeting their—and everyone else's—expectations of her. Valedictorian of her high school class, beauty pageant queen, *Harvard Law Review* editor and, let's not forget, the lead role in "The Littlest Fairy," her third-grade class musical that started the whole mess. She was tired of being perfect. It was time to do a little rebelling.

She opened the drawer and withdrew the keys.

The location of the personnel files was no secret. They were plainly marked in a brown metal cabinet behind Ms. Stillwater's desk, in between drawers marked "News Clippings" and "Post-its, Pens, and Envelopes." She didn't know for sure whether Ms. Stillwater's circle of keys contained the proper one for the cabinet, but it was a good bet that such an organized woman would link everything together. It took less than a minute to find a likely looking suspect and spring the lock on the top of the cabinet.

She was proud of herself for not pulling her own file or those of Phil and Arthur. She would have loved to read what her professors had said in their letters of recommendation (she got the job—they must have said something good!), but she denied herself this pleasure and pulled nothing but the Bastaigne file. Then, she shut the cabinet, locked it, and brought the manila folder into the library. She sat next to a stack of books, ready to slip the file into her briefcase and feign reading something else in the unlikely event that one of her co-clerks returned late to meet a deadline.

The story of Carolyn Bastaigne emerged slowly in the letters, school transcripts, and notes lying before her. The first mystery—how someone so lazy could have gotten the job in the first place—was solved fairly quickly. Melanie knew that Carolyn had gone to Yale Law School, but she had forgotten that Yale did not give letter grades, nor any indication of class rank or honors. As a Harvard graduate, she had heard her classmates and professors ridicule the presumption made by Yale that all of its students were so talented that any quality distinctions made between them would be spurious and misleading. She looked at the transcript and couldn't make heads or tails of the "Ps" and "HPs" next to each course Carolyn had taken.

For a Yalie, like Carolyn, letters of recommendation would be key. The first two were standard and uninformative, probably penned by professors with more important work to do and laboring under the assumption that anyone who could get into their school was *prima facie* fit for a federal appellate clerkship. The third letter was more striking. Carolyn Bastaigne knew the governor of Georgia, and he had written her a glowing letter. Her father had practiced law with the governor, and he had known her since she was a small child. Having grown up in Georgia, Melanie understood what an impact the letter must have had. Before Governor Jackson had taken office, he had made his reputation as the state's attorney general, working hard to enforce the Judge's civil rights decisions. Faced with a stack of talented applicants from the usual selection of elite schools, the letter probably tipped the balance in Carolyn's favor, although it gave no indication that the governor had ever read a single word she had written.

The penultimate page in the file was a folded piece of yellow legal paper. It contained two sets of notes, one dated a year before Carolyn started work and another dated the day before she died. "Pleasant enough . . . helped Jackson on his campaign . . . no strong feelings about death penalty . . . favorite teacher BZ!" Melanie guessed that BZ was Brent Zwicki, the author of Melanie's constitutional law textbook and the Judge's most successful clerk in academia.

The entry at the bottom of the page was written in bolder strokes. "CB late . . . denies all knowledge . . . more upset by Cravath call than by fucking me over!" More was scrawled, but Melanie could not make out the handwriting. A low whistle escaped her lips.

A letter from the Justice Department clipped to the back of the yellow sheet provided a final clue to Carolyn's fate. It was addressed to the Judge from Ross Pritchard, a former clerk writing on Antitrust Division letterhead. *It was great to see you at the reunion last month! Marilyn's doing great and sends her love. I wish that I had better news to report about Ms. Bastaigne. Your instincts, as usual, are right. I contacted a colleague at the SEC, and a check of recent market transactions showed that she purchased over five thousand shares of the stock you mentioned two weeks ago. We won't proceed without your go ahead. We're pretty busy with the S&L crisis, as you might imagine! Hope to hear from you soon . . .*

So, after learning about Carolyn's insider-trading scheme from his ex-clerk in the Justice Department, the Judge had followed up with a career-killing call to Cravath and then a fraught interview with the perpetrator herself.

The image of Carolyn fleeing the terrible news delivered in the Judge's chambers flitted through Melanie's mind. Distraught and careless, years of education wasted and her future in a shambles, she might easily have tripped and plummeted down the stairs. It made for a vivid picture.

Melanie read through Pritchard's letter to the Judge one more time and put the file back in Ms. Stillwater's cabinet. Once it was safely locked away and the keys replaced in the desk, Melanie went back to her office, slipped on her coat, and left the chambers. The exit light above the stairwell door provided the only illumination in the hallway. She could barely see the door to Judge Meyers' empty chambers down the hall. What had happened five years ago? The source of Carolyn's distress that night was obvious, but why head for the stairs without her shoes? And wouldn't a barefoot person be less likely to trip on a marble staircase than someone in heels?

A critical question suddenly occurred to her. Had Carolyn been wearing hose on night she died? If she had been, a slip would be much easier to understand.

★ ★ ★

The Judge entered the library and announced that a new round of briefs had arrived. He watched his minions sort through them as he set forth the timetable for the rest of the spring. Melanie would attend the late-February sitting of the court in Atlanta. Phil was slotted for Miami in early April, and Arthur for Tallahassee the last week in May, which would be Phil's final month before he left Clarkeston for a firm in San Francisco.

"Don't lose your focus now that the rest of the year is mapped out. The home stretch can be tricky sometimes." To emphasize his constant scrutiny of their labors, he sat down and leafed through the pile of briefs. Humming and chewing the corner of his mustache, he skimmed a case and tossed it at Phil.

"Mr. Garner, this looks right up your alley. Employment discrimination, an appeal to the NLRB, and an illegal strike all in one case." He relished the look of surprise on the clerk's face.

Did they think he didn't notice the pattern of the cases they chose to work on?

"Miss Melanie, here we go, another prison case. No blood and guts, but an interesting looking First Amendment claim."

He squinted at Arthur. "I haven't really detected a clear trend in your choices, Mr. Hughes. You did an excellent job with Gottlieb, though, so maybe I'll make you my Death Clerk."

The Judge watched Arthur laugh nervously. Judge Lindsey in Orlando was infamous in the Eleventh Circuit for designating one of her clerks every year to handle all of her death cases. Her theory was that the cases were complicated and that she was better served if one person mastered the complex web of procedural issues that repeatedly cropped up. The unlucky designee gained instant notoriety and bore the brunt of grisly jokes whenever clerks gathered for drinks after a sitting of the court.

"How come you don't have a Death Clerk, Judge?" Melanie asked.

"Oh, it would be unfair to let one clerk have all the fun." He winked at Arthur but then spoke seriously. "You all come here to get a deeper and broader education into the law. I'd be cheating you if I forced you to spend all your time on habeas cases. That's why I let you choose your own cases and why I do a lot of the death work myself. You may not know it, but I only dump habeas cases on you when I'm swamped. And then, I ask the person who's made the most progress with the rest of his work. That's kind of a perverse incentive, but it usually works out to be fairly random."

They nodded their understanding, and the Judge felt a wave of good will wash over him. It had been a decent year so far. A little too much talking in the library, but most of it was work-related. The three clerks helped each other out, and the work benefited from their diverse talents. He would not want them to closet themselves in their offices all day long.

"I don't usually pat my clerks on the back—although Stillwater says I should—but you've done a good job this year. Just don't let down your guard and start dreaming about leaving here and making money." He frowned and stood up to leave. "That said, let me share an article that I just read in the *Legal Times*. It says that the governor of Florida has finally got his pen out and will be signing a slew of execution warrants next month. His theory seems to be that victims' rights will be better served if the habeas attorneys who take these cases get completely overwhelmed. That's their problem, of course, but it will eventually become ours. Don't fall behind on your work, because you'll need plenty of time to deal with the mess he's going to create."

As it turned out, the Florida governor got involved in winter session politicking and held off until the end of January before signing the warrants piling up on his desk. During the interlude, the chambers attacked a fresh batch of federal cases: a sex discrimination class action, a bad faith bankruptcy filing, a teacher fired for being overly critical of her principal in the local paper, and the usual criminal procedure cases arising from drug arrests. The state law cases were interesting too: a negligence action for burns suffered in a trailer fire, a breach of promise not to compete, and a convoluted case involving the wrongful repossession of a farmer's combine. The clerks scurried from library to office, and back again, trying to get as far ahead on the work as possible.

The Judge was energized by the frenzy of activity. He visited the conference room more frequently, asking questions about bench memos or sharing courtroom war stories about the days before his appointment to the appellate bench. Ms. Stillwater fueled the productive mood by leaving snacks on the conference table—brownies, cookies, and homemade cheese straws. The clerks appreciated the food, but the Judge did not.

"Stillwater, you're gonna make my clerks fat and slow," he growled at her as he left the library. She always treated his clerks like elementary school children. "They're supposed to be working in there, not making a mess and attracting roaches!"

"They spend less time eating than they do listening to the stories you make up!" she snapped back at him. The Judge caught Arthur winking knowingly at Melanie across the conference room table and getting rewarded with a giggle and a small air burst of brownie crumbs. *You're bad,* she mouthed at the young man as the Judge turned and headed back to his office.

★ ★ ★

The week before the death cases arrived, Arthur arranged to meet Phil at the Wild Boar after the Thursday evening practice of the *King David*. After Ms. Henderson dismissed the group, Arthur asked Kennedy, the history professor, if he would like to join them.

"Absolutely," the professor replied as they walked through the lamp-lit fog of the south quadrangle, "we earned a beer with that rehearsal."

"How often does Henderson fly off the handle like that?" Arthur asked.

"Oh, she usually reams out the group once a semester. We old farts take it more philosophically than the students do." He laughed and kicked a pine cone out of their way. "It's kinda funny, though, they seem to like being abused—sort of like law students." He gave Arthur a mischievous grin. "President Assad of Syria used to bite the heads off snakes to fire up his troops; she likes to bite the heads off sopranos."

Practice had been going quite well until she heard a couple of sopranos scooping for the high notes. "When you sing a sizeable ascending interval between two notes, like a fifth or an octave," she explained patiently after the first offense, "you should not audibly slide through the pitches in between the lower note and the higher note."

The second time, she demonstrated sarcastically exactly what an offending scoop sounded like.

"Did you learn to sing by watching MTV?" she yelled when two sopranos made the same mistake a third time. When the altos giggled nervously, everyone was chewed out for their lack of concentration. In retrospect the scene seemed somewhat contrived, but her anger had been effective. The group perceived no evil motive—just honest passion. She cared about the music, and they refocused and sang with previously unmustered intensity for the last thirty minutes of practice.

When they got to the tavern and found Phil, Kennedy bought the first pitcher. "I want your expert advice," he explained as he poured. "The History department is considering making an offer to one of two faculty candidates. The new professor will teach our constitutional law and legal history courses. They're equal in every way, but one has a PhD from a top-ten grad school but a law degree from a mediocre one, while the other has a PhD from a mediocre program, but a JD from a great law school." He took a long draught of his beer and wiped a dollop of foam off his beard with the sleeve of his jacket. "Since I spent a year in law school and I've got a doctorate, I'm supposed to advise the hiring committee."

The professor was twenty years older than the two clerks, but his brown eyes twinkled with a boyish enthusiasm. And why not? Arthur thought. Kennedy had a job where big decisions came in discrete, nonthreatening packages, amenable to discussion over a pint of imported beer in a warm bar on chilly winter night.

After Arthur and Phil agreed that the quality of the new hire's law school degree was most important, they plied the professor with more beer and questioned him. He spoke eloquently about being forty-five and still in love with his wife, about not having won the Pulitzer Prize, and about the occasional student who returned to thank him. He talked about music and feigned annoyance at a buxom junior who seemed to unbutton yet another button every time she met for her tutorial.

While they talked, an almost mystical sense of community enveloped Arthur for the second time that day. Just hours earlier, after the sopranos had stopped scooping and everyone was finally together, they had sung virtuously, transcending pitch and rhythm, eventually finding the pure center of the sound. When the rehearsal ended, they fell completely silent for a moment. The eventual performance two months later no longer mattered because for a brief time they had occupied a place outside themselves, and it was utterly unimportant that no audience had heard. Now, a similar magic threaded its way through the smaller community constituted by Phil, Kennedy, and Arthur. They were not singing as such, but something about the sublime rhythm of their conversation suspended for a moment all of Arthur's doubts about the existence of God, the communion of saints, the resurrection of the dead, and the life everlasting, even as they talked of basketball, beer, their love lives, and the source of the Judge's mood swings.

★ ★ ★

Suzanne rocked on the porch, arms crossed against the cold as she watched and waited. Do you say something to your lover when you're only one day late with your period? Do you pile more grief onto a plate that's already full? Of course, much depended on whether Arthur was just a fun and confidence-building diversion or something much more serious. As she spotted him striding happily up the street to the house, her usually reliable intuition took a leave of absence.

"Oops, I better wipe away the telltale lipstick." He teased her, rubbing his forearm across his mouth as he climbed up the steps.

"I don't have to worry about that, do I?"

She stood up and hugged him tight. He nuzzled his face into her hair and assured her that he was incapable of cheating on her.

"Now, that's a fine promise to make with Boar's Head breath and cigarette hair." She smiled and hoped that he would not notice that her eyes were red.

"Are you okay?" he asked.

She didn't reply, but clung to him as they entered the warmth of the house, content to linger in the incomplete comfort of his arms.

XXI.

PASS THE CHAMBER POT

In the middle of February, as tiny-petaled phlox bloomed in endless shades of purple, rose, and violet among stalks of early daffodils, the law clerks of the Eleventh Circuit waded knee-deep in gore. The governors of Florida, Alabama, and Georgia had signed more than one hundred execution warrants within a week-long period, and almost every affected prisoner responded by filing a petition for habeas corpus. About one-third of the strongest cases earned stays of execution by state supreme courts willing to monitor their own lower courts rather than watch them be slapped down by the feds. Another third were first-timers, prisoners who had never filed a habeas corpus petition and were entitled under an informal rule of the Eleventh Circuit to an automatic stay of execution and a close look at the merits of their cases. That left thirty or so death row inmates on the fast track. With twelve judges comprising the circuit and three clerks per judge, virtually every clerk would have a case to call his or her own.

As soon as Arthur entered his office, he saw a thick file sitting ominously on his desk. A yellow sticky note bearing Ms. Stillwater's spidery handwriting declared the subject of the file to be "Averill Lee Jefferson." The name did not ring a bell. He turned his back on his desk and looked out the window at the dandelions polluting the courthouse lawn. Perhaps someone should take a scythe to them.

He spent the first half of the morning reading the pleadings in the Jefferson case and then walked into the library where he found Phil and Melanie.

"You know how most petitioners make at least a dozen whacko claims?" He sat down and thumped the top of the case file. "I've got a petition that makes only two arguments."

"Maybe it's good strategy," Phil replied. "If you raise too many issues, the best argument gets lost in the clutter and you piss off the clerk who has to sort through the garbage looking for it."

"What's the gist of it?" Melanie asked.

"Well, there's a plausible *Hitchcock* claim, arguing that his constitutional right to a fair sentencing hearing was denied by the jury's failure to hear important mitigating evidence. Have you heard of *Hitchcock*?" His co-clerks both shook their heads. Melanie seemed curious, but Phil wore a scowl of disapproval at his friend's academic approach to life and death issues.

"It's not complicated," Arthur explained. "The Supreme Court established in a series of opinions ending with *Hitchcock v. Florida* that a trial judge can't exclude evidence offered by a convicted murderer to show he deserves life in prison rather than the death penalty. A defendant gets to show that he was or is a drug addict, a drunk, a victim of child abuse, a good husband, a model prisoner, a regular churchgoer, or anything else that might make him look better."

"Before you get into that," Melanie interjected eagerly, "have you checked whether this is his first or second petition? You remember Gottlieb."

"Yup. I checked." He nodded. "Unfortunately for Mr. Jefferson, this is not the first habeas petition he's filed. So, his *Hitchcock* claim, which looks really strong on merits, is in serious trouble. He should have raised it in his first habeas go-round, so he's barred now from complaining about all the evidence the jury should have seen." He flipped back through the documents to a copy of the petition filed on Jefferson's behalf two years earlier just to make sure that there was no mention of *Hitchcock*. "By the way, his first petition was truly a piece of shit. And check out the signature line on the last page . . ."

Phil was reluctant to play along, but he scanned the last page along with Melanie. "Well, I see the attorney's name, followed by his state bar number and . . . oh fuck . . . his patent bar number."

"Welcome to criminal justice in the South!" Arthur whistled. "Nothing like asking a patent attorney to practice criminal law! The local bar's *pro bono* guy was really on the ball making assignments that day."

"So, Jefferson might die because a charity attorney couldn't recognize that a blatant error was committed when he was sentenced to death?" Phil stared hard at his friend, daring him to approve of such a harsh result even in theory.

"That's exactly why the Florida legislature now funds a special office of attorneys in Tallahassee to represent death row inmates in habeas cases," Melanie explained as she took the Jefferson petition from Arthur. "Look at this: his current attorney comes from that office, but it didn't exist at the time of his first petition." She pushed the papers back in front of him. "I'll bet I can predict his second claim."

He smiled. Phil might be his best friend in the chambers, but Melanie understood the perverse excitement of working through the maze of habeas corpus. "Go for it."

She cleared her throat. "I'll bet he argues that his first habeas counsel was incompetent, thereby denying his constitutional right to effective counsel."

"You are a prophetess!" Arthur reverenced her briefly with both arms outstretched like a bleacher bum worshiping Andre Dawson at Wrigley Field. "Under the Sixth Amendment right to counsel, having a totally incompetent attorney is the functional equivalent of having no counsel at all. So, I've got to look at all the evidence after all."

Phil opened his mouth as if to say something, but did nothing more than shake his head and turn back to his work.

Arthur brought the file back to his office and looked at the petition again. According to its concluding paragraph, a three-inch stack of affidavits from friends, family, and clergy, along with reports from psychological and medical experts, would demonstrate that even though Averill Lee Johnson had intentionally murdered an eight-year-old girl, he did not deserve to die.

★ ★ ★

"Hello, Mr. Dumont? This is Margaret Hill again, from Aetna Insurance." Melanie spoke brightly into her living room phone. "I'm sorry to keep bothering you, but I've got one more question that I'd like to ask you."

"No, you're not."

"Excuse me?"

"Maybe your name is Margaret, but you're not with Aetna." His rumbling voice relished revealing the lie. "The Judge told me a while ago that the federal government self-insures. No insurance company has any policy on the courthouse. Who are you anyway? A private investigator?"

Melanie froze. Although the reporter couldn't see her, she felt completely exposed. As much as she wanted to know whether Carolyn was wearing a slippery pair of nylons on the night of her death, she was unprepared to impersonate a private eye. She gripped the phone hard and slammed down the receiver.

"Shit," she said through clenched teeth. "Shit, shit, shit, shit."

She reminded herself that the reporter had no way to trace her identity and began to calm down. She was safe, but no closer to learning whether Carolyn was wearing hose when she slipped. If the dead clerk had been, an accident was much more plausible, but if she'd been barefoot, then there were a lot more questions that needed to be asked. Suddenly, she realized that Dumont was not the best source of information on what Carolyn Bastaigne was wearing at the time of her death. Surely, the coroner's official report would provide the answer.

But what if someone in the courthouse noticed her request for the report and told the Judge? He might put two and two together and demand to know why Melanie was snooping around. He might even fire her.

The next day, she chanced upon a solution to the dilemma as she walked to lunch with Phil.

"I can't believe I'm so stupid!" She slapped herself on the forehead.

"I can't either." Phil grinned. "Maybe there was a lot of lead paint in your house growing up."

She bumped his shoulder and propelled him against the brick wall of a store.

"Look, I need to tell you something. I called Sydney Dumont again. I wanted to see if Carolyn was wearing nylons on the night she fell. If she did, it was more likely a slip, right?" She glided next to him and took his arm while she spoke. Sometimes the lack of romantic spark was a good thing. She had never had a brother to lean on before.

She continued. "Imagine Carolyn getting really upset after the Judge tells her that he's called Cravath. She races out of the chambers, desperate just to get away from the scene. Maybe she even pounds on the elevator button, but it's too slow and she just has to get out, so she impulsively takes the stairs instead."

"Well, it's a better theory than Ms. Stillwater's chocolate bar. What did Dumont say?" His stride matched hers perfectly as they walked down the sidewalk. "And why do you think you're stupid?"

"Well, Dumont told me nothing and accused me of impersonating an insurance agent."

"Fuck!" Phil stopped and turned to her, eyes wide with concern.

"Don't panic," she reassured him. "He said he talked to the Judge—I have no idea why—and knows that the building is not insured. I just freaked out and hung up. He has no clue who I am"

"You know your little obsession is going to get you in trouble."

"Not if I'm more careful." She led him down the street again. "Anyway, I thought about getting the autopsy report. After all, it's a public document, but everybody knows everybody in the courthouse, and I was afraid it would get back to the judge."

"You can't take that chance."

"But I haven't been thinking straight," she explained as she stopped him on the sidewalk. "There should be two documents. First, we already know about the closed inquest held by the feds. That was meant to determine the cause of death and whether any crime had likely been committed. I'd love to read that document, but even if there's a copy in the federal courthouse, we don't dare ask to see it."

"Damn right," Phil confirmed.

"The inquest, however, must have had access to a doctor's autopsy of the body. That would have been conducted by a local official. I doubt the feds have their own doctors examining all dead federal employees. Carolyn died here in Clarkeston and was undoubtedly carted off to a local funeral home, and I guarantee some local official examined her and filed an autopsy report. The report may have been part of the evidence submitted at the inquest, but I'll bet it was also filed in the local coroner's office."

Phil sighed and started trudging toward their lunch destination. "You might be right, but I bet you still have to show some identification to the county folks to look at the coroner's files."

"Well, we'll just have to find out." She offered him her biggest smile. "Because after lunch, you're coming with me."

When they had finished eating, they walked across a small urban park to the county courthouse. Compared to its federal counterpart, the red brick building looked quaint and a bit forlorn. It sat in the middle of a quiet tree-lined square surrounded by park benches and flower beds. A memorial obelisk to the Confederate fallen split the sidewalk on its way to the courthouse steps. They strode cautiously up the stairs, determined to retreat if they saw anyone they knew.

They made it to the Coroner's Office on the third floor without seeing anyone at all. A middle-aged woman looked up from a novel as they entered.

"Hello!" Melanie said cheerfully. "What do we have to do to see an autopsy report?"

"One filed recently?"

Melanie shook her head.

"Because sometimes Fred will hold on to them for a while after an inquest, but any one older than six months will be in the back room." She led them a dozen paces into a room occupied by two wooden chairs, a small table and three large metal filing cabinets. "Which one do you want?"

"Bastaigne, Carolyn." Melanie spelled the last name.

"Don't remember that one, but I've only been here two years."

"It should be about five years old. I don't know the exact date."

"It doesn't matter. We've got an alphabetical cross-index." She flipped through the top drawer of the second cabinet. "Here you go. You gotta keep it in this room while you read it. I'll be happy to make a photocopy of it and mail it to you later if you want."

"Thanks!"

"And here"—the woman put the file on the table and pointed to the cover—"please sign your name and date it right here." She handed a pen to Melanie and waited.

Concluding that the chance of discovery by the Judge was minimal, Melanie signed and waited for the woman to leave. She had not yet opened the folder, but already the visit was bearing fruit, for in clear black letters, right above her newly entered name was the signature of Jennifer Huffman, Carolyn's best friend in the courthouse. The date was six weeks after the death and just two days after the report was filed.

"Well, what do you know?" Phil said. "I wonder why Carolyn's friend was so interested in seeing the report?"

"Good question."

"I had a classmate die in college . . . I must say that it never occurred to me to make a trip to the county courthouse to read any documentation."

"Same here." Melanie traced the signature slowly with her fingertips. "I mean, I'd never think to do it either."

"Maybe she was just playing detective. Maybe she thought the death looked funny and was checking things out like we are." He reached for the folder, but she grabbed it first.

"Maybe." Melanie stared at it and pushed back a strand of hair out of her eyes. "Let's see what's inside."

The report itself was dry and filled with technical medical jargon but it was not hard to understand that Carolyn had died of massive brain trauma cause by her fall. She had not been under the influence of drugs or alcohol. Although forty pounds overweight, she was otherwise in perfect health at the time of her death. An appendix to the report listed the personal effects found on the body: two hair clips, a pair of glasses (broken), one dental retainer, one necklace, two earrings, a dress, a bra, a slip, and underwear.

"No nylons." Phil said.

"Nope."

"Is that unusual? I mean, don't woman normally wear nylons to work?"

"It depends. If the dress were long enough, she might not wear any. And I've seen her shoes—Ms. Stillwater's got them stored in a box in the photocopy room with her stapler and some sticky pads. Carolyn could have worn them without socks or nylons." She laid the report down on the table and chewed meditatively on her pen.

"Well, Nancy Drew, are you satisfied?"

She just raised her eyebrows at him: *What do you think?*

★ ★ ★

Phil knocked on Arthur's door when he returned to chambers. He had a vague notion of describing his trip to the courthouse, but mostly he wanted to check in on his friend. Something compelling happened to Arthur's expression when he tackled a problem, a focus and single-mindedness that was intriguing even when he was headed down the wrong path. He wondered what Averill Lee Jefferson was writing on his friend's face.

"Hey."

Arthur was sorting through several piles of paper scattered over his desk. He had devoured the thick case file in less than two hours. "Hey," he responded automatically.

"Did you skip lunch?"

"Yeah." He looked up, briefly made eye contact and then glanced out the window. "What's up?"

"Oh, more twists and turns in the Bastaigne affair," Phil confided. "Carolyn wasn't wearing nylons when she fell."

Arthur looked at him without comprehension.

"Means it's less likely that she slipped."

"Oh." He polished his glasses with his shirttail and shook his head. "I'm glad Melanie's got something to be excited about . . . but I don't really care. I love a good mystery, but this habeas shit teaches you that in real life, you always know whodunit. Or at least almost all the time. The only mystery is what happens after."

"I suppose." Phil watched his friend carefully. "But how can habeas be a mystery when you get to write the story?"

"Because these fucking cases are impossible," he replied fiercely. "You want to hear about Jefferson?"

"Sure." Phil moved two books off a chair and sat down.

"Bottom line: this guy is just fucked." Arthur gestured to the papers in front of him. "He was a prison guard without any kind of criminal record. In fact, the guy seemed to be some kind of pacifist. All of his redneck relatives talk about him being the peacemaker during hunting trips and family reunions." He picked up an affidavit. "Great with children too. The whole family used to dump their kids on him. Still would, if you believe this."

"So what did he do?"

"He picked up an eight-year-old neighbor girl on the way to work and strangled her."

"God . . ." He waited for his friend to say more, but Arthur just stared at him. "Any clue as to why?"

"Sort of. His wife was cheating on him and spent the night before the murder with a coworker of his right across the street from their house."

"Did he rape the girl?"

"Well," Arthur sighed, "he tied her up, put her in a garbage bag, and dumped her in the woods. Wild dogs ate the lower half of her body, so no one knows."

"What does he say?"

"He says that he doesn't remember any of it."

Phil shook his head incredulously. "Trauma-induced amnesia? Good luck with that."

"Oh, it's way worse than that." Arthur picked up a file and gestured with it. "According to the psychologist's report, this guy was always pretty slow, barely graduated from high school, but when he was thirteen, his parents got worried that he wasn't maturing as quickly as his cousins, so they took him to this doctor—now in prison on drug charges, I might add—and got him put on growth hormones." He snorted with disgust. "It says that they were worried about the size of his penis."

"You've got to be kidding." Phil shifted uncomfortably in his chair.

"You can't make this shit up," Arthur replied grimly as he put down the report. "Anyway, apparently the doc injected him with these hormones, which another affidavit tells us is highly dangerous and is never done anymore, and Jefferson shoots up to about six foot three inches and turns into the jolly green giant, except that he gets excruciating migraines as a side effect and spends every other night banging his head against the wall in agony."

"His shrink claims that the hormones turned him into a killer?" Phil asked.

"No"—he shook his head approvingly—"and that makes the report more credible. The psychiatrist just wants to paint a picture of a hulking and alienated high school boy who's functioning on the margins. He withdraws whenever presented with any kind of conflict and is basically unhappy until a new girl moves into town his senior year and sweeps him off his feet."

"He can't have been totally alienated if he had a girlfriend."

"Well, by the end of high school, he's kinda doing okay. He's so big that he's starting on the football team and even though school pretty much sucks, he's still got all of his cousins to go hunting and fishing with in the backwoods of north Florida." He rolled his chair back and forth on the hard plastic mat behind his desk. "By all accounts the girlfriend is pretty slutty, and even though his fundamentalist parents go ballistic, he marries her and does a one-year junior college course to become a prison guard. By their second anniversary, she already regrets the marriage and stays out partying to all hours of the morning, but he still absolutely adores her. She shoves this final fling in his face and he cracks."

"By killing an innocent little girl?"

"Apparently so . . . he confessed as soon as he was caught."

Phil waited for Arthur to finish the story and provide the missing connection, but he was disappointed.

"He called the parents a couple of times, rambling incoherently about knowing where their daughter was," Arthur explained. "The cops caught him with a phone tap."

"That's it?" Nobody deserved the death penalty, Phil thought, but the killers should have to explain why they did what they did. Without an explanation there's no closure, no path to mercy and forgiveness.

"Oh, that's much less than it," Arthur sighed. "With the confession, the trial lasted a day. The jury never saw any evidence of his background. They had no clue who they were sentencing." He stacked up the papers and put them back in the accordion folder on top of the desk. "I've just given you a taste of the psychiatric and character testimony that the jury never heard. He may have been a killer, but everyone agrees that he only spent one morning of his life being anything but a sweet, damaged kid."

Was Arthur himself swayed by the evidence? He looked disgusted by the course of events at Jefferson's trial, but he had put aside his qualms to send Gottlieb to the chair. Jefferson, however, was no Gottlieb. Surely in this case, no matter what the law said, his friend would do the right thing. Surely. Their eyes met and Phil almost asked, but he didn't want to know the answer. He let their shared sense of injustice linger a while before he nodded and left.

Phil walked slowly down the hall and waved at Ms. Stillwater who sat typing at a right angle to her desk. She gave him a curious look as he opened the door and entered his office. He could sense that something was not quite right. He scanned the room and saw that his normally clutter-free desk top was occupied by a large brown file folder. He circled it cautiously and then leaned against his chair and peered downward, as if he were looking down a deep well. On the top of the file was a single Post-it marked "Thomas Watkins."

XXII.

BAD MOON ON THE RISE

The day that the habeas cases arrived, Phil decided to shake things up. Instead of his usual quick lunch at the Chinese buffet on Court Street, he suggested to his co-clerks that they walk to a friendly soul food restaurant on the edge of town. Arthur and Melanie followed, willing this one time to clog their arteries with mouth-watering chicken and potatoes fried in bacon grease. The sun shone brightly as they crossed the railroad tracks and approached a small cinder block house. A short line of racially mixed laborers and businessmen waited outside the door, but the lunch rush was almost over, and they got a seat in less than fifteen minutes.

"Let me ask you guys a question," Melanie said as she poked at her coleslaw. "Do you think that the Judge didn't give me a death case because I'm a woman?"

"Trust me," Phil interjected, "you don't want one."

"That's not the point!"

"Maybe he thinks you're too bloodthirsty." Phil was trying to make Melanie laugh, but he could see the gears turning in her head. She wanted desperately to make a good impression on the Judge and probably resented being denied the chance to show what she could do with the toughest kind of case. She was the hardest working of the three clerks. He wondered if the Judge appreciated the ridiculous hours that she put in.

"Forget it," she dropped the subject, "why don't you tell me what y'all ended up with."

"Well," Arthur explained while dissecting a crunchy battered chicken breast, "I've got this basically nice, kind of pitiful guy, whose wife was cheating on him. But instead of killing the wife and boyfriend, he snatches an eight-year-old off the street and chokes her to death."

Melanie turned, incredulous. "That's his excuse for murdering a kid?"

"Actually, he didn't make any excuses. He admitted doing it." Arthur popped a piece of chicken into his mouth. "You know me. I don't deal in mysteries."

"Did he take the stand during the trial to explain what was running through his mind when he strangled her?"

"Nope."

"Did his attorney argue for second degree murder, heat of passion excuse, that sort of thing?"

"Nope." He took a noisy slurp of Coke through his straw. "The evidence suggested strongly that his actions were deliberate."

"Then he's a monster."

She put down her silverware and shook her head. She was quite charismatic when she was passionate about something, her careful professionalism cast unconsciously aside. "No feeling human being could deliberately kill a child in cold blood . . . I can understand taking a shot at the wife and lover, but not killing some random kid."

She looked hard at Arthur. "You're not trying to find a way to get this guy off, are you?"

"Calm down, I just started my research today." Arthur took another sip. "I didn't know you were such a fan of capital punishment."

"In theory, I'm not," she explained. "Some of the prisoners I worked with at our law school clinic were bigger victims than the people that they killed, but when it comes to Gottlieb and your new guy, it's hard for me to be a bleeding heart."

For a few minutes, the three clerks ate in silence, deep in the middle of a true southern experience: soul-satisfying food in a laid-back neighborhood joint, a friendly buzz of conversation with state-sponsored death for dessert.

A smiling waitress poured them all more drinks and gushed, "You're welcome, sweetie," when Arthur thanked her.

"You're pretty quiet." Melanie turned her attention to Phil. "What did you get stuck with?"

"Not a monster." He finished his last bite of chicken and pushed his slaw to the middle of the table. "This guy Watkins was a decorated black army sergeant who got drunk with a friend. In the middle of the night, the friend decides to rob his ancient, half-deaf uncle out in the country somewhere down in rural south Georgia. For God knows what reason, the sergeant goes along. When the uncle opens fire in the dark at them, the sergeant reflexively shoots back and kills the old guy. He felt so bad when he sobered up the next morning that he marched straight down to the sheriff's office and confessed."

Phil dunked a french fry in ketchup and sighed. "He then waived his right to counsel and a jury trial. Unfortunately, he was in a super redneck county and got the death sentence, even though he had no prior criminal record. I'll bet even the Grim Reaper here—"

"Hey!"

"—would agree that this is not the especially nasty sort of murder that the Supreme Court says capital punishment is reserved for. The problem is that it doesn't look like any of his constitutional rights were ever violated during the course of his arrest and trial."

Arthur crunched a corner of Texas toast. "So, I've got a monster who might get off, and you've got a respectable dude who's got no chance."

"You wanna trade?"

Arthur thought about the offer for a moment. "Nah, you can keep your guy. I wouldn't know what to do with someone who wasn't a nutcase."

"Shoot, and I was going to offer you Watkins and two drug cases to be named later."

Suzanne sat at the kitchen table, picking at her supper and wondering what was wrong with her intuition. She should not have to take a pregnancy test to discern her condition. She should just know, like she had when Maria was conceived. After a few more bites, she took her plate to the sink and wondered if she had been listening for the wrong future. Joy and disaster echoed on different bands of the spectrum. This was not like before. Despite her appreciation of Arthur's wit and kindness to Maria, she had trouble seeing him as a husband. He was too immature, too moody, too focused on his own goals, all of which destined him for a life in Washington instead of Clarkeston.

She stared at the unopened home pregnancy test on the table and slipped it into her purse. Taking the test when Arthur got home had seemed a good idea at first, but now she hesitated. Before she dealt with his reaction, she needed to determine her own. Maybe a hypothetical talk about pregnancy was a good interim step. She was considering how to broach the subject when she heard the front door slam and Arthur's heavy footsteps echo down the hall.

"You want some leftovers?" She opened up the oven and gestured to two small pieces of cod. "I've got some tater tots too that Maria didn't finish."

He gave her a kiss and sat down at the table. "Sure. That'd be great."

She fixed him a plate and slid a bottle of ketchup and a cold beer alongside it. "There you go."

She sat down across from him. "Now, tell me about your day, and then let me ask you a question."

He spoke and her face clouded as he summarized the facts of the Jefferson case. The victim had not been much older than Maria. Why had he attacked this child instead of his wife and her lover? She stared at him with a mixture of sympathy and distaste. "So, this is how you're going to spend your time over the next week?"

"The legal issues are pretty straightforward, so it shouldn't be too bad." He shrugged and popped a tater tot into his mouth.

Did he owe his cool nerves to bravado or simply a poor memory of the Gottlieb case? "I don't know how you can just stick to the issues when you're dealing with a child murderer, but that's your job, I guess." She reached over and took a sip of his beer. "In a way, this guy sounds worse than Gottlieb."

"What do you mean? He only committed one crime in his whole life."

"Yeah, but what a crime! Can you imagine the terror that little girl felt when he started to choke her?" She peeled the label from the beer bottle with a brittle intensity. "At least Gottlieb knocked most of his victims over the head when they weren't looking." The wet paper ripped and she looked up. "I'm not saying we should give Gottlieb a medal or something, but can you even begin to understand how Jefferson could have done such a horrible thing?"

"God! Do you really wish I had that vivid an imagination?" He got up, put his plate in the sink, and ceded the remains of his beer to her. "Well, to change this delightful, uplifting subject, what's your question?"

"Huh?" She tossed the beer label in the wastebasket. The kitchen felt polluted, and she had no desire to talk about anything personal. "Later. It's not urgent right now."

★ ★ ★

Later that evening, on the way upstairs, Arthur peeped through the door of the television room and saw Maria curled up on the sofa with her favorite blanket and a circle of talking animals. The three smallest were sick, and a doctor Bear and nurse Fox consoled the mother Bunny worried about her sick ones. The doctor was not sure what was wrong, but nonetheless prescribed painful injections of medicine to his patients. The victims squealed and the doctor comforted them in as deep a voice as the little girl could muster. Arthur tried to imagine what it would be like if one day Maria did not come home from school. She saw him as he stood in the doorway and put a finger to her lips and cradled her arms to show that the sick animals were sleeping. He smiled and put a finger to his lips in return and then trudged up the stairs to his bedroom, numb to what lay before him the next day.

★ ★ ★

By eleven thirty in the morning, he felt like the nation's expert on when the failure to introduce mitigating evidence constituted ineffective assistance of counsel. It was a toss-up what was more disgusting in the cases he read, the grisly details of the murders or the grossness of the errors committed by the attorneys and judges in the trials. The precedential cases were an education on how not to conduct the penalty phase of a capital case. He only noticed toward the end of his reading that all the cases involved errors made by the defendant's attorney at trial and not errors made by habeas counsel years later.

"What's the word on your guy?" Phil asked as he emerged from his office to join Arthur in the library.

"Well, as far as I can tell, a minimally competent attorney would have pushed for admission of relevant evidence about Jefferson's background." He leaned back in his chair and looked up at his friend. "And now that I've read what the jury never saw, it looks pretty damn relevant. Lots of courts have held that work records, medical and psychological histories, and other proof of good character have to be admitted to help the jury with sentencing. There's no doubt that Jefferson's trial counsel was constitutionally defective."

"So," Phil said as he sat down and pushed away enough books to create a space for his file folder and legal pad, "his main problem is the failure of the patent attorney to complain about those errors when he filed the first habeas petition."

"Right, that was the chance to point out the errors made at trial. In order for Jefferson to get a new sentencing hearing, he needs a case that condemns the incompetence of his first *habeas* attorney." Phil nodded attentively, sunlight reflecting off the reading glasses he sometimes wore. They sat comfortably in leather-covered chairs, dressed in their best wool suits. They were both only twenty-four years old.

"What I eventually found was a one-page 1956 Supreme Court opinion holding that the constitutional right to counsel does not extend to the preparation of habeas corpus petitions." Arthur sighed as he dropped his bomb. "In other words, there's no remedy for a prisoner whose first habeas lawyer was grossly incompetent. If a defendant's constitutional rights are violated at trial, his very first petition had better set forth all the errors. If it doesn't, then he's fucked, because you can't complain about how shitty your first habeas lawyer is."

"So, your memo's going to say that he's not entitled to a stay of execution." Phil's eyes pleaded for Arthur to reveal some precedent that would save Jefferson's life. He had looked hard. There was none.

"What choice do I have?" Arthur wanted to lay his head on the oak table and sleep.

He expected Phil to object. Melanie and Suzanne would not shed any tears over Jefferson, but his co-clerk had decided long ago what the answer was in all these cases.

Instead of arguing, Phil took off his glasses and massaged the sides of nose between his thumb and forefinger. He apparently had his own problems.

"Watkins?" Arthur asked.

"Yeah. It's his first habeas petition, so he doesn't have any of Jefferson's procedural problems." Phil smiled weakly and shook his head. "It's just that there's nothing for his attorney to complain about. Watkins made a knowing confession that he won't renounce because he still feels bad about the killing. And since he pleaded guilty, there was no trial, so there's no trial mistakes to find."

"So the real problem," Arthur concluded, "is that the sentence was just too harsh."

"Yup."

"And that's not unconstitutional."

"Nope."

"So what are you going to do?"

When Phil had announced his opposition to the death penalty months ago, Arthur had wondered what would happen if his friend got just this sort of case. Much of the time the law was fuzzy and there was room to massage it into a memo recommending clemency. But Watkins was worst-case scenario for someone like Phil.

"What are my options?" He doodled for a moment on his legal pad and then set down his pencil. "I could write a memo arguing that the death penalty is unconstitutional."

"Except that the Judge doesn't believe that."

"Or, I could tell him that I won't work on capital cases because I don't believe in the death penalty." Phil's voice was grim.

"Then he'd know that you lied to him in your job interview."

"Not to mention that it would be letting Watkins down."

"Any other options?" Arthur asked.

"I could throw the Judge under the bus . . . fabricate some sort of argument from an old case, ignore later precedent, and hope to fool him."

"You'll get caught."

"I know." He snapped his pencil in half and picked up his things. "I'm going to read through the petition again and look for more cases. There's got to be something out there." He walked to the door but turned before he left. "What are *you* going to do?"

Arthur inclined his head toward the Judge's office. "I'm going to consult the Oracle of Delphi."

Ms. Stillwater was gone, so Arthur knocked on the Judge's door and entered in response to an inarticulate grunt. Once in the room, he could barely see the Judge's back as he fished around for something in his credenza.

"Good morning, Judge."

The white-bearded old man straightened up, a pack of cigarettes in one hand and a lighter in the other.

"I need to ask you a quick question before I write my memo in the Jefferson case."

The Judge lit a cigarette and winked at him conspiratorially. He took a deep drag. "Mr. Hughes, you're way ahead of schedule."

He motioned for Arthur to sit down. "The pipeline's so clogged Jefferson's case probably won't make it up here until Friday." He flicked an ash into his top right drawer. "But go ahead and tell me what you've got."

Assuming the Judge had already read Jefferson's file, he explained that the case presented a strong *Hitchcock* claim that should have been argued in Jefferson's first habeas petition. While he was deriding the competency of the first habeas attorney, the Judge interrupted—

"And, of course, you found out that there's no remedy for the damage caused by an ineffective habeas counsel."

"That's the bottom line, Judge. I just wanted to make sure you didn't see anything I was missing. If that's still the law, then it's a pretty straightforward denial of stay." He clutched the file in his left hand and started to stand up.

"One thing I've learned," the Judge drawled contemplatively, his voice stopping Arthur in his tracks, "is that there's no such thing as a straightforward death case." He tapped off another bit of ash and waited until his clerk sat back down. "Before you write the memo, would you do a little further research just to ease my mind?"

"Sure." While Arthur waited, curious to learn what he missed, the Judge balanced his cigarette on a stapler and started rummaging through one of his massive bookshelves.

"I've read the Jefferson file all the way through twice, mostly because I just couldn't make any sense of the crime. I felt like even with all those doctors' reports and affidavits something was missing. Ah, here it is." He turned and revealed a paperback collection of Greek drama that looked like it had not been opened for forty years. "It's been a long time since I've read this, so you'll have to humor me. Give the first play a read and tell me whether it helps explain what's missing in Jefferson's file." He nodded at his clerk but provided no more guidance.

Realizing with a chill that he was seeing the first manifestation of senility in one of the great jurists of the twentieth century, Arthur promised to read the play as soon as possible and quickly retreated as the Judge rearranged the mess on the credenza.

He went straight to Phil's office.

"What now?"

"I think the old man has finally cracked. I told him that there were no valid grounds for granting Jefferson's petition and he gave me this to read." He held up the book.

"So? He gave me a law review article to read just yesterday." Phil reached over the desk for the book and then looked up quizzically. "*Euripides's Medea and Other Plays?*" He laughed. "Awesome stuff, but I can't say that I've seen it cited in too many recent cases."

He handed the volume back to his co-clerk. "What does he want you to do with it?"

"Just read it. I guess our next conference is going to be like a book club." Arthur shook his head in disbelief. "Maybe he'll bring some brownies."

"Look, I don't know what he's up to," Phil said, "but I haven't seen any sign that he's losing his mind. And besides, isn't it more fun to read a play than a bunch more cases?"

Arthur grudgingly conceded the point and went back to his office. He put his feet up on his desk and began to read.

XXIII.

THE LAST ONE YOU EVER LOVED

Melanie sat in her apartment and looked across the parking lot at the pennants fluttering over Toys"R"Us. Her co-clerks were still at work, fussing over their habeas cases. Without one of her own, she had finished early, and for the first time since her arrival the previous July, she had left the chambers before Arthur and Phil. It was pointless being mad at the Judge for the special treatment she was getting. He was a southern gentleman, a victim of his upbringing, unconsciously relegating her to second-class status. Even so, the absence of a bloody, violent, disgusting, convoluted, and disturbing capital case gnawed at her until she left the apartment, wandered through the miles of asphalt surrounding her building and settled on the newest Clint Eastwood film as a temporary diversion.

As she left the theater two hours later, she decided that maybe she did sort of have a death case. Carolyn Bastaigne was just as dead as the victims of Arthur's and Phil's killers. The logical next step was to contact Jennifer Huffman, but she was a possible co-conspirator with Carolyn in the securities fraud scheme, so a phone call to her was out of the question. In addition, Melanie wanted to see the face of the ex-clerk for Judge Meyers when she answered questions. Unfortunately, she was broke, and the Judge was unlikely to bless a vacation in the middle of a busy session.

The next morning, after handing the second draft of a bench memo to Ms. Stillwater, Melanie marched into Phil's office without knocking. She plopped herself down in his chair with a spectacular pout.

"Phil, why don't you find me an excuse to go to New York to talk to Jennifer Huffman and then give enough money to fly me there?"

"Okay," he said with a smile as he reached into his pocket. "Do you take credit cards?"

"No," she whined, "just call and book me a ticket!"

"Boy, you've really got it bad haven't you?" Phil laughed and leaned back in his chair. She could see a bankruptcy treatise on his desk; he was taking a break from the Watkins case.

"She's the only person left who might know something more about the case."

"Except the Judge." Phil motioned across the hall. "Why don't you talk to him?"

"Very funny." She pursed her lips and frowned. "I'm being serious. I need to see the expression on Huffman's face when I tell her that we know Carolyn was trading on inside information."

"You think she's going to confess or something?"

"I don't know, but I'm pretty good at telling when people are lying."

"The pulsing vein in the temple gives them away?"

"Something like that."

He squeezed his eyes shut for a moment and muttered something under his breath. "I can't believe I'm going to suggest something this unethical." He let out a huge sigh. "Why don't you call up Jennifer's firm and ask for an interview? They'll fly you up at their expense, and the Judge probably won't begrudge you the trip."

To an outsider, the suggestion would have seemed absurd, but clerking for the Judge meant that she could call any major firm in the United States and instantly get an interview, and the biggest firms wouldn't even blink at paying her travel expenses.

"But I've already decided that I want to work in Washington," she replied. "I can't stand New York."

"That's why it's unethical, dear."

Melanie stood up and put her hands on Phil's desk. "It would work though, wouldn't it?" She felt a surge of energy. "And it would give me a great excuse to talk to Jennifer, and to learn about the firm, of course."

"And if I were a Jesuit," Phil said cryptically, "I could even justify it on moral grounds."

"How so?"

"Don't you think Cravath would want to know if they have an insider-trading sleazebag working for them?"

★ ★ ★

After Melanie said good-bye to the recruitment coordinator at Cravath, Swaine, and Moore, she stared at the phone and marveled at the credibility she had earned simply by working for the Judge. The eager young woman on the other end of the line did not even inquire about her level of interest in the firm or in New York City. Who wouldn't want to work at the highest-paying firm in the country? She had just asked Melanie to fax a resume and immediately began arranging the details of the interview trip. Melanie asked Ms. Stillwater to run the dates of her absence past the Judge.

On the way back, she stuck her head in the library and saw Arthur chewing on the end of a pencil and reading a small paperback that was obviously not a volume of federal cases. "Finished with all your work already?" She leaned against the door and put her hand on her hip. "You're a clerking machine."

He looked. Then shut the book and tossed it casually on the table toward her with a curious look on his face. "Behold my work."

She leaned over and picked up the book. "So this is what Phil meant when he said that the Judge gave you some literary homework." She handed the book back to him. "I saw a performance of *Medea* a long time ago, but I don't remember much."

"You remember Jason, of Jason and the Argonauts fetching the Golden Fleece fame? It's mostly the story of him being a shitty husband." He shrugged at his reductive summary, but she was intrigued enough to sit down.

"He goes through all sorts of adventures to get the Golden Fleece," he explained, "none of which he could have survived without Medea, his wife. She's sort of a sorceress who double crosses her own family to help Jason. Without her, Jason gets nowhere."

"That sounds vaguely familiar."

Sometimes when Arthur talked, his eyes looked up and to the right, as if he were seeing what he was describing. She could study his face without her gaze being misinterpreted.

"Well, after getting the fleece and having some more adventures, they land exhausted on the shores of Corinth where the king offers to let Jason settle down with one of his daughters as his new wife." He looked at Melanie. "Turns out that Medea is from some barbarian tribe and her marriage to Jason doesn't count in the eyes of Greeks, even though she and Jason have two kids."

"Anyway, Jason is middle-aged, tired, and the king's hot daughter looks pretty good to him, so he announces that he's accepting the offer and divorcing Medea, all for the so-called good of the family. Worst of all, instead of apologizing, or at least acknowledging Medea's loyalty, he refuses to accept any blame and tries to put the breakup all on her."

"I remember now," Melanie replied, images of the play flashing in her mind's eye. "It's basically a primer on how not to break up with somebody."

"And a pretty good one too," he sighed, "even if it was written 2500 years ago."

"What do you mean?"

His eyes had wandered again and he looked pensive.

"When I was a senior in college, one of my roommates broke up with his fiancée to date this gorgeous graduate student.

He was constantly at her apartment, so I ended up having to deal with his ex all the time. She used to call our room crying, wanting to talk with him."

"That must have been fun." Melanie stacked two fists on the table and rested her chin on top while Arthur shook his head in disgust.

"No kidding. He told me not to tell her anything and to just hang up, but instead I told her that pleading with him to come back was a waste of time. He was totally into his new girlfriend and couldn't be bothered to go to class, much less find time for her."

"That's pretty harsh," Melanie sympathized, "but I would have done the same thing."

"Well, she didn't want to hear it. She kept saying that if he only knew how much she hurt, he would change his mind. If he only knew, he would stop." He picked the book back off the table thumbed through it absentmindedly. "I was afraid that she was getting suicidal, so I gave her the phone number of the new girlfriend's apartment. She called and he told her that they were never really meant for each other. Then, he just hung up on her."

He ran his finger along the spine of the book and continued. "That was a big mistake. She started stalking him and vandalized his car. Finally, she spray-painted a big red *"A"* on his back after one of his classes. They got in a shoving match, and she was suspended from school for a semester. As a condition of getting readmitted the next year, she had to get counseling."

"No guy is worth that much trouble," Melanie whistled. "Get drunk, cry for a weekend, and then just get over it."

"That's easy for you to say—I'll bet you've never been dumped!"

She blushed at the compliment and then started to protest, but he cut her off. "It gets worse. A couple of weeks later, I get this phone call from her therapist who's looking for my roommate because she's threatened to kill him in her sessions. Since the threats were credible, the doctor had to call him."

"Great introduction to tort law disclosure duties!" She smiled and reached for a cookie from a plate that Ms. Stillwater had left on the table. She offered him one, but he waved it away.

"I suppose the therapy worked, because my roommate survived, graduated, and still works in Chicago for a brokerage firm, but I always thought the whole mess could have been avoided if he had sat down with her, admitted his attraction to the new woman, apologized like crazy, and let her cry on his shoulder for a while. She would have still been miserable, but she probably wouldn't have gone off the deep end."

"I get it…Jason was as bad at breaking up as your roommate."

"Yeah, and when Medea's tears and anger fail to make the slightest dent in him, she kills the king's daughter and even though she adores her sons, she stabs them to death with Jason's own sword. Of course, even at the end Jason's clueless, screaming that everything's her fault."

"Doesn't Medea get away?" She flicked a small pile of cookie crumbs into the wastebasket. "If I remember right, she denies Jason the body of his sons for burial—a huge deal back then—and is carried off by Apollo to sanctuary somewhere, right?"

"That's right. The gods don't punish her for her crimes."

"She gets off," Melanie said with a frown and made a silent promise to let down her next boyfriend extra gently when the time came to cut him loose.

★ ★ ★

Arthur sat at the table, beginning to think that the Judge's intuition was not totally off base. Talking with Melanie had revealed some connection between Medea and Jefferson, but he still couldn't see where the Judge wanted him to go. The two child killers had some traits in common, but a comparison was not immediately fruitful. Medea's behavior was horrific, as was Jefferson's. They both were cheated on by their spouses, but then again, so were a lot of people who managed to respond much more appropriately. The play didn't provide any explanation why Medea resorted to infanticide rather than throwing the ancient equivalent of darts at a picture with Jason's face on it. It certainly didn't explain why a previously nonviolent young man would murder an eight-year-old girl whom he had previously been kind to.

And what to make of the end of the play? Was the Judge suggesting that, like Medea, Jefferson should not be executed? If so, he had failed to give Arthur any legal grounds for writing an order granting a new sentencing hearing. He slumped in his chair and watched the clouds outside his window without coming to any earth-shattering conclusions about the play or Jefferson. He sighed and rang up Professor Kennedy and asked if he might enjoy discussing classical drama over a pitcher of beer after rehearsal that evening.

The rehearsal went badly as Arthur's mind kept wandering back to Jefferson's case and to Medea and to the worried look in Suzanne's eyes the night before. To make matters worse, the year's first round of pollen settled in his throat on the walk to the college, and the quick sip of water he snatched outside the rehearsal room went down the wrong way. Physically and spiritually distracted, he missed a cutoff in the first part of the *King David*.

"That was a beautiful note, nameless tenor," Ms. Henderson remarked to the delight of the chorus. "So nice of you to sing it when we could all hear it." His other transgressions were thankfully harder to pinpoint from the podium.

"Somebody's breathing after measure 84." She peered around the room. "There's no breath marked there; you only breathe when I tell you to."

When rehearsal was over, Arthur and Kennedy slipped out into the cool night air and made their way to the bar. The darkness provided a blessed escape from the hawk-like gaze of their director.

"So, why the sudden interest in Euripides?" Kennedy asked as they crossed the street in front of the Wild Boar. "Switching careers to ancient drama critic?"

"God, no. *Medea* is sort of related to a case I'm working on."
The middle-aged professor gave him an intrigued look.

"But I'm not quite sure how. That's why I want to talk to you."

"Well, I haven't read it since I was an undergrad, but I saw a production the drama department did about three years ago." They walked to the back of the bar. The place was crowded, so they were stuck in the corner booth next to a pair of chain smokers.

"What did you think of the performance?"

"Well, it was kind of a weird feminist production. Jason was the villain and Medea the victim." He sipped the beer and tilted the mug at Arthur. "I don't think they changed the dialogue, but the way the lines were delivered and the costumes and casting, even the advertising, all had a very modern feel. Making it relevant to our times, that sort of thing."

"But did you like it?"

"Not really. I'm an historian." He straightened his shoulders and explained. "I want to imagine myself sitting like a good Greek citizen two thousand years ago, experiencing the cathartic purge of the tragedy."

"Like a fresh bran muffin."

Kennedy was a rather doughy fellow, with a quick smile that lit up his entire face and a nervous habit of brushing his sandy-colored hair out of his eyes with a flick of his left hand. He spoke with a faded northeastern burr but spiced his conversation with the vocabulary of the South. "Do y'all have a case with a woman who murdered her kids?"

"No, no women on the docket, thank goodness." Arthur paused for a second, trying to figure out a way to get the professor's opinion without specifically mentioning the Jefferson case. "Look, does Medea deserve the death penalty?"

"I don't believe in the death penalty at all . . . so no."

"God, you sound like Phil." He sighed and tried another tack. "Just tell me . . . in a state which has the death penalty, like this one, is she the sort of killer who qualifies for it?"

He took a second to consider his answer and then peered over his glass. "Well, she's a multiple child killer. If you're going to have objective categories of really nasty murderers, that would be a logical place to start."

"Yeah, but if you had made it to your second year in law school"—Arthur smiled—"you would have learned that in *Woodson v. North Carolina* the Supreme Court declared that fixed categories, where every murderer of a particular type gets the death penalty, are unconstitutional." He paused and took a long draught of his beer. "You've got to consider the mitigating circumstances in each individual case."

"Well, if you want me to play devil's advocate." The professor warmed to the task. "I'd say she's a poor candidate for the death penalty."

"How come?"

"First, I don't think she killed her kids out of some sick pleasure of killing. She's not a psychopath. All the evidence prior to the crime indicates that she loved them. She doesn't kill for personal gain, monetary or otherwise. In fact, she's pretty ripped up by the whole experience. She gets nothing out of it; it's a very self-destructive act."

"You mean she's committing some kind of symbolic suicide? Killing her kids in despair? Why not kill herself too?"

"No, I don't think that's it. The murders are a last-ditch effort to communicate with Jason. None of her other attempts to get through to him worked. The murders are a sick way of expressing her pain."

"Interesting theory, counselor."

"Thank you"—he laughed and stood up—"but it's actually my wife's. We had a fight on the way home from the play, and that was her explanation why I shouldn't hate it."

He left for the bathroom, and Arthur cracked peanuts and contemplated the patterns in the veneer overlaying the table. Did Kennedy's theory include mercy for Medea?

"Okay," Arthur started before his friend could sit down, "I assume your wife doesn't endorse child killing as a reasonable means of self-expression. Most murderers, at some level, have reasons why they kill, or at least we can guess at their motives. How do we tell which reasons deserve a life sentence and which ones don't? Should we automatically give the death penalty to people who don't seem to have any reason at all?"

"Pam was just trying to defend the ending of the play—why the gods help Medea escape to Athens rather than punish her." He shrugged. "I'll invite you over to dinner and you can ask whether she has an overarching theory about capital punishment."

Kennedy changed the subject and described the candidate his colleagues wanted to hire to teach their law courses. He tried to explain departmental politics while Arthur's mind stumbled over the blood-slippery terrain left by Medea and Averill Jefferson. Had Jefferson, like Medea, been reduced to communicating his pain through an outrageous act of violence?

According to the comments in his file, Jefferson had poor verbal skills. Because of his respect for his evangelical parents and their disapproval of his choice for a wife, he could not confide in them. Although he had hunting and fishing buddies, he had no close friends. His wife disdained his complaints and suspicions, treating him like a dumb beast, incapable of feeling. Violence might have become the only means to let the world know of his suffering. But the law must assume, he argued with himself, that violence is always a choice among other constructive options. It cannot let people off the hook just because they have a comprehensible reason for expressing their pain in a totally unacceptable manner.

Suzanne was not waiting for him when he arrived home, so he crept quietly upstairs, undressed in the bright moonlight, and crawled into bed. When he pulled back the covers, he was greeted by the sight of a voluptuous figure bundled warmly in black tights and a sweatshirt. He crawled into bed and positioned himself to receive the maximum force of the heat generated by her back. Suzanne grunted and muttered something unintelligible as he snuggled closely to her. Sneaking his left hand over the curve of her hip, he brushed the bottom of her sweater aside and ran the tips of his fingers over the lower part of her rib cage and in between her breasts.

"Unh, unh . . . sleepy," she murmured, but his hands kept wandering until she grunted again, rolled on her back, raised her hips, and slipped off her tights.

Thirty minutes later, they were both wide awake. While he brushed his teeth, she slipped her night clothes back on and sorted out the tangle of sheets and blankets.

Thick dark hair streamed over the mound of pillows propping up her head. "Have you finished with your case yet?"

He spat into the bathroom sink.

"Having exhausted my legal sources, I spent the day examining the Euripides angle."

"What?"

He explained the Judge's strange request and summarized his conversation with Kennedy. She had seen the same performance and shared his wife's sympathy for Medea.

"Fine, but how can you reconcile your total loathing of Jefferson with your sympathy for Medea?" He lay back down next to her. "They both commit horrible crimes in response to infidelity, and I'll bet you a million dollars that if Jefferson and his wife had kids, he would have killed them instead of the little girl."

"Now, that's a novel approach"—she scowled—"defending a man by arguing that he would have preferred to kill his own kids."

"You're avoiding the question! Do we agree that Medea and Jefferson both killed to communicate the pain of being rejected by their lovers?" He propped himself up on one elbow to look more easily into her face. "Putting your revulsion aside, do you think Jefferson should die?"

Intelligent individuals are natural lawyers and Suzanne, no exception to the rule, responded with her own question. "Did you feel bad when you recommended that Gottlieb be executed?"

"Not at the time." He thought about it a moment. "It's irrelevant now."

"Would you feel bad if you wrote the memo that got Jefferson executed?"

"I don't know," he admitted. "Should I?"

"What's the difference Gottlieb and Jefferson? Just the number of people they killed?" He pushed himself upright and sat cross-legged across from her.

"No, it's not just the number. The big difference is those creepy interviews with Gottlieb. He had this hungry part of him that enjoyed controlling someone's life. Maybe all of us—or maybe just men—have this horrible little remnant deep inside. Instead of locking it away, he fed it."

"What about Jefferson?"

Arthur shrugged. "He fell in love."

She rolled over and looked at him.

"He indulged in a perfectly understandable passion for a sexy young woman. Passion leads to violence all the time, but we still think of love as a good thing. Everyone tells us we're supposed to fall in love." He watched her smooth out the blanket with the palm of her left hand. "Shouldn't you be nodding your head at all my brilliant insights?"

She smiled weakly. "I'm thinking about an article I read in the paper last week. It was about a guy in San Francisco who received his final divorce papers on a day he had custody of his daughter. After he signed them, he put her in the stroller, walked out onto the Golden Gate Bridge, threw her off, and jumped in after her."

"Medea raises her head again?"

"Maybe so." He flipped the lights off and they lay back down in each other's arms. She burrowed her head deep into his shoulder and eventually fell still as he lay awake, wrestling with the problem of finding a legal box in which to put Medea.

XXIV.

CALL ME

When Arthur got to work on Friday, Ms. Stillwater told him that Jefferson's petition had already worked its way through the state courts. It was in the hands of a federal district judge and was expected to arrive officially in chambers later in the afternoon. The execution was scheduled for Monday morning at 6:00 a.m., so the Judge would be casting his vote as a member of a three-judge appellate panel over the weekend. Arthur spent the morning searching for exceptions to the rule that prevented Jefferson from introducing his evidence, but nothing excused the patent attorney's failure to argue that the jury should have seen it before sentencing him. He found several cases holding that newly discovered evidence of a petitioner's innocence could constitute grounds for granting a stay of execution, but he found little hope for someone who had admitted his guilt.

Just before lunch, he ran across a cryptic paragraph in a Supreme Court opinion that hinted a narrow exception might be available in some circumstances when guilt was admitted. Unfortunately, the language was nearly incomprehensible. The Court mysteriously suggested that it might excuse procedural failures like Jefferson's if new evidence demonstrated that he was "actually innocent of his death sentence," as opposed to being innocent of his crime, whatever that meant.

The case was three years old, and he checked to see how later cases had interpreted the language. After a couple of minutes of searching on the computer, he leaned back and stared at the screen. The relevant language had been quoted in a dozen opinions, but not a single judge had taken the Court up on its invitation to find someone "actually innocent" of a death sentence. In fact, a number of judges had metaphorically thrown their hands up in consternation over what the phrase could possibly mean. One thing was clear: If the Judge ordered a new sentencing hearing for Jefferson, he would run the risk of being reversed. The legal history of 1960s proved that he was not afraid of controversy, but it was impossible to say whether he was still willing to make new law in the 1980s. Innovation was a job for judges, not for law clerks, he reminded himself as he went back to his office to write his memo.

The report reminded the Judge of how the incompetency of Jefferson's first habeas attorney prevented the court from considering his evidence. Arthur summarized the contents of the affidavits and medical reports and discussed the theoretical possibility of arguing that Jefferson was actually innocent of his death sentence. In conclusion, he noted the great reluctance that other courts had shown in implementing the exception, but unlike previous communications with the Judge, the memo did not make a recommendation. Jefferson would be saved only if the Judge were willing to blaze a trail for him. All Arthur could do was inform him of the route he might take and warn him that it passed through uncharted territory.

He did not mention *Medea*. He would talk with the Judge about the play when he handed him the memo. Discussing the Medea archetype with Kennedy and Suzanne had changed his mind about one aspect of Jefferson's case. For him, the crime was no longer "especially heinous," the only aggravating factor that provided the legal justification for his sentence. If the jury had felt the same way, Jefferson might not have been condemned. Did that mean he was innocent of his death sentence? This was a question to raise with the Judge as they discussed the play. He held the memo tightly in his hand as he walked down the hall to the Judge's chambers.

"Can I talk to the big guy?"

"He's on the phone, Arthur," Ms. Stillwater replied.

He slid the papers on her desk. "I'll come back in a couple of minutes, then."

He walked into the library to wait and found Phil massaging his temples, head bowed over a stack of *Supreme Court Reports*. He brushed his friend's shoulder with his hands as he walked by.

"I'm coming up empty, Art." Phil looked up, his eyes almost feverish. "What if there just isn't any ground to grant a stay of execution?"

"Then tell the Judge that." Arthur sat down. "Just lay out everything you've found. That's what I'm doing."

"And then Watkins dies."

"Maybe . . . but that's not your fault," Arthur insisted. "It's the trial judge, the prosecutor, Congress, and Georgia voters who are responsible. Let them feel bad."

"Do you think they will?" Phil spat out his frustration. "I don't think any of them give a shit."

"Just leave it for the Judge."

"Since when do we do that anyway?" Phil argued, fists clenched on the table. "How many times has he overruled our memos since we got here?" Arthur was silent. "How many?" he repeated.

"None."

"That's right." He shook his head and dared his friend to disagree. "On the one case that really matters, I'm not going to just punt and leave it for the Judge."

"I get it." Arthur nodded. "You do what you have to do. Just remember, you're not God."

"Yeah, I know." Phil sighed. "If I was, I could give Sergeant Watkins his old life back."

"Maybe"—Arthur smiled—"but I don't see your image on the ceiling of the Sistine Chapel."

"Huh? Oh . . . God giving life to Adam." Phil returned his friend's smile and extended his arm, finger crooked downward across the table in imitation of the white-bearded creator in Michelangelo's fresco. Arthur leaned his head sideways, trying to capture the doleful look on Adam's face as he reached his own bent finger across the table to receive the spark of life.

"What are you boys doing?" Ms. Stillwater stared in wonder.

"Uh," Phil replied sheepishly, "I was just giving life to Adam."

"Is the Judge off the phone yet?" Arthur asked before the confused secretary could comment further. "I really need to talk to him."

"He just left, but I did give him your memo."

"Is he coming in tomorrow morning?" Calling the Judge at home to discuss *Medea* was not an appealing prospect.

"I'm sure he will," Ms. Stillwater assured him. "I'm certainly going to be here, and you know as well as I do that he's got work to finish this weekend." She sniffed. "And we all know that he never comes in on Sunday."

"Well then, Ms. Stillwater, here's something I hoped never to say on a Friday afternoon: see you tomorrow morning."

The house was empty when Arthur got home and the weather mild, so he opened the windows in the television room and sat down to look at the mail. Among the catalogs and invitations to apply for new credit cards lay a small cardboard box that contained a recording of *King David* that he had ordered several weeks before. A fragrant breeze filled the room as he read the liner notes. Although the performance was only a few weeks away, a few passages continued to elude him, so he fetched the score and put on the music. He listened through the choruses, forcing himself to sip a beer whenever he felt the urge to sing. In practice, he seldom had the luxury to relax and listen to how all the vocal parts were woven together. Professor Henderson constantly admonished them to "listen to each other," but he usually took this as a challenge to stay in tune, rather than to appreciate the structure of the piece. He turned up the volume so that the passersby could hear.

He leaned his head back, put his feet up on the coffee table, and let the music wash over him. But he could not get comfortable. Images of Gottlieb and his father and Jefferson flashed in his head, and he could not shake the feeling that his life was fraying bit by bit. The logic of his decision making, his commitment to law itself, was assaulted by the emotional chaos of the music. Phil's despair in the library suddenly seemed a more honest response to their predicament then his own fatalism.

When the last chorus finished, he drained his beer, got another, took up his score, and started to run through it from the beginning. As he was wailing away on the last measures of the longest section, he heard the door shut behind him. Assuming it was Suzanne, he finished with a dramatic flourish and spun to face her.

"Bravo!" Melanie stood in the hallway, smiling and jangling a set of keys.

"Hey." He turned the stereo down and patted his front pants pocket. Empty. He had left his keys at the office. He hadn't noticed because Suzanne, as usual, had left the door to the house unlocked. "You didn't have to bring those! This is way out of your way. You should have just called."

"Well, Ms. Stillwater did call, but I guess you couldn't hear the phone." She nodded at the stereo and looked around the room and down the hall. "Nice place! I wish I could walk to work."

"It is pretty sweet. You want a beer?"

"Sure."

Arthur offered her a seat on the sofa and went to the kitchen.

"When's the performance?" she asked when he returned and handed her a bottle of Beck's. "I'd love to come."

They made small talk for a bit, first about the house, which she was seeing for the first time, and then about the Judge, their usual topic of conversation. She was lovely with her hair tied back and more relaxed than Arthur had ever seen her, feet up on the coffee table, seemingly oblivious to the amount of thigh she was showing or the warmth she projected whenever she made eye contact and smiled.

A treacherous little part of him wondered what would happen if he gave her a tour of the house that ended in his bedroom. The mere thought prompted his beer to go down the wrong way, and he fought a losing battle to keep from spraying the room with a regurgitated mist of barley malt and fine German hops. He stood up and pounded on his chest, while Melanie laughed and rubbed his back. When the coughing subsided, she snaked her arms around his waist.

"Do you need the Heimlich maneuver?" she whispered in his ear. "I'm pretty good at it."

His back tingled with the pressure of her firm belly, but the specter of a surprise return by Suzanne jolted him from temptation. He shook his head harder than was absolutely necessary, and she slowly withdrew her hands. As he straightened back up and cleared his throat, she leaned against the door frame and observed his recovery. Her expression was inscrutable, something between mildly offended and amused.

"Someday I'll learn to drink," he gasped and forced a grin.

She smiled back. "Well, I better be going. Thanks for the drink!" She turned and left with a provocative flounce.

He breathed a sigh of relief and watched her through the window as she walked to her car. When she drove away, he turned to the picture of King David on the cover of the album. "That's how you should have dealt with that Bathsheba chick."

★ ★ ★

As she drove away from Arthur's house, Melanie wondered what had come over her. Not that she was embarrassed. Where she grew up, playful flirtation was not necessarily meant to lead anywhere. And he had felt uncomfortable, so she had backed off. No big deal. But the attraction she had momentarily felt seemed real, and that could be a problem. After a rocky start, they were now working well together. His comments on her work inevitably made it better, and she felt like he was finally taking her seriously. Developing feelings for him would upset a delicate equilibrium.

He's just so cute, she thought, *and I haven't been with a guy since last summer.* This season of celibacy was wearing thin.

Instead of going home, Melanie drove her car back to the courthouse. She had decided to contact Jennifer Huffman and arrange for them to meet when she made her interview trip to Cravath, Swaine, and Moore. When she got back to her office, she dialed the number she found in the Martindale-Hubbell directory of American lawyers.

"Could I speak to Jennifer Huffman, please."

"I'll connect you," then, "Hello?"

"Hi! I'm Melanie Wilkerson, and I'm currently doing a federal clerkship in Clarkeston, Georgia." She spoke brightly, an eager young prospect trying to impress a potential future colleague. "I'm coming up to New York to interview with y'all next Thursday, and I was hoping we could get together for a cup of coffee. It'd be awesome to talk with someone who's already made the transition from Clarkeston to Cravath."

"I'd be happy to." She sounded friendly and honestly interested in helping out a fellow high-flier. "I'm not on the interview team this year but that doesn't matter. How did you know that I clerked in Clarkeston?"

"I met April Duncan. When she heard I was interviewing at New York firms, she said that you'd be a good person to talk to." She was making a big assumption that April and Jennifer had not been deadly enemies. "I'm not quite sold on moving to New York versus staying closer to home in Atlanta. It'd be nice to hear the thoughts of someone who's actually spent time in Georgia."

"Of course." She paused for a moment. "I don't know how much help I'll be. It was quite a traumatic year. I'm sure April told you that one of my friends died."

"She did mention it." Melanie wondered whether she should say anything more or drop the subject. Since Jennifer had first broached it, she decided to put out a feeler. "It must have been horrible, and no one's forgotten about it here. We've got Carolyn's mother constantly calling the chambers to bug us."

"Are you kidding? I thought she only bothered me. That woman is whacko. She thinks everyone in the courthouse conspired to kill her daughter."

"What do you tell her?"

"The truth. I saw Carolyn that evening, and she was hopping mad at the Judge about something. I tried to calm her down, but she just kept getting more and more worked up. By the time she charged out of my office, she was practically foaming at the mouth. It's no wonder she slipped."

"Wow!" She feigned surprise at the news. "Did she say what the Judge had done? Or why?"

"Not really," Jennifer said as she expelled an audible breath. "She was pretty vague about the details. But she wasn't vague about how she felt about him. Her last words to me were, 'I'm gonna kill that sonofabitch.' I didn't tell Mrs. Bastaigne that, though. No sense throwing fuel on the fire."

She was taken aback by Huffman's frankness. She could not think of a quick follow-up question and decided she should wait until they were face-to-face. "Well, this year has been a lot less exciting, thank goodness. I'm really looking forward to seeing you in New York . . ."

Jennifer rang off cordially, leaving Melanie to sit in her office and ponder the information that had fallen into her lap.

The image of Carolyn charging out of Judge Meyers's chambers was not difficult to conjure. She had always imagined Carolyn as a spoiled brat who never lacked anything. How would she react to running into a brick wall like the Judge, someone who could smash her dreams without a hearing or appeal? She could imagine the frustration and surge of emotion. And to whom else had Carolyn complained and blustered? What other threats had the enraged young clerk made? Anyone who loved the Judge, anyone who wanted to protect him, would have plenty of motivation to defend him. A violent argument with Carolyn could have ended in a tumble down the stairs. Misadventure or accident were more likely than murder given the volatile person that Jennifer Huffman described. Where had April been that evening? Or her co-clerk?

One thing at a time, Melanie thought as she headed home. Go to New York, get as much information as you can, and then reevaluate.

★ ★ ★

When Arthur got to the courthouse on Saturday morning, the old limestone building was devoid of its usual bustle. Only four cars, none of them the Judge's, were parked in the gated lot. He let himself in through the loading dock door at the back of the building and walked silently down the cool marble halls, meeting no one until Ms. Stillwater greeted him from behind her desk.

"Arthur! I tried to call you a while ago but you'd already left home." She frowned, distressed at her inefficiency. "You can go back if you want. The Judge called a half an hour ago to say that he and Judge Byrd and Judge McIntosh had tentatively decided not to enter a stay in the Jefferson case." He stared at her and bit his lip. "Since they were in agreement, they did everything by phone. I'm sorry that I couldn't get a hold of you earlier."

Arthur went back to his office and spun helplessly in his chair. The train had left the station, and he had missed it. He drummed his fingers rapidly on the table and reminded himself that the Judge was just one vote out of three. Arthur could not change things unilaterally even if he wanted to, even if he could convince the Judge that *Medea* was somehow relevant to Jefferson's case. His stupid thoughts about a play didn't really matter. But then why had the Judge given him the book? For that matter, why was he working here in the first place? Suddenly, he was tired of being passive. He wanted the Judge to save Jefferson's life, and he walked quickly back down the hall to Ms. Stillwater.

"There's something I forgot to put in the memo," he said forcefully, before he lost his nerve. "That's what I wanted to talk to him about today. Do you think I could call him at home? I don't have his number."

"He wouldn't mind at all, Arthur, but he's gone into Atlanta with his wife. They're not going to be back until late this evening, but I'm sure it'd be fine for you to call him on Sunday."

She wrote down the number, and he drifted through the rest of Saturday, working in a desultory fashion until late afternoon, trying to catch up on the bench memos due for the next sitting. He was just about to leave when he got a phone call from William Redwine, chief attorney at the Office of Legal Counsel. He reminded Arthur of their meeting in Washington and apologized for the office's delay in getting back to him. Then, without any further elaboration, he offered Arthur the job of his dreams. He could start on July 15, and all his reasonable moving expenses would be paid for by the government. Due to time pressures at OLC, he would need to respond to the offer within ten days.

Someone had once told him that smart offerees always say "thank you" and then pretend to consider the offer for a reasonable period of time, but he had no stomach for mock indecision. He told Redwine that it would be his pleasure to join the most exclusive group of lawyers in the United States.

When he left, Ms. Stillwater had already gone, and there was nobody around with whom to share the news. He called Phil, but his friend's answering machine reminded him that he was out of town for the weekend. He resisted the impulse to call Melanie and left for home. Suzanne was visiting her sister in Augusta, so he rocked on the porch of the empty house and watched television before making supper. When she returned late in the night, Suzanne found him on the sofa and tucked a comforter gently under his chin before carrying Maria to bed.

XXV

MOTHER AND CHILD REUNION

The next morning, Suzanne lured Arthur out of bed with the smell of gourmet breakfast. After packing Maria off for an early play date, she wafted the aroma of fresh ground coffee and frying bacon up the stairs like a smoke signal and soon heard the shower running. The comfort of the warm kitchen soothed her nerves and steadied her for the conversation they were going to have. Eventually, she heard his footsteps down the hall and felt him sneak up behind her and kiss the fine hairs on the back of her neck while she stirred potatoes and onions in a heavy black skillet.

"Stop it!" She reached back and shoo'd him away. "I'm going to burn myself! Pour a cup of coffee and sit down."

Sunlight streamed through the back window as she moved from range to cabinet to refrigerator and finally spun around to present him with a steaming plate of homemade hash browns, bacon, and a cheese omelet. He attacked the food, but she had little appetite. A nibble of bacon cramped in her stomach, and she dumped extra cream into her coffee to cut its bitterness. When Arthur finally came up for air, she leaned back in her chair and let out a deep sigh.

"I sent Maria over to Judy's house so we could talk." She reached over the table and squeezed his hand. "Arthur, I've thought a long time about how to tell you this, but I just don't know a good way." She met his gaze and held it. She was filled both with love and the poignant certainty that she was stronger than he was.

"I found out last Friday that I'm pregnant."

The compressor on the refrigerator kicked on and hummed quietly. Arthur said nothing. He stared intently at a mole on the back of his hand, unmoving, as if stillness might dissolve the whole scene and ravel it back to some safe place.

"I know this is out of the blue," she spoke in a quiet voice. "Let's go sit in the living room."

She took his hand as they walked slowly into the parlor. She sat down first, then scooted closer to him on the sofa where they had first kissed five months before.

"Talk to me."

The secret out, she was calmer. After a few silent moments, she managed a weak smile. "You look like I just hit you over the head with my skillet."

"You sort of did."

She imagined him trying to see into possible futures of marriage, birth, adoption, abortion. He looked like he might lay his breakfast on the thick wool rug covering the living room floor.

Arthur hunched forward on the sofa. Suzanne rubbed his back through his flannel shirt and said, without any trace of guile or regret, "I know what you're thinking, and I'm not suggesting we get married." She felt another wave of nausea hit him.

"Why not?" he managed weakly.

"You know why ... My home is here. I'd rather be a single mother in Clarkeston—hell, I already am—than be a lawyer's wife up north." She put her hand on Arthur's knee and squeezed with emphasis as she spoke. "I love my life here. We've talked about this before, and I understand your dreams. You'd be miserable here wondering what you might have done in Washington."

They sat and looked at anything but each other for a long time, examining cracks on the walls and listening to mowers start up around the neighborhood. She hoped he wasn't working up the courage to *do the right thing* and nobly sacrifice his career for her imagined well-being. Judy would think she was crazy. All she saw was a nice, handsome guy with unlimited potential. She hadn't seen the clouds gathering around him. She hadn't seen his reaction to the pressures of the Judge's chambers. Immature and wounded was not an attractive characteristic in a future spouse. She loved him and would heal him if she could, but imposing a marriage on him was out of the question.

"Suzanne, will you marry me?" He looked up at her, still half-crouched over the floor. Sisyphus rolling his stone looked more enthusiastic. "We can stay here in Clarkeston. It'll be easy for me to get a job after working for the Judge. Things will work out."

She shook her head.

"Thanks, Arthur, but this isn't a fairy tale." She sat up straight and explained the facts without hesitation. She had spent the last forty-eight hours working things out. "I've had longer to think about this than you. I've had one less than perfect marriage, and I'm not going to risk another because I've frustrated my husband's lifelong ambitions." Her voice picked up intensity. "And I'm not willing to risk Maria's feelings either. The last thing she needs is another family to fall apart on her. And I don't even know whether I want another baby. It's a huge responsibility, and there's nothing fun about being pregnant . . . Marriage is not the answer."

She thought she could see relief on his face.

"If you keep the baby, I'll support you completely." He straightened up and finally made eye contact. "I'll be making enough money in Washington to help all the way through college. I'm not perfect, but I'm not a prick."

"I know that. That's one of the reasons why I love you."

"I love you too."

They held each other tightly, but the warmth and comfort that had seen them through a winter of uncertainty had faded, and Suzanne released him and wiped a tear out of the corner of her eye. She slid back into the corner of the sofa. There was more to talk about. The decision not to marry answered only one important question, and she wanted to know what Arthur thought about other matters.

"What would you think if I decided not to keep it?"

"I've got no legal right to interfere with that decision," Arthur replied immediately.

"I understand, counselor." She sighed at his knee-jerk legal correctness. "But I'm not asking for a legal opinion. I'm asking how you would feel if I terminated the pregnancy?"

Arthur's mouth was set in a thin line as he leaned back in the sofa and studied the grooves etched in the beaded board ceiling. His left temple pulsed as he ground his back molars against each other.

"I'm sorry to be sarcastic," she added gently. "You've probably never thought through this before." But a sudden wince told her otherwise. "Oh . . . you want to tell me about it?"

He shut his eyes, as if to keep errant memories from slipping through the cracks of his consciousness. "We should talk about you today, not me." His voice strained to the breaking point.

"Maybe so, but right now I'd like to hear about you."

★ ★ ★

When he finally spoke, Arthur found himself back in college, sitting in the student health clinic, watching an ashen-faced Julia return with the news that her IUD had somehow failed to prevent the union of sperm and egg. They were nineteen. It was the spring of their sophomore years, and they were utterly unable to comfort each other. Pointless questions abounded: "How could this happen?" "What should we do?" The answer to the first question was self-evident and the answer to the second was so elusive that all attempts to find it ended in bewilderment and frustration.

Being engaged to be married complicated rather than eased their predicament. If they had been casual lovers, the choice to terminate the pregnancy might have been more easily made. Preventing a disastrously forced marriage or single parenthood might have justified drastic action. As it was, they loved each other and planned to spend the rest of their lives together. Those plans, however, did not involve one of them quitting school and caring for an infant. Or working a job at night to make extra money. Or explaining to their parents why they could not wait to marry until after graduation. Or changing anything in their enjoyable routine of attending class, studying, socializing, making love, and sleeping late.

Arthur suggested having the baby and putting it up for adoption, but Julia would not consider an option that involved all the discomfort and scandal of an unwed pregnancy without any of the countervailing joy of being a mother. He understood her attitude but thought that abortion might be a big enough sin to justify the trouble. Arthur was concerned with the question of sin. His intuition told him that abortion was wrong—at least for two intelligent middle-class people capable of caring for a child. And it was such a conscious premeditated wrong, not like his usual transgressions of inadvertence or omission.

Julia was more afraid of the procedure itself than the detrimental effect it might have on her immortal soul. Given she was raised a Roman Catholic, Arthur found this bizarre. Although his liberal-minded splinter of the Lutheran church supported a woman's right to choose, she had been relentlessly taught that abortion was a mortal sin. She nonetheless displayed a childlike faith that God would understand, irrespective of how many priests and nuns had warned her otherwise. He hesitated to argue that she did not understand her own religion, for fear of making her as miserable as him.

She eventually told him that the university clinic had made an appointment for her at an excellent facility in the northern suburbs of Chicago. Her eyes, dark brown, intelligent, and passionate, told him that her decision was irrevocable. Her complexion was perfect, hair thick and golden, her beautifully proportioned body not yet betraying her condition. He did not argue. Instead, he promised himself to make her choice bearable, even if it meant being quietly miserable.

His tale sputtered to a halt, and Suzanne urged him to go on. "I'd really like to hear the rest . . . "

"I've never told anyone before." He squeezed his eyes shut and pressed his fingers against his temple. "I don't know why you want to hear it."

"I always like to hear the truth, Arthur."

"Yeah, but honesty isn't always a good policy." He considered saying more, but stopped himself. "If you really want to know what I think, let me get something."

He went up to his room and returned a few minutes later with a thin sheaf of papers. "This is as far as I ever got in sorting things out. It's a stupid short story I've never shown to anybody —written in the first person by the Devil." He handed it to her and shrugged. "Don't make fun of my writing—I was nineteen and pretty drunk when I did this."

The Devil and Lemroy Webster

On the evening of February 23, 1979, Lemroy Webster found himself with a severe stomach ache. His girlfriend Eileen was pregnant, and he was staring an abortion right in the face.

Now, abortions are odd things, and I always pay attention to people who have the bad luck to get themselves into the unwed pregnancy situation.

Some unimaginative people do not think twice about driving down to the clinic, nodding their heads at the counselor's words of wisdom, and laying down to listen to the low murmur of their problem being aspirated away. A much smaller group hates themselves so much before, during, and afterward that even I find their mental state unattractive. However, others, like Lemroy, tend to view the event as a more complicated threat to their morality and the rightness of their relationship to The Big Guy. These people can be fun.

I was initially drawn to the utter hopelessness of Lemroy's position. Having been hypothetically opposed to abortion all his life, he suddenly found himself being seduced by this seemingly straightforward solution to his problem. It was senseless cursing the sperm who had fought its way past Eileen's IUD; he had tough decisions to make.

What were his options? Having the baby and embarrassing two families who considered unmarried pregnancies an historical relic left behind on the journey to upper-middle class? Being chained to an unknown other for at least eighteen years? Maybe even dropping out of school? Life should not end at twenty. That left mortal sin as the only reasonable choice.

I've found that people who are not used to committing mortal sins usually have a great deal of trouble with their first one, especially when it has to be premeditated and anticipated. So, I decided to pay Lemroy a visit.

Lemroy had a sense of humor, so I crept up behind him and whispered in his ear.

"Boo!" He almost hit the ceiling. It was a cheap laugh, but I couldn't resist.

"Who are you? How'd you get in here? The door is locked!"

"You know who I am."

He stared for a moment through narrowed eyes and said, "You mean . . ."

"Yup."

He looked firm, determined—not really scared. People of real faith are always a pleasure to deal with. He spoke clearly. "Why don't you leave? You know where I stand. I'd rather be tortured than give up anything to you. There's nothing for you here."

"Don't be so defensive. I just want to talk."

"About what?"

"I think you know."

"I suppose I can guess." He paused a moment. "Well, you should be happy. We've already made an appointment at the clinic for next weekend. So, you're only going to be wasting your breath."

I gave him an amused look. "What makes you think I'm so pro-abortion? Every procedure means one less potential soul to add to my collection."

"Nice rationalization, but I don't believe it for a second. I know God can't be too wild about them, and I'm sure they give you plenty of good opportunities."

"True, of course. But, Lemroy, it's more complex than that, isn't it? You see, there's a wrong decision for everybody in all situations, and we really haven't worked out a bright-line policy to apply in all cases."

Lemroy looked a little perplexed and put down his pen. He tilted his head at me and spoke while unbending a paper clip on his desk.

"That means I've been wasting my time worrying and feeling guilty, because I might really be doing the right thing?"

"Or the wrong thing," I added.

"Now, don't give me this flexible morality, each to his own, bullshit. If that's the way things really worked, you wouldn't be here, would you? There's a right thing to do and a wrong thing to do, period."

"Well, Lemroy, if that's the case, then which are you going to choose?"

"You know which . . . and I know it's wrong."

"How do you think that's going to go over upstairs?"

"Probably not too well."

"Exactly, then maybe there is something for me here after all?"

This had him worried. He started breathing more deeply, and he leaned forward. He shut his eyes, opened them again, and then shut them for a long time.

"So, I've really no choice but to have the kid and go through all the parenting bullshit, since Eileen won't even hear of giving it up for adoption. Yeah, I'm going to make a wonderful father—I hate the brat already. But with my soul at stake, I really only have one option, don't I?"

"What makes you say that?"

"Well, what do you think? I'm not too keen on spending eternity standing knee-deep in shit with you watching reruns of *The Love Boat.*"

"You need to remember what I said. Maybe raising a child with your attitude would really be the wrong thing to do."

"So, what is the wrong decision then?"

"There's a hefty price tag on that." He was pissed off by my rather juvenile attempt at soul purchasing.

"Oh good. I sell you my soul and you tell me how to save it. How do you fool anybody with lines like that?

"No sense getting abusive."

"Look, what is the moral of all this? If there is no right or wrong, then you wouldn't exist. If I were damned if I do, damned if I don't, then you wouldn't have bothered me. And if there is a right and a wrong decision, then there's apparently no way for me to independently determine what it is."

"That sounds like a good moral. Don't you feel better?" I faded out with a cheerful, "Have a nice day."

Lemroy did feel somewhat better for a bit, marveling at the fact that although things looked hopeless, he at least would not be making the wrong decision premeditatively, because the wrong decision was no longer so cut and dried. It took Lemroy about five minutes to realize that he felt better as a result of a visit from me. His heart sunk, and what he planned to do weighed more heavily on him than before.

Humming to myself, I headed off to continue my rounds.

★ ★ ★

Suzanne finished reading and looked up. "You know, that was pretty good. It's really hard not to be preachy when you talk about this stuff."

"Not when you don't know what to preach."

"Do you still feel so conflicted?"

"Pretty much, I guess."

Suzanne cracked the window to let in the fresh spring air. One of the neighbors fired up a leaf blower, but the din was distant enough not to disturb their conversation. "I'll make some coffee and you can tell me the rest of the story."

Arthur got up and opened the window wider. The gauzy curtains blew far into the room. When Suzanne arrived with two steaming mugs, Arthur was sitting on the edge of the sofa, staring at the empty porch swing as it glided silently in the breeze.

★ ★ ★

After a lot of hand wringing, Arthur decided to approach a former roommate about borrowing a car for the trip to Chicago. He had not talked to Don for a year, but the awkwardness of renewing their acquaintance paled in comparison to the alternative of revealing to one of his close friends (and therefore to all his close friends) that he and Julia were stupid enough to get pregnant and venal enough to take the expedient way out. Don, who had once confided to Arthur that he had a similar problem in high school, readily agreed to the loan of his battered Plymouth Valiant. He assured Arthur that he could keep it overnight if Julia were unable to travel after the procedure. Given Don's promise of silence and his disconnection from their usual group of friends, the chance of any public stain on their reputation was slim.

Julia and Arthur conversed little as they sped through the bleak winter landscape to Chicago. She dozed much of the time as he piloted the boxy sedan through a narrow corridor of snowy cornfields, keeping his eyes on the black asphalt of the interstate and away from the glare of the brilliant white countryside. When they got to the outskirts of the farthest-flung suburbs, Julia straightened up in her seat. This was her home turf, and she seemed comforted by the familiar procession of exits and malls.

She turned to him. "You know you didn't have to help me."

"What else was I supposed to do? Abandon you? I'm not a shithead."

"I know, but you might have fought with me."

"And what good would that have done?" He chanced a glance at her as a semi roared by.

"I would have gone ahead anyway," she admitted firmly, "even if you were totally against it."

He wondered for a bright moment whether the clarity of her statement relieved him of responsibility. Did it mean that her decision was not his burden? Yet, Arthur could not make himself feel like a mere bystander. He could still have convinced her to marry him and have the baby. She might have resisted initially, but in the end she would have acquiesced. He had not even tried. Success would have meant becoming a father.

Eventually they arrived at the nondescript clinic, and a friendly, middle-aged receptionist confirmed the 9:30 a.m. appointment and handed Julia several pages of paperwork. "Hand those to Nurse Charone at the back desk when you're done."

Arthur had brought a novel to divert his attention while Julia was with the doctor, but he felt uncomfortable starting it while she was right beside him, so he absentmindedly flipped through back issues of *Time* and *Sports Illustrated* while she filled out the forms.

The waiting room was comfortable but unimaginatively decorated and furnished. Vinyl and fluorescence were dominant themes, relieved only by a couple of plants next to the nurse's desk. Limbo might be similarly appointed.

"Are you okay?" Arthur laid a hand on her back and awkwardly tried to massage through her thick winter coat.

"The closer it gets, the less real it seems."

"I love you."

"I love you too."

Arthur took her hand but did not embrace her. The stiff and worried postures of the others waiting around them deterred overt shows of affection. When the nurse returned, Julia brought her the papers, then walked back to Arthur and handed him her coat and purse. "They're ready now. I've got to talk with a counselor for a while and then they'll take me to the doctor."

She was grimmer and less sure of herself than before. "I'll see you after." Then, she turned and disappeared beyond the double doors at the far end of the waiting room.

Arthur spent the next three and one-half hours alternating between supplications to the Almighty and efforts to read his novel. He bargained with God for Julia's safety and peace of mind. He pledged a huge percentage of his future income to charity, promised to give up drinking, and resolved to tell his father to leave his share of the farm to his brother. He knew such offers were improper, if not blasphemous, but he knew no other way to seek comfort without begging forgiveness for something he had willed to happen.

At about one thirty, the double doors opened and a tight-lipped Julia emerged. She walked directly to Arthur and bent down to pick up her purse. She spoke softly. "Let's get out of here."

He helped her into her coat and followed her to the car. Icy ridges of snow lined the single-file trail to the parking lot, preventing him from supporting her with his arm as she walked. She picked her way across the glazed snowpack without incident and slid down into the passenger seat of the Valiant.

Arthur warmed up the car and asked gently. "How are you feeling?"

"Like I'm having a really bad period, but other than that, okay. What I really need is some food in my stomach before I retch."

The lines of fear and anxiety that had creased her porcelain skin for the last three weeks were gone. To his relief, they had not been replaced by trauma or grief. She looked tired, but strong. She returned Arthur's stare and nodded convincingly, "I'm okay."

After a quiet lunch, they filled a painkiller prescription and drove back. Before long, the sprawl of Chicago was just a gray smudge in his rear view mirror. He gazed at the sleeping figure beside him and realized with a sigh that they had gotten away with it. Neither one of them would have to drop out of school. There would be no painful scenes before parents and siblings. There would be no gossip or pity from friends and classmates. Not only was the problem gone, but the solution had been efficient and secret. Even the timing had worked out—they had only skipped Friday's classes and Julia would have all weekend to rest and recover.

When they got to the dorm, Julia crawled into bed and pulled the covers high up under her chin. "Turn off the light and bring me a glass of water, will you, sweetheart?"

He put his hand under her back as she leaned up to drink and set the half-empty glass on a desk within her reach. He kissed the patch of smooth cheek left uncovered by her down comforter.

"Do you want me to stay here and read to you?" She shook her head firmly, so convincingly at peace that Arthur gave her a final chaste kiss and departed quietly without misgivings about her safety.

Within a week, Julia was back to normal. Arthur could discern no difference in her attitude or mood. One awkward conversation about their trip to the clinic confirmed that he was the only one obsessed with affixing a meaning to the event. She saw no point in ruminating over something that was finished and irreversible. Arthur never broached the subject with her again, at least not until he needed ammunition in the middle of their divorce.

In the weeks after their trip, he brooded on what they had done and finally concluded that although they were equally culpable in theory, he was far more in the wrong. After all, she did not really consider it a serious sin—if she thought it a sin at all. She had not intentionally spit in God's face. Her actions were the moral equivalent of Arthur's failure to declare his penny ante poker winnings on his tax return. But he had known better. He knew the gravity of the wrong and the malice aforethought with which he had helped carry out the plan.

He eventually started avoiding Julia, taking his meals at odd hours and playing basketball every day at the university intramural complex until it closed. They talked on the phone when she called, but he found excuses not to visit her dorm room in the evening. She was annoyed, but too proud and independent to make any demands on him. They might have drifted completely apart, were it not for a chance encounter in front of the University Student Union.

In between classes, Arthur had stopped to listen to one of the rabid itinerant preachers who descended on the campus to harangue the students about the evils of their constant fornication, drug use, and substitution of rock and roll for God. The combination of their ridiculous literalism and heckling by the students provided some of the best free entertainment that the university had to offer.

"I know what sort of sinfulness you all engage in every night: FOR-NI-CA-SHUNNNNNNNNN!" Jeb thundered, a rail-thin figure in a stained down jacket who might have been mistaken for a street bum in another context.

"Could you point out some of the girls you're talking about?" a gawky student asked while Jeb was drawing a breath for his next tirade. "I've been trying to fornicate all semester, but I can't find anyone to fornicate with!"

Then, Jeb began reading lengthy passages from Saint Paul's letters in support of his thesis that all of the women on campus should be at home, either married and caring for their children or making their parents' lives easier. Purporting to speak for the outraged women in the audience (who had been maintaining an amused silence), a bearded graduate student attacked Jeb's thesis obscenely, screaming that Jeb was a "pea-brained shithead," punctuating his points with fist-shaking fury. Arthur listened to the two ideological enemies yell, the venom in their voices poisoning the splendor of the day around them. Prompted by some innate sense of fairness, Arthur found himself yelling to his classmate, "You're a philosophy major. Why don't you try using some logic?"

The sudden outburst earned him the curious stares of the onlookers and a string of invective from the student philosopher.

Jeb had no comment. He hated getting any support from the crowd. Arthur turned and walked quickly into the anonymity of the Student Center. As the butterflies in his stomach subsided, he sat down and watched the fountain misting in the interior courtyard of the spacious building. A moment later someone sat next to him.

"Excuse me. My name's Alan Whitehead, and I run the Presbyterian Student Center on Campus." The stranger looked to be in his midthirties, dressed in jeans and a flannel shirt. His face bore an expansive and genuine smile. "This may seem like a silly question, but I was wondering why you defended Jeb out there."

Arthur looked at the young minister and scooted around in his seat to face him. "I wasn't defending him—Jeb is a moron. It just bothers me to see a guy whom I know is a totally rational Marxist let himself get dragged down to Jeb's level . . . Rage isn't the right response to Jeb's blather, especially since he loves it so much."

"What is the right response then?" Whitehead asked. "That's something I struggle with because, as you can imagine, people like him don't help business very much."

"I don't know." Arthur shrugged. "You just have to forgive him for being such a fucking idiot. But that's kind of conde-scending, I suppose."

"I don't think it's condescending at all." The minister laughed. "I'm quite certain Jeb needs forgiveness—all he can get. I suppose if God can forgive some serial killer, then we should be able to tolerate old Jeb." He got up with a final word of praise about Arthur's skills as a theologian and left.

Arthur remained seated, watching the sunlight play on the mote-like spray of the fountain and wondering whether he agreed with Whitehead that God could forgive a serial killer. In theory, he thought He could. God could do whatever He wanted, which meant that theoretically God could forgive any-body for anything. Of course, that did not mean that He had to. But it never hurts to ask, thought Arthur. So, he did.

He stared at the fountain for a few minutes longer while the burden of his pride lifted a little. Before the abortion, he had never really done anything he thought was deeply wrong, but now he was no better than anybody else. He was surprised by the sense of freedom that came with the simple admission that he had failed. Having irretrievably lost perfection as a goal, he put his conceit behind him and breathed in deeply again and again. When the clock at the top of the student center chimed 1:00 p.m., Arthur remembered that the woman with whom he was desperately in love would be getting out of her math class in fifteen minutes. Forgetting his hunger, he rushed out of the building to find her.

★ ★ ★

The Georgia sun was warm on their backs when he finished his story. Arthur's focus remained inward as he stared vacantly across the room. Suzanne did not trust herself to speak. She felt an overwhelming longing to touch him, to heal him, but she could not move toward him. The impossibility of having him weighed on her like never before. Before she lost control, she stood up shakily and left the room.

XXVI

THEN EVERYTHING FALLS APART

Melanie sat in her office on Monday morning and imagined Carolyn Bastaigne's fury at losing her chance to work in New York, her desire to slander the Judge and somehow punish him for discovering her brilliant insider trading scheme. To whom had she raged? A number of different scenarios seemed plausible. She might have complained to her co-clerks or even Ms. Stillwater. Wanting to spare the Judge her anger, a protective person in his chambers could have hustled her into the hall and away from his office. A confrontation could easily have resulted in Carolyn fleeing into the stairwell, or perhaps an argument could have spilled into the stairwell itself where the unlucky girl might have tripped and fallen.

Of course, she might have threatened the Judge directly. It was hard to imagine the Judge chasing her, but it was possible. At a minimum, the Judge must have suspected something beyond an innocent slip on the way to get a candy bar. According to both Ms. Stillwater and Suzanne, the Judge had become withdrawn about the time of Carolyn Bastaigne's death. The closed curtains and his sour disposition suggested that he blamed himself for something. One thing seemed certain, someone knew more about Carolyn's fate and had covered up their involvement.

Her restlessness eventually drove her out of her office and down the hall to the library. She found Phil in his favorite seat, feet propped up on the conference table, reading cases.

"You want to go out for a cup of coffee?" she asked.

"In the middle of the morning?" He held up his coffee mug and gave her a questioning look. "What's wrong with Ms. Stillwater's brew?"

"Nothing. I just want to get out of here for a bit. Let's go," she pleaded. "The Judge isn't going to notice." He shrugged and stood up.

"Should we get Arthur too?"

"No," she replied with a shake of her head. "Leave him alone. He came in this morning looking like a zombie and locked himself in his office."

They slipped out of the courthouse into the cool morning air. A café had just opened in a former bank building, and the smell of fresh roasted coffee hit them as they turned the corner onto College Avenue. Melanie waited to speak until they were both served and seated.

"You're going to think I've gone nuts."

"I already think you're nuts." Phil smiled and dumped three packets of sugar into his mug. "Go ahead. What paranoid theory have you come up with now?"

She edged forward in her chair and pushed her drink to one side. "I spoke to Jennifer Huffman, and she started talking about Carolyn without being prompted. In fact, I kinda cut her off because I was getting freaked out. She says that on the day Carolyn died, she said she was really pissed at the Judge."

"So, Carolyn went down to Judge Myers's chambers after he talked to her."

"Definitely. What's even more interesting is her state of mind at the time. Jennifer said she was hopping mad and even threatened to kill Judge."

"Well, that's a pretty common turn of phrase." He shrugged and gave his coffee a stir.

"Yeah," she admitted while still pressing her point, "but Jennifer swore she was really worked up. She didn't say it, but it seems likely that Carolyn returned to chambers for another confrontation."

"Is there a record of a second meeting in the personnel file you looked at?" He blew on the top of his coffee and the small lenses of his wire-rimmed glasses fogged up.

"Nope. But remember that Sidney Dumont said that the Judge was the last person to see her alive, not Jennifer Huffman." She took a deep breath. "I've been thinking about this all weekend. Tell me if I'm crazy." She laid out her theory as if she were presenting a memo to the Judge. "I'm starting from the premise that Carolyn did not slip on the stairs on the way down to get a chocolate bar. I stood in that stairwell this morning and kicked off my shoes to check the traction." She stuck her feet out to show that she was not wearing nylons.

"It's virtually impossible to slip on marble in bare feet, even if you're in a hurry or careless. I think there must have been some sort of confrontation."

"Are you suggesting," Phil asked doubtfully, "that someone pushed Carolyn down the stairs?"

"Not necessarily," she cautioned with a tip of her mug. "But I can imagine her rushing in to yell at the Judge for ruining her career. Can you imagine how someone in the chambers would take that? The Judge threatened by a felon who broke the most sacred confidentiality rules in order to commit securities fraud?"

"One might get a little upset. I'll grant you that."

"A little? If she burst back into chambers spoiling for a fight, an argument could easily have spilled into the hallway.

"Think about it," she continued, caught up in the reenactment of the imagined events. "The biggest part of this mystery is why Carolyn took the stairs. She was lazy; she always took the elevator. But if someone was pursuing her, she might not wait for the elevator and face the music. She might be tempted to flee down the stairs."

"Maybe." He considered her version of events and nodded. "It makes some sense."

"Remember the coroner's report?" Melanie pushed her theory further to see his reaction. "It reports massive injuries to the back of her head. Now, that might have resulted from her twisting in the air as she fell, but it's also possible that she was facing away from the stairs when she tripped or . . ."

"Or what?" Phil asked, daring her to complete the thought.

Melanie frowned at him and sighed. "Or was pushed."

"You don't believe that, and neither do I." Now it was Phil's turn to frown. "It's true that the Judge is depressed, and we all know he's a hard-ass. But there's no way that someone in the chambers intentionally pushed Carolyn Bastaigne."

"I know, I know. But something happened in that stairwell. Something had to have happened. And I really can see someone following her into the hall."

"Fair enough," he replied. He took a sip of coffee and thought for a minute. "It's as plausible as the candy bar theory and provides a reason for the Judge's mood swing five years ago. He wouldn't be too broken up about a lousy clerk who had an unfortunate accident, but he might be bothered by a death caused directly by his phone call to Cravath."

He gave the coffee a couple of quick swirls and then looked up. "Is there any mention in Carolyn's file of Jennifer Huffman?"

"Definitely not." She shook her head. "And there was certainly nothing in the letter from the Justice Department."

"Okay," he admitted reluctantly. "But we're still missing something. For example, if Carolyn were having a knock-down, drag-out fight out with someone in the hallway, then why didn't anyone hear anything?"

★ ★ ★

The work week began for Arthur with a hot cup of coffee and a frustrating proofread of an opinion Melanie had written. Preoccupied with Sunday's drama, he took twice as long as usual to find typos and make substantive suggestions. He scanned the paper with little immediate comprehension, rereading the same paragraphs over and over before deciphering their meaning, unable to hang on to his ideas for how to improve it. The draft was already quite good, amenable mostly to minor changes, but fine tuning came only with a sharpness that Arthur lacked. Instead of concentrating, he measured with his fingernail the depth of the scratches on his desktop and analyzed each sound floating up from the bustle of Court Street. Shaking his head to clear his mind only served to remind him that the hair flicking in his eyes needed cutting, and he wondered whether he should go back to the old Filipino barber who said he liked everything about Clarkeston except its lack of bowling alleys.

With new appreciation for people with learning disabilities, Arthur got up to fill his mug from the coffeepot in Ms. Stillwater's office. As he poured, he noticed that the fax machine had just finished spitting out a one-page message from the Circuit Executive's office. He picked it up and smoothed it against his chest. The message was worded similarly to the one received on the morning that Karl Gottlieb had been executed. The only difference was the name of the subject—Averill Lee Jefferson—and the time of death—6:48 a.m. that morning.

Arthur had forgotten about Jefferson.

He stood in absolute stillness for several moments. The fax machine was at the end of a long electronic pipeline, running from Clarkeston to the headquarters of the court in Atlanta, from Atlanta to the death chamber in Starkville, Florida, where electricity had delivered its final message for the State. He held the sheet, connected to everyone involved, executioner, governor, attorneys, witnesses, and judges. None of them believed the death of Averill Lee Jefferson would deter even a single future murder. The state had exacted retribution; no other purpose had been served. Arthur looked at the sheet of paper and felt that retribution retrace itself across the miles and through his trembling hands. Starkville was over three hundred miles away, so the lights had not dimmed when the switch was pulled, but he could feel something happen in Clarkeston nonetheless, a faint seismic tremor of the soul.

After several minutes, he tried to drop the fax on Ms. Stillwater's desk, but it stuck to his hand and fell to the floor. He left it there and stumbled back to his office where he pushed away Suzanne's pregnancy to a far corner of his mind and locked away in another compartment the death of the man he had never met.

★ ★ ★

He worked through lunch, eating without tasting a sandwich brought from home, while he scrolled silently through several dozen bankruptcy cases on the computer. Phil had left to run an errand for the Judge in Atlanta, and Melanie was closeted in her office completing another opinion

Arthur, walled off from all distractions, worked without speaking until the early afternoon. As he sat at his desk, outlining a bench memo, he heard a tap on his door and saw the Judge come in. The rare visit to his clerks' offices usually meant the assignment of extra work, but Arthur cared little whether he had to write another memo or do some extra research for the Judge, as long as he wasn't bringing another death case.

He sat down and asked Arthur if he could smoke. Arthur gestured vaguely. "The window's open."

"I know it's a little late to ask you this, but did you ever read that play I gave you?" The Judge blew a narrow stream of smoke over his left shoulder away from Arthur. It snaked languidly into the bookshelves, pushed softly by the spring breeze. Hearing disappointment and disapproval in the Judge's voice, Arthur dared to deflect the fault for their lack of communication before Jefferson's execution.

"I read it as soon as you gave it to me, but you left early on Friday afternoon and didn't come in on Saturday. I wanted to call you, but Ms. Stillwater said that you'd gone out of town for the day. And Sunday . . ." Arthur looked down and his voice trailed off. "I didn't think that you wanted to be bothered on a Sunday."

"Don't worry about it." He flicked an ash into Arthur's wastebasket. "Something about Jefferson's case struck a chord in me and I remembered the play. I'm not sure why." The Judge paused a moment and sighed. "He was no Gottlieb, was he?"

"No, he wasn't." Arthur stared at his shoes, avoiding the piercing gray eyes.

"Well"—the Judge gathered himself to leave—"he was more sympathetic than most of the petitioners who come through here, but I couldn't see any way to get over the procedural hurdles in front of him."

Arthur slowly looked up, and something in his expression must have stopped the Judge in his tracks. What the young clerk offered up was not a confession, but a deliberate leap into the pit. He retraced for the Judge the beginnings of his research and his conversations about Medea with Kennedy and Suzanne. He included the false starts and his growing doubts that Jefferson deserved to be executed. "Why couldn't we argue that Jefferson's crime—unlike Gottlieb's—was not especially heinous? Jefferson believed what society told him, that passion and erotic love are good things. He was just mentally unable to handle the pain that comes with the territory."

"Maybe," the Judge murmured.

Arthur made his points as forcefully as he could, hoping fervently that the Judge would see some obvious flaw in his line of argument, but the old man just nodded at him to continue. "That's not to say Jefferson's innocent of murder—he's guilty as hell—but isn't his crime pathetic rather than heinous?' Arthur leaned forward as he explained. "Gottlieb was evil incarnate. He's the poster boy of heinousness. Wasn't Jefferson something different? And doesn't that make him innocent of his sentence and free from the procedural bars that prevent him from arguing his lawyer's incompetence?"

A long section of ash fell to the carpet and broke apart. The Judge sat silently, ignoring the mess he had made, looking over Arthur's shoulder at the vast expanse of blue sky stretching cloudless all the way to the coast. He sighed and looked at Arthur with pity and admiration.

"Not bad, son. That's creative and powerful reasoning . . . I might have gotten Judge Byrd to go along with it. McIntosh would never have voted for a stay, but Judge Byrd might have, and all it takes is two votes." His voice trailed off. He seemed to be imagining making Arthur's argument to his long-time friend on the bench.

The Judge shook his head and stood up. He stubbed out his cigarette on the corner of the glass-covered desk and swept the butt and ash into the trash with his hand. "Welcome to the shitty side of judging, Arthur. I'll tell you a secret. I never second-guessed myself in the old days. Never. Now, I do it all the time, whenever I grant a stay and whenever I deny one."

Arthur shook his head slowly. He could have saved Jefferson.

The Judge offered a weak smile in return.

"Don't let this get to you. You're a good clerk. Just forget about it and plow ahead." With that unsatisfactory benediction, he slipped out the door.

For a moment, Arthur's stomach cramped as forcefully as it had the previous morning, and for the first time, he regretted coming south. Slowly, the wave of nausea passed and a strange calm fell over him. He looked from where he had fallen and understood that there would be no climbing back this time. With the realization came no desire to reflect on his present desolation, nor how he had gotten there. His passion for the bench memos dissipated, replaced by the need to be seated in the Wild Boar consuming large amounts of beer and multiple shots of rye whiskey. He strode down the hallway purposefully to make his appetite for destruction known to Phil.

Ms. Stillwater watched Arthur emerge from his office and lock it. "He's not there, Arthur," she said brightly. "He got stuck in that Atlanta traffic and won't be back until later."

"Well, shoot," he replied with equal brightness. "I was going to convince him to leave early today and be bad." He grinned wickedly. "Maybe I can corrupt Melanie?"

"She's still in her office." She made it sound like Melanie was in a highly guarded bunker. "She's working real hard on something. I know that she got here extra early this morning."

He looked up at the clock. "It's four o'clock. Maybe she'd like to take a break." Without waiting for a response, he walked down the hall and rapped on Melanie's closed door.

"Pizza World," he announced, sticking his head into her office, "I've got a proofread opinion to deliver."

"What do I owe you?" Melanie pushed her chair back from her computer, a movement that revealed the neat tailoring of her lightweight spring dress.

"If you buy me a pitcher of beer at the Wild Boar, we could go over my edit."

"When?"

"How 'bout right now?"

"I'll tell you what." She looked at her watch. "Save a window seat and I'll meet you in an hour. I've got to finish this and get it on the Judge's desk before I leave."

"Deal." Arthur gave her a broad smile and walked down the corridor to the elevators.

★ ★ ★

As she drove to the college an hour later, Melanie wondered about Arthur's invitation. The dangerous look in his eyes suggested that his intention was not entirely businesslike, but given his cool response to her flirtation on Friday, it seemed unlikely he was looking for anything more than a drinking buddy. She wondered about the ambiguous nature of her relationship with him. Never without a steady boyfriend since the age of fourteen, she had dedicated herself so completely to work in Clarkeston that her love life had degenerated into a breezy weekly phone call to her last law school beau. Arthur, who sometimes seemed disdainful of her, was not a likely prospect to improve even that tepid situation. To be fair, his attitude had improved over the year. He had been very nice since Christmas and was especially cute on Friday afternoon. And it was hard not to notice those striking dark eyes, when he bothered to make eye contact, that is.

As she approached the tavern, she saw him at a window table with a basket of popcorn, a glistening glass of beer, and a nearly empty pitcher. He held up the pitcher and communicated with raised eyebrows that she should immediately visit the bartender. She nodded and tried to decide whether she preferred straightforwardness in a man or a more gentlemanly style. It was always a choice between Rhett Butler and Ashley Wilkes for southern girls.

When she got to the table, she moved the empty pitcher to the window ledge and replaced it with a fresh one. "I don't think I've been out on a Monday night since I started law school. Do you want to go over my draft?"

"Sure, but have a sip of this draught first."

"Clever."

He poured her mug at an expert angle designed to minimize the head on her beer.

"Are you always this bad on Mondays?"

"Only when I've lost a client in the morning." Arthur leaned back in his chair and fixed his eyes disconcertingly on hers.

"A client? Oh, you mean Jefferson." She took a sip and sat back in her chair. "Ms. Stillwater told me that he was executed this morning." She squinted at him and wrinkled her nose. "I remember you telling us about the case. Should I be sorry?"

"Don't be sorry about anything." He gestured expansively. "It's a beautiful day, and you've written an excellent opinion that should settle important areas of uncertainty in the messy world of qualified immunity." He pulled out her draft from his briefcase. "I'll show you the few comments I have."

He took her work out of a manila folder. She scrutinized him for any sign of irony, but he was sincere. His suggestions for improvement were all rhetorical, made with evident appreciation for the tight structure of her logic. She sometimes doubted herself, and she was surprised to get so much praise from someone whom she had referred to in her more bitchy moments as *Mr. Perfect*.

"Thanks for the suggestions, Arthur." She topped off his glass with a smile.

"You're welcome." He shut the briefcase and turned his attention back to her. "Have you decided yet where you're working next year?"

"It's between McKittrick Brown or Schiarra Wildenthal in Washington, although I do have an interview with Cravath in a couple of weeks." She had not told Arthur about her conversation with Jennifer Huffman or her plans to see her in New York. "Do you know what you're doing yet?"

Arthur looked startled and then slightly embarrassed, as if he forgotten something important. "Actually, I took a job at the Office of Legal Counsel a couple of days ago."

"Why didn't you tell anybody?" she said, barely managing to keep from squealing. "That's amazing! We've got something to celebrate now. I'm really impressed. Will you introduce me to the president next fall?"

"You'll probably meet him first," he said generously. "Didn't McKittrick Brown represent all of his friends during the last campaign contribution scandal?"

Arthur turned the conversation back to her, and as the afternoon wore on, he continually deflected any attempt she made to talk about Jefferson or his new job.

"Didn't you clerk in LA last summer?" he asked after he brought another pitcher to the table.

"Yeah, at the LA office of a big New York firm. You wouldn't believe what went on out there! The big summer party was a cruise out to Catalina Island, and I saw one of the partners lighting up a joint with some of the summer associates. It was unreal."

"Was it good dope?"

"No!"

"Home grown, huh?"

"No," she sputtered. "I didn't have any! I was just watching."

"I'll bet the New York office was a little more uptight." He smiled and poured them both another glass. "How come you didn't just commit to them after your clerkship?"

"I really didn't like the firm. And when I discovered that McKittrick Brown and Schiarra Wildenthal had two of the highest ratios of women partners in the country, I decided to think harder about going to Washington."

"Lots of women?" He slapped the table and grinned. "Excellent! I'll need to go somewhere for after OLC, you know."

"You pig! I'll tell them not to hire you." She smiled at him and sipped her drink. "I just want to go to a place that will give me an honest chance. McKittrick Brown also has a great pro bono program. They don't penalize you for taking on public interest work."

"As long as you bill your two thousand hours."

"Probably."

"What led you to law school in the first place?"

Melanie had not thought about this for a while, and she surprised herself by admitting that it was initially just to please her parents and to change the minds of people who saw her only as some sort of empty-headed beauty queen. Arthur kept asking questions, mining deeper into her past as the crowd in the bar forced them closer and closer together. He seemed fascinated by what she had to say, watching her intently and punctuating his own comments with a brief touch of the hand or tap on the knee. She had never seen him like this before, never felt this boundless energy focused solely on her.

Between the beer and Arthur's unexpected charm, she felt a little disoriented as she got up to visit the ladies' room to check her makeup and collect her wits. She was not used to drinking so much and so quickly. They had to work together for three more months, and she promised herself not to do anything stupid as she vigorously brushed her hair. If there was really something going on, it could wait until they both got to Washington. Frowning into the mirror, she stuck her tongue out and headed back to the table.

★ ★ ★

While she was gone, Arthur stared across the road toward the college. Between the Administration building and the Alumni

Affairs office, he could see a shady spot under a large oak tree where a guitarist played for a small group of students. It was too far away for Arthur to hear the music. He could see the right hand strumming chords and the left moving gracefully up and down the neck of the instrument, but no sound penetrated the barrier of traffic noise and the buzz of conversation in the tavern. He was deaf to the music. He averted his gaze, suppressed all thought of song, and drained the rest of his glass with a smile as Melanie approached the table.

By the third pitcher, Arthur and Melanie were leaning shoulder to shoulder, and by the fourth, her hand was resting casually on the top of his thigh. He pulled her closer so he could be heard above the din in the bar. "Want to go somewhere for dinner?"

"Sure. Pizza?"

"Had it for lunch."

"Chinese?"

"Maybe."

"I've got some pasta salad in my fridge and some fresh bread." She looked straight into his dark eyes. "We could just go back to my place."

"Sure."

He gave no hint of the destructive nature of his appetite.

They had both driven to the bar, but neither gave thought to the dangers of driving while intoxicated. Arthur followed her car through downtown, past the perimeter road and into the vast parking lot of her apartment complex. The upstairs apartments had balconies, while the first-floor units had small patios populated by cheap lawn furniture, bicycles, and rusty barbecue grills. Arthur and Julia had lived in a similar complex in law school. He put his arm lightly against Melanie's back as they ascended to the second floor.

"Well, here it is, in all its rattan glory." She waved at the beach decor surrounding them. "I swear, this is not my taste in furniture, but the students snapped up the better places before I got down here to look." Before Arthur could comment, she ducked into the kitchen and kicked her shoes off into the hall-way. "Could you put on some music while I get the food?"

Arthur found her stereo on the bottom shelf of a tippy wicker entertainment unit and put on a greatest hits collection by Sade. Within moments, "Smooth Operator" was filling the room with its languid rhythm, and he stood up to study her bookshelves.

Half of the space was filled with pictures, including a couple of sexy swimsuit shots taken during her days as a pageant contestant.

What the fuck was he doing there? Melanie was a nice person—there was reason to treat her like a whore or a mental punching bag or a convenient means of self-flagellation. But fine points of ethics mattered little in a world where there could be no life with Suzanne and no reprieves for Jefferson or for his father or for a child pushed away years ago.

She emerged with a couple of plates and silverware, and set them on her small dining room table before gliding smoothly behind him.

"I don't think I could fit in that suit anymore." She rested her chin on his shoulder.

"If you can't," he murmured as he turned slowly and put both hands on her hips, "then it's for some very sexy reasons." He kissed her fully while he traced the curves of her body from her waist until he held her face in his hands and felt her own hands begin to unbutton his shirt.

They never got to the pasta salad. Or the bread.

★ ★ ★

A little before 2:00 a.m., Arthur crawled shakily out of bed and went into the bathroom to splash some water on his face. Melanie, wide awake, studied him as he bent over the sink. She wanted him to spend the night, to feel his lean body finally at rest, but the length of time he was spending staring into the mirror meant he was contemplating leaving. He walked back into the bedroom and sat on the bed with his back to her.

"I need to go home and sleep in my own bed tonight." No question or apology, just a brief statement of fact.

"I suppose it would look a little strange if we came in to work together in the morning." With two cars, this was pretty lame, but she wondered if he would use the excuse as an escape hatch.

"You don't want to see the look on Phil's face if we walked in all rumpled and wasted?" He laughed for the first time that night. "I just don't want to cause any problems with Suzanne back at the house."

"Well, I'll see you at work then." She laid on a little guilt with her voice, but not too much. She understood his situation. After the beach trip, Phil had said that Arthur and Suzanne had something going on. She probably had a crush on him, and Arthur generously saw no need to stimulate any jealousy. That problem would come up all too soon, she supposed.

* * *

Arthur left the bedroom without another word and gathered the clothes strewn on the living room floor. This is how Grover must feel, he thought as he tied his shoes. See a beautiful girl, then fuck her and go home. He cast a good-bye in the direction of Melanie's bedroom and walked out into the night.

The drive home through the cool night kept him alert, and he wound his way through the town listening to the radio, gliding through the flashing yellow lights that hurried late-night travelers along the main thoroughfares. He delayed his arrival, criss-crossing the downtown streets a half a dozen times before turning into his adopted neighborhood.

"I'm back from the 'burbs," he said to the tree-lined avenue as he slowed to make his final turn. "It's a jungle out there."

When Arthur appeared at the breakfast table later that morning, Suzanne commented on his frayed appearance and his late night.

He leaned over his bowl of cold cereal, shoveling Wheat Chex into his mouth for a moment before responding. "I told everyone about the job at OLC, and we stayed out late celebrating . . . I think I'll go in and then have a little nap." He looked up and saw Suzanne smile at him. A tidal wave of remorse washed over him. He forced a smile in return and refocused on spooning the cereal into his mouth.

As he walked to work, he made a weak attempt to rationalize what he had done, but soon gave up. His list of regrets was now too long for an extra demerit to claim his undivided attention, but he did vow not to tell Suzanne. He owed her at least that much.

Arthur sat motionless at his desk for most of the morning, catatonic but for a sporadic and unsuccessful attempt to tackle the memos he had started the day before. The encounter with Melanie had intensified rather than erased the memory of his last conversation with the Judge. Jefferson was just one victim of his failure. Had the Judge accepted Arthur's argument and convinced at least one of his colleagues, their opinion would have been groundbreaking, the first definition of what it meant to be "actually innocent" of a death sentence. That meant likely Supreme Court review and a lost opportunity for the ultimate court to throw a lifeline to dozens of others like Jefferson. No stay had meant no new precedent.

XXVII

DAVID, THE KING

The Judge sat at his desk reading Seneca's *De Ira* for the third time in as many years. After finishing the first chapter, he looked up from the text, rubbed his eyes, and fought off the urge to finish the pack of Camel non-filters hidden in the bottom of his desk. Several years earlier, he had given a speech at a prominent law school and observed that the criminal justice system was more an expression of society's anger than its inclination toward mercy. Afterward, a classics professor in the audience had suggested that he read Seneca. Since then, he had been trying unsuccessfully to harmonize what he admired about Roman stoicism with his role as a judge.

He understood what Seneca was saying: Punishment inflicted in anger or for purposes of retribution ultimately rebounded on the punisher. One must eradicate retributive motive from the criminal justice system, not out of pity or weakness, but to protect those who administer the system. The Judge had succeeded in purging his own anger at the murderers who populated his docket, but he knew that the public had not. His fellow citizens favored the death penalty and, more significantly, believed that retribution provided the soundest rationale for maintaining it. He had seen what happened when Mike Dukakis failed to get angry about crime. He lost votes for failing to sin; that would be Seneca's conclusion.

He found Seneca's writings on the death penalty to be fascinating. In general, the Roman was against capital punishment. It was too likely to be an expression of retribution, of collective anger, with a corrosive effect on all those responsible for the death. Institutionalizing retributive feelings in law meant institutionalizing the most dangerous emotion. Not only would anger then rebound upon the executioner, but upon the collective mental health of the society itself. Seneca only approved of capital punishment in a rare class of cases where the execution was a kindness to the accused. The Judge remembered a habeas petition filed years earlier by the mother of an inmate on death row. The murderer himself wanted to die, and the petition included an extraordinary document confessing both the inmate's remorse and his continuing uncontrollable impulse to kill young boys. Being alive was pure agony for him. The inmate's own words echoed Seneca's rationale: Let me die out of your sense of mercy.

But such cases were few and far between. Mostly, he was just an instrument of the angry people of Georgia, Alabama, and Florida. The worst thing was watching what it did to his chambers. Phillip was stressed out, and Arthur was coming unglued. What working on Gottlieb had begun, Jefferson had finished. Arthur had followed the rules of habeas corpus with precision, but obedience to the law provided no protection.

He shut the book and laid it down. Reaching into his desk with a sigh, he pulled out a cigarette, lit it, and inhaled quickly. I need to go on some sort of a monastic retreat, he thought. No cigarettes or whiskey, just a lot of green vegetables and quiet time.

★ ★ ★

Arthur went straight to his office and buried himself in the pile of unfinished memos sitting on his desk. He skipped lunch and wrote steadily through the afternoon without so much as a coffee break. When he finished his second draft opinion of the day, he looked at his watch and realized he was about to work through the final regular rehearsal of the *King David*. He pushed his papers aside and bolted out the door, disposing of Melanie's smile with a wave of his hand and an urgently whispered, "Rehearsal!"

He jogged through downtown and across the river, arriving at the beginning of warm-ups out of breath and barely in time to participate in the limbering exercises that Professor Henderson always required of the chorus. The pain of stretching felt good to him—his neck was stiff, his back muscles were knotted, and his jaw was so tight that his ears popped whenever he moved it from side to side. When he finished massaging the neck of the girl next to him, he asked her to pound on his back as hard as she could. Her small fists barely dented the tension that sheathed his torso from his shoulder blades to the small of his back.

At the beginning of the vocal warm-ups, Arthur proved the truth of Professor Henderson's dictum that a tight body is not good instrument. His voice broke on the highest notes and went flat on the descending scales she asked the choir to sing. Eventually, he stopped singing entirely. He took a deep breath, leaned his head forward and rocked it from side to side, humming through the next few minutes of warm-ups until he built up some confidence that his voice would do what he wanted it to do. When he finally joined back in, the director nodded her head slightly in approval, rare acknowledgment that any particular individual existed apart from the group.

The rehearsal consisted of singing through the entire work with the soloists, but without orchestral accompaniment. Henderson had so far concentrated on preparing each section of *King David* separately until they were individually polished to her satisfaction. That afternoon everything was put together. The next two nights would be dress rehearsals with the orchestra, and on Sunday night they would perform before a sold-out house.

For the most part, Arthur sang raggedly. He was frequently behind the beat, late on his entrances and groping for the pitch whenever the tenor line wandered chromatically. The music spun like a school yard merry-go-round, and he was unable to grab on and ride with the rest of his friends. When the central motifs swelled to forte, he was left behind, unable to add anything substantial to the intensity of the sound. On occasion he joined the group fully for a couple of measures and felt the sense of wholeness at the center of the sound, but mostly he listened helplessly from the sidelines.

To make matters worse, the biblical story of David told in the lyrics did little to help reconnect him to either the choir or to himself. David died the best-loved king in the muddy history of the early Hebrews, but along the way he took the crown from his best friend's father, sent an innocent man to his death in order to screw his wife, and saw his son die leading an aborted coup d'état. Arthur had always found David to be a morally ambiguous character. Now, he looked upon him with disdain. Honneggar, who focused on the glories of David's reign, was not nearly judgmental enough for Arthur.

In spite of the uninspiring text, the music had remarkable power. It somehow transcended both the story of David and the tumult of the post-WWI period when it was composed. But as Arthur stood trying to join with the other tenors, he found himself on the wrong side of the divide, in the middle of history, standing outside the music.

After, the marathon practice, Arthur slipped through a side door to seek the oblivion of the moonless night. As he stopped under an archway and let his eyes adjust to the dark, he heard someone behind him.

"Do you have time for a drink tonight?" Kennedy touched his shoulder from behind. "There's something I want to talk to about."

★ ★ ★

Arthur sat down in a secluded booth at the back of the bar. Tuesday night was slow, a time for the management to experiment, as evidenced by the candle-topped wine bottles flickering on every table. Arthur pinched a burning wick between his thumb and forefinger and pushed the bottle to the side.

"I've got a proposition for you," Kennedy said hopefully. "I doubt it'll seem too attractive compared to the other options you have, but let me give you the chance to say no." He leaned both forearms on the table and gauged Arthur's reaction. "The History Department made a job offer to a candidate with a law degree from the University of Michigan. Unfortunately, he waited two weeks to get back to us and then decided to blow off the teaching market altogether to take a law firm job that pays five times what we were offering. Of course, we went back to candidate number two, but while we were dicking around with candidate number one, he accepted a job at a college in his home state.

"That leaves us in the shitter." He gave his beer a disgusted look. "Clarkeston College sells itself as a great preprofessional school. The History Department attracts a lot of young people who want to go to law school after they graduate, but this year we taught no undergraduate legal reasoning or legal history courses, and because of this fuck-up, we may not be able to next year either."

Arthur sipped his beer and tried to focus on Kennedy's problems instead of his own. "You want me to call my old profs and see if they know anybody who could do it?"

"Not quite." Kennedy paused a moment. "We were wondering if you might be interested in taking the job yourself for a year. It wouldn't be a tenure-track appointment, but we pay our full-time instructors close to an assistant professor's salary. You'd get no fringe benefits, but you'd really enjoy the experience."

He painted an attractive picture of academic life at a well-regarded small college, extolling the flexible hours, the friendliness of the students, and the close-knit character of the liberal arts faculty. "It's a nice place to spend a year or two, and we can definitely offer something a law firm can't—five weeks of vacation at Christmas!"

The professor's face was so earnest that Arthur hated to let him down, but anyone with the slightest understanding of law would understand why he was going to Washington. "In college, I used to dream of being a history teacher," he explained, "but I just accepted a position with the Office of Legal Counsel starting this fall."

"Holy crap!" He filled up their glasses for a toast. "The main thing I remember about OLC is that it's next to impossible to get a job there."

"The office basically gives legal advice to the executive branch of the government." Arthur let Kennedy clink his glass. "It settles disputes between federal agencies, offers opinions on the legality of legislation, and generally deals with the president's legal problems."

"Well, I'll tell the committee that you turned us down to work for the president. They can't blame me for that one!" Kennedy's broad face beamed. "Is Suzanne going to move up to Washington with you?"

"Unh, unh." Arthur shifted uncomfortably in the booth. "I mean, no, she's not. Why do you ask?"

"Well, just the way you've talked about her." He paused. "To tell you the truth, I figured a bit of romance would help us. Suzanne would entice you to stay for a year. Then, you'd fall in love with teaching, and maybe her, and get rooted in Clarkeston. If you did a good job with the classes, then I could convince the department to consider you for a tenure-track position, and you could practice a little law on the side." He looked genuinely surprised. "I guess I was off base with Suzanne."

Arthur shook his head and then looked down at the table. Kennedy was almost old enough to be his father, and he felt the urge to unburden himself, to share his secrets with someone who seemed to have life figured out. "No, you weren't wrong. Suzanne and I were lovers, but I never asked her to come to Washington with me." Arthur leaned his head back against the top of the hard wooden booth and stared vacantly at the faux Tiffany light fixture over the table.

"I've totally fucked that up." He set his beer mug down before it could slip out of his unsteady hands. "Suzanne is great ... it's hard to explain how amazing she is ... but I spent Monday night having sex with Melanie Wilkerson."

Kennedy exhaled loudly. "Arthur, when you go to Washington, things are going to be a whole lot less interesting around here." He leaned back and tried to rest his arm on the back of the booth, but the ledge was too high and it slid back down beside him. "I don't know whether to ask how it happened or what it was like."

Arthur managed a faint smile. "I'd say gentlemen don't tell, but that would be claiming to be gentleman."

"Does Suzanne know?"

"No." He responded emphatically. "And she's not going to." He fumbled a moment for the right words. "Suzanne is about the coolest person I've ever met in my life, and Maria is the first little kid I ever liked since . . . since I was a little kid. They can't know any of this."

"What if Melanie told Suzanne? Such things can happen."

Arthur thought for a moment. "I don't think she would. I don't think she's that kind of person. Besides, I'd tell Suzanne that she was lying."

"You're pretty protective of Suzanne, given . . . uh . . . subsequent events with Melanie." Kennedy looked at him quizzically. "Dude, what happened?"

Arthur had no satisfactory answer. On the one hand, any single man would be crazy to turn down the chance to be with Melanie, but on the other hand, the world was full of attractive women and Arthur had never just hopped in bed with anyone before. He considered the possibility that Suzanne's Sunday revelation was connected to his fling with Melanie. That's what I'll tell Kennedy, he thought bitterly, I'm fucking Melanie because I got Suzanne pregnant.

Kennedy saw the look on Arthur's face and withdrew the question. "I'm sorry to pry into your private life. I'm just worried, that's all."`

Arthur shrugged. He could not explain why he was behaving more like Titus Grover than the reliable Midwesterner who had arrived in Clarkeston eight months earlier. He pushed his beer away.

"I don't know, Ken." He shook his head and frowned. "But feel free to worry. I've never been this big a shit before."

The need to visit the restroom provided a good excuse to drop the subject, and when Kennedy returned, they spoke for a while about the upcoming performance and parted with an awkwardness new to their friendship.

As he left the bar, Arthur decided to walk the long way home alongside the river. He moved slowly, hands in his pockets, trying to prolong the distraction that movement brought to his restless mind.

The night was cool but not brisk. Spring had taken firm enough root that when the temperature dropped at nightfall, the pungent breath of new growth buffered the air against the chill. The cry of crickets and tree frogs drove out the last vestiges of winter that lingered in the undergrowth. Arthur walked along the levy, following the moon's reflection on the river until the lights of the bridge drove it from the surface of the inky water.

At the crossing, his stomach cramped for a moment, and he rested one hand on the concrete railing. He felt a sharp pain and bent over briefly as it knocked the breath out of him. As he gathered himself, two cars roared past him in a mist of warm exhaust, and he moved quickly over the bridge to safer ground. Spooked by the close call, he did not stop walking until he got to Oak Street. He trudged the last five blocks, head down and clutching at his side.

He did not look up until he reached the foot of the porch stairs, and when he did, he saw Suzanne bundled in a sweater, sipping a mug of something steamy and rocking gently on the porch swing in the cool night air.

"Hey," he said softly. He wanted to sit next to her, but the pain in his side redoubled and he collapsed instead on the top step where he could draw his legs up close to his chin.

"Hey, yourself," she replied. "Why don't you sit up here with me? I don't have cooties, you know."

"I've got some kind of a stomach cramp."

She silently slide off the swing and flicked a wet oak leaf off the edge of the porch. She sat next to him and gazed out over the street while he studied the paint job on the bottom step.

"Another late night, huh?"

"Nothing special. Kennedy offered to buy me a beer after rehearsal, which went on forever because we only have two left before the performance." Arthur stole a side-long glance at Suzanne's profile. He was unable to read her expression, and his stomach bent him over again. When the cramp subsided, he asked whether she had found a sitter for the performance.

"Yeah. Judy's going to come over. The girls can play, and they'll have a good time." She reached over and rubbed his back. "I called up Helen Stillwater today and asked her if she wanted to come. Her husband doesn't want to go, so we're going to sit together."

Arthur nodded.

"Are you sure you're okay?" She squeezed his shoulder.

"It's just a stitch in my side from walking home."

He could feel her eyes upon him. He didn't deserve her sympathy. He'd taken way too much from her already. He sat motionless, resisting the pulse of her sympathy, knowing eventually she would get up and leave.

XXVIII.

I'LL FLY AWAY

Why, Melanie asked herself, do I always sit next to the screaming baby? Wedged in the window seat next to a young mother and a beet-red child, she stared out over the piedmont of the Carolinas and tried to concentrate on her visit to New York. The law firm interview would be easy. She knew what the Cravath attorneys wanted to hear, but the meeting with Jennifer Huffman would be more delicate. If the former clerk got suspicious, she would probably just clam up. A careful plan was called for, but images of Arthur in her bedroom kept interrupting her planning.

She seldom just jumped into bed with a man. She wanted to make sure that he felt something for her first, that he was not going to run straight back to his friends and brag about screwing the beauty queen. Trust could be built up fairly quickly, but never after just a couple of beers in a sleazy bar. But then again, she had worked with Arthur for months and come to know him pretty well. There seemed little chance he would be shouting his conquest from the rooftops.

Their lovemaking was best characterized as acrobatic and frantic rather than tender. It had been mutually desired and mutually fulfilling, but when it was over, she had lain exhausted and content, while he had been restless and, unless she had lost her ability to read people, touched by remorse—an emotion she had never seen a man exhibit in her bedroom before. She resolved to be wary. He would have to convince her that he wanted to be more than friends who had too much to drink one evening. Until then, she resolved to put off her own complex feelings about him.

By the time she got to the law firm, she still had no clear idea for how to deal with Jennifer Huffman, and her interview schedule allowed little time for further reflection. She spoke with small groups of partners and associates from ten o'clock until noon and then had lunch with the hiring partner and the recruitment coordinator. All of her conversations went well, and she found herself considering the firm as a viable option if things did not work out in Washington. By the time her afternoon coffee date with Jennifer rolled around, her moral qualms about accepting the airplane ticket and occupying the attorney's time had completely subsided.

She was dropped off at Jennifer's office at two thirty, and the two made small talk while they walked to a café one half block from the firm.

"Have we made a good impression on you?" Jennifer asked while they waited in line to order their drinks. She was a tall brunette with a slim figure, obviously dedicated to a careful diet or hours of aerobics a week, and probably both. Melanie had calculated she would be about twenty-eight, but she looked older.

"Absolutely," Melanie replied enthusiastically. "I had no idea you all had such an extensive pro bono program."

Jennifer mentioned other perks of working at the firm and ordered Melanie a coffee and herself a mineral water. They sat down in a private corner of an impressive walnut-paneled salon. "And the proximity of Café Bijou is a nice bonus too," she explained when she saw Melanie admiring the space. "It originally opened in the late twenties and used to be quite the hang out for Russian ex-pats. It's a great place to get out of the office for a few minutes."

"It's fabulous. I love the chandeliers and all the wood." Melanie beamed. "Was the coffee shop in the old bank building on College Avenue open when you were in Clarkeston?"

"No, we had to go to that awful diner across from the courthouse."

"It's not this nice, but the coffee is better than Ms. Stillwater's brew."

"You mean she's still there?" Jennifer managed to be surprised and disapproving at the same time. "How old is she? She's must be a hundred."

"I don't know exactly, probably more like seventy."

Melanie searched for the most seamless way to bring up the subject of Carolyn Bastaigne. "Do you ever miss Clarkeston? We Atlantans tend to look down on it a bit, but I'm kind of enjoying the place."

"Like I said on the phone, it was a rough year." She took a sip from her glass of Perrier. "Judge Meyers was a disappointment. He'd faded quite a bit by the time I got there, serious memory issues, stuff like that. And you already know about Carolyn." She waved a busboy over and asked for a lime. "I got out of Georgia as soon as I could and went straight to see my boyfriend in England. I ended up spending the whole summer there studying for the bar. Trust me, London is nicer than Clarkeston or New York."

She got her lime and squeezed it into her water. "Has Carolyn's mother called again?"

"No, thank goodness."

Melanie began her next question with her eyes on her coffee, but raised them slowly as she spoke. "Do you mind if I ask you a question about Carolyn? What do you think she did when she left your office on the night she died? You said on the phone that she was pretty upset."

Jennifer contemplated the question, giving no sign that the subject matter troubled her overly much. "I think she probably went back to confront the Judge."

"Did she say why she was so angry at him?"

"No." She shook her head and sighed. "I wish I knew. It's frustrating to realize that we'll never know what really happened."

"Yeah, you can sort of see why her mom is going so crazy." She posed the most baffling questions in the mystery. "Why take the stairs? Why no shoes? How did she slip?"

Jennifer nodded. "The choice of the stairs is a mystery, but I'm not sure the slip is. She was always going around without her shoes and that marble is damn slippery."

Melanie started to argue with her about bare feet and cold marble but held back. "I've never taken them myself."

"I was working late one evening and went to get Coke in just my nylons—I landed flat on my ass." Jennifer laughed at her carelessness. "I don't have any trouble seeing Carolyn slipping."

Melanie sipped her coffee and thought frantically. Jennifer didn't seem like someone who was too lazy to put on her shoes to make a trip to the courthouse lounge. Given her prim appearance, Melanie had trouble imagining her ever venturing into a public space looking less than perfect. "That makes a lot of sense. So, she was wearing nylons?"

"Oh yes."

The young lawyer offered a sad smile and shook her head.

"You're sure?" Melanie wanted to be certain Jennifer was lying before she played hardball.

"Of course." She still showed no signs of wariness. "Why do you ask?"

"Because I know for a fact that she wasn't wearing hose that night." Melanie looked Jennifer in the eye and held her gaze. "I've looked at the coroner's inquest, which lists everything she was wearing when she died. It inventories everything from her contact lenses to her earrings and underwear. There's no mention of any nylons."

Jennifer did not immediately respond. She stared at Melanie, her mouth set in a tight line.

"And moreover," Melanie added, "you know it too. I saw your name on the report. You checked it out and read it."

Jennifer sat up straight in her chair and brushed a crumb off the top of her skirt as if she were brushing away her antagonist. "I think it's time this interview was over." She laced the word "interview" with momentous disdain and stood up to leave. She was two steps from the table when Melanie responded.

"Too bad. I was just going to ask if you knew anything about the merger of two soft drink companies."

Jennifer stopped in her tracks and turned with some effort. Panic and anger were quickly mastered with a plastic smile.

"Why don't you sit back down? You don't have to go back quite yet, do you?"

"I may have a bit more time." Jennifer looked at her watch and sat down. "I'll give you five minutes." She was now on full alert. No more choice clues would be slipping out unnoticed.

"I'd like you to tell me about the death of Carolyn Bastaigne." Melanie spoke assertively, but she was glad they were in a public place. This hardened version of Jennifer Huffman did not look like someone she wanted to be alone with.

"Why should I do that?"

"Because if you don't, I'll tell the Justice Department about the little scheme you and Carolyn hatched to buy stock in soft drink companies before the appeals court reinstated the merger." She watched to see if her guess hit home.

"Nice try." Jennifer laughed. She had fully regained her composure. "Even if your fantasy were true, do you really think I'd buy stock in my own name?"

Melanie's knowledge was limited by the Justice Department letter to the Judge. It had identified Carolyn but no one else. "Are you saying you had no idea that your best friend was committing securities fraud right under your nose?"

Jennifer laughed again and shook her head in disgust. "That little toad was hardly my best friend."

Melanie knew immediately who had dreamed up the insider trading scheme and who had written the impressive memo on the merger to the Judge. Jennifer would have completely dominated a weak partner like Carolyn.

"Look," the lawyer continued, "we seem to have gotten off on the wrong foot here, but I'll satisfy your curiosity, if you want.

"Carolyn was a mess when she came into my office that night, just like I told you. She told me that the Judge had called the firm, so I asked her why. That was the first time that I heard about the stock scheme." She spoke with evident pity for the poor misguided creature. "I tried to calm her down, but she was totally out of control. When she decided to go back to confront the Judge, I tried to convince her that was a horrible idea, but she insisted." Jennifer radiated good–friend-trying-to-avert-disaster.

"I ran into the hall ahead of her and blocked her way back to the chambers. She got frustrated and ran in the opposite direction. There's really nowhere to go except back into Judge Meyers's office or down the stairs, so she yanked open the door and disappeared."

Melanie knew where the story was going, but she saw no way to challenge Jennifer's version of what happened. And she saw no advantage in showing her disbelief—she felt in her bones that Jennifer had killed Carolyn. Why else would she lie about the nylons? She had master-minded the plan, written Carolyn's memo for her, and then killed her when the story threatened to get out. "So that's what happened?"

"That's it," Jennifer concluded with a shrug of her shoulders. "I wasn't about to chase her all over the building. I went back to my office and left shortly after that."

"And you never looked down the stairwell?"

"No. I always took the elevator. That's why I went to look at the coroner's report. I wanted to know if she died instantly." She smiled sweetly. "I couldn't abide the thought of her laying there and suffering because I hadn't bothered to open the stairwell door to follow her."

As Jennifer sat, composed and attentive, like a sleek, satisfied cat, Melanie finally discerned a motive for murder. What if Carolyn had threatened to reveal Jennifer's role? What if she had not wanted to go down quietly and alone? Self-preservation was a powerful reason to kill, but Melanie made no accusation. Given the lack of hard evidence and the passage of time, her suspicions were never going to send Jennifer to jail. At the end of the day, the best strategy was not to further antagonize a dangerous person.

"I'm sorry that I made you relive that horrible night," she offered in a conciliatory voice. "I've become a little obsessed with her death. I hope you don't mind me prying."

"Don't worry about it." Jennifer smiled. "And you've certainly done your homework. How did you discover Carolyn's securities scam?"

"Just a lucky guess." She was not about to reveal the contents of the Justice Department letter in Carolyn's personnel file. "I read all of her bench memos, and the merger one stuck out like a sore thumb. It was really comprehensive. I asked myself why she should care so much about the result in the case and put two and two together."

"That's precious," Jennifer replied. "And so typical of poor Carolyn: caught in a moment of competence."

Jennifer accompanied her back to the firm for a final round of interviews before dinner, dropped her off at a partner's office with a firm shake of the hand, and walked away without looking back.

★ ★ ★

Jennifer shut the door to her office and walked to her window. She looked down on the bustle of the city street below and smiled, confident that the stuck-up young bitch from Georgia was satisfied with her story. It was mostly true, anyway; that was the beauty of it. She had not bought any soft drink stock, but her boyfriend in London had. And she had chased Carolyn down the hall and stopped her from going back to see the Judge. The stupid twit should have known better than to threaten to rat her out in some insane hope that the feds would go easier on her. And Carolyn had inexplicably fled to the stairwell. She had not tripped, however. No, she had stood defiant at the top of stairs, assuring Jennifer that her bright young career was over too. Too bad, Jennifer thought, that Ms. Melanie could not see the look on Carolyn's face as she felt the hand on her chest propel her into space.

XXIX.

FORGIVENESS, EVEN IF . . .

On the evening of the *King David* performance, Arthur sat in a small downtown restaurant eating a bowl of seafood chowder and tugging on the collar of his rented tuxedo. As he slowly sipped each spoonful, he reviewed his score one more time, paying special attention to the places where he had circled a note in the accompaniment and penciled a line to his own note to prompt his memory of the proper pitch. Since Jefferson's execution, only music had any power to divert his attention. He kept a small radio on in his office while he was working and made sure he had a fresh tape in his walkman the rest of the time. When he was home, he played the *King David* compact disc so incessantly that Maria knew several of the choruses by heart.

She had provided the only lighthearted moments of the week as she twirled about the living room in a dozen scarves from her dress-up drawer dramatically lip-synching the deep-voiced narrator of the story. Her expression was so stern and the contrast between her slight form and the booming bass voice so great that Arthur could not help but smile. When Maria exited amid a trail of silk and nylon, he felt the impulse to confess everything to Suzanne, to purge himself and recapture their carefree life together in the house. The ridiculous fantasy left him clutching his score against his racing heart, fighting the urge to curl up on the sofa in a tight ball.

As the downtown church bells chimed 6:00 p.m., he got up from his chair and headed across town to the college's performing arts center. The sun was still visible over the western tail of the river, but its light penetrated with little force between the downtown buildings. Arthur walked through the lull that settled over Clarkeston around dusk, the time when municipal workers were gone but students and young couples had not yet come to the bars and restaurants. As he crossed the river, the quiet gray of the city gave way to the lamp-lit bustle of the Watson Music Hall. He climbed the steps at the back of the elegant brick building and emerged into the scurry of pre-concert activity backstage. He avoided everyone he recognized and ducked into the men's bathroom where he splashed his face with water and waited for the call to line up with the other tenors.

When he followed the tuxedos and black dresses onto the risers, he saw the glare of the spotlights did not completely obscure the audience that filled the large auditorium. The chorus stood immediately above a small orchestra, about eye level with the people who sat in the middle of the main floor. He could see Phil, Suzanne, and Ms. Stillwater, but not Melanie. She was scheduled to fly into Atlanta from New York that afternoon and was not sure she could make it. The Judge had not planned on coming. He said he no longer went to concerts.

Although the room seated almost 1500 people, heavy tapestries and dark-stained hardwood floors lent it an intimate feel. The space was so acoustically alive that wall curtains were necessary for dampening the sound and keeping it from ricocheting too brightly around the room. The Atlanta Symphony Chamber Orchestra loved the vibrancy of the space so much that it routinely recorded there. When the house lights dimmed, Arthur could no longer make out the audience or the details of the auditorium's architecture. From the opening strings of the overture, only director and music existed.

It seemed like Dorothy Henderson kept her eye on him throughout the concert. She certainly watched him during the tenor section's most difficult and exposed section. She had challenged them in practice to sing quietly, yet with enough support and movement in their voices to carry the whisper of their words all the way to the back of the hall. The beatific smile on her face and a nearly imperceptible nod conveyed that they had produced precisely the sound she wanted. But it mattered little whether she had looked at him, or the men next to him, for they sang with the same voice. The endless hours of warm-up and exercises had created a sound of such unity that individual voices within the chorus were not discernible. At no point in his life had he ever felt so completely a part of something. Not only did his voice merge with those around him, but his senses expanded so that he heard with the ears of the group and saw with its eyes.

They had not sung the piece for an audience before, and Arthur was amazed by the change it wrought in the music. Rehearsals had been aesthetic events, and at times even ecstatic ones, but they had not been acts of love. As he sang, he felt a bond that extended from Dorothy to his friends, to those in the audience whom he had never met, to the composer of the music, and to the author of all music. And the chasm that divided him jolted slightly narrower. She had warned them during warm-ups that performing was about relationship, that they could not hold themselves apart and still sing well. The music did not heal him, but sometime during the performance he began to yearn for reconciliation, with the people he loved, and with the various parts of himself scattered around Iowa, Clarkeston, and the acrid bowels of the prison in Starkeville, Florida.

When the concert ended, the applause was lengthy and deafening. The chorus waited through three curtain calls before they began to file off. They left the bleachers row by row through a small teak door on the right side of the stage. Dorothy waited just past the exit, shaking the singers hands as they walked by. Arthur shuffled quietly in the reception line until she put out her hand. He ignored it and surprised her with a quick embrace.

"Thank you," he whispered intensely in her ear, and before she could respond, he let her go and walked quickly past the crowd gathering for punch and cookies in the Green Room.

He spoke to no one, content to listen to the music echoing in his head as he pushed through the back exit from the performance hall. He walked slowly to his car, still parked by the restaurant where he had eaten, and savored the light breeze as he looked back at the crowd exiting the Watson Center. He slid exhausted behind the wheel of the aging hatchback and piloted it resolutely away from town and out to Melanie's apartment complex.

The absence of her car indicated she was not home, so he parked as closely as possible to the sidewalk leading to her unit and waited for her to come back. When she arrived several hours later, delayed by Atlanta traffic, she found Arthur asleep, head against the driver's side window, a thin thread of spittle connecting the corner of his mouth to his left shoulder. In response to her tap on the window, he jerked awake and gave a brief uncomprehending stare. When he realized where he was, he cleared his head with a shake and followed her to the second floor landing and through her door.

★ ★ ★

Suzanne and Ms. Stillwater waited for Arthur in the lobby of the Watson Center for forty-five minutes while the crowd slowly spilled out the doors of the auditorium and eventually trickled away to nothing.

"You know," the smartly dressed older woman concluded reluctantly, "I don't believe he's going to make an appearance."

"I think you're right." Suzanne took one last look at the lobby before she turned and walked down the steps.

"He has been kind of erratic lately." Ms. Stillwater gave Suzanne an inquiring look, but got no reward for her digging.

"He's got a lot on his mind," Suzanne replied as they found her car in the parking lot. "Well, what should we do?"

"About Arthur? I have no clue about him," she replied. "But I don't see why that should keep us from getting some ice cream."

After indulging in a double-dip of Rocky Road at the campus town Baskin Robbins, Suzanne stopped by the video store on the way home to find a movie for Maria that would neither warp her young daughter, nor bore herself to tears. She gambled on a new feature-length cartoon, and they passed a quiet evening watching television and reading stories.

The little girl woke up from a nightmare in the early hours, and Suzanne comforted her with gentle questions about the creature in her dream. She laughed fearlessly at her daughter's description of the beast and knew everything was all right when Maria asked for a glass of water, only to fall back asleep before her mother could bring it back to her.

When Suzanne passed the stairwell on her way back to the kitchen, she ignored her best instincts and crept quietly up to visit Arthur. As her eyes adjusted to the play of moonlight and streetlight on Arthur's bed, she realized that he wasn't there and given the late hour was unlikely to return. She flicked on the lights to cauterize the tears forming in her eyes and slumped down in the worn plaid chair next to his bed. All of a sudden, she felt very tired and old. She did not know for sure that Arthur doing something reprehensible, but her cluelessness to his whereabouts highlighted their separateness, garishly evident in the empty mystery of his bed. The pathetic image of herself as anguished lover released an anger that had been growing inside her for a week.

She did not rage against Arthur. He had behaved no differently, and maybe better in some ways, than the typical man. She was angry with herself—angry for falling in love with someone so clearly destined to leave, angry for relying on a knowledge of her own body's rhythms to avoid pregnancy, and above all, angry with the grotesque joke growing unbidden in her womb. In her disgust, she found the will to make hard decisions. Suzanne stood up abruptly, switched off his light, and left the room without looking back. Certain of what she wanted to do with both Arthur and his child, she crawled back in bed but never found the oblivion of sleep.

★ ★ ★

Arthur emerged from Melanie's apartment around eleven that night and slipped quietly down the stairs. He marveled at her as he crossed the lot to his car. There was much more to her than met the eye. Cursing his missing rearview mirror, he rolled down his window to back out and sped away from the complex. Preferring the undifferentiated noise of the swiftly moving night, he kept the radio off and the window down, left arm hanging out, claiming ownership of the dark small town streets.

When he pulled up to the house on Oak Street, he contemplated going in and talking to Suzanne, but then he abruptly pulled away, circling the neighborhood twice before eventually making his way to Kennedy's house across the river. Although it was almost 2:00 a.m., he knocked at the door until the wary professor flipped on the porch light and let him in. After telling his wife to go back to sleep, he led Arthur into his den and brewed a pot of tea. They talked until shortly before dawn. When the morning sun finally arrived, it found Arthur asleep on an overstuffed sofa in the sitting room, covered by a comforter sewn years earlier by the local chapter of the Daughters of the Confederacy.

XXX

HAVE A CUP OF TEA

"So, how was the trip?" Phil sat in the library, eating a doughnut and tapping his pencil on the empty yellow pad in front of him. The precedent needed to save Sergeant Watkins from execution continued to elude him. He had been in the library over an hour and had written not a single word of the required memo. Resigning from the job was looking like the only ethical course of action.

"Oh, the firm was really interesting." Melanie sat down and laid two books on the table. "I'm really glad I talked to them."

"I didn't mean that part of the trip."

"Oh, you mean my little chat with Jennifer Huffman?"

"Yes!"

"Well, when I think about it real hard," she said with a sly grin, "I think she convinced me that she killed Carolyn Bastaigne."

"She did what?" Phil got up and shut the library door. "What exactly did she say?"

"Ironically, I tripped her up with the nylons." Melanie leaned back and grinned. "When she insisted that Carolyn was wearing them when she died, I told her about the inquest report, threatened her with the merger story, and asked her to tell me what really happened. She claimed not to know about the securities scheme until the night of the accident. She said that she prevented Carolyn from confronting the Judge by stopping her in the hallway, but that Carolyn ran back down the hall and through the stairwell door." She put her palms on the table and gave him a knowing glance. "Jennifer says she never saw her again after that."

Phil thought for a moment, more than willing to be distracted by the story. "It's all plausible. Why don't you believe it?"

"Because Jennifer Huffman is one of the smuggest, most obnoxious narcissistic bitches that I've ever met. She wouldn't have chased Carolyn down the hallway out of some altruistic impulse to save Carolyn from herself. Jennifer only thinks about the well-being of Jennifer. If she chased her down the hall, it was to save her own ass." She leaned over the table, her eyes bright with excitement. "Given what we know about Carolyn, does she strike you as the type to go down alone? Would she take the rap by herself while her friend goes off to a promising career in New York?"

"My guess is Carolyn threatened to tell the Judge about Jennifer. Sure, Jennifer chased Carolyn, but it was to save herself. And once she was in the stairwell, just one little push would take care of her problem." She screwed up her face in an expression of disgust. "And she struck me as someone who'd enjoy doing the job."

"You've got no evidence." He scrutinized her carefully. "You're not going to the police are you?"

"No! She'd just deny that she ever said anything to me. There's no physical evidence that she did it, and there's nothing to link her directly to the securities fraud either. She's way too smart to have bought any stock in her own name." Melanie shook her head emphatically. "I might even get the Judge in trouble."

"So, you solved the mystery, but it gets you nowhere." Phil smiled. "I don't remember any Nancy Drew books ending like that."

"Like Arthur says, 'welcome to reality.'"

"Not too pretty, is it?"

"Nope." Melanie leaned back in her chair and looked up at the ceiling. Phil could see she was thinking hard. She stood up and paced about the room, running her index finger over the spines of the books lining the walls.

"Do you think I should tell the Judge?"

"What! Are you crazy?"

"Maybe."

"He'll figure out it was you calling Sydney DuMont," he exclaimed. "He'll know it was you snooping around."

"I know, but there's nothing illegal about calling a reporter or looking at a coroner's inquest."

"Technically true." He did little to conceal his horror at what she was contemplating. "But what about snooping around in a federal judge's personnel files?"

"I've thought about that." She pushed in a volume that was sticking out over the edge of the bookshelf. "If he asks me how I know about the securities fraud, I'll tell him that I made a guess based on her bench memos and that Jennifer confirmed it. She'll be my source for why Carolyn was fired too."

"So now you're gonna to lie to him?" His arguments were having little effect. "Why would you want to do this?"

Melanie sighed and finally sat down. "Because I think he blames himself. Why else the five-year depression? Why else has he been sitting in the dark? He's got the right to know that Jennifer's responsible, not him. I'm going to talk to him after lunch."

"You're playing with fire."

"Maybe. But it's just playing, isn't it?" She looked at him sympathetically. "Not like what you've got sitting in front of you."

★ ★ ★

By the time Arthur arrived home the next morning, Suzanne had already left to keep a hastily made appointment with her gynecologist. No one witnessed the curious grin on his face when he arrived, nor the furrow that creased it when he realized she was gone. He washed and dressed slowly, hoping she was just running an errand, but as ten o'clock approached, he gave up and wrote her a note, pinned it under the butter dish on the kitchen table, and walked briskly downtown to the Judge's chambers. He was dangerously late, but he didn't care.

★ ★ ★

The office was humming with activity. Phil was scheduled to leave Sunday with the Judge for the final sitting of the spring term. The Judge was studying his bench memos and charging out of his chambers with alarming frequency asking questions that sent his clerks scurrying back and forth from bookcase to computer. Amid the activity, Phil sat in the library and wondered whether he would have a job by the end of the day. The Judge had requested his memo on Watkins' habeas case by 5:00 p.m., and he had resolved to hand the file back to the Judge without writing one. The law was clear: Watkins had to die. But Phil would not participate. Moreover, he would refuse to explain why to the Judge. Reporting the case was hopeless from the petitioner's perspective would be tantamount to delivering an oral memo of condemnation. Worst of all, his decision had not left him feeling virtuous. He felt like a failure. Perhaps there was something perversely admirable in Arthur's ability to take a cold look at a case and do his job.

As midday approached, the pace of work quickened, so Ms. Stillwater risked the Judge's wrath and ordered pizza for a late lunch in the library. The Judge claimed that the spectacle of food in the office was inconsistent with judicial propriety, but the three clerks confirmed her opinion that a quick in-chambers meal would increase the chance that they would finish that afternoon. If the preparation for the upcoming sitting was not completed before the Judge left, then everyone would have to work on Saturday. She took their orders and told the courthouse marshals to call as soon as the delivery boy came.

When the phone rang fifteen minutes later, Phil assumed that lunch had arrived, so he was surprised to hear Ms. Stillwater call Arthur's name. His friend got up from the library table and picked up the phone. Ms. Stillwater entered room and handed Phil a typed revision of a draft opinion.

"Hey, thanks for calling me back . . . Why don't you come down to the office?" Phil saw a look of concern crease Arthur's face. "I'm sorry you're not feeling well. You know, we're breaking the rules and having pizza delivered in a few minutes. Why don't you take a couple aspirin and eat with us?" He looked over at Ms. Stillwater to see if such an unprecedented invitation were permissible. She cast a glance toward the Judge's office and nodded.

"Please? Even Ms. Stillwater says it's okay." Another pause. "Well, come if you can."

When the food finally arrived, Ms. Stillwater found some paper towels to use as napkins and then sat down with the hungry clerks. As they attacked their first slices, the Judge stuck his head in the library and frowned his disapproval, but before Ms. Stillwater could defend their violation of the chambers sanitary code, he grunted and told her to bring him a couple of slices later. When they heard his door shut, they let out their breath and giggled like school children just excused for drawing a naughty picture of their teacher.

"We need to do this more often, Mrs. S.," Phil teased, "now that the Grinch is on board."

"Believe it or not," she replied as she gingerly patted the grease off her mouth with a paper towel, "we used to have covered dish lunches here about once a month, to celebrate birthdays or welcome a new clerk. The Judge used to sit right down with us." She continued her story solemnly, "In fact, his wife, God rest her soul, used to give him something to bring."

"You've got to be kidding." Melanie goggled. "I can't see him strolling into the library with a plate of fried chicken instead of an armload of file folders."

Ms. Stillwater lowered her voice and the clerks leaned over the table in one motion. "He wasn't always as distant as he is now. He used to do a lot more socializing before we started getting those awful death cases." A look of disapproval crossed her face and she shook her head. "That's when he started smoking again too. Anyway, he can deal with a little food in the chambers." Then she winked at them. "And I'm sure it does him good to be poked at once in a while."

After a moment's contemplation of Ms. Stillwater's revelations, the group finished their meal and plotted the most efficient way to complete the day's remaining tasks, but as they got up to leave, they heard a rap on the open library door.

"I hope I'm not bothering y'all." Suzanne stood in the doorway dressed in jeans and a T-shirt advertising her daycare center.

Melanie looked at Arthur warily as he invited her in with flourish of his cheese-encrusted paper plate.

"Sit down!" Phil scooted over to make room for her. "We've got a slice of mushroom for you right here."

"Thanks, but I'm not feeling very hungry."

She looked nervous and pale, plainly uncomfortable amid all the gray wool outfits. An awkward silence settled over the group, and Arthur stared intently at her. He looked anxious to say something, but then the Judge appeared suddenly in the doorway next to Suzanne.

"I thought I heard the voice of my favorite goddaughter." He broke into the broadest smile they had ever seen crack open his hoary face.

Suzanne returned the warmth with a tight hug and a peck on the cheek. "It sure is good to see you God-Judgie."

"*God-Judgie?*" Phil mouthed to Melanie with mock horror.

Suzanne chided the old man as she reluctantly detached herself from his embrace. "You've been neglecting your duty to guide my spiritual development."

"You're absolutely right, but I do get progress reports from Arthur and Ms. Stillwater. All is well with Miss Maria, I hear?" He gave her a mischievous grin. "What brings you to the halls of justice at lunchtime? And don't tell me it's the smell of onions. These people"—he flicked his hand at the table—"think we're running a restaurant here."

Everyone laughed and Arthur jumped into the brief silence that followed. "Judge, I asked Suzanne to come in today." All eyes turned to him and his face colored, but he stumbled on. "Uh, I haven't been the easiest person to live with recently, and I wanted to apologize to her for the last couple of days." At this bizarre announcement, Suzanne gave Arthur a distressed look that begged him to maneuver the conversation in a different direction. Melanie stared at Arthur with eyes like saucers.

"More importantly, I've got an announcement to make." He gestured with his arm around the room. "I'm really glad you all are here." He cast a nervous glance at Suzanne and continued. "I had a big day yesterday ... I don't know how else to explain it, but some things matter more now than they used to, and others don't seem to matter as much anymore."

He had the group's undivided attention and his voice gained strength. "Anyway, this morning I called up the Office of Legal Counsel and told them that I wouldn't be joining them next July." He paused and let the news sink in. "I told them I was accepting a temporary position in the History department here at Clarkeston College."

Phil let out an audible gasp. Melanie and Ms. Stillwater sat motionless at the table as Arthur walked toward the Judge and Suzanne. The young mother's expression resembled that of a doe that sees an eighteen-wheel truck bearing down on her at seventy miles an hour.

"Judge, since Suzanne's parents are gone, I want to ask your blessing ... what I mean is that I'd like you to marry us—that is if Suzanne will have me." His look of supplication turned to alarm as he saw the stunned expression on Suzanne's face.

For a moment, the room was absolutely still. Phil, assuming that the couple had already fully discussed the proposition, offered his hand to Arthur. "Congratulations, old boy! You're a lucky man."

Suzanne's shoulders slumped, and she slowly shook her head, tears welling in her eyes. "Arthur ... don't," she whispered and bolted from the library with a sob.

Arthur chased her to the door, but the Judge grabbed his arm and dragged him protesting into his office, leaving the others to assess the aftermath of the meltdown.

"I can see why the Judge doesn't like food in chambers," Phil said as he took the stunned ladies' plates and dumped them in the garbage before tiptoeing back to his office.

★ ★ ★

"Judge," Arthur said urgently, "I need to go to her right now!"

"Sit down."

"But, Judge—"

"I said sit down," he bellowed and forced Arthur into a chair with eyes that had terrified attorneys for thirty years. The Judge rifled his drawers until he found a pack of Lucky Strikes. He lit one with great deliberation and sunk down next to Arthur in an overstuffed wingback chair. He took a couple of deep drags and let the clerk stew for a while before he spoke.

"Son, I'm not the world's expert on women, but my advice would be to let Suzanne calm down and let all of this"—he searched for an adequate description of the scene he had just witnessed—"all this crap sink in." The boy's fidgeting gradually stopped, and he stared at the carpet pattern at his feet.

"Arthur. Look at me!" The Judge snapped his fingers. "Do you think you could explain what happened out there because I gotta confess I can't make any sense out of it." He exhaled a long stream of smoke with a sigh that suggested the forthcoming interview was unlikely to be a short or pleasant.

"Well, I thought that it would be romantic to ask her to marry me in front of everybody." He started to explain further, but his voice trailed off into nothing. He picked at the fabric on the arm of his chair for a moment and then added, "And I thought that it would be harder for her to say no. That's why I explained about the job first, so she'd know that I was really serious."

"So, you'd never brought marriage up with her before?"

"No," Arthur said before abruptly correcting himself. "Well, actually we have, but not really."

The Judge rolled his eyes toward the ceiling and settled himself deeper down in the chair as Arthur struggled to explain.

"You see, I did ask her before and she said no, but that didn't really count—"

"Wait a minute: You put her on the spot with your job-switching story *after* she had already turned you down?" The Judge began formulating an impromptu speech on how to treat a southern lady properly, but Arthur looked too miserable to absorb the lesson. The red-faced young man leaned forward in his chair, desperate to be understood.

"Sir, you've got to believe me. I thought I was doing the right thing. I was absolutely *sure* I was doing the right thing." The boy clearly had some sort of secret that he didn't want to reveal, and the Judge tried to figure out what it could be while Arthur rambled on.

"Uh, Judge, I know that you understand the need for discretion . . . um . . . Let's just say that the first time I mentioned marriage to Suzanne, there were circumstances that made her doubt my sincerity. I don't think she turned me down because she doesn't love me." This assertion got a raise from the Judge's eyebrows. "I had every reason to think that she would agree this time."

"She loves you?"

"I can't read minds, but she has said it." He leaned back in the chair, obviously unable to puzzle out what had gone wrong with his brilliant plan.

The Judge studied the heavily starched curtains behind his desk while he added together two and two. He had spent more than thirty years listening to hundreds of witnesses and attorneys spin facts far more complex than those presented by Arthur and Suzanne's love life, and it didn't take him long to make four. His logic began from the premise that 90 percent of all clumsily timed marriage proposals are made for the same unfortunate reason. He imagined several possible explanations why Suzanne did not take

Arthur's first offer seriously, the most likely being that it was made out of duty and not desire. If so, he thought, then Arthur's strategy of first committing to stay in Clarkeston at incalculable cost to his career was plausible, although highly risky.

"You proposed here in the office because you needed to put your money where your mouth was, so to speak."

"That's it, sir." Arthur's feelings were written plainly on his blotchy, perspiration-beaded face. "I need to make her see how much I love her."

The Judge, lost in his own thoughts, gave no immediate response. Arthur's tale had summoned vivid memories of his own romantic shortcomings and of his most monumental failure to communicate his own feelings. He shut his eyes, contemplated his own legacy of stupidity, and wondered whether someone as young as Arthur could appreciate his story.

"Maybe I should just give it up, Judge," Arthur sighed and started to get up. "I don't want to hurt her anymore than I have already."

"No." The answer to the question exploded with unexpected violence from the Judge's lips.

The old man got up from his chair and circled deliberately around his massive walnut desk. Without a word, he pulled open the shades and let the afternoon sun flood his office. He squinted over a bookshelf filled with copies of the Supreme Court Reports and took out a volume. He flipped it open and studied it briefly before handing Arthur a picture that had been pressed tightly between its pages.

"Do you know who that is?"

Arthur looked first at the Judge, then carefully at the picture, and then back at the Judge again. "It looks a whole lot like the picture of Suzanne's mother sitting on her mantel."

"It is."

The Judge took the photo back and laid it on his desk, looking at it from time to time while he spoke, as if to get approval that his story was fit to be continued. He had never had any reason to tell it before.

"You shouldn't give up yet." He sighed and gestured to the picture. "Eleanor and I became very close during the last few months of her husband's life. Suzanne will have told you that he was my old law partner and friend. He and my wife became ill about the same time, but Mary died quickly, just a few months after she was diagnosed with leukemia. Jim lingered and was eventually institutionalized."

He stubbed out his cigarette and flicked it in the trash before he continued. "It was the most natural thing in the world for us to get together. We'd known each other since we were in high school. In fact, we might've gotten married thirty-five years earlier if Jim hadn't swept her off her feet their sophomore year in college."

As he spoke, he pulled out a pint bottle of Jim Beam yellow label and two shot glasses from the bottom drawer of his desk. He poured both of them a small tot and reverenced the photo with a tip of his drink.

"Anyway, we both had very happy marriages and never worried about what might have been, at least until the very end of Jim's life." He rocked back in his chair as he contemplated the string of bad luck five years earlier that had cost him a wife, a friend, and a lover. "Once he lost consciousness and was put in the nursing home, I felt no shame about being with her. My mistake was assuming that Ellie could handle it too. But when he died, her guilt lay so heavy that she wouldn't even look at me at the funeral."

He took a sip of the sweet rye whiskey from his tumbler and watched the sunlight play on the fluid as it slid back down the side of the glass. "I left her alone for a month or so, not wanting to start any gossip and figuring that she would eventually realize that we hadn't done anything wrong. I had no idea what she was going through. When I finally paid her a visit early one evening, she was dressed from head to toe in black, cold as a statue, and looking determined to join him as soon as she could. I stayed a couple of minutes and slunk on out."

The Judge finished his whiskey, and seeing that his clerk's glass was still full, he hesitated before pouring another. Arthur gulped his drink in response and held out the empty glass.

"Did you ever get through to her?"

"No, but I didn't push very hard. . ." He looked at Arthur and hoped he had made the right decision to trust the boy. "I'm not of your generation, so I'll dispense with a recitation of my feelings, but you'll have figured out my advice by now: do whatever you have to in order to make Suzanne see how strongly you feel." He drained his glass again. "I gave up way too easily; don't make the same mistake."

Arthur raised the glass to his mouth, drinking in parallel movement to the Judge. As they sat violating federal alcohol regulations and despairing of the complexities of love in a place usually reserved for legal analysis, the gap between generations closed a bit. And if they had thought hard about it, they might have come to the conclusion that it was not just failed love binding them, but also their shared roles in the deaths of two men.

They sat in silence for several minutes. A pigeon's deep vibrato rumbled from an outside drain pipe and played counterpoint to the Judge's soft wheezing. Finally, he put out his cigarette, shifted in his chair and, leaned in Arthur's direction.

"Just out of curiosity, why do you think Suzanne reacted so strongly to your proposal out there?" He stifled a cough. "I mean, it was tacky, but she seemed really upset when she should just have been embarrassed."

"Or just have agreed," Arthur added.

"Or just have agreed," conceded the Judge.

"I don't have any idea." He replied, but then sat bolt upright. "Oh SHIT, oh shit, oh shit . . ." Arthur murmured in descending degrees of audibility and in ascending degrees of agitation.

"What?" The Judge momentarily stemmed the chant of obscenity from Arthur's mouth.

"Oh shit," breathed Arthur one last time, "she must know about Melanie."

"Know what about Melanie?"

"Oh shit." Arthur squirmed in his chair. "After Suzanne turned me down—the first time—I had a brief, uh, relationship with Melanie. Suzanne must have found out somehow."

"Oh shit," the Judge murmured. Arthur started to speak again, but the Judge waved him silent and tried to work out the ramifications of Arthur's confession. He ran back over the lunch scene in his head.

"Wait a minute," the Judge sputtered, "Melanie was right in the room when you proposed to Suzanne." He gestured spastically in the direction of the library. "What kind of an idiot are you?"

"No, Judge," Arthur protested, "Melanie's cool." The Judge looked at him uncomprehendingly, and Arthur told him about his last visit to his beautiful co-clerk.

★ ★ ★

When Arthur had gone to Melanie's apartment after the concert, his goal had not been more sex, but rather a radical reversal of their relationship. The problem was figuring out the right approach. He had never broken up with anyone before, and he doubted whether any guy had ever broken up with Melanie. When she unlocked the door to her apartment with a smile, he frowned and asked her to sit down with him on the worn couch in her living room. He sat on his heel with his knee bent on the sofa cushion, maintaining safe distance between them

"Melanie," he declared earnestly, "we need to talk about something important."

Her expression suggested that she expected a romantic pronouncement, but whether she desired intimacy or was worried that he was moving to fast, she was going to be blindsided.

"What's on your mind, Arthur?" She looked at him with eyes that hinted the best thing to do might be retiring to her bedroom, putting off serious conversation to a later date. She touched his arm. "Are you sure you just want to talk?"

"I'm definitely sure."

"What is it then?" She settled back in the sofa.

"I don't really know where to start, but I need your help. I need it really bad." He took a deep breath and searched for a logical starting point. The main problem was not knowing whether Melanie cared for him or whether he was just a temporary diversion.

"Um . . . let me ask you a question." He grimaced with embarrassment. "How would you describe your feelings for me."

"I think you're terrific. You're nice and smart and a good lover . . . and it would be great to see you when we move to Washington." She offered him a generous smile.

"Crap." He shut his eyes and massaged his right temple forcefully with his thumb. "Melanie, you're wrong. I'm not a nice person. In a second, you'll be hating me."

Melanie twisted her hair with her left hand and looked at Arthur warily.

"I'm not sure where to begin, but it doesn't really matter, because the ending's the same: I've misled and used you and I hope you can forgive me."

Now, he had her full attention, and he stumbled quickly on.

"After I moved to Clarkeston, it didn't take very long for me and Suzanne to fall in love. She's wonderful, and even though I never liked kids, Maria actually makes it better. Anyway, things were going great." He watched Melanie's face grow colder and colder. "But a problem came up a couple of weeks ago—"

"So you hopped in bed with me."

"No," he pleaded, "I mean, not consciously. I haven't been doing anything very consciously . . . "

Melanie got up from the sofa.

"Wait, don't go," he cried.

"What do you mean, 'don't go'?" She stamped her foot on the floor and looked like she was going to spit at him. "This is my apartment, dumb ass. I'm just moving over here so I don't get any slime on me!" She planted herself firmly in a wicker rocking chair across the room, arms crossed, eyes burning a hole in the middle of Arthur's forehead.

"Please hear me out." He sat on the edge of the sofa and leaned forward, trying to communicate his sincerity. "You are amazing, gorgeous, and incredibly smart, and the thought of taking the job at OLC and seeing you in Washington is unbelievably tempting." He searched for more convincing words. "Any other guy in America would jump at the chance, but I've got to stay here."

"You've got to what?" She was stunned. She shook her head and held her palms up as if to fend off the craziness. "Wait, you're not going to OLC?"

"No, I'm going to stay here and ask Suzanne to marry me." He stared down at his feet and tried to convey his regret for treating her so shabbily. "I'm sorry that I hurt you before I realized what I wanted."

"Don't assume you can hurt me, Arthur Hughes. I'm a lot tougher than you are."

It was a hopeful sign that she was more angry than disappointed. He looked up at her when she spoke.

"Do you know what you're getting into?" she asked. "What are you going to do down here anyway . . . for a job, I mean?"

"I'm not worried. I'll find something."

"Holy shit," she murmured as she struggled to make some sense out of his decision to ditch his career. "Are you out of your mind?"

"I think I actually was for a while, but not now." He tried to find the right words to explain what had changed. "During the concert tonight, it just hit me—I've done nothing but death all year long, and now I've got the chance to do something positive, something wonderful."

"It just hit you while you were singing?"

"Yeah."

"You are crazy." She moved back to the sofa and gave him a hard look. "And I'm still pissed off with you, but are you sure that you know what you're doing by withdrawing at OLC? A chance like that only comes once in a lifetime. Wait, if you do the math, way, way less than once in a lifetime!"

"I know it does." He nodded vigorously. "You're absolutely right, but there are more important chances here that I need to take." He saw her wince. "I'm sorry. I've ended up hurting both of you. Maybe you can forgive me someday and see that I'm just trying to make things right."

Melanie's anger appeared to fade in the face of Arthur's shame and derangement. A tear welled in her eye, and she let it fall before giving here head a violent shake and laughing abruptly. "You know, nobody's ever dumped me before."

"I'm not surprised."

"Well, it could be worse," she added. "You might be leaving me for Phil. I always wondered about you two guys. Don't you realize that the Wild Boar is a gay bar?" She managed a smile, and a strange calm descended on them both.

"What do we do now?" Arthur asked.

"Well, we could try just being friends. We never really gave that much of a chance."

"Maybe even have dinner together?"

"Well, guess what," she said, "I do have some leftovers in the fridge."

For the first time since they met in the fall, they sat down as friends, talking and eating, sharing a secret that they swore Suzanne would never learn.

★ ★ ★

The Judge opened his mouth to comment on the fantastic tale, but no comprehensible sound emerged. He finally got up and moved behind his desk, a bulwark against the mess of Arthur's life that threatened to spill all over the floor of his chambers. "Son, you don't need a wife. You need a janitor."

Arthur nodded his agreement. His frankness provoked a smile from the Judge and a glimmer of understanding as to how Melanie was converted from a potentially deadly enemy into a sympathetic supporter.

He offered one last bit of advice to conclude the interview. "Arthur, just pray that Suzanne doesn't know, and if she doesn't, don't you ever tell her." He sent Arthur toward the door with a wave. "There are no clear guidelines here, but I do think you're trying to do the right thing. The universe will be a bit more balanced if you succeed."

"Get her back," he said as Arthur slipped from the room. And redeem an old fool, he added to himself. He stared for a while out at the balmy spring afternoon. Then, he opened the window and pitched his pack of Luckies out into the air.

XXXI.

CRAWLING FROM THE WRECKAGE

Melanie watched Phil brush the last crumbs from the conference table into a green metal garbage can and then plop down with a groan into the chair across from her. She offered a smile in response to the dazed expression on his face.

"That was hard to watch, wasn't it?"

Phil nodded. He was genuinely distressed by the scene they had just witnessed. "I didn't see that coming at all."

"I don't think Suzanne did either."

Neither had Melanie—life had gotten wildly unpredictable in Clarkeston lately. Even her own plans about the future were starting unravel a little. After meditating on her trip to New York, white shoe law firms were looking less interesting to her. Commercial lawyers would never send her out to track down a murderer like Jennifer Huffman. On the other hand, the Justice Department and the US Attorney's office were desperate for people who had a nose for uncovering dirt.

"Nope," Phil replied. "She looked totally stunned." He pushed the trash container away with his left foot and spun the chair parallel to the table, sticking his legs out and slumping down even farther. "I can't believe he didn't tell me." He shook his head and rested an elbow on the table. "I thought we were closer friends than that."

She studied him for a moment. He seemed hurt by Arthur's failure to confide in him. Or maybe by something else. Phil didn't seem the jealous type, but you never knew. "You are his best friend, Phil. This looked really impulsive."

"Come on," he protested with a wave of his hand, "you don't just suddenly decide to junk your career, stay in Clarkeston, and marry your landlady."

"You do if you're Arthur Hughes," she replied with a sigh.

Phil looked at her sharply. "What do you know anyway? You haven't been snooping around his office, have you?"

"I wouldn't snoop around . . . "

His expression dared her to complete the sentence and get a lecture on her ethical shortcomings.

"Okay, so I'm a little nosy," she sniffed, "but I haven't been snooping around the corners of Arthur's love life." She almost didn't go any further, but this seemed to be a day when all bets were off. "I kind of got myself in the middle of his love life."

"You did what?" He turned and leaned against the table.

"You heard me." She sighed as she gathered her thoughts. "Arthur and I had a little fling, and he came over last night to talk to me." She got a perverse kick out of the look of horror on his face. "I didn't expect him to ask Suzanne to marry him today, but I knew it was coming sometime."

"What?" he sputtered, and then asked sarcastically, "What did he do, come over to ask your permission?"

"Well," she said with a scrunch of the face and sideways look to escape his eyes, "yeah, sort of."

"Unbelievable." He shook his head slowly and swore. "Un-fucking-believable . . . I thought I knew him . . . ." He looked up at her. "Shit, I thought I knew you too."

"Well, don't be pissed at us! It just happened once, and then Arthur felt like he needed to warn me that he was actually in love with Suzanne and was going to stay in Clarkeston."

"Well, if you don't mind me saying so, the fact that he slept with you doesn't say much about his real feelings for her." Was he jealous or just blindsided? Either way, she set him straight.

"Look, I think the Jefferson case really fucked him up. He never showed any interest in me until after the execution, and when he did, it was pretty . . . uh . . . mostly feverish, if you know what I mean." Phil looked like he didn't. "I really think something in him just snapped, and I just happened to be in the way."

Phil got up and walked over to the window. He stared out for a while, resting the knuckles of his hands lightly on the sill. When he turned around the churlishness was gone, replaced with worry and concern. "I told him this would happen."

"You told him he would sleep with me if he worked on habeas cases?"

"No," he snorted, "I told him that the law can't insulate you—you can't be a tool of retribution and not get tainted."

She started to protest. She didn't like the idea that Arthur's running to her was an allergic reaction to his job, but it was hard to characterize their night of passion as anything but frenzied.

"What I don't understand," he continued, "is why the blowback wasn't an act of violence." His brow furrowed. "Violence usually begets violence . . . I would have been less surprised to hear that he'd slapped Maria for whining or gotten drunk and hit Suzanne or something like that."

At first she recoiled from the thought. Arthur would never hit anyone; the idea was ludicrous, but then she remembered the intensity of the sex and his hurry to leave her bedroom, his inability to look her in the eye the next day. To be honest, there was no way to call it lovemaking.

She spoke in a level voice, pretending her question was merely rhetorical. "What's the difference between that and using someone?" He flinched and looked away. "With the wrong attitude, hitting and fucking can both be pretty violent."

Silence. If Phil were worried that his friends did not confide in him, he could rest easy now. After a long pause, he sat back down across from her. He reached over, touched her hand, and smiled.

"So, what did Arthur say to you last night?" he asked. "How come he came in today without a black eye? Or two?" He laughed. "Or maybe as a soprano?"

"Oh God," she sighed, "he was so pitiful. He was like a whipped puppy." She shook her head and leaned back in her chair. "I was furious, but when he told me about some epiphany he'd had during the concert—I swear he sounded like he was on a mission from God—then I realized that he just knew deep down the right thing to do. He just knew. And then I knew that I could fuck it up if I wanted to be a bitch."

Phil nodded his head.

"I didn't want to be that bitch. Arthur may be a little prig sometimes, but . . . ."

"Yeah, I love him too."

"It's good you can say that."

"Well, I don't mean—"

"Yeah, yeah, I know what you mean . . ."

★ ★ ★

An hour later, Phil knocked tentatively on the Judge's door.

"Come in!" He entered and was immediately taken aback by the change in the room. The Judge was sitting in his chair, shoes off, feet perched on the sill of an open window. When Phil set the Watkins file on his desk and sat down, the Judge pushed himself back to the desk and glanced at it.

"What does your memo say?"

"There isn't any memo."

"No memo?" He squinted the question at his clerk. "Why the hell is there no memo?"

"I can't work on the case, Judge." He felt like a piece of scripture being scrutinized by a studious rabbi. After a while, he dared to look up and meet the Judge's famous stare. "I don't believe in the death penalty."

"Pretty shitty case, isn't it?"

"Yeah." It was safe to admit that much.

"Conscience bothering you?" the Judge asked. "That's a serious problem."

Phil dropped his head and stared at his knees. He was completely drained, but however dreadful the Judge's verdict, he would submit to it. For a moment, his time in Clarkeston flashed before him and he realized how happy he had been in the cloister of the Judge's chambers working side-by-side with Arthur and Melanie.

"A very serious problem indeed." The Judge repeated himself. "You can go now, Mr. Garner."

Phil got up and walked slowly to the door, but as he was about leave and collect his things from his office, the Judge cleared his voice and stopped him.

"Mr. Garner." There was an unexpected lilt in his voice. "You may have noticed that I'm the senior judge on the panel hearing Watkins' appeal."

"Yes, sir."

"You'll remember, I'm sure, that it's the senior judge who gets to assign the job of opinion writing once the case has been heard."

Phil nodded.

"I get to decide which of us drafts the opinion, and you might be interested to know that I plan on assigning myself that job."

He gave Phil a faint smile.

"See this spot on my credenza? After the hearing, the file is going to sit there for a very long time waiting for an opinion to be written . . . maybe until I retire. Maybe the law will progress between now and then. That's the best we can do for your sergeant." He nodded his dismissal. "Don't worry about it, and make sure you have a beer with Arthur tonight. He may need one."

★ ★ ★

Melanie knocked on the door an hour later. When she entered, she saw the Judge, bathed in bright sunlight, rearranging the

311

drawers in his desk. He turned around and gave her a curious look. She stopped in the doorway, speechless at the state of the room, the expression on his face, and the three packs of crumpled Lucky Strikes on his desk.

"Yes?" he asked. "Do you need something?"

The story of Carolyn Bastaigne refused to come out, and the Judge no longer looked like he needed to hear it. And maybe the image of the guilt-ridden jurist had always been a figment of her imagination. And what was the point of the story anyway? Jennifer Huffman would never be prosecuted for murder, and maybe the chambers were better off living with the comfortable tale of a trip to get a candy bar gone awry. Was there any justification for the revelation other than her own vanity, her own desire to impress the Judge with her cleverness?

As he stared at her, she realized that her motivation for telling him was part of the same desire to please that led to pageant victories and straight As in law school. It was a useful desire, often a productive one, but one that she needed to let go of. She needed to please herself. She needed to junk the law firms and join a team of Justice Department prosecutors instead.

And she needed to start by keeping a well-earned secret to herself.

"No," she replied as she turned to leave the room. "I was just looking for a file."

★ ★ ★

"Well," Phil asked as Melanie walked into the library, "what did he say? Was he impressed or did he fire you?"

Instead of sitting down, she leaned against the bookshelves next to the door. "Neither. I didn't tell him." She absentmindedly pulled a book halfway out and popped it back in with a rap of her knuckles. "There's just no point."

Phil let out a long sigh. "I know that I told you not to tell the Judge, but I have to admit that I was kind of looking forward to seeing him go after Jennifer Huffman. It just doesn't seem right that she should be able to get away with securities fraud and probably murder."

Melanie smiled. "Well, look at you. Mr. Retribution finally comes out of the closet."

"I'm not saying that she should get the death penalty!" He smiled back and dared Melanie to contradict him. "But a little prison time for her would not be amiss."

"Well, we've got no evidence for a murder charge, and even the Hatcher memo only mentions Carolyn in the securities fraud."

"The Hatcher memo?"

"Yeah, the memo from the Justice Department in Carolyn's personnel file."

A broad grin spread across Phil's face and a rumble of sinister amusement filled the room. "You don't mean Glenn Hatcher?"

"Yeah." She drew out the syllable as she sat down and tried to figure out why he could not stop smiling.

"Glenn was at the beach." He paused for a moment. "Glenn is awesome, and I'll bet he would love to get a phone call from you ratting out Jennifer's little stock scheme." He watched Melanie process the suggestion and tried to anticipate her objections. "He could keep the Judge totally out of the investigation, and once he tracked down the stock purchase, he could swoop in and take her down."

"But how could he do that?" She looked doubtful. "Jennifer would have bought the stock through a third party. Hell, she admitted as much to me in New York."

"It's the Justice Department!" he exclaimed. "They can track her financial records around the relevant time and find any deposits that look suspicious. One thing the feds know about is following the money."

Melanie nodded slowly in response and then more vigorously as she remembered her conversation with Jennifer. "And I think I know where the feds should start looking," she added excitedly. "Jennifer mentioned spending the summer after her clerkship in England with her boyfriend. Having him buy securities on the London stock exchange would be too fucking clever. I'll bet that's how she financed her little vacation over there too."

"Could be," he replied enthusiastically. "We'll never get her for murder, but a little jail time for fraud is way better than nothing." He studied his co-conspirator and asked her to deliver the verdict. "So, what do you think?"

"I think"—she paused a moment while a smile spread across her face—"I need to get Glenn Hatcher's number from Ms. Stillwater." She walked across the library and kissed Phil on top of the head.

As she was leaving the room, she paused at the door. "And I need to ask him about a job too."

XXXII.

WATERLOO SUNSET

Arthur's walk home showcased Clarkeston at its springtime best. The architecture of both man and nature were defined to cookie-cutter clarity against a cloudless sky rinsed clean by an early-morning shower. Even the tardiest of trees and flowers were leafing out, celebrating the end of winter with spectacular blossoms that filled the air and covered the ground with a cloak of rose and white. But the scene provided no comfort. For him, Clarkeston had become a huge pitcher plant, a seductive invitation to disaster.

He walked slowly down the street, reliving the last twenty-four hours. In a brilliantly short period of time, he had burned his bridges with the Office of Legal Counsel, confessed to Melanie and the Judge, taken a job with Kennedy, and proposed marriage to Suzanne. Whether the decision to stay in Clarkeston was going to be an act of contrition or a chance at redemption was up to her.

When he got within a block of home, he squinted to see whether she was waiting on the front porch. Unable to tell, he walked a dozen more steps before checking again. Not there. When he arrived, he crossed the yard and looked behind the house to see if Suzanne's car was parked. The worn patch of gravel and grass was empty.

He climbed up on the porch and slumped down on the top step. Squirrels were busily searching for edible treasures buried the fall before, but no other humans intruded on their domain. He attended to the details of squirrel society, studying them until he no longer felt like crawling out of his skin. I'll sit in the swing and wait, he told a particularly fat squirrel who was sharpening its teeth on the lattice work underneath the house.

For two hours, he swung quietly, conducting an unrelenting critique of every major decision he had made since his arrival in Clarkeston. He understood many of his mistakes, but he had no confidence that he could avoid the traps fate might lay for him in the future, nor was he sure that some irremediable and innate character flaw was not really his problem. Worst of all, he concluded, his own happiness had become dependent on forces outside himself and out of his control, contingencies from which he could not wall himself off. Slightly nauseated, he went to the kitchen to fetch a Coke and left Suzanne a note on the back door. Then, he went back out to the porch to continue his vigil, resolving to stay there overnight if he had to. When she arrived, she would find him perched where she had so often waited for him. Perhaps she would see that he had learned something.

★ ★ ★

Suzanne picked up Maria after a preschool field trip and treated them to a restaurant supper. They took their time eating and then had ice cream for dessert. She let Maria color, while she listened quietly to the last half of the evening public radio news broadcast. Fortified by a large hot fudge sundae and a report on anti-Pinochet rebel activities in the mountains of rural Chile, she drove home and chanced a confrontation with Arthur. She set the parking brake with a creak as the station wagon's tires crunched to a stop behind the house. Exhaling deeply, she unloaded Maria, grabbed an oversize shoulder bag, and walked up the back steps to find Arthur's note taped to the door:

I'M OUT FRONT ON THE PORCH IF YOU WANT TO TALK

"What does it say, Mom?"

"It says that *All little girls have to immediately take a bath.*" Suzanne read in as deep a voice as she could muster.

"It does not! What does it really say?"

"It really says that *All little girls have to go immediately to take a bath or they will get a huge spanking!*"

Maria squealed and ran through the door. Suzanne followed her through the hall and bedroom and into the bathroom where she let Maria soak in the tub as long as she wanted.

"Mommy, will you read 'Bongo Has Many Friends' to me in the tub?"

"Sure."

When the last bit of soap was rinsed out of her daughter's hair, Suzanne scooped up the wrinkled little girl, slipped a clean nightgown on her, and plopped her in bed with a picture book.

"It's still a half an hour before your bedtime, but you can read for a little while if you're nice and quiet."

"Okay. Mommy, but it's still light out." She studied the fairy-tale castle on the first page of her book while her mother combed her hair.

"The sun stays up later this time of year, darling. I'll come back and tuck you in, all right?" The girl nodded and unable to find any further excuse to delay, Suzanne walked out to find Arthur.

When the front door swung open, Arthur looked over and expelled a quick apology.

"You'd better be sorry!" Suzanne fought to lower her voice to keep the neighbors from hearing. "That was the single most embarrassing moment in my entire life!"

Arthur scooted over so she could sit beside him, but she continued to stand, glaring at him.

"I know . . . I'm sorry . . . but can you see how I thought it was a romantic idea?"

"Arthur, you must live in some sort of fantasy land. When are you going to get a clue? Do you really think anyone wants to be proposed to over pizza in front of four other people? Two of whom, for all you know, might see me pushing a baby carriage around town seven months after your announcement!" She spoke quietly, but her anger and contempt bled through.

"You mean you've decided to keep the baby?" Arthur's face lit up.

"What?" She let out a squeal of frustration. "You don't get it, do you! This is my home town—the place where I live—you just can't barge in and fuck everything up."

"But I want it to be my home too," he pleaded. "If you marry me, no one will care about the timing. You can't tell me that we're going to be shunned if the baby comes a little early."

"Of course not." Her voice lost some of its hard edge as she tried to make him understand that she could not consider marrying him. "That's not what I meant; we're talking about two different things, Arthur."

She sighed. "I know you're a sweet guy deep down, but I've got to protect myself and Maria from your kind of chaos. I'm really sorry, Arthur, but I'm not going to take any chances."

Arthur stopped arguing. He sat still on the porch swing, as if afraid that his slightest movement would set off an even more final and deadly judgment. He studied Maria's Duplo creations crowding the near corner of the porch and said nothing for a full minute.

"You know, right after you left," he said softly, "the Judge dragged me into his office and made me confess my sins. He chewed me out for a long time."

"You didn't tell him I was pregnant, did you?"

"No, I didn't. But I told him that I love you more than anything in the world." He snuck a peek up at Suzanne but she was unimpressed by his revelation. He carried on nonetheless. "He told me that I should do everything I can to get you back. Even he sees that we should be together."

"Arthur, look at me." She sighed again and waited until he met her gaze. "Getting the Judge's recommendation can get you a job anywhere in the country, but it doesn't count as much where my life is concerned."

"Well, what does matter then?" he asked hopefully. "Love, maybe? I haven't heard you say that you don't love me." He looked straight into her eyes as if he were playing a trump card. "I'll stop my begging right now, if you tell me that you don't love me."

Suzanne's posture lost a bit of its rigidity and she sank into the seat next to him. "Arthur, love is the least of my concerns. We've both been married before. So, you know as well as I do that romance has very little to do with making a marriage work." She put her hand on his knee and squeezed. "I do love you, and I doubt that I'll ever stop, but this can't work."

Frustration and anguish colored his response. "Am I that horrible? I don't even deserve a real explanation why you're so goddamn sure that marrying me would be such a terrible mistake."

"Arthur, I can't predict the future. I'm going with my intuition." She shook her head and looked out over the street. "Today, you tried to coerce me into marrying you. You tried to blackmail me after a night when you didn't even make it home!"

"But it's not just that. Quaint as it sounds, predictability and reliability are virtues. I don't know who you are anymore."

He began to protest, but she refused to be sidetracked.

"But most of all, and please don't take this the wrong way, I could see the look of absolute horror in your eyes when I said I was pregnant. That told me all I needed to know." She paused, expecting an argument from him, but he was no longer looking at her and said nothing. "Arthur, none of these things means that you're a bad person; they just mean that you're not the kind of a risk I want to take."

A long moment passed when neither spoke. A car drove slowly past the house, its driver gazing with appreciation at the neighborhood and the dogwoods blooming along the avenue. As the car pulled away, the porch door opened and Maria walked out to chide her mother for failing to tuck her in. Suzanne stood up, using the interruption as a way to end the conversation, but Arthur jumped over to the near corner of the porch.

"Maria! Why don't you show me these new guys you made?"

"Sure, Mr. Arthur." She let go of her mother's hand and sat down close to him. "This is Ziggy. He's giraffe." She held up a tower of thin multicolored blocks with a clump of thicker blocks attached to the top. "That's Piggy. He's rhinoceros." She pointed to another blob of blocks with Ziggy, whose head clattered off onto the floor of the porch.

"Ooopsie." Arthur picked up the head and pressed it back into place. "Who's that guy next to Piggy?"

"That's not a guy." Maria laughed. "That's Quiggly. She's a lion." She grabbed a pile of blocks and climbed up into Arthur's lap. Then, she picked up another unnamed pile and made smoochy kissing sounds as she rubbed it against her Cubist lion. She played happily, taking the creatures on an imaginary journey from Africa to the Atlanta Zoo and back again, flying them through the air. Eventually, Suzanne sat down and began to swing slowly back and forth, looking over the street and down at the two playmates.

"I know what you're trying to do, Arthur." When he did not respond, she leaned over them and began picking up. As she reached for her daughter, she saw tears streaming down Arthur's cheeks.

"Please don't make me go," he whispered.

Unable to respond, Suzanne got up and paced to the far end of the porch. She placed both hands on the railing overlooking the neighbor's side yard and noticed for the dozenth time a wild-looking mimosa pushing its way out of her neighbor's garden and toward her house. She felt a sudden desire to fetch her limb-loppers, but she stood instead studying the serrated edges of its deep green leaves. Eventually, she tilted her head and ran her fingers through her thick dark hair. When she turned, she could see that Arthur's shoulders were heaving, even as he played with Maria in his lap.

She walked slowly toward them, still not entirely sure what she should say. A loose floorboard creaked as she approached and Maria looked up at her mother with eyes full of worry and expectation. Suzanne smiled at her and put a hand on Arthur's shoulder, unsure how she had come to her decision. "Maria, would you like to have a baby sister?"